GRIST

MILL

ROAD

ALSO BY CHRISTOPHER J. YATES

BLACK CHALK

GRIST MILL ROAD

A NOVEL

CHRISTOPHER J. YATES

PICADOR   NEW YORK

GRIST MILL ROAD. Copyright © 2017 by Christopher J. Yates. All rights reserved. Printed in the United States of America. For information, address Picador, 175 Fifth Avenue, New York, N.Y. 10010.

Epigraph from "Feelin' Good" by Anthony Newley and Leslie Bricusse.

picadorusa.com • picadorbookroom.tumblr.com
twitter.com/picadorusa • facebook.com/picadorusa

Picador® is a U.S. registered trademark and is used by Macmillan Publishing Group, LLC, under license from Pan Books Limited.

For book club information, please visit facebook.com/picadorbookclub or email marketing@picadorusa.com.

Library of Congress Cataloging-in-Publication Data

Names: Yates, Christopher J., author.
Title: Grist Mill Road : a novel / Christopher J. Yates.
Description: First edition. | New York : Picador, 2017.
Identifiers: LCCN 2017028306 (print) | LCCN 2017030199 (ebook) |
    ISBN 9781250150318 (ebook) | ISBN 9781250150288 (hardcover) |
    ISBN 9781250189929 (international edition)
Subjects: LCSH: Triangles (Interpersonal relations)—Fiction. | Life change
    events—Fiction. | City and town life—Fiction. | Friendship—Fiction. |
    GSAFD: Suspense fiction.
Classification: LCC PR6125.A8593 (ebook) | LCC PR6125.A8593 G75 2017
    (print) | DDC 823'.92—dc23
LC record available at https://lccn.loc.gov/2017028306

Our books may be purchased in bulk for promotional, educational, or business use. Please contact your local bookseller or the Macmillan Corporate and Premium Sales Department at 1-800-221-7945, extension 5442, or by email at MacmillanSpecialMarkets@macmillan.com.

First Edition: January 2018

10 9 8 7 6 5 4 3 2 1

To my mother, June,

for all my first stories

Scent of the pine, you know how I feel

PART I

PATCH

I remember the gunshots made a wet sort of sound, *phssh phssh phssh,* and each time he hit her she screamed. Do the math and the whole thing probably went on for as long as ten minutes. I just stood there and watched.

I don't know when I realized I was counting. Eight, nine, ten. For a long time it seemed as if all sensation, everything but my eyesight, had been switched off. But once I realized I was keeping track of the shots—eighteen, nineteen, twenty—it felt like something I could cling to because my sense of balance had been switched off along with everything else. I was standing on the nauseating brink of something I didn't want to fall into, a world beyond comprehension.

Twenty-six, twenty-seven, twenty-eight.

This wasn't real life, this was a show. And this show wasn't for me, I wasn't even allowed to stay up late enough to watch this sort of show. No, none of it made any sense, a silent movie with Russian subtitles.

And yet I watched.

What does it mean to *watch*? When a crime takes place in front you, what is watching? Is it a failure to act or is it simply keeping your eyes open?

I was twelve. I was twelve years old.

Forty-one, forty-two, forty-three . . . although the newspapers reported Hannah had been shot only thirty-seven times with my Red Ryder BB gun, so maybe Matthew missed a few times, or more likely some of the pellets simply glanced off the ropes. He had used so much rope, I imagine he had to be taking careful aim at the gaps. We were both pretty good shots by then—I could plunk a soda can one-handed from thirty steps and Matthew no doubt thought himself a better shot than me. No way, José.

I figured everything was winding down now. Hannah's screaming was slowly becoming less and less. And between the screaming there was crying and that also was becoming less and less.

Until—

When Matthew pulled the trigger the forty-ninth and final time, there was only half a scream, a sharp yelp that died quickly in Hannah's throat. And that yelp was a sickening enough sound on its own but it is the absence of the second half of her scream that rings loudest in my memory.

I can still picture it as well, the way Hannah's head twisted despite the rope tied around her neck, a reflex that had come absurdly too late.

The woods fell ever more silent. It felt like the moment in a storm when you see the flash of lightning and wait for the thunderclap. Is it closer?

And then Hannah's head drifted back. And her chin dropped to her chest. And her long dark hair fell over her face.

Matthew stayed as still as a lead soldier and I did the same, fused to a plate of the earth, not even breathing, just trying to exert some small measure of control over my life for a few final seconds. The world at that moment was reduced to a thin sort of strip like a newspaper cartoon, a ribbon of life that started with Matthew, the butt of the rifle wedged at his shoulder, and ended two frames later with Hannah, motionless, tied to a tree.

But then came a sound that snapped us both out of it, something small scurrying through the undergrowth, Matthew's head jolting and his body coming alive. He leaned the gun carefully, almost respectfully, against a rock and began to creep forward, stopping an arm's length away and peering in at Hannah like she was darkness in a cave.

He picked up a stick and prodded her arm.

Nothing.

He jabbed again, Hannah's flesh like dough, a small crater of skin filling itself back in. Raising the stick higher, he hesitated a moment. What kind of world might exist beyond the curtain?

And then Matthew parted her hair. That's when I first noticed the blood dripping from Hannah's chin, soaking the neckline of her T-shirt, its pink collar crimsoning.

I spun around and spat on the ground, my eyes beginning to scope the woods, looking to see if anyone else might have witnessed it all. When I turned back, Matthew still had his stick under her hair, standing there with his head to one side, as if reading spines in a bookstore.

Hey, come take a look, he said.

I pressed the heel of my hand to the bridge of my nose, trying to push out the gathering sense in my forehead, a new universe exploding.

The BB's gone right through her eye, said Matthew. Straight into her brain. She's stone-cold dead.

I couldn't rub my forehead hard enough to make the pressure go away so I started to hit myself instead, *thump thump thump*. Still to this day the heel of my hand fits perfectly into the hollow between my nose and my brow.

I said come here, said Matthew, turning to me. We haven't got the whole damn day, Tricky.

It was only Matthew who called me Tricky. To everyone else I was Patch or Patrick, or sometimes Paddy or Paddyboy to my dad. But Matthew was Matthew to everyone, me included. He'd never let you shorten his name, would even correct adults if they tried on a Matt or a Matty to see if it fit. My name's Matthew, he would say every time, very calm and straightforward.

Sniffing, I started to move, feeling like old kings must've felt taking their final steps to the executioner's block—which is a selfish way to think of it but that's just how it was at the time. I walked as steadily as I could toward the two figures connected by a stick and when I stopped, Matthew pulled me closer, positioning me at the perfect spot. What do you think, Tricky? he said.

Swallowing hard, I ran my eyes along Hannah's measled arms, up to the circle of rope burn like a choker around her neck. And then, not turning to face her, but with grimacing eyes, I peeked beneath Matthew's stick. There was nothing but blood and mess and some of the blood was already congealing. Blackness and wetness and skin. Hannah's left eye socket looked like it was housing a dark smashed plum.

Yeah, I said, trying not to cry. She's dead.

Matthew dropped the stick.

We didn't check for breathing. We didn't feel for a pulse.

I stood there for a moment and then Matthew tugged me, not unkindly, hooking his fingers in the back of my shirt to break the spell.

We didn't make the sign of the cross. We didn't pray for her soul.

There are layers of rock piled high everywhere in the Swangum Mountains like stacks of pancakes. Our failures were mounting as well. We didn't even cut her down.

I DON'T KNOW WHAT AN ideal childhood is, but I know until that Wednesday, one hot yellow day of 1982, I believed I was living it. Believed my parents were happy, that I was growing up in the best place on earth, probably still believed in ghosts, UFOs, tarot cards and the purity of major league baseball.

My hometown was Roseborn, ninety miles north of New York City, far enough away from that inferno that we felt safe from its everyday dangers of casual pornography, recreational murder and heroin on tap. Best of all we had the Swangum Mountains, a ridge of blazing white rock like a wall at our town's northern edge, the world's greatest backyard for an adventurous boy.

There were pitch pines up there and blueberry bushes and turkey vultures overhead. And sometimes you might get a hiker come by but mostly you wouldn't see anyone, not on weekdays at least. I loved it best in the dog days of summer vacation, heat stippling the air, incessant shrill of insects.

My favorite place was the lake. I told Matthew it was the ice caves but really it was the lake. The smooth water made the air feel loose, especially when the sun was out and the world with a breeze.

I remember our time up there all bleached like old photos, the sky more bright than blue, rocks with a hazy glare and our bicycles two different shades of baked orange. The year before we had ridden them up there, three panting miles, the whole summer long.

Beneath the wide mountain skies we could be whoever we wanted—Luke and Bo Duke, Starbuck and Apollo, the Lone Ranger and Tonto—playing our parts without inhibition, inventing our own boyhood games away from the critical gaze of adults. Rifle Range, Deer Patrol, Houdini. We were free to roam wherever we wanted—in my case, so long as I was home and scrubbed up in time for dinner—but also we had our own base, a secret spot you reached by pushing through a thicket of mountain laurel. That was where we built our secret fort, mostly from stuff we scavenged from the abandoned blueberry pickers' huts. We kept supplies there and plunked soda cans with my Red Ryder BB gun, an air rifle named for that comic strip cowboy, designed to look like a Winchester rifle. The same kind of gun you see in the movie *A Christmas Story,* the one Ralphie dreams about—*You'll shoot your eye out, kid!*—only mine didn't have a compass in the stock or a thing to tell the time.

The Red Ryder was our weapon of choice for Deer Patrol but as well as the BB gun we had a hunting knife with a scrimshaw handle and a Swiss Army knife. One time we crafted a spear from a piece of bamboo we took from Effy Scott's yard, the tomato plant collapsing under the weight of green fruit. We used rubber bands and a big nail we found at one of the old cement works. We took everything up to the Swangums to piece our weapon together and spent a lot of time making intricate adjustments, weighting the thing with small stones inside for the right sort of balance, ensuring the nail was tight enough to the bamboo that it wouldn't deflect when it met with its target. We wanted to be sure the point of the spear would embed. It took us an hour or more but the conclusion of the whole episode was over in just a few seconds.

Matthew had hold of the spear when we agreed it was ready and he told me to run, just that one word barked out like I'd made him angry for no particular reason.

What?

Run! he repeated, higher-pitched this time.

He had started to get a sense of the spear's weight, holding it lightly at his shoulder and feeling for the right sort of grip, fingers fluttering as if playing the flute.

I find it hard now to believe his intention took me so long to discern. I stood there awkwardly, unsure what to do, while Matthew closed one eye and started to line me up along the shaft of the spear, this spear we had made together. I really do think it took me three or four seconds before everything finally clicked.

And I ran.

I ran, not looking back until I heard the rippling sound it made pushing its knuckled length through the air, turning just in time to glimpse the spear a moment before it sunk its nose into my calf. When it dug in, it dug in far enough that it stayed there for seven or eight paces as I started to slow, the tail of the spear rattling on the stony ground below.

Now comes the hardest part of the story for me to relate to in adulthood and yet I'm certain this actually happened. I turned and picked up the spear, which had now disengaged from my leg a few yards behind me, and took the thing back to him. Like some kind of bird dog.

Matthew, looking immensely proud, reached out with both hands, palms facing skyward. Closing his fists around the shaft, he flexed the thing, gave it a slight and single shake. It was a good spear. It had flown true. Twenty, thirty yards.

He rested our weapon against a tree, gripped me by the shoulders and turned me around while whistling one of those long dying notes like when you read how much money some lucky guy has just won on the lottery.

When I twisted to peer over my shoulder, down past my shorts, I saw the hole in my calf and the blood. Not so much blood but enough to trickle down into the heel of my sneaker.

Cool wound, he said.

I looked over at the spear. The nail at its tip was pretty rusty and I don't remember if I knew about tetanus back then but I knew I should probably tell someone what happened. Although I suppose the reason I didn't speaks volumes about me as a kid. I would never have said anything because I felt ashamed, worried it was me who would get in trouble. So instead of telling anyone, I wore long pants for a week and fretted over how I would answer the question if somebody asked me why. Although why anyone would have asked me why I was wearing long pants, I have no idea.

OK, stay put a minute, said Matthew, moving for the spear again, me twitching like I might break into another sprint. Hey, I said don't move, Matthew shouted, pointing his finger.

Run. Run. Stay put. Don't move.

I began to notice the sting in the hole in my leg.

Matthew took off his T-shirt and I swear I thought he was going to bend down and smear himself all over with mud or the juice of crushed berries. When he picked up the spear, I closed my eyes.

A few seconds later I heard a tearing sound. Opening my eyes, I saw that Matthew had the arm ripped off his tee and was using the tip of our spear to make a notch in the cloth. Next he tore the thing into a strip and beckoned me turn. And then Matthew spat into his hand and wiped the blood from my calf, me wincing when his spittly fingers stung the raw wound. Once my leg was clean he bandaged it with the cloth, stretching it taut, wrapping it twice and tying a firm knot at my shin. When he was done, he pulled on his lopsided tee.

Let's go find some deer, Tricky, he said.

———

THE SWANGUM SHOOTING, AS IT came to be known, took place almost exactly a year after Matthew stuck me with our spear. We'd spent every day of that previous summer together. But in 1982, things went a little differently.

First of all, six weeks before the shooting, there was the accident, news of which spread around Roseborn the day before July Fourth. I was bummed because for a long time after that I didn't get to see Matthew, my parents having told me that I had to give him some space, that Matthew needed time to grieve with his family. So the next time I saw him, Wednesday, August 18, it felt like we'd lost a whole summer together.

Before heading up that morning, I'd arrived at our usual meeting spot only to see a girl alongside Matthew, Hannah Jensen straddling her bike. She was in dark jeans and a pink T-shirt with a cartoon ice-cream cone on the front. I suppose I thought her being there must've had something to do with the grieving, maybe Matthew needed the emotional support of the female sex or something like that. To be fair, I wouldn't have been much help on that front. And although Hannah was also in seventh grade, she wasn't in our class, so her being there didn't exactly make sense to me. Anyway, whatever the exact reason for her presence, I felt pretty sore about Hannah's intrusion.

I assumed the plan was to show her the usual spots and do the usual things. It was the first time we'd taken anyone with us, let alone a girl, and probably we wouldn't find any deer and then we'd show her our secret fort and plunk some soda cans and maybe Matthew would try to make out with her. Because although we were just kids, Matthew was a country mile further along that snaky path toward manhood than anyone else in seventh grade. Me especially.

For several weeks after his arrival in Roseborn, the major talking point for everyone in our class was that Matthew had grown up in New York City. But it wasn't only his big city upbringing that made him seem more grown up than the rest of us, he actually was more grown up, having been held back a year before moving upstate. And so being an older kid—over a year and a half older than me—when Matthew got dropped into our class at the beginning of sixth grade, he landed with an almighty splash. It was as if a stone giant had been thrown among us, not just a street-fighting kid from Gotham but a taller, stronger, more developed creature. Matthew could easily have passed for sixteen, even eighteen maybe, and for weeks everyone was too intimidated to talk to him, this hulking brute from another world. Eventually, when I did begin to befriend him, I would realize that Matthew wasn't just factually older than me, he was light years ahead of my curve, perhaps light years ahead of everyone in Roseborn Middle School, possessed of such a single-minded fearlessness that perhaps my initial suspicion that a stone giant had been cast into sixth grade wasn't all that far off.

But, of course, this is easy to say looking back twenty-six years. At the time, Matthew just felt like an older brother to me—even more so than my actual older brother. I feared him and loved him in equal measure.

I suppose we'd never really discussed girls in any sort of making-out sense but I think Matthew had had sex already, probably more than once. If I'd asked, I'm sure he would've told me. But I didn't ask, the whole thing made me feel incredibly uncomfortable. For several months I'd seen him looking at girls in a way that would slowly become familiar to me—if I'm being honest with myself, I probably resented that.

So it didn't surprise me much when, not long after we'd trekked to our secret spot with Hannah, Matthew sent me away on my own. It's a new game, he said, called Reconnaissance. And then Matthew tried to sell it to me like I was a spy and now I'd get to sneak around and if I spotted anything, like deer or a hiker, I should report it when I returned.

Oh and Tricky, he added, just as I was leaving. Take your time, OK.

So I skulked around for thirty or forty minutes, making it as far as the trailhead for Sunset Ridge, not seeing any hikers or deer. But I did almost step on a huge black rat snake, a dark flurry whipping over the fiercely lit rock, at which point, figuring I'd been gone long enough, I started to head back, feeling proud to be returning with something cool to report. Maybe Matthew would suggest a game of Snake Hunt and we'd go back to the spot with our entire arsenal of weapons. Also I was thinking about the look of shock on Hannah's face when, with my arms spread wide, I would hiss the word *snake*, six feet long and as thick as my arm.

Perhaps at the time it should have occurred to me that, the same as with cats, when a black snake crosses your path it's an omen. And what if I'd taken such a hint? What if I hadn't returned through the mountain laurel back to our secret spot? Then I'm certain that, twenty-six years on, my story would now be heading toward a different end. Not that I believe my being there, my being a witness, made any difference to what Matthew did that day. But certainly it changed me, changed me in such a way that the conclusion to my story now seems like an inevitability. So much so that the right ending has come to feel like my purpose.

Pushing my way through the last of the branches, I broke onto the scene and there they were, already in position. I remember being amazed at how much rope Matthew had used. It reminded me of old silent movies, the victim mouthing screams as she lies on the railroad tracks, already cocooned by the caped villain.

Matthew fired his first shot. Hannah cried out in pain. Everything was rolling now.

NEW YORK, 2008

His wife is already in bed.

Patrick swirls the last inch of Jim Beam in his glass, the ice barely smaller than when he poured himself the large shot. Lights off, TV on, sound off. Letterman swimming onstage in his huge suit, the monologue in mime. It looks twice as phony without any sound and he turns it off.

Now the room is lit only by the white blaze of the city. He walks his drink over to the high windows for the wide-screen view, the nebulous glow of Times Square hanging low in the sky to the north. And then Patrick's gaze pulls to the east, the Empire State Building lit up tonight like a Popsicle, its tip colored cherry and lemon.

It never gets old, he whispers.

No, but you do, Paddyboy.

One last gulp to ease him sleepward, his reset button at the end of another jobless day. Thirty-eight years old and cast out.

In the kitchen, dark beyond the city light, he cracks the fridge door to see what he's doing, ditches the ice, leaves the glass in the dishwasher and heads to the bathroom. Brushes and flosses. Swooshes the mouthwash extra long, bourbon-free, minty fresh.

When he creeps into the bedroom, his wife is asleep. Patrick undresses quietly in the dark, peels back the covers and tries to drift down like a feather. But as he lets the mattress take the last few pounds of his flesh, it happens, the very thing he was trying to avoid. And although not unexpected, it comes out loud enough that he jumps.

His wife screams.

He spins and hits the switch on his bedside lamp. Turning back he sees her fighting the sheets, her body twisting and bucking, a sense of arms pinning her down in her shrieks.

Shh, he says, it's me, just me. It's Patch, there's nothing wrong.

As he touches her shoulder she screams again, harder, arms scrabbling free of the bedclothes. Now he knows to be careful, she's trying to fight her way out. Only once before has it gone that far, once before when she screamed about a man holding a gun to her head, ran to the kitchen, pulled a knife from the rack and started to prowl. That night he had stayed pressed to the bedroom wall calling out to her, It's Patrick, hun, Patch, honey, holding a pillow doubled up at his chest. It had taken her five minutes to wake. Murmuring, shivering, pacing. Where am I? she said to him when she returned to the bedroom empty-handed.

He found the knife stuck in the backrest of the leather armchair, a long gash spilling fluffy white guts. He had used it that day to debone and butterfly a half leg of lamb.

And that night, the night on which she had eviscerated the armchair, Patrick's mistake had been to reach for his wife too hard. So tonight he knows he shouldn't grab, he has to whisper her loose from the dream without becoming part of it.

And now she's halfway free, legs kicking the covers.

It's Patrick, *shh,* it's Patch, just Patch.

She pushes the sleep mask onto her forehead, wincing at the lamplight.

What is it? she asks, quieter but still terrified.

It's me, honey, nothing happened.

What did I do? she says.

Nothing—he strokes her arm—you did nothing.

She flinches but doesn't recoil, her jaw rigid, her good eye wide and blinking. Nothing happened? she says. What did I say?

Nothing, he says, soothing her, shushing her.

She frowns and pulls down her sleep mask. There was a pen, she says, I lost the pen.

We'll find the pen tomorrow. There's nothing to write now.

No, the pen for the rabbits, silly, she sighs. Too much snow.

Shh, he says, stroking her hair, go to sleep.

Don't let him hurt me, she says, pulling herself under the comforter. You promise you won't let him hurt me?

Shh, he says, *shhhh.*

Mornings after, she remembers only the screaming, not the words. But even so he can't lie to her. Because how can Patch make a promise to his wife that he's already broken?

Go to sleep, Hannah, he says, stroking her hair. *Shhhh.*

THURSDAY, FIRST THING, THEY DON'T speak of it, weaving themselves between each other's mornings, talking weekend plans when they cross. She doesn't remember and he doesn't want to remind her. Not today. Because there is something else she has forgotten but he will wait for her to bloom with the sunlight. Every new day for Hannah begins with a gradual unfolding, forty minutes of groggy, the fog of night slowly fading.

Her morning *grog*, he calls it, like living with a drunken sailor. Stumbling about, swearing at stubbed toes, spilling coffee, dropping things that bounce under the bed or skid beneath the sofa.

And then, transformed, Hannah outshines the day.

Patrick maintains the same routine, the same apartment patterns as a month ago, before he got fired.

Let go, Patch.

Sorry, Hannah. Before I got *let go.*

Once he hears no more splashing from the shower, he starts to make coffee. When he takes the mug to the bedroom she is sitting at the edge of the bed, wrapped in a towel, brushing her dark hair. And yet not dark, he supposes. Because it is bright. Hannah's hair shines like brown glass.

She smiles as he lowers the coffee, droplets of water on the ridges of her shoulders, in the scoops of her collarbone. He likes her like this, freshly misted, free of makeup.

Hannah reaches for the eyepatch and pulls it over her head, lifting her hair up and over the elastic. Thank you, she says, adjusting the patch, a glossy black satin. For a moment it makes him think of a mussel shell. A shell cupping her absence.

Sipping her coffee, she looks up at him with her good eye. *Mmm,* she says.

Bright blue eye, dark-but-bright hair. Married for exactly four years and still she surprises him, not only with her beauty, the unique blend of her, but most of all with her presence, the improbable fact of her close to him.

Patrick pulls his hand inside his sweatshirt sleeve and dabs his wife's wet shoulders. The card is tucked behind him in his waistband. Happy anniversary, Hannah, he says, producing the envelope.

For a moment she looks disappointed, gripping the towel at her chest and accusing him with her fierce eye. And then he realizes that her look isn't disappointment in him.

It doesn't matter, he says. You can get me one later. Or, you don't have to.

Yesterday Hannah worked the crime scene of a triple homicide in Chinatown, three women gunned down in a nail salon at lunchtime, the shooter's ex and two customers. She spent the afternoon gathering the facts, trying to speak to Detective McCluskey—who always slips the best details to Hannah—filing her copy for the newspaper by five. And when she came home, she started to cry, one of the deceased three months pregnant. So is he supposed to feel hurt that Hannah didn't find a spare half hour to track down a card store and trawl through its colorful racks?

Anyway, this has become an annual tradition of sorts, her forgetting their wedding anniversary. Three times out of four. Almost quaint.

No, it's not OK, she says, sucking her lips into her mouth.

Don't worry, he says. Open it, then.

The flap is glued down only at the tip. She works her finger in and pops it up without tearing. She even saves the envelopes.

Hannah takes out the card, reads the words to herself. Closes it. Holds it to her chest.

You're so sweet, Patch, she says.

Don't tell anyone.

They already know.

She beckons him down and they kiss.

I have a dark side, he growls.

PATCH

Walking away from Hannah, her blood already fading to brown, I remember thinking that I had just seen my first ever dead body.

How did that make me feel, having watched a girl tied to a tree and shot forty-nine times? Flesh, blood, death?

What if it thrilled me? Oh God, what if it *thrills* me?

We ducked out through the thicket and by the time we hit the trail, I was already twenty yards behind Matthew, too dazed to keep up as we headed back to Split Rock, where we always hid our bikes. All I remember of the trek out that day is the sight of Matthew moving farther and farther ahead of me, hauling me along in his wake.

He waited for me near the bikes, standing with one foot on the rock, looking like a dad snuck off for a smoke at a church picnic. When I got close, he unslung the bag from his shoulder.

EVERY TIME WE HEADED UP to the mountains, we took these two bags with us. We'd found them the summer before going through my dad's junk in the garage, old fishing bags for two-piece bamboo rods, made of camouflage-patterned canvas. Wearing them over our shoulders we felt like soldiers out on patrol.

It was Matthew's idea. He said one of the bags would be perfect for hiding my Red Ryder BB gun, although if anyone had looked closely enough, the gun was actually an inch too long for the bag. Matthew knew this might look suspicious, so he worked out a plan in case anyone ever stopped us.

We saved up enough money and cycled thirteen miles over to New Paltz, where there was an art supply store. Matthew had been right, I could see it was perfect as soon as he showed me the carry tube made of clear plastic. We bought the tube along with some good paper to roll up inside and also a tin of pencils. The plan was that if anyone stopped us in the mountains we'd tell them we liked sketching the scenery and I'd roll down the top of my bag and show them the tube full of paper, maybe even pull out the pencils.

Well, it turned out to be an excellent plan because one time we did get stopped by an old guy who worked for the Conservancy—the same old guy who sometimes came to our school to give us talks on geology and trees, all the good stuff kids find so fascinating. He called out to us, hurrying over and pointing at the bags, Boys, boys, you know there's no fishing in the lake.

I'd already slipped the camo bag from my shoulder and was pulling at the string that cinched the opening. When the old guy got closer I began to scrunch down the canvas to show him the clear tube full of the good drawing paper. It's OK, I said, we're not fishing.

And then Matthew said, Tricky likes to sketch the lake, sir. Tricky's really good with water, it always looks like it's moving.

By now I'd pulled out the tin of pencils and started rattling them softly to keep all the attention on me, in case the dark inch of muzzle peeking out from Matthew's bag caught the Conservancy guy's eye. He seemed to be buying into our whole act, was even smiling at us like we were an unexpected pleasure, scratching at his half-white beard.

Shouldn't you be home playing Atari? he said. That's all my sister's boys ever do these days. No, sir, I prefer to draw, I said. So you like to sketch water? he said. Yessir, I said. You ever sketch Jakobskill Falls? he said. All the time, sir. Well I guess you can't come to much harm, he said. No, sir, I said. Just remember, though, said the old guy, half turning away already, no fishing in the lake, boys. Yessir, said Matthew.

After that we'd see the old Conservancy guy occasionally. Matthew even made me sketch Jakobskill Falls and then we had to carry the drawing around with us. One time we showed him my sketch and he pretended to like it. And when he came into school to give one of his talks he seemed to deliver most of the words in the direction of Matthew and me, as if we were the only kids who cared about this stuff. I couldn't have cared less. But anyway, I suppose it was better to have the old guy on our side rather than chasing us away from the ridge. I'd say it's a fair guess we probably broke several Conservancy rules while we were up in the mountains playing our games.

MATTHEW REACHED INTO THE CAMO bag, pulled out the gun and tossed it over to me. Instinctively, I caught it.

It has your fingerprints on it too, Tricky, he said.

I looked down at my hands, one curled around the stock, the other on the barrel. Of course it had my fingerprints on it, it was my damn gun. Only something about holding it right after the crime made it feel worse, as if mine were the fresher of the two sets of prints they might find.

So now we need a plan, said Matthew.

God, we always needed a plan. *We need a plan* might as well have been Matthew's mantra. We couldn't ride our bikes around aimlessly, there had to be a final objective, our time in the Swangums always having to come with a list of activities. Rifle Range, Trail Race, Lake Swim, Lone Ranger . . .

Plus it was always Matthew who made the damn plan.

And I was always Tonto.

Shouldn't we tell someone what happened? I said, not daring to look at him.

Are you fucking stupid? They'll put us both in jail for-*ever*.

We could tell them how we were playing a game, I said. Maybe it was all just an accident.

Matthew's tongue was slipping from one side of his mouth to the other, his eyes somewhere else. Right, he said, this is what we do. First we ditch the gun. But the lake here's too obvious, they'll dredge. And nowhere in these woods. We should cycle over to Mannaha, we'll throw it in the lake over there or bury it somewhere.

Mannaha was another one of the skylakes in the Swangums and also the name of the state park surrounding it, seven miles farther down the ridge. Sometimes we cycled over there even though it wasn't so different from our own skylake and our own stretch of the mountains but there were days when we just wanted to loosen our legs, pedal hard down a different road.

I started to feel faint, dropped the gun next to our bikes and sat down on the rock. Tipping my head back to take in some air, I was half-blinded by sunlight and as I screwed up my eyes, a dark blot passed overhead. I knew what it was right away even though I couldn't make it out properly—and in that instant, I knew exactly what it was I had to do.

Come on, Tricky, let's get going, said Matthew, pulling me up by my hands.

And then I saw it again, farther down the road. Sure enough it was a turkey vulture, wings spread wide and its body flat, as if it were sliding over plate glass. I remember back then how I used to think of those turkey vultures as the vampires of the air, their gaunt bodies cloaked in plumage, prowling the skies on the lookout for their next taste of blood.

Blinking up at the sun, I pictured one of the vultures swooping down on Hannah, the thin stalk of its neck turning its red wrinkled head and its pale beak parting her hair, just like Matthew's stick.

Hannah's split eyeball was the path of least resistance and now I could see the turkey vulture going at her, its beak dragging out strings of flesh like snapped rubber bands, gobbling up wet dabs of brain, the vulture's hooked beak penetrating her over and over . . .

Dammit, I was only twelve, this doesn't have to mean anything. I had already failed to do the right thing. You think I haven't regretted that ever since? I've waited my whole life for a chance to make amends. And at least in that moment twenty-six years ago, thinking about Hannah and the turkey vulture, I finally acted. Isn't that what matters most of all?

We have to cut her down, I yelled at Matthew, and we have to bring her back and we have to tell someone what happened.

Matthew's muscles tensed but for once I acted faster than him, turning side on, dropping my shoulder and charging, my speed and weight tackling him square in the chest. He went flying back, the air punching out of him as he landed on the road. And then I broke into a sprint.

NEW YORK, 2008

Hannah kisses him goodbye but then, halfway out of the apartment, she turns as if she has forgotten something. Oh, one more thing, Patrick, she says. Are you buying any food today?

He is.

Then don't forget the cabbage, Patch, she says, blowing him a second kiss as she closes the door.

How is it that Hannah manages to come up with something new every time, playing with words as if they were plastic bricks?

Be sure to remember the sugar, sweetie.

Can you get us some veal, baby?

Buy whatever's most expensive, dearest.

Don't forget the rice, Paddy.

He goes to the kitchen, makes coffee and thinks about the long hours until she comes home. But at least there is one pleasant task today, their anniversary meal. He is making steak, a huge bone-in rib eye for two with sautéed potatoes. And that's it. He won't have a plate of steak adulterated by green vegetables. No salad, no spinach, no broccoli.

Steak and broccoli? Had Hannah actually once said that or was it just a bad dream?

But she will want *something* green tonight. Green means health. Hannah wants them both to live forever, or at least until flaky parts of them start to drop off.

Can't say I find the idea wildly appealing, he thinks, lifting up the slab of beef and sniffing, the meat well aged and just high enough. He sniffs again. Green pasture with a hint of sweetness like fresh-baked meringue.

No salad, no spinach, no broccoli. Instead he will make a green appetizer, an emerald riot of health. He starts writing a list. Zucchini and sugar snaps. Asparagus, Granny Smiths, pea shoots. He'll whisk up a lemony salad dressing. Maybe he should also buy chervil, every mouthful of salad alive with green sap.

It is a fine-looking piece of beef, aged enough to have taken on the deep red of old leather tomes, thickly edged with rich white fat.

He can picture the look she would be giving him, sitting at the kitchen table, assessing the piece of beef with a wary eye. *You can always cut the fat off, Hannah,* he imagines saying to her, his tone playful, half-challenging.

Fat is where the flavor is, she replies, mimicking one of his favorite sayings. And then somewhere in the back of his head, he pictures her sighing an affectionate sigh.

Patrick salts the steak and slides it into a large vacuum pouch, fetches his jar of bacon grease and smears some over the meat. He clamps the pouch in the vacuum sealer and starts the machine, which begins sucking all the air from the bag, its plastic shrinking until it wrinkles up tight to the flesh, the machine whining as it applies heat, sealing the pouches airtight.

He puts the beef back in the fridge, enough prep for now. Later he will drop the pouch in a water bath, 134 degrees Fahrenheit. There are machines for this as well, *sous vide* machines, but a year ago he decided he wanted to build his own. He had even wanted to make his own immersion circulator. The electronics looked simple enough but the soldering was an issue.

If they lived in the country he would have a workshop. But Hannah will never move to the country, so instead he bought himself a temperature controller and hooked the thing up to his rice cooker.

He pictures her at the kitchen table feigning a swoon. *Immersion circulator?* she says. *Temperature controller? God, you make tonight's anniversary dinner sound so darned sexy, Patch.*

This is Hannah's favorite way to speak to him about his more esoteric cooking techniques. Mostly sarcastic. Not wholly without love.

It's called cooking sous vide. *That's French, Hannah. What's sexier than French?*

You're right, Paris was so romantic. Le Jardin des Tuileries, Paul Gauguin, le Musée d'Orsay . . . Wait, sous vide, Patch? Isn't that the thing you explained to your brother by referencing Death Valley?

OK, it was true, Patrick had explained it that way to Sean and his wife, Beth, thinking that something more muscular than *gentle water bath* might have appealed to his older brother.

Look, Sean, this is how it works. The highest temperature ever recorded on earth was at Death Valley, Nevada, in 1913. One hundred and thirty-four degrees Fahrenheit. And one hundred and thirty-four just happens to be the perfect temperature for medium-rare steak, exactly how you like it, right? That means you could fill up a bucket with water on the hottest day in Death Valley, wait for it to reach the ambient temperature, drop in a steak sealed in plastic and you know the water temperature's never going to rise above one-thirty-four. You literally can't overcook the thing. You leave it for an hour or two, take it out, brown it quickly in a hot pan. And there you are, perfect steak, one-thirty-four.

You mean, tournedos à la Death Valley? *Mmm,* sign me up, Patchman. Can I get a side of pommes de Sahara with that?

Potatoes have a completely different molecular structure, Sean. You'd need something like one-eighty-three. You could use a hot spring, perhaps.

Something like one-eighty-three? Total nerd! OK then, how about a little creamed spinach Kalahari, bro?

A week later Patrick had invited Sean and Beth to their house for dinner, even printed up a fake menu. He made them

Tournedos à la Death Valley but he crisped the potatoes at four-sixty and called them Pommes de Venus. Sean licked his plate clean and admitted the meat was maybe the best he'd ever eaten.

Remembering all of this gives him an idea. Patrick finds his computer, brings it to the kitchen table and pours another coffee.

Meat loaf sous vide, Patrick types into the document labeled *Blog Recipe Ideas* and then drags his hands down his face. You're thirty-eight years old, he says. Thirty-eight and you write a blog. Isn't it time to grow up?

It's temporary, Patch. Until you find another job.

He clicks through to the webpage. Red Moose Barn. His blog has a concept.

Yeah, let's hear it for the big ideas, Paddyboy.

The posts he writes for Red Moose Barn work through the development of one dish at a time, the gradual invention of a restaurant menu, plate by plate. The blog is his test kitchen, his yays and his nays, a test kitchen for a nonexistent restaurant, the kind of place Patrick dreams of opening one day. Red Moose Barn, not a restaurant in the city but somewhere upstate among the apple orchards. Only he isn't trained, he knows cooking but he doesn't know restaurants, the business. So he writes fantasy menus on his fantasy blog. Creates fantasy dishes and cooks them for Hannah. Shoots them, eats them, posts them.

On his blog.

Blog. God, the word sounds so ugly, a word that should be a slang term for one of the less glamorous bodily functions.

He glances over to see the time on the stove, his appointment with Dr. Rosenstock not until three this afternoon, five hours away. He has been seeing Dr. Rosenstock since the incident several weeks ago, although he's still not sure he sees the point.

You forgot how to breathe, Patch. Don't you think it's been good for you, finding someone to talk to?

Four weeks earlier, he and Hannah had been in the backseat of a taxi, on their way to meet friends for brunch, the driver with the radio on, a report about how America was in danger of suffering the worst financial crisis since the Great Depression. Patrick had sent his résumé to only three places right after losing his job, thinking perhaps he could be picky in his search for new work. Not one of those places had called him in for an interview. Not even a preliminary round.

. . . the Dow Jones has tumbled over a thousand points in less than two months, with experts warning this is just the beginning . . .

He remembers trying to swallow in the back of the taxi. Nothing. And then he had tried to breathe in. Nothing. And then nothing had followed nothing, more nothing and more.

Patrick had felt so stupid, struggling for air while Hannah checked messages on her phone, unaware that her husband couldn't remember how to swallow, the world turning too fast beyond the taxicab windows. Breathing, one of the most basic human functions. How could anyone forget how to breathe?

And so a week later he started seeing Dr. Rosenstock, every Thursday afternoon at three. At first they spoke about his job, how he had been fired, and then they spoke about how he felt about losing his job, how he felt now.

A tightness in the chest.

That's where the feeling is, Patrick?

Yes.

Does the feeling have a color?

No.

Does the feeling have a shape?

He would have felt rude saying, Of course it fucking doesn't.

Now Patrick has started to wonder if he is the only person in the world whose feelings come in shapeless monochrome.

After a few weeks, the sessions had moved onto his childhood, which had been easy enough to speak about, right up until the point at which he neared the end of his twelfth year, August 18, six days short of his thirteenth birthday. That's when he had felt his breaths starting to shorten, an inability to swallow, and he couldn't get the words to come out.

Would you like to try writing it down for me, Patrick?

I don't know.

You don't ever have to show it to me. Not unless you want to.

———

HE OPENS IT ON HIS computer, the page blank but for a title, *1982*. Every attempt to write about it has ended in deletion. A delete button cleanse, a delete button peel. He stares at the screen for a while trying to recall all of his colorless, shapeless feelings.

Nothing.

And so Patrick decides instead to describe the mountains, the pitch pines and blueberry bushes, the smooth water of the lake.

Sure, Paddyboy, start out with the stuff that really matters.

He looks away from his laptop angrily and now the only thing he can think about is the way Dr. Rosenstock's mostly bald head reflects the light from his reading lamp.

Patrick never knows how much he should say, how much to reveal in that room with its unruly ficus and glimpses of Central Park through the window. What if Dr. Rosenstock has a duty to report him to someone?

Not that Patrick is planning to kill anyone, not exactly. And probably everyone has thought about such things. To some degree, at least. No?

Although often Patrick wonders how much potential he has, because if you think about something often enough, when does going through with it become inevitable?

He looks back at his laptop and types a line.

And again he can picture his wife sitting across from him at the kitchen table, Hannah nodding approvingly. It's like I always say, Patch. Don't bury the lede.

He looks back down at his computer—

I remember the gunshots made a wet sort of sound, phssh phssh phssh, *and each time he hit her she screamed.*

The line shocks him. His wife is right, of course.

GLANCING ACROSS AT THE TIME, Patrick sees it is nearly twelve o'clock, three hours to kill before his appointment with Dr. Rosenstock, and he tells himself not to but he knows that he will. He can feel it in his shoulders, something dragging him up. Don Trevino has started to fill the empty hours of his life. Trevino is fast becoming another hobby.

Patrick closes his laptop and goes to find shoes.

Outside, the sidewalk is strewn with salt, little manufactured pellets like crumbs of polystyrene, but the promised snow hasn't yet fallen on the city. Patrick heads uptown and east, his route a boxy zigzag as he tries to avoid the red hands of the crosswalks, only getting caught at the curb a couple of times. He likes it when the lights fall kindly for him—recently things as small as this have become capable of almost making or breaking his days.

The traffic slides around him like blocks of a puzzle, pictures coming together and then dismantling again across the vast grid of midtown Manhattan.

As he walks, he thinks about the perfect abandoned barn he has conjured up in his imagination. He thinks about its restoration, helping out in overalls, tired limbs satisfied at the end of the day. And there it stands, finished, the words RED MOOSE BARN printed on a wooden sign that hangs by the road, the red silhouette of a moose beneath the words, the same symbol they will stamp onto menus, cards, brown paper napkins. Everything is finished, the barn freshly painted barn red with white sugar-frosting trims and white roof. Red Moose Barn, sixty, seventy miles north of the city, far enough that country food would feel right, close enough that city people would have weekend homes in the area. Country food made with modern techniques. Comfort made perfect.

Eventually they could turn the land around the barn into a vegetable garden. Golden zucchini blossoms, scarlet tomatoes, sweet green peas . . .

The voice inside interrupts him. *Enough already! This is nothing but a doll's house, Paddyboy. You're thirty-eight years old. Listen to me—you need a good job, not a goddam blog.*

The air is arctic cold and Patrick's ears begin to burn. He puts on his watch cap as he reaches his destination, pulling it down all the way to his eyebrows.

Forty-Seventh Street, opposite the building in which he used to work, the building in which he was fired.

Let go, Patch.

He checks his watch, almost twelve thirty, so maybe he's missed him. Don Trevino fails to keep especially regular hours. Patrick stamps his feet to ward off the chill and holsters his hands deep in his pockets.

After thirty minutes of waiting, Patrick sees him through the glass, stepping out of the elevator, alone and sprightly, gray cashmere coat and Russian-style fur hat. Don Trevino's nose is a veinous red even before it has been slapped by the cold. He pushes through the barrier, nodding jovially to security, and marches out onto the street.

Patrick has opened his laminated tourist map, half-covering his face, but keeps his eyes on his quarry, Trevino heading right and Patrick following, fifty yards back on the opposite side of Forty-Seventh, Trevino's head bobbing along on the yellow surf of taxi roofs.

And Patrick begins to picture it again, bumping into Don Trevino by chance on the street only a week after Trevino had fired him. He remembers the prickle in his shoulders. Even his nose had buzzed with a sense of the moment. Hit him. Hit him. Hurt him.

Hello, Patrick, Trevino had said, looking perfectly unfazed, as if he were doing nothing more than greeting a neighbor.

Patrick had said nothing, his actual assault on Trevino no more than a brief snort, a look of disgust.

Over the several weeks since, Patrick has replayed this scene in his head numerous times, picturing the details of the street, pasting them into various fantasies.

The brass poles of an apartment building's awning. Patrick could have grabbed Trevino beneath the chin and pushed him up against the metal before making him gasp and cough with a punch to the gut.

The window of an Irish bar. He should have grabbed Trevino by the collar and driven his fur-hatted head through the plate glass, whereupon a neon sign would have shattered and crackled with approval.

A blue mailbox. He imagined smashing Don Trevino's face into the metal studs on its side. Or sometimes he pictures the mailbox open, Trevino's head and shoulders stuck inside, his legs wheeling away, the last desperate kicks of a flipped bug.

There are intricate variations of each scenario, some comical, some grotesque, and when lost in these thoughts, Patrick barely has to remember his actual inaction that day several weeks back—an impotent snort, his pointless disgust, another one of life's great passive-aggressive victories.

But maybe today is the day.

Trevino turns right and Patrick skips over the street, through the knee-high fog of taxi fumes, around the corner. Patrick's eyes follow Trevino's hat above the jostle of Fifth Avenue. Trevino turns right, opens a door and disappears.

The same door as last week, three times. And the week before, twice. Trevino will reemerge in five minutes, his leather-gloved hand holding the string handles of a white paper bag. Sandwich, soup, drink.

But Patrick waits anyway, a little farther down Fifth Avenue, and when Trevino reappears, strolling back toward the office, Patrick follows, just in case.

Yeah? Just in case what, Paddyboy?

And the sky, now swollen, starts dispensing its snow.

PATCH

Without having to look, I knew Matthew was behind me. I could sense his rage in the heat, another harmonic alongside the electrical hum of the bugs.

The summer before, challenging each other to Trail Races, I'd managed to win most of the time. I had natural pace. And because I was smaller than Matthew, I was nimble over the rough ground. But Matthew must've grown an additional foot since then.

On our very first day at school, getting changed for gym, every boy in the locker room had stolen a look at the small nest of hair between Matthew's legs, something noticeably absent from our own bodies. And now that hair was thicker still, not only between Matthew's legs but below his knees as well. There was even a hint of mustache above his top lip, Matthew's whole body bursting with the strength of Samson.

Which meant now I wasn't sure whether I was faster than Matthew. I was running flat out through the stifling heat, hoping that my advantage still held, pushing my smooth hairless legs as hard as I could.

The trail to our secret spot carried you on a thin path that ran along the top of Swangum Ridge. To my right the ground fell away steeply to a valley with Sunset Ridge on the other side but that was nothing compared to the sheer drop to my left, a cliff face that ran straight down to the Hudson Valley. It must have been more than a thousand feet, the valley floor below nothing but haze.

Even walking that path was tricky, so running was downright dangerous. The topsoil was thin, the trail a tangle of tree roots, an assault course of half-buried rocks. But I sprinted as fast as I could and despite the danger and my fear of Matthew, I remember feeling exhilarated, my lungs sparkling with life, my body performing at its absolute peak for that first quarter mile, when suddenly a bad thought leapt into my head.

Maybe I could get to Hannah first but even if I won this race, what then? Matthew wasn't going to offer me a gentlemanly handshake. You win, Tricky, well done. We play by your rules now.

Now I was thinking too hard about this problem and the overthinking was hindering my movement. My stride was losing its focus and I could feel my uncertainties mixing together, frothing up like the insides of a bottle rocket. How close was he now?

I believe I can actually remember thinking the words *don't turn around* but it's like that old thing about being told *not* to think of a white cat. Instantly you go ahead and think of a damned white cat.

It was only a glance, a quick peek over my shoulder, but one glance was enough. I went down hard like the sprung bar of a mousetrap.

I don't know what it was my skull thudded into, tree or root or rock. All I remember is the sense that my head felt made of stone in the moment of impact.

EVERYTHING WAS A BLUR WHEN I awoke. And then blur turned to treetops and sky sliding by. Matthew was pulling me off the trail by my arms.

At the point where I'd tripped, the path ran maybe thirty feet in from the edge of Swangum Ridge but I'd fallen close to a spur, one of several along the way that would bring you right up to the edge of the cliff for the panoramic view. He was dragging me along one of those spurs.

Everything hurt. I let out a moan and Matthew let go of me, the pain shooting higher as my hands smashed down against rock and my head hit the ground. That's when I noticed a sharp damp pain in the back of my head, my skull singing high notes.

Now Matthew was on me, pinning my wrists, straddling me the way he sometimes did if he wanted me to cry uncle in a play fight, threatening to make me eat grass or dirt or a live frog. As he glanced around, wiping his mouth, I thought I could see all the thoughts spinning behind his eyes like the wheels of a slot machine.

All you ever do is watch, Tricky, he said, not sounding mad at me, just weary. You stand to one side, watching and watching like a statue. You think because you didn't join in, that's OK? You're off the hook?

I didn't say anything, staring at him as I tried to think away the pain.

So you're telling me the first time you ever decide to do something is when it's too late? When it screws me over and screws you over and Hannah's still just as dead? Matthew's voice had shifted from weary to bitterly amused. It's too late, Tricky, he said. You didn't even say anything.

He gave me a hard look, daring me to disagree, but I didn't speak. I don't know why but something told me I had to lie there playing possum, the grand tactic of my life.

Matthew's eyes fixed on my hands. Quickly he moved one of my wrists on top of the other so that he could grip them both at the same time. I had slender wrists but even so, and as weak as I felt, maybe I could've wrenched free of his grip but I was in a lot of pain.

Matthew began to rise, pulling me up with him.

Once we were standing, he started backing me up. I didn't look around or fight him. I was trying hard not to cry out in pain as we moved together like awkward prom dates stumbling across a dance floor.

When we stopped, I think I felt an updraft from the valley floor. If I were an eagle I could have soared away. The screech of the pain was so loud that I let my body surrender to him, like the moment when the lady in old movies collapses into the hero's arms.

Him Tarzan. Me Jane.

I let my eyelids fall as Matthew took his hand away from my wrists and then my shoulder. Open your eyes, Tricky, he said.

But I couldn't, it was as if I were standing on a high-wire and even the slightest movement might be enough to overbalance me.

Matthew yelled at me, I said *open your eyes*.

Still I didn't do what he said, thinking instead about the time we found a fat timber rattlesnake and when Matthew shot it, it moved like a whip and we ran for our lives screaming and when we stopped running we laughed so hard we thought we were more in danger of dying from the laughter than we ever had been from that snake.

Tricky, I swear . . . Just open your goddam eyes right now.

I thought about lake-swimming, deer-stalking and can-plunking. We'd had a lot of fun together in the Swangums.

My chest felt like it was painted with a bullseye.

I thought I could sense something moving, only the breeze per-haps, but then after a long pause, I heard Matthew speak, the sound of his voice having moved farther away. OK then, OK, he muttered. OK, Tricky.

I opened my eyes. Matthew was ten paces back, his shoulders slumped and a look of defeat on his face. He smiled bitterly at me. By the way, your head's cut pretty bad, Tricky, he said, reaching into his back pocket, pulling out his red bandana and draping it over a rock. You know, he said, you realize no one ever needs to find out you were actually there. Really it was nothing to do with you at all. I'm sorry, Tricky.

And with that, Matthew turned around, giving me a dejected wave as he headed off into the trees, back toward the bikes.

———

I FELT FAINT IN THE heat, the sickly pine resin air. Stepping away from the drop, I wanted to sit down and sleep but the pain in my head flared again. I reached back and started pushing my fingers timidly through my wet hair. I had a huge thatch of hair back then—people said I looked like a young version of Bobby Ewing from the TV show *Dallas*—and maybe that proved to be lucky, as if my head were wrapped in layers of gauze. The hole was right at my crown and all sticky. My fingers moved down and just kept on moving, down, farther down.

And then I swear I heard a squelching sound, like a boot landing in mud, and yanked my hand away in shock thinking I must've touched my brain. Looking at my hand it was almost as if the blood couldn't be mine. Too bright, too thick, too much. I wiped the hand on a rock, picked up Matthew's bandana and pressed it to the back of my skull.

I had to get to Hannah but my head was all swirly in the sick-making heat as I started to wonder how long it would take for a corpse to rot in this weather. When would her body start to smell? And now I couldn't stop thinking about Hannah hanging there, meat for the vultures, blood dripping from the milky white hooks of their beaks.

NEW YORK, 2008

The griddled zucchini lie in a bowl banded with faint stripes of char, flecked with pepper and basil, soaking up olive oil and sherry vinegar, while the steak cooks slowly in water and the potatoes, parboiled and dusted with rice flour, dry off in the fridge.

Rice flour, don't ever tell anyone your secret, Patch.

All the better to crisp them with.

He sits at the kitchen table reading the comments on his blog as he waits. He will begin preparing the salad as soon as Hannah calls to say she is heading home, his signal to start peeling asparagus into a pile of pale ribbons, trimming the sugar snaps, acidulating apples.

Jorgé, the doorman, has been enlisted to help with Patrick's plan to make everything perfect tonight. When he sees Hannah coming through the door, he will buzz their apartment, three quick blasts their agreed-upon signal, and then Jorgé will delay Hannah, complimenting her hair, tutting over the weather, the snow, her poor shoes.

Please, how long do I keep her, gentleman? A minute would be great, Jorgé. No problem, gentleman. Thank you, Jorgé.

And action. Deep greens and pale greens will be tossed in the lemony dressing. He will make a wreath of tangled pea shoots on the plate and scatter everything else from above, seemingly at random. The composition of a salad always makes Patrick feel like Jackson Pollock dripping paint.

No delusions of grandeur in that whatsoever, Paddyboy.

Once the salads are plated he will begin crisping the potatoes in duck fat and heating his large slab of cast iron on which the steak will be seared to a crust. A half hour of preheating and the metal will take on the appearance of charcoal, hints of white ash in the shimmering iron.

By the time he carries the salads to the table, Jorgé will have released Hannah, a thirty-second elevator ride to their penthouse floor.

Patrick will slip off his apron and fetch champagne. When she walks through the door he will be standing by the table in his wedding suit, the same tie as four years ago, the same silk handkerchief in his breast pocket and a white napkin wrapped around a bottle of Pol Roger.

Soft pop. Happy anniversary, Hannah.

Hannah will clap and kiss him.

Everything must be made to happen just so, with perfect timing. Everything for her.

And then Patrick wonders if the salad needs some crunch. *What about pistachios?* he thinks. There is a bag in his pantry, vivid green nuts speckled with patches of dusty violet skin.

HANNAH TRIES TO INITIATE HOME-HANNAH mode, anniversary-Hannah, leave-the-streets-for-the-day-Hannah as she rises from her desk in The Shack.

NYPD in the elevators, NYPD in the corridors, NYPD in uniform, NYPD in suits, the ugliest fourteen-floor stack of stone you ever saw, all clay-colored bricks, little blocks piled high to form a squat square building, all shithouse glam and checkerboard curves, address 1PP, looks exactly like a cubist giant has lain a terra-cotta turd (Detective McCluskey liked that one, she'd heard him steal it more than once, only he dropped the *cubist giant* and *terra-cotta* motifs), the most important building in the city, at least if you value not being slain in your bed on a nightly basis, 1PP, One Police Plaza, the headquarters of the NYPD—Major Crime Squad, Real Time Crime Center, Police Commissioner—the place that Hannah calls (among other scatological names) her office, or when she's talking to anyone in the know, The Shack, because they all call it The Shack, the crime reporters who work there, 1PP's second floor set aside for the journalists of eight news organizations, rivals fraternizing, hanging out in the same small space, the thin schmear of mustard in the fat pastrami sandwich of the NYPD HQ.

NYPD in the elevators, NYPD in the corridors, NYPD in uniform, NYPD in suits, the rub of it, The Shack in the 1PP stack, Hannah loves it, she lives it, she breathes it.

So that leaving it behind is bittersweet every night—a news day low on blood is a good day for the city, it's true, but red streets at night, tabloids' delight. And today? Just a light shade of blush, a good thing, probably, for her anniversarial mood. Is that a word, *anniversarial*? Possibly not, probably she's confused it with *adversarial,* and then she thinks to take the stairs, only a single flight down, not the elevator, because enough cops already, she will see more on the way out anyway, and she does, Officer Kohn (Jets, Mets, Nets, hates hockey, two daughters).

Four and twelve, Brian? she says. Four and *twelve*? Unbelievable.

Yeah, well, we stank up the whole season. But what can I do? When you're a Jet you're a Jet, right? Thanks for reminding me, Hannah.

Would I do that to you, Brian? No, I meant your daughters, four and twelve, right?

Oh, I see, playing smart, Hannah, huh? You know, we could do with some of that, maybe you could coach the Jets instead of Mangenius—dumbest nickname I ever heard. The girls? Seven and nine. Gang Green? I'd take seven and nine in a heartbeat.

Come on, dream big, Brian, turn that frown upside down— nine and seven! You know, nine and seven could sneak you into the playoffs next season.

Right, dream big, sure. Look, I love my kids, Hannah, but I'd sell both their sweet little souls for nine and seven. You have a great weekend now.

You too, Brian. Maybe take up watching hockey instead. And give Jasmine and Kaylee big hugs and kisses from me.

Out into the night, the day's snow no more than a haze in the plaza lights now, and incoming Daniel Ochoa (Knicks, Yanks, fiancée) and Marty Russell (Devils, Springsteen, *seven* boys).

Still don't have my invite, Officer Ochoa.

Still don't have a wedding date, *New York Mail*.

What gives, Danny? Marty's sons will have seven brides for seven brothers before you make an honest woman of Isabel. (Hannah's phone starts to ring.)

She has like twelve thousand cousins. And they all eat, you know? I'll be saving up till Judgment Day.

Now Marty wants in. Hannah, why leaving so early? Come on, Friday night's just getting started.

Maybe I was born to run, Marty.

They wave her away like a bad smell, but laughing, as she picks up the phone, Jen's number on the screen, best friends from the first day of kindergarten, and she answers, Hey, Jen, you got snow up there?

Snow? No. I called to say happy anniversary, Hannah.

Hannah hangs back from saying anything more for a moment, her marriage to Patrick still one of the sore points between her and Jen, not that Jen openly disapproves, would never voice disapproval, but Jen hadn't *understood why,* and four years ago, Hannah had felt hurt by nothing worse than a pause after she told Jen the news of her engagement, and then they hadn't spoken in almost a year, all because of a pause not much longer than this one ballooning now . . . Thanks, Jen, she says. Four years already, I can't believe it.

You have plans?

Patch. He's cooking something special.

Lucky you.

(Another call coming through.) Yep, lucky me. (Hannah looks

to see who it is, the news editor.) Oh shoot, I have to take this other call from . . . Sorry, it's work, Jen. Let's talk over the weekend. Tell the girls *arrrrr* from their Aunt Hannah.

I will. You have a good night, Han. Love you. Say hi to Patrick.

Hannah hangs up the call and pauses a moment before taking the next, noticing the sound of helicopters in the distance, a sense of fourteen floors behind her beginning to hum, sirens winding up everywhere, and she knows she should let the call from her news editor drop to voice mail, she can say she was stuck underground, delays on the subway, and that's what she absolutely should do, their fourth anniversary, because if she waits thirty minutes before talking to work it will probably all be too late, whatever it is, the news will have broken, and Hannah will be into her first glass of champagne, Patch always buys them the same one they drank in a restaurant, before that first night she had spent in his apartment, so very sweet, Patrick is so very good to her.

But she answers.

PATCH

I was halfway down the trail to Jakobskill stream when I heard what I thought was a blue jay squawking, so it wasn't until I actually made out the word *help* that I realized Hannah was alive.

At this point I should probably describe the huge sense of relief I felt and how it had been like I was carrying a great weight, only now the burden was lifted. But exactly what that twelve-year-old boy was thinking and feeling is often a mystery to me. I'm not sure I know who he was beyond a bunch of things that happened to him.

You might as well know a calendar. A grocery list.

What I do remember is trying to run. But running was difficult, what with me holding a blood-soaked bandana clamped to the hole in my head. Plus, the trail was steep and strewn with sharp rocks and now the world was overlapping itself, like when you see a 3-D comic book without the glasses, so I went as fast as I could, stumbling down the scree, stones scraping and slipping under my sneakers.

As I crossed Jakobskill stream and scrambled uphill, the sounds she was making became clearer. Sometimes the word *help* or sometimes a strained scream, halfway between effort and pain. Other times just a horrible, feeble sound.

I pushed the bandana into my back pocket as I darted off the trail. When Hannah heard me crashing through the last of the branches, she turned her head as best she could. Her face was twisted with a wild and desperate look. And seeing me, she screamed again and started fighting the ropes.

I can still picture the perfect angles of her face as she strained at those knots, the neat curve of her chin, a soft arc of jawbone rising up to her ear. Writing this now makes me think of turning over in bed Sunday mornings to see if she is awake, hoping she stays asleep so that I can wake her with coffee, bagels and newspapers in bed.

How am I supposed to reconcile any of these things?

I tried to say something comforting but Hannah was still crying and writhing and I don't think she heard. So I didn't move close right away but circled around to where she was facing, keeping my knees bent and hands raised.

Hannah, I promise I won't hurt you, I said, getting down into a kneel, still showing my hands.

Her head carried on twisting like she couldn't stand the sight of me. And then, slow to catch on as usual, I realized what she was doing—Hannah was trying desperately to see if Matthew was with me—and I yelled, He's gone, Hannah, Matthew's gone. I promise, he's not coming back.

Her body began to fight less and less.

When finally she faced me, I dropped my fists to the ground and started to cry. I'm sorry, Hannah, I didn't know he would . . . I'm sorry, I should never . . .

Hannah sniffed hard, her head shivering in disbelief. Oh my God, she said. Oh my God, Patch. What will my mom say? Patch, my mom's really gonna kill me.

I just stared at her. How was I supposed to respond to something like that?

Hannah clenched her teeth and cried out in pain, *Uuurgh,* my eye, he shot my eye and it hurts so much. And now I can't see from my eye, I can't see from it, Patch. I can't see from my eye, she said, her breathing starting to stutter. Patch, what does it look like? What's happened to my eye? Is it bad? I can't see from it. Is it really bad?

Hannah tilted her face, having no clue that I couldn't make out her mashed eye for all the blood-matted hair that was over her face.

I gulped. It doesn't look so bad, I said, still on my knees, which made the lie seem that much worse. I started to get to my feet.

But what's it like? Will my mom be able to tell?

No, it's kinda bloodshot, I said. There were dried leaves stuck to my hands. I wiped them away.

Why can't I see anything from it?

I started to kick lightly at the ground with my toe. Maybe it's kinda . . . shocked, I told her, like unconscious. And the next thing I said was something I actually believed. But if there's anything wrong, I'm sure the doctors will fix it.

Hannah's good eye just blinked.

I stood there uneasily, as if there existed a zone between us through which I wasn't allowed to pass, and said to her, Is it OK if . . . ? Can I come over and help you, Hannah?

She nodded at me, so I walked forward gingerly and then leaned around the tree to eye up the knots. Hannah's breathing was loud. I have to go get a knife, I said.

The ropes creaked. *Nooo,* she pleaded. Don't leave me here, Patch.

It's not far, I said. We keep supplies over there, it'll take less than a minute, I promise. Don't worry, I'll whistle a tune so you'll know I'm still here, I said.

Heading deeper into the woods, I started to whistle. The only tune I could think of was *Whistle While You Work.* And I could whistle the singing bit pretty well but I wasn't so good at whistling the whistling bit.

We had this place where we kept all the stuff we'd take up there, everything hidden beneath a tarp kicked over with leaves. Weapons-wise, there was a slingshot, our spear and a load of BBs in tins and plastic bottles. We had soda cans for playing the game we called Rifle Range and sets of paper targets. We had a bunch of food in cans and a can opener, obviously. There were some bones and antlers we'd picked up here and there, although we never really found a good use for them. A compass we didn't need, a pair of weak plastic binoculars, a hip flask that we'd fill up from the stream and take sips from like we were real men drinking liquor. There were pickle jars for frogs, a couple of cigarette lighters, a pair of toy handcuffs. And we had two knives, a little Swiss Army knife that was nine-tenths blunt and also a scrimshaw hunting knife, its bone handle etched with a grizzly bear marauding down a piney bluff. Matthew loved that hunting knife so much we hardly ever used it, which is why the Swiss Army knife was nine-tenths blunt.

When I got to the place, I saw the tarp pulled all the way back. And right away I could tell he'd used every single rope we had.

We used the thinnest ones for tripwires and the thicker ones to play Tarzan—which mostly involved swinging over streams— or to make lassos. Oh and also for an escape game we called Houdini. And I was definitely the best at Houdini. Not because I was the best at knots but because I had thinner hands and was the best at wriggling free.

Anyway, I knew exactly where the two knives were kept, so right away I could tell Matthew had taken the hunting knife. I wondered if he'd thought about cutting my throat when he had me pinned down thirty minutes earlier.

That's when I heard Hannah screaming my name and realized I'd stopped whistling. So I started to run back, not pulling the tarp back over our supplies, calling out that everything was OK.

Sorry, I said, getting back to the tree, using my least-chewed-upon fingernail to ease the blade from the Swiss Army knife.

Patch, hurry up, said Hannah, shivering now in the near-hundred heat.

That blade was so blunt it probably would've been just as quick had I gnawed through those ropes with my teeth.

NEW YORK, 2008

He waits for Hannah to call again, watching the story as it sprouts fresh limbs on the television news channels. By eleven most of the details are in, the story playing on loop.

. . . worked for two years at the jewelry store in the West Village. But Johnson was sacked after the store owner, Elias Petridis, received several complaints about Johnson's behavior toward his customers. Tonight, it seems Michael Johnson followed his former boss from the store after Mr. Petridis locked up for the night, and what happened next, in nearby Washington Square Park, took place in the full view of hundreds of witnesses. Again we want to warn our viewers about the graphic nature of this shocking crime. More details from our reporter at the scene, Dan.

Yes, thank you, Michelle, at around 6:00 P.M., just around the corner from here in Washington Square Park, the snow still falling, Michael Johnson, having followed his former employer, Elias Petridis, owner of the jewelry store you can see behind me on Eighth Street, screamed out for his ex boss to stop, yelling the instruction several times with the addition of several expletives. At this point, turning and seeing Michael Johnson, Mr. Petridis started to quicken his pace, at which point Johnson pulled out a handgun and shot Elias Petridis, the bullet apparently striking him in the leg and Mr. Petridis falling to the ground. What came next horrified the hundreds of shocked onlookers. Witnesses have described how Johnson then ran at his ex-boss like a madman—with a crazed look in his eyes, as one witness told me—and then from a back-pack pulled out what's been . . . there are some suggestions it was a meat cleaver or perhaps a large carving knife . . . and then, with this big, big knife, Johnson tried to . . . again, please be aware that some of you might find this extremely disturbing . . . Michael Johnson attempted to decapitate Elias Petridis, all the while yelling the words, Now who's losing his head, now who's losing his head? Witnesses to this grisly crime, many of them clearly traumatized by what they've seen here today, have described how the park, at this point, became a scene of great panic, many witnesses speaking about a sense of hysteria, hundreds of people in the park screaming and running, but not everyone it would appear was sure what they were running from or where they should be running to. And it was during this frenzied, chaotic stampede that police officers Michael Karp and Anthony Lorenzo, having heard the gunshot, arrived on the scene, drew their weapons, and instructed Johnson to drop the knife. Now, here's where we have a number of conflicting reports, Michelle, some witnesses saying that Michael Johnson dropped the knife and then stood up, turning toward the police with his hands raised and empty. Other witnesses, however, stated that when Johnson stood up, he was waving the knife at the police officers and looking as if he was about to run at them. Yet others recalled that Johnson was still holding his handgun, that he jumped to his feet and then turned, pointing his weapon in the direction of the cops, leading to suggestions that this might have been a case of suicide by cop.

Let me stop you a moment, Dan, could you explain to any of our viewers who haven't heard the phrase exactly what you mean by suicide by cop?

Certainly, Michelle. Suicide by cop describes an incident in which an individual provokes the police into shooting them, for example, by pointing a gun at them, knowing that the police will then employ lethal force, as may have been the case today. But just to reiterate, the details are still not completely clear. What we do know for certain is that whatever it was Johnson did after being instructed by the police to drop the knife, the two police officers then opened fire, some witnesses describing Johnson, who died at the scene of multiple gunshot wounds, as being

*taken down in a hail of bullets. Now, Michelle, as I say, there are con-
flicting reports about this, we don't know for example if Johnson was
holding the handgun the whole time, if he maybe even discharged the
gun, what we do know is that during this terrible incident, seven
bystanders were hit by stray bullets and/or debris and that, unfortunately, one of those innocent bystanders, a man in his twenties, as yet
unnamed, died on his way to the hospital after sustaining a gunshot wound. Now, was that from a shot fired by the police officers or a
shot fired possibly by Johnson? It's too early to say, but obviously what
took place here today was truly a brutal crime, just a ghastly spectacle,
something that none of the witnesses present here today will ever forget,
and a terrible, terrible tragedy. Back to you, Michelle.*

*Thanks, Dan, and for more on this incredibly shocking story we
join . . .*

WHEN THE PHONE RINGS IT is almost eleven.

Patrick hadn't realized that Jorgé's shift ended at ten, so he is
unprepared when Hannah comes into the apartment. No wedding
jacket, no Pol Roger, only a tired hug and Hannah's apologies. She
needs to take off her shoes right away, she says, but she doesn't
take off her shoes, she sits in the armchair, closes her eye and covers her face.

Patrick goes into the kitchen and pulls on his jacket.

But the champagne is good and the salad is fine. Gradually
Hannah slips away from her long day at work and back into
the home around her, the romantic meal. Most nights are the same,
as if some part of Hannah has remained back at the day's crime
scene and has to be reeled in. Only tonight this takes longer than
usual.

She doesn't talk much about the incident in Washington Square
Park, he doesn't ask, but she does say that McCluskey could tell
her almost nothing more than Patrick has seen on the news.

So pointless, she whispers to herself.

Hannah takes her champagne to the bedroom. When she

emerges, she unclips her hair and lets it fall over her shoulders. She adjusts the elastic of her eyepatch and then the thin straps of the dress into which she has changed.

Patrick has to turn the potatoes and by the time he returns, Hannah is almost restored, memories of their wedding day beginning to flower on her lips. He kisses her forehead and she pulls the silk handkerchief from his breast pocket as he leans over, twisting it quickly and wrapping it around her wrist. You wore this on our wedding day, no? she says, Patrick nodding. Do you remember how you couldn't get the words to come out? she asks him. Ahd . . . I duh . . . I do.

The air was so dry in there, he says.

More like you were so choking up, she laughs.

He leaves her with a Bordeaux to uncork as he sears the steak, which crackles as it hits the fierce cast iron, the smoke so sweet Patrick can taste hints of caramelized meat in the corners of his mouth.

While the steak rests he checks the potatoes, which have crisped to a golden shell, and then checks on his wife, who has warmed and now looks almost relaxed at the candlelit table. She swirls her wine and insists on another anniversary toast. When he comes close, she grasps his tie and pulls him down into a kiss. The kiss is insistent, Hannah's mouth pressing hard against his, the breath loud from her nose. She bites his lip gently and draws back, not letting go, the lip unfolding in the pinch of her teeth. It starts to hurt and, sensing his pain, she growls and lets him go.

Now bring me my meat, knave, she says, slapping her thigh.

The pleasantly lingering pain of the kiss stays with him as he bastes their steak with melted butter.

When he brings the food from the kitchen, she claps, just as he'd hoped she would clap upon arriving home, and when he cuts into the steak, it is perfectly pink from one thin edge of the dark crust to the other. The potatoes are perfect as well, first a quick smack of salt and then the crisp shell shattering down into light, pillowy flesh. Hannah takes a bite of the meat and as she groans and sighs, he says to her, I cooked steak because . . .

You wanted to remind me of the first night we kissed, says Hannah, reaching under the table and touching his knee. But back to our wedding day, she says. Now, correct me if I'm wrong, but I seem to remember you looked like a soldier standing to attention. She makes her body stiff and widens her eye. Oh, it was so romantic, she says, exactly how I always imagined it.

I was concentrating, he says, waving his fork in circles. I was taking my vows very seriously, Hannah. I still do.

Aha! she says, reaching up to wipe his cheek with the handkerchief she has knotted around her wrist. Now I understand why you needed this thing.

He gives her a doubtful look at first. But then he says, I honestly thought every cell of my body was about to dissolve into tears.

Her head tips down, she smiles and when she looks back up at him, Hannah says, So, tell me about your day, Patch, what's going on?

My father called again, he says. Same thing, wants to set me up for a chat with this guy from Goldman who owes him a favor.

You should do it.

Come on, Hannah, you know I don't want anything from him.

I know, I know. And I get it, I do. I just want to see you happy.

I am happy, aren't I? I have you, Hannah.

That's sweet, she says. But think about it, Patch.

OK. But I can do this myself, you know, I can find another job.

I know you can, of course you can, she says, touching the back of his hand. When she looks into his eyes, Patrick blinks at her as if he is empty in a place that only she can fill. You know what? she says, a fresh tone in her voice, a change of topic. I think I'm definitely going to need more wine.

He picks up the bottle to pour but she covers her glass.

No, I mean another bottle.

Is there something wrong with this one?

No, she says, I just need another one.

He holds the bottle up to the candlelight. Half full.

Please go and get some more wine, Patch, she says. I want the one at the far right end of the rack that's on top of the cabinets.

He looks confused.

Do it, she says.

He has to use the step stool to climb to the wine rack above the kitchen cabinets. But he can't reach all the way to the right so then he has to clamber up onto the granite counter. When finally he pulls out the bottle at the far end, he sees it is white. Are you sure you meant the far right, Hannah? he calls out. This is Chablis.

Oh, maybe I meant the far left. Bring any bottle you like, that's OK.

He looks through the reds and picks out a Malbec, wiping the dust away. Do you want me to open it? he calls out.

No, just bring it here.

Shaking his head, Patrick returns to the room.

When he gets there, he sees that everything has been pushed to the far end of their dining table—plates, bottle, candlesticks, cutlery, wineglasses—while Hannah's head rests at the other. She lies on her back, looking past her shoulder at him, stretched out and naked, her body shining where it is lit by the small flames of candlelight. Breast, belly, flank.

Sorry I was late, Patch, she says.

Her dark hair feathers the tops of her breasts. And between her breasts, as if at the neck of an hourglass, is where she has nestled the first slice of meat.

I thought you might like to start at the top and work your way down, she says.

The meat, like small steppingstones, descends invitingly, its slices running down past her navel, bisecting her pelvis, pink flesh bright against her eggshell skin, the beef rising and falling where it rests on her belly. His gaze trails down, farther down, until the pink and bloody path disappears between her legs.

Will this be enough? she says.

The red juices streak her hips and her ribs.

He swallows and nods.

Well, don't let everything go cold, Patch, she smiles, crossing her hands behind her head.

He puts down the bottle of wine and undresses quickly.

PATCH

Staying at the back of the tree, I started with the ropes around Hannah's neck and worked my way down, sawing away diligently but in silence.

When the blunt knife finally made it through the last rope, Hannah fell to the ground, curled into a ball and covered her head. Her arms were all pimpled and scratched and some of the pimples were already bruising, flesh turning brown like cut apples. As she lay there, making herself small, I noticed that the back pockets of Hannah's jeans were embroidered with cartoon characters, Sylvester the Cat on one side, Tweety Bird on the other.

I stood there not knowing what to do, clouded with shame and convinced that everything had been my fault. Looking back at that boy all these years later, I want him to bend down and scoop Hannah into his arms. But no, his biggest test in life had come to him too young. How do you make up for something like that?

At last, having exhausted her sobbing, Hannah reached out to me and I pulled her to her feet but I couldn't look her in the eye, so my gaze fell on the cartoon ice-cream cone in the middle of her pink T-shirt. Only now the ice cream was streaked with red where once had been white, as if someone had drizzled it all over with cherry syrup.

Hannah crossed her arms and held herself as if she were cold. Patch, she said, I really want to go home now.

I felt a rush of relief at her suggestion. A plan. Home. Yes, that's where I wanted to be, home forever. OK, this way, I said, turning around.

But as I turned, Hannah gasped and said to me, Oh my God, Patch, what happened? The back of your shirt, is that blood?

Oh, that? I said, looking over my shoulder. Yeah, I tripped on a rock. Knocked myself out cold. It was pretty bad, you know, but I'll make it.

Such a noble show of bravado. I turned away again to conceal the sickly look on my face and then we set off, me helping Hannah through the thicket, moving branches aside for her, worried she might get jabbed in the other eye and then what would we do?

Once we reached the trail, I led the way but when we came to the edge of Jakobskill stream, I paused, waiting to help her across the rocks. Hannah had her hand over her eye and I could see she was in a lot of pain. Telling her to wait a moment, I pulled the bandana from my back pocket, washed out as much of my blood as I could and then folded the damp cloth into a sort of cold compress.

When I reached out to give it to Hannah, she just stared at me.

I took her hand by the wrist, pulling it away from her face, and started to move the wet bandana toward her. Now I had to look at the eye again. When Matthew made me look before, it had been mostly blood but now the blood was dry, brown streaks caking one side of her face. I could just about make out her eyelid, which was shut, and a line of clumped lashes. But as I moved the bandana closer, Hannah's eyelid started to flutter and that's when I saw something else in there among all the dried blood.

Like scrambled egg-white but only halfway cooked. I almost threw up on the spot.

This is the image that keeps coming back to me, twenty-six years and I can't forget what I saw in that moment, the memory making me nauseated all over again.

Hannah breathed hard and flinched when the damp cloth touched her face.

Shh, I said, *shhhh.* OK, keep it there like that.

Hannah did what I said as I led her by the hand over the stream.

I DON'T REMEMBER ANYTHING ELSE being that hard as a kid. I remember times in my childhood when I was tired or exhausted or hurting. Nothing was truly hard. Hard is something I associate only with being an adult.

But that walk back to the bikes was hard. I wanted to curl up and surrender every second, so I tried to think only one step at a time. Whenever one foot landed in front of the other, it was another minor victory.

We didn't talk. I offered my hand to Hannah every time the way got steep or there was a rock that needed clambering over. What would we have said?

When finally we reached Split Rock, Hannah seemed barely conscious, so I said I could take her on the back of my bike. Thank God the road to Roseborn was downhill all the way.

I had it in mind that I should take Hannah to the doctor but the only doctor I knew would've been another couple of miles, so as soon as I saw the first house, I freewheeled straight into the driveway. Hannah's chin was a dead weight on my shoulder.

Coasting up to the house, I saw an old-looking lady in her kitchen holding a glass up to the sunlight, her fingers all sudsy. Seeing us, she jerked her head and soon enough came running out the front door, dish towel thrown over her shoulder, yelling, *Oh my goodness, oh my God,* over and over. That's the last thing I remember because at that point everything started to go gray and speckly, the way untuned television screens used to look.

And I wouldn't wake up, my fractured skull bandaged tight, until that particular Wednesday in the calendar of August 1982 had flipped over to Thursday.

NEW YORK, 2008

The winter melts into a cold, rainy season at the tail end of which the first buds appear hesitantly on the trees. Days later, the true spring weather arrives, a feeling of freshness and warmth, the city's population seeming to triple overnight, streets teeming with newly bared flesh. The freshness lasts for three days before Manhattan turns hot, temperatures leaping suddenly from the sixties to the nineties.

His father calls twice and leaves messages, becoming insistent about the guy in Goldman who owes him a favor. Patrick doesn't return the calls, but less picky in his search for new work now, he sends out his résumé another eleven times and fails five interviews. Hannah might not like the word *fail* but what other word should he use? And he needs to find a job soon—the financial crisis is becoming more severe with each passing day, every news bulletin. What was it Trevino said? *Tornadoes with a 50 percent chance of Apocalypse.*

He cooks more and more, making frequent trips to the greenmarket, returning with his wicker basket full of roots and apples before the spring produce arrives. And then with fava beans, asparagus, sorrel, baby artichokes. The frequency of his blogging increases and the numbers for Red Moose Barn show a steady improvement, more and more traffic to his website, a rise in the number of page views per visit. He was worried that increasing his posting would lead to saturation, boredom, but instead he seems to be feeding some sort of need. And then his brother is on his back about allowing their father to help him. Eventually they fight on the phone, Patrick hanging up angrily when his brother scoffs at the word *principles*.

He embarks upon a personal mission to cook every recipe from the book *La Cuisine Précise* by Jean-Jacques Rougerie, a Christmas gift from Hannah, described by *The New York Times* as the most challenging recipe book ever written for the home cook. When he is not dreaming up meals for Red Moose Barn he is filling a paint gun with chocolate to spray melon-ball-size scoops of ice cream, or turning chicken fat into a powder that he scatters over microgreen salads like a dusting of crumbled feta, or poaching egg yolks in clarified butter, droplet by droplet, so that when he is finished the plate appears to be covered in hundreds of kernels of corn.

Here and there he starts to slip Jean-Jacques Rougerie's modern techniques into the homey cooking of Red Moose Barn. But everything must stay hidden, he tells himself, the magic behind the curtain.

His technique is rapidly improving. Sometimes he looks at a plate of food he has produced and feels that something beyond him must have guided his hand.

And yet still Patrick knows he has to find a job and he spends hours trying on interview clothes, as if a certain shoe–tie combination or a particular pair of socks with this shirt or that, his blue suit or his gray, might make all the difference.

He fails three more interviews, the third of which he was sure he had nailed.

Gray suit, pale blue shirt, brown silk tie.

Meanwhile he continues to follow Don Trevino. There are no set days assigned to the task but he feels the frequency increase. One weekend he realizes that he followed Trevino on four of the previous five workdays, *weekdays,* and promises to limit himself to two days a week.

En route to these clandestine missions, or when returning home, it becomes increasingly important to Patrick that he take a route that will entail his not having to stop and wait at a single crossing light. He feels desperate that he should achieve perfect efficiency of motion and wonders if some part of him supposes that efficiency of motion might make up for the increasingly wasted hours of his life.

Often he imagines running at Trevino, charging like a bull, the liberating roar that would sound from his lungs. He pictures the moment of recognition on Trevino's face when he realizes that the crazy bellowing and running down the street is an ex-employee and that he, Don Trevino, is the target. Sometimes Trevino has time to turn and flee but Patrick chases him down, *pow!* Or if he doesn't catch him, Trevino runs into moving traffic. Oh, the distance a body might fly. Other times Don Trevino is frozen by uncertainty and Patrick leaps and tackles him, their bodies sailing horizontally offscreen.

He reads an article about professional pasta extruders and later that day imagines feeding Trevino's arm into one of the machines. Linguine.

He recounts these daydreams to Dr. Rosenstock, who reassures him that such thoughts are perfectly natural. Patrick's mind clearly has need of these fantasies. But he doesn't tell Dr. Rosenstock about the actual stalking, not least because the word *stalking* strikes him as too extreme, and neither does he feel ready to share what he has written down about the events of 1982. Whenever he's ready, Dr. Rosenstock reassures him, adding that he's immensely pleased with their progress, he should be very proud of himself, Patrick feeling infantilized by the praise.

He starts to delight in the use of cheaper cuts of meat—beef shanks, pork shoulder, neck of lamb—and learns to debone a whole chicken, taking great pleasure in the task of butchering bird after bird, popping joints, snapping bones from their sockets, severing cartilage. Every time he finishes, he cleans and hones the knife, stroking the blade afterward, checking the deathly sharpness of its edge until he can almost hear a high-pitched ringing in his ears.

He continues to write about his food adventures for his blog on which he has now placed ads and created links to buy products he uses. In March he makes $147.40. In April he makes $202.68. He wonders about investing in a better camera.

When his next interview proves fruitless, Patrick realizes that his number of failures has risen to nine. He worries that it might mean something definitive should the total reach ten. He takes his résumé from the printer, crumples it into a ball and makes a perfect throw into the wastebasket.

He gives up having his hair cut expensively by Takahashi in a NoHo loft every four weeks and buys clippers instead, cutting his own hair while standing naked in the bathtub, the vacuum cleaner close at hand. While the clippers buzz he thinks about how undignified this scene would look to anyone witnessing the process.

The home haircuts are just one element in his effort to cost-neutralize his existence. Now that he cooks most weeknights, instead of two or three, they must be saving more than a thousand dollars a month on restaurant meals. His blog is making only pocket money for now but two hundred dollars is at least something to throw into the equation. Plus, they have no mortgage to pay—thanks to Hannah's inheritance, finances have never been a genuine concern. If he can cost-neutralize himself perhaps Patrick can justify not having to find himself another job so soon.

Thoughts of the continuing job search make him sick, the process having quickly made him feel undignified. As undignified as he might feel were someone to observe him standing naked in the bathtub, the vacuum cleaner close at hand, his pale body covered in short lengths of dark clipped hair.

Every day the picture in his head of Red Moose Barn gains a little more detail. The interior of the restaurant has been clear to him for some time, so his imagination begins to wander farther and farther outside. He sees a meadow rising behind the barn, climbing eventually to an apple orchard. The restaurant's nearest neighbors are retired professors who live in a converted school-house and take the same table early every Thursday evening.

Back in the real world of their condo, Patrick begins to perform domestic chores beyond the kitchen, which means they have to let go of their housekeeper—there remains nothing for her to clean. He fears an angry scene but it is worse, their housekeeper cries and tells him they have a beautiful apartment and she is grateful to have worked there. Hannah says that letting go of Marta was a mistake, Patrick will soon find a job and they will struggle to find a housekeeper as good.

But not using Marta will save them almost five thousand dollars a year. So he scrubs and he dusts and he polishes. He washes their clothes and folds them neatly away. One day in their apartment building's laundry room, a woman tries to help him add time to the dryer. But he knows how to add five minutes to the dryer. He's a man, not an idiot. This is not genetic fucking knowledge.

Patrick smiles and thanks her.

Returning to the apartment, he discovers that a picture of sorrel soup with blackened shrimp that he sent to a food photo submission website has been accepted. Nearly seven hundred people are funneled to his own website that day. One visitor, TribecaM, writes such a kind and gushing comment about Patrick's recipe-writing style that he asks Hannah whether she has invented the character TribecaM so that she can compose uplifting comments on his blog to bolster his mood.

She says that she has done no such thing, then looks uncomfortable, as if wondering whether she might be guilty of some negligent omission.

One night, before the weather is quite warm enough for it to be comfortable outside, they make love on their building's roof terrace, almost getting caught by neighbors who come out to show the view to friends. Patrick and Hannah are behind a long wooden planter and they hear the neighbors whispering about people in the building they dislike. Hannah and Patrick are not on the list but some of their dislikes surprise Patrick and he feels hurt on other people's behalf.

Another night, after watching *The Seagull* on Broadway, they eat at a Mexican restaurant and Hannah slips her hand under the table and up against his groin. They fuck urgently but almost silently in the men's bathroom before returning to plates of *léchon* and carne asada.

They no longer talk about his efforts to find a job. He doesn't tell Hannah that his blog has started making money. It seems as if she has closed her eye to him and is silently praying for things to get better. But until they do, she doesn't want to watch, she can't take on his pain. Perhaps they love each other too much to talk about what is happening to him, that the sun is slipping from Patrick's world.

It had always seemed to him that Hannah's nighttime screaming occurred approximately once a week. At the end of January he creates a document on his laptop to keep a record of these episodes and discovers that the true figure, over a three-month period from February to May, was 1.23 times a week. But there are no particularly severe episodes. No knives, no slashed upholstery.

He expands the document to include figures that will allow him to analyze his *tailing* of Don Trevino—having decided that *stalking* is definitely too harsh a word—and then adds a section for recording the average frequency of his and Hannah's lovemaking.

One afternoon late in May, he snips all the collars from his work shirts, using a pair of kitchen shears he bought years ago to cut the backbones from chickens. The next day he tosses his ties in the trash chute, all of them except for the tie he wore on their wedding day.

TribecaM has become an increasing presence on the pages of Red Moose Barn. She or he is always complimentary and Patrick wonders, with an embarrassed blush, whether he has a fan. A female fan, he hopes, his blush deepening.

Perhaps the *Times* will include him in a list of top food blogs one day. He performs frequent web searches for *Red Moose Barn* to see if there are any new mentions. Soon this hopeful web searching becomes a biweekly habit. And then daily. But maybe his audience will simply reach a tipping point on its own. He looks

out for any surge by keeping a close eye on his website analytics—
the graph of daily hits, the audience pie chart with its red *new
visitors* wedge. He becomes aware that he is staring at his phone
and computer too often every day now, praying for new messages,
statistical bumps, hoping that something transformative will simply arrive, that one day his life will forever be changed by a new
arrangement of pixels on a screen.

What else is there to do?

June arrives. The sky is mostly blue. And Patrick's number of
failed interviews remains stranded on nine.

PATCH

I was unconscious until Wednesday ticked over to Thursday, so I don't know exactly how everything played out, but I suppose that initially, as far as the police were concerned, all they had to go on was this—

One 13yo girl, Hannah Jensen, brought to the hospital with a BB gun pellet lodged in her left eye, recovering from emergency surgery. One 12yo boy, Patrick McConnell, suffering from blood loss and head trauma. One witness after the event, Alice Welcher, 62, who stated that said boy, unknown to her, had cycled into her driveway with said girl, also unknown to her, on the back of his bike. Situation—the injured parties were seemingly the only two people who could explain what had happened and yet both said boy and said girl were, for the time being, unconscious.

Meanwhile my father, Joe McConnell, Ulster County's chief assistant district attorney, rising Democrat and would-be New York State assemblyman (the election was little more than two months away), did not hesitate for a moment before telling the police as much as he could. Yes, his son owned a BB gun, a Red Ryder. No, the gun could not be found at home. Following this my brother, Sean, having been swiftly hooked out of soccer camp, told the police that I was best buddies with Matthew Weaver and that we often cycled up into the Swangums with the BB gun concealed in a fishing rod bag.

So now, at least, I was not the only suspect.

Next, I presume, someone was dispatched to find Matthew, only to discover that he wasn't home. In fact, Matthew had ridden over to Mannaha State Park, concealed his bicycle in a large patch of ferns and begun living survivalist-style somewhere near Jakobskill Falls, hoping to stay alive on a diet of wild blueberries. Possibly, were it not for his close encounter with a large black bear four days later, an encounter that sent him running almost directly into the arms of a park ranger, he might still be there now, the Mowgli of Mannaha.

Meanwhile, back to the hospital, approximately an hour after I awoke, an hour after my mom had soothed me and informed me of my fractured skull but explained that I was going to be fine, my father and two police detectives entered the room.

If I told them I didn't remember anything, touching my shamed and bandaged skull as I did so, it was not intended as any kind of deliberate tactic. And yet, as it turned out, my temporary amnesia was a masterstroke, because it quickly became clear that Hannah had regained consciousness a few hours before me and the police detectives had already spoken to her. Shaking their heads, they took out their notebooks and that's when I learned, from the mouths of others, the story of everyone's role, my own included, in the tragic loss of a thirteen-year-old girl's left eye. And it went like this—

Matthew Weaver, Hannah Jensen and I had ridden up to the Swangums together on our bikes the previous morning, setting out from the parking lot of O'Sullivan's Dive Inn at or around 11:00 A.M.

Matthew had led the three of us to a spot in the woods where he and I often hung out.

Arriving at the spot, Matthew sent me away.

I departed.

Matthew tied Hannah to a tree.

Matthew proceeded to shoot at Hannah for several minutes with my BB gun.

Hannah passed out from shock when one of the BBs struck her left eye.

It was unclear how long she was unconscious but a few minutes after Hannah awoke, I returned to the scene.

At this point I was stumbling and faint, bleeding from a hole in the back of my head.

Nevertheless, I cut Hannah down from the tree and helped her back to civilization.

At which point, I passed out.

Yes?

Oh, just spectacular.

You see, sometimes you do nothing at all and everything turns out just peachy.

Next the detectives asked me what put the big hole in my head and I paused, as if waiting for a fog to clear, and told them I was strolling around killing time after Matthew sent me away but had gotten spooked by a snake. Fearing it was a rattler, I turned around and ran but, panicking, tripped and fell. No, I had no clue where Matthew might be now. Yes, I certainly could describe to them the spot where the shooting had taken place and tell them what it was we did up there. I was happy to help as much as I could.

Dad grasped me warmly by the shoulder. Good work, Patch, good work, he said. And now that I think about it, I'm fairly sure that was the last time in my life that my father ever looked proud of me.

ALTHOUGH HANNAH WAS JUST ALONG the corridor from me, I didn't get to see her at all in the hospital.

In fact, it would turn out that our family's time in Roseborn would soon come to an abrupt end and I wouldn't set eyes on Hannah Jensen again for another two decades, until our accidental meeting on the concourse of Grand Central Station. So I never did get to ask her why she didn't mention anything to the police about the fact that I was there and did nothing—not that I would ever have asked such a question at that age. Instead I became haunted by the thought that one day the police would find out about my cowardice and I would be sent to jail where, with good reason, my fellow prisoners would abuse and torture me for my role in such a despicable crime. If I had thought about Hannah's silence as to my presence, I probably would have guessed it was some kind of tit for tat situation. OK, so I had done nothing to stop Matthew from shooting out her eye. However, I did go back for her. I did cut her down and help her get out of that place. Perhaps Hannah thought we were even.

Only it would turn out that the explanation for why Hannah Jensen had said nothing to the police was something completely different. But I wouldn't learn this new side to the story for many years to come, several weeks after seeing her at Grand Central, a revelation that I overheard accidentally as she spoke on the phone. And now this revelation has become the monstrous secret that paces the perimeter of our marriage, like something that prowls in the shadows, a dangerous creature awaiting its moment, the right time to strike.

When it comes to our relationship, we have only ever stated one rule out loud, a rule made at Hannah's request. We don't talk about that day. Ever. And if Hannah doesn't want to talk about it, then certainly neither do I.

So if I haven't shown this account to you, Dr. Rosenstock, perhaps this is the reason why. Because to have kept the truth to myself for so long feels like a crime in itself, a terrible secret I couldn't bear for anyone to learn.

Hannah least of all.

I TURNED THIRTEEN ON THE following Tuesday, one day after my return from the hospital and two days after Matthew's arrest and immediate confession, which I found out about because, being Ulster County's senior prosecutor, my father had privileged access to all the information on the Weaver case, despite the potential conflict of interest, his son being, to use his increasingly desperate phrase, *only very loosely associated with the matter.*

Summer birthdays were never riotous affairs—half of my school friends would always be away at camp or off on family vacations when the day fell. If you were lucky you might rustle up a half dozen boys for a trip to McDonald's, followed by a matinee at the local movie theater. We'd watched *Raiders of the Lost Ark* for my twelfth birthday but this time around, on the day I officially became a teenager, there was an especially conspicuous lack of festivity. No school friends, no Happy Meal, no Ark-stealing Nazis and melting of faces by God-fire.

When I woke up, instead of having a present to unwrap, my mom handed me a card with some money folded inside. My parents had never given me money for my birthday and I would find out later from my brother they'd actually bought me *Asteroids* for my Atari but that, all things considered, the game being a shoot-'em-up in which the object was to blast apart objects of a roughly circular nature, my father had deemed the gift inappropriate and returned it to the store.

Anyway, what I'd really wanted was *Pac-Man*, so a few days later, that's what I bought, Mom taking me to the store, although I told her I could easily cycle there on my own. But no, she insisted on driving. And then, seeing the looks cast at us from the faces of our fellow townsfolk, looks that suggested there was a foul smell in the air, quickly I understood why. Something was rotten in the state of Roseborn. Over the past several days, rumors had started to circulate and something had soured.

The looks on everyone's faces? That foul smell in the air? It was me.

NEW YORK, 2008

The dark rump of the Lower East Side, seventeen minutes after McCluskey's message, a rare day of Manhattan work (Brooklyn her bread, the Bronx Hannah's butter), homicide two floors above the Chinese car service, brick tenement building with red-painted fire escape, body still inside, probably nothing, probably drugs, but not much happening elsewhere, and besides, she likes to keep in with Manhattan South Homicide. The sound of screaming children issues from the schoolyard at the corner of the block, another same-old day about to start at the sound of the bell, and fifty yards up the street, outside the crime scene, more of the same-old as well, street gift-wrapped in yellow-black tape, two uniforms on the door, crowd milling about, the neighborhood starting to stitch its own story into the breeze, and McCluskey comes out, losing the gloves, clapping the first uniform on the back, shaking hands with the second, his eyes reaching for the distance, long breath as he buttons his suit jacket, rubs his nose back and forth, and then, eyes returning, sees Hannah there, waves. Smoothing his gray crest of hair, McCluskey stoops to climb through the tape—POLICE LINE DO NOT CROSS POLICE LINE DO NOT CROSS POLICE LINE DO NOT CROSS—surprisingly nimble for a ten-ton truck of a man.

Hey, Aitch, how's tricks?

Detective McCluskey. Detective Colón not with you today?

What, I'm not good enough for you now? He's off procuring vital supplies.

Glazed or jelly?

Jeez, Hannah, you freakin hacks, you're so full of clichés. That's what you think, after what I just feasted my eyes on?

Sorry, Detective.

Yeah, well, at least whoever did this was good enough to take the *bath* part of bloodbath to heart.

So the body was in the tub, right?

Sure. Nine-tenths of him. But look, Colón can fill you in. I gotta go make a call, says McCluskey, pulling his phone from his jacket, but then looking at the screen as if he's forgotten how to turn the thing on, tilting his head back to her, Oh, one more thing, Hannah—did someone tell me you were writing a book?

Supposed to be. True crime. Apparently that's my wheelhouse.

You got a particular case in mind?

A couple of thoughts, nothing fixed.

You know what I think? You should do the Angie Bell homicide.

Sure, only I need something with an ending, McCluskey.

Oh, I've got your ending. It's the psychic, no-brainer. The facts that little creep knew? What, from the magic fairy vibes in the air? No way, Hannah, that guy's about as psychic as my big Irish balls.

McCluskey stands there, looking at her as if, after the gentle toss of a softball, Hannah has failed to go deep, hasn't even taken a swing.

Hey, what gives, Hannah? Something up?

No . . . Go make your call.

McCluskey puts his phone back in its pocket. Come on, Aitch, this is me.

It's just . . . Patrick, you know, my husband? He still can't find another job. So . . . I don't know. I don't know what to do.

Tough freakin economy, Hannah. My neighbor, young go-getter, something in banking, the guy gets canned four, five months ago, now he lives out of his Lexus, trunk full of fancy suits, shaves every morning in Burger King . . . But Patrick? You know, I only met the guy once but I remember he cooked us the best brisket I ever ate. So maybe I was high on the meat vapors or something but he seemed kinda solid to me.

He is. Patch is. Solid.

And he's not taking it out on you. Because, you know . . .

No, nothing like that.

Any money worries? If there are, just say the word, Aitch, I can . . .

On a cop salary?

What? I'm living the Miller High Life now. The boys are all packed up and gone. Hey, Lindy just started a business, she does this tai chi massage thing.

Tai chi?

Yeah, something like that. So anyway, shit's good, Aitch. It's like a Cinderella story, only this one's Aladdin.

Go on then.

Rubs to riches.

She smiles. Cute, McCluskey, how long have you been holding on to that one?

It's been stinking up the locker a few days, I won't lie to you.

Thanks, she says. Moneywise everything's good. But thanks.

Whoa, then that means you were talking about emotional stuff . . . Wait, about that phone call I gotta make . . . But McCluskey doesn't reach for his phone.

Emotions? she says. I wouldn't do that to you, Detective.

And he turns his head, eyes reaching for the distance again. Look, Hannah, he says, I'm sure you tell your husband you . . . whatever, you love him and everything, right? But make sure he knows you've got his back. No matter what. *No matter what.* Me? I'll take loyalty every time. McCluskey nods as he looks up the street, squinting, and then lifting one of his double-big fingers. Hey, here he comes now, he says.

Hannah turns and sees Detective Colón, paper bag in one hand.

Just in time, says McCluskey.

So those are your vital supplies? Inside the Dunkin' Donuts bag?

McCluskey snorts. Freakin hacks, he says. You know, Aitch, it just so happens they make excellent coffee, OK?

EVERY MEAL AT RED MOOSE Barn could begin with free snacks to nibble, popcorn served in brown paper bags. Sometimes the popcorn would be covered in salt caramel, on other nights buttery and dusted with flecks of crispy chicken skin. Or customers might be greeted with a mixture of nuts freshly roasted that day and flavored with an herb-scented sea salt. Rosemary, chives, sweet basil. Miniature pretzels, right out of the oven, cheddar and black onion seeds studding their crusts.

He writes it all down, saving it for later before clicking onto his email. And then, seeing the message and opening it in a hurry, Patrick stares in excitement at his computer screen, this new arrangement of pixels—

TribecaM   Thu 6/5 9:58 a.m.
Re: Contact Form submission from Red Moose Barn

Dear Patrick,

Congratulations on your stunning website. Since stumbling across it several weeks ago, it has become by far my favorite place to spend an hour. I'm a terrific admirer of your blog.

Listen, I don't want to waste anyone's time—particularly yours—so why don't I come out and say it:

I have a small business proposal for you. I promise you this could be very interesting indeed, and I'd value the opportunity to put my case face-to-face if you think that might be possible. Even if nothing were to come of it, I'd appreciate the opportunity to meet.

However, I realize that a message such as this one, coming out of the blue, could come across as creepy. (What if I'm some kind of weird food blogger stalker?) I don't wish to make you uncomfortable, so here's my suggestion. Allow me to buy you lunch at an exceedingly expensive and perfectly public restaurant. At the very least you receive a good meal and some fine wine in return for your valuable time.

Now, forgive me if I'm wrong about this, but some of your recent recipes/techniques have hinted to me that you might be familiar with the cuisine of Jean-Jacques Rougerie (I loved the close-up of you spraying melted chocolate from a paint gun), and I just happen to be able to score a reservation at Le Crainois. Jean-Jacques is a very close personal friend of mine.

What do you say? How about one o'clock sometime? I can do tomorrow and Saturday. Or otherwise any day next week?

Yours,
A fan (TribecaM)

It feels like something is flowering in Patrick's chest, the air blooming inside him. He reads it again. He reads it again. He feels the tears trying to push their way out.

Perhaps TribecaM works in publishing and wants to suggest a Red Moose Barn cookbook. He starts to think about test kitchens, photo shoots, book signings, cooking demonstrations on daytime TV . . .

Sure, Paddyboy, don't go leaping too far ahead of yourself.

But food bloggers get offered book deals all the time. He sees them interviewed in magazines, on morning TV. They even made an entire movie out of one woman's food blog.

Although what if it all means nothing? What if nothing comes of this?

At the very least you receive a good meal and some fine wine in return for your valuable time.

He wipes his eyes, checks the website for Le Crainois and discovers that the next available lunchtime slot is over seven weeks away. To snag a dinner reservation requires taking part in an online lottery. In April, Le Crainois was voted the number one restaurant in the world by a food magazine, and ever since Jean-Jacques Rougerie has been featured in every newspaper and magazine that has ever breathed a word about food. Several that have not.

This is what the wait has been for, thinks Patrick. This is it. The point at which everything changes.

OUT OF THE SUBWAY AT Twenty-Third, daylight surrendering to taillights and headlights, the walk home one long block, one short, a few golden minutes, Hannah's workday slipping away, and then into the building, fresh flowers in the lobby, and the doorman Jorgé there to greet her, Hello, lady, I hope you had a pleasant day, Thanks, Jorgé, you have a good night, and she makes it into the elevator with no neighbors in tow, thirty seconds of peace, a few golden breaths, not exactly a wildly successful day, not really much point.

A man was found dead in his bathtub yesterday on the Lower East Side, hacked to death in an apparent drug-related attack, police sources said.

The victim, whose name was withheld pending family notification, was found at 8:43 a.m. in an apartment at 47 Ludlow Street.

Police responding to an anonymous phone call recovered drug paraphernalia including scales.

And that's it, ten hours' work reduced to fifty-eight words for the *New York Mail's* CRIMINAL RECORD column, page sixteen or so, maybe as high as twelve, now that Obama v. Hillary is mostly played out, but when they go big they go big, Hannah missing the thrill of her weeks after the bloodbath in Washington Square (*Jeez, what a job*) when it was she who broke the news that the innocent bystander had been killed by a bullet from the gun of a cop (*But oh, what a week*), because it is she, Hannah Jensen, who cracks wise with the Manhattan South Homicide squad.

Open door, kiss husband, sit down, kick off shoes, maybe he seemed brighter, Patch stepping back into the kitchen, tiptoeing away as he does every night after their kiss and a confirmation of okayness, a few more golden minutes, which, for some time, she has been needing more and more, not that her life spent with Patch has become dark, but he is saddened and hurt, and she can't fix him, but she loves him, and sometimes after a hard day at work, a tough job, she just wants to . . .

McCluskey would take loyalty every time. And she's loyal, surely Patch knows that she's loyal. She throws her shoes in the closet and steps into the kitchen.

You seem in a good mood, she says. Did something happen?

His back to her, stirring risotto. No, he says. Well, an email. But it might not mean anything.

Tell me about it.

I'll tell you if anything comes of it.

Good, she thinks, *good, then everything's taken care of,* and she tells him about her morning on the Lower East Side, the body in the bathtub, details McCluskey passed on to her that didn't make the story, because just another drug homicide, another humdrum New York murder, not really much point.

PATCH

The perpetrator had confessed, the victim had effectively absolved me of blame and so, legally speaking, I was off the hook. And yet, much to my father's chagrin, there was still a case to be heard because I hadn't yet been cleared of any wrongdoing by the second most important authority of the land, the Supreme Court of Public Opinion.

While I rested my fractured skull at home and Mom fussed over me, Sean returned to soccer camp and my father continued his work at the Ulster County district attorney's office, the town of Roseborn began to gather—at supermarkets and gas stations, in hardware stores, diners and bars—to sift through and scrutinize every last detail of The Swangum Shooting.

Dad would arrive home each night in a terrible froth, additional snippets of grapevine gossip having trickled down to him, and although he directed his anger physically at the front door and then vocally at the checkout-line numbskulls of town, I felt that the party his anger was really turning toward was me. But to be fair, the election was fast approaching and the Supreme Court of Public Opinion holds some sway in such matters.

Before too long, every time my father looked at me, I started to see my approval rating dropping. Yes, at the very least I was guilty of stupidity. Hadn't everyone been saying for years that

Matthew Weaver was trouble? How had I gotten myself into such a preposterous situation?

It was now becoming clear that the self-appointed jurors of Roseborn would find me guilty of something—my crime, at the very least, was one of first-degree association—but it was not only the legal opinions of a misinformed public that my father had to contend with, because then opinion became rumor and rumor became lie and soon my father's froth turned to fire.

What in hell's name? It was nothing but a pack of lies to suggest the police had stumbled across the bodies of several dead animals near the scene of the shooting, animals tortured to death and their limbs removed. (In truth, the police may have found some frogs in pickle jars. And I certainly remember us saving a few bones and antlers we'd picked up here and there.) Goddammit, how dare anyone suggest that his son had helped tie Hannah to the tree, this was slander of the worst kind. Are you damn well kidding me? If Patrick had really fired half the shots did these imbeciles not think for one second that the police would have arrested him? Why not ask the girl herself, listen to her own words?

And then, one morning, Joe McConnell, chief assistant district attorney, rising Democrat and, until recently, a shoo-in for election to the New York State Assembly, awoke to discover that someone had tipped a gallon of yellow semigloss all over the hood of his blue Chevy Impala.

Yes, the electorate had spoken. Our motor vehicle was dripping with poll numbers. And it was time for us to leave.

At least that's how it felt to me at the time, a violent shift to the dramatic, our family chased very suddenly out of town by paint, a protest aimed squarely at me and my spinelessness.

Although when I turned thirty, my brother organized a bar crawl for me and a few friends and at the end of the night, I was speaking to Sean about these and other events from our childhood and he told me, over the space of several whiskey shots, that there was more to the story of our leaving Roseborn than I'd ever understood at the time.

And how did Sean know all this? Well, apparently our dad told him everything one night—also in a bar, whiskey also the culprit—after they'd both attended a fund-raiser for Bill Clinton's 1992 presidential campaign.

Sean told me he had long suspected the truth of the matter—from the moment right after everything unraveled a few years after our exit from Roseborn. But I had suspected nothing at all.

Anyway, back to 1982, my father had long remained friends with an old college roommate, another lawyer with a small practice in Portland, Maine, and after a series of increasingly buddy-buddy phone calls, conversations my father strategized as carefully as his electoral campaign, it was agreed that the two of them would join forces.

Which meant that not only was my father withdrawing from the New York State Assembly election but also that he would be switching from prosecution to defense.

I suppose the whole episode had prompted an ethical shift.

Hence, or at least as it seemed to me at the time, my spinelessness didn't just run the family McConnell out of town, it also ran us clean out of New York State, a six-hour drive across Massachusetts and up through New Hampshire, all the way over to the fronded coastline of Maine.

THE REASON WHY MY FATHER'S election to the New York State Assembly had, until a certain Wednesday in August 1982, been a near-certainty was not only because he'd been laying the groundwork for years but also, and more important, because my father was so enormously well liked and respected.

Joe McConnell was a smart-yet-approachable man. Joe McConnell had a firm handshake and steady eye. Joe McConnell was both supremely confident and solidly down-to-earth.

These were just some of the tricks of the trade he was keen to pass on to his sons, because a political career wasn't something my father dreamed of only for himself. No, Joe McConnell, son of a Long Island baker and his German immigrant wife, had a longer-term scheme in mind.

The McConnells were going to be the next Kennedys.

The plan was trickle-down, political empire-building that began with paterfamilias Joe as the capstone of the political pyramid. Next down would come his two fine sons, Sean and Patrick. And after that, his sons would bear grandsons who would also be nudged along the same glittering path. Breed and repeat, breed and repeat, a plan for the ages.

I was five years old when I was presented with my first suit, bought for neither a wedding nor a funeral, but on the occasion of the seventieth birthday of Mrs. Effilinda Scott, a nonrelative but a party grandee and something of a local kingmaker. And wow, you should have seen us, Sean and Patrick in matching blue gabardine. Cute as hell!

Along with the suit came a series of important lessons from my father. Soon my cocktail-sausage fingers had learned how to tie my tie and tuck my shirt and part my hair. Dad showed me how to roll up my shirtsleeves, reminding me as he did, We want to look like we're doers, not bankers or playboys. When we take off our jackets, we roll up our sleeves and get on with things, right?

Dad also gave lessons in glad-handing, oration and debate. Plus guidance on how to treat friends and spot enemies. At weekends we handed out buttons, waved pennants and allowed ladies even older than Effilinda to maul us with their grabby hands. I lost count of the endless hours we spent playing with kids we didn't really want to play with at various fund-raisers, rallies and potlucks.

Whenever we stood on a platform or walked through town together, it was in a formation that had been drilled into us—Mom on Dad's right, my brother first on his left and then me. When I complained one time about being on the outside, it was explained that it was all about height order, a family triangle with Dad at the apex, and if I ate my greens and grew taller than my brother, I would take his place.

I think I was the only kid at Roseborn Elementary who actually liked the taste of broccoli.

The execution of the plan should have been perfectly straightforward, a timeworn march into power. Sean and I would both go to good colleges and then on to law school. Next we might work in the Justice Department or on a congressional subcommittee, or clerk for the right judge, or become assistant district attorneys.

I knew my chosen path in life long before I understood what it is an assistant district attorney actually does. At a young age, all I understood about my father's work was that he kept the world safe from bad guys—I thought my dad was a superhero. And if this was my father's dream for me then I wanted it too, I wanted it like hell.

Only now the plan had gotten horribly bent out of shape, meaning that, 250 miles northeast of the seat he had earned by dint of his hard work and the power of his smile, my father had to start working all over again. Except this time around, the scheme would require one minor constitutional amendment.

It remains one of my more vivid childhood memories, the moment I learned of my de-selection from The Kennedy Plan. I was sitting on the living room floor playing *Pac-Man* when I looked up and saw my brother in his suit for the first time in months. And then I noticed my father, also splendidly besuited, the two of them edging toward the front door. No explanation was needed—I'd been struck from the ballot paper for good, there being some question concerning my suitability for office. But in all fairness to my father, as he stepped out of the house, he did offer me a look of intense consolation, the sort of look you might give a toddler with a hearing aid, or a seven-year-old with only two weeks to live.

Mom let me stay up later than usual that night to watch *Dynasty*. We lay in the recliner together, her filling me in on the internecine squabbles of the various characters. What I remember most about that show, for reasons that will become obvious, was the scene in which two attractive women, one blond, one brunette (Alexis Colby and Krystle Carrington), had a catfight in a lily pond. I stared wide-eyed at the TV as these vengeful beauties flailed at each other in the shallow waters of the pond, their expensive and low-cut gowns clinging to their numerous curves, the two of them splashing and whaling and sprawling. Yes, that was the moment, snuggled up against Mom's left hip, that my body decided to present me with the very first erotic stirrings of my life. I couldn't have been more horrified had a cat dropped a headless bird in my lap.

I knew pretty much what it was, this stirring down below. For some time I'd heard boys my age talking of similar seismic activity. Jonny the Spin's first erection had leaped unexpectedly from the flap of his pajamas almost two years earlier—in front of his grandmother, as he told it. So the shock I was experiencing wasn't fear of the unknown. No, it was the mortifying thought that my mom might notice my interest piquing. Which meant that, while trying not to move a muscle, trying not even to breathe, at the same time I desperately wanted to leap out of the armchair and run up to my room.

Thankfully, if she did notice, my mom didn't say anything. The fight ended with stern words for both women delivered by a handsome gray-haired man (Blake Carrington). And as the show wound down, eventually so did my first ever erection.

That night in bed, and with some success, I tried mentally to re-create the frisson I'd experienced during the lily pond scene, going over it again and again in my head. Blond, brunette. Brunette, blond. And it was a tough choice but before too long I'd come down firmly on the side of the brunette, an allegiance I suppose I've retained to this day.

DON'T ALL BOYS ASSUME THAT they're clever? At least until some point in their lives? And although I wasn't exactly top of the class, my grades at school were decent. I thought maybe I might be an intellectual late bloomer, just as I had been a late bloomer when it came to matters of puberty and height—the broccoli thing having never quite worked out. Plus, I've always been good at math. Numbers feel right to me. If I can quantify something, I feel I have a better chance of understanding it.

But at fifteen years of age, two years after our move to Portland, I realized I wasn't clever at all. No, worse than this, I was in fact stupid. This became rapidly and dazzlingly clear because, smarty-pants me, I had continued to believe all this time, as I had done my whole life, that my parents were blissfully and ceaselessly happy together.

And they were not.

When, one Sunday afternoon after church, they told me and my brother they were divorcing, the news totally scrambled my head. How could two people so clearly in love, *my* parents, be splitting up? I had never glimpsed so much as the shadow of a sign, not even for one second, that there was anything but an undying love between them.

Later that day, speaking to my brother about this bolt from the blue, he laughed disbelievingly at me. Are you a dumbass or what? he said. They argue all the time, Patch, right in front of us. Especially since we *mooh* . . . And then in a rare display of sensitivity Sean put me in a headlock and gave me a noogie instead of finishing the sentence.

It took about one microsecond of reflection to realize what my brother had said was patently true. My God, how could I have failed to notice? The information was all there being fed into me like data, only what came out the other end wasn't just the wrong conclusion, it was a table lamp. A swordfish.

When the day came for my father to move out, I'd been dreading the farewell scene for some time. It wasn't that I couldn't stomach the thought of him not living with us anymore. I could, the idea even held some appeal. It was the thought of the final exchange that made me feel queasy—the handshake, the hair ruffle, the words of wisdom from a man who was running away from us. *Now you look after your mother, boys.*

It went as badly as I'd feared. Then it got worse, because when he wound down the window of his car to wave one last goodbye, my father looked me square in the eyes. He didn't actually say anything but I could hear the words in my head as clearly as if he'd spoken them out loud. *This is all your fault, Paddyboy.*

And then, following an almost respectful period of solo divorcé-hood, my father went and found himself a better family—or that's how I viewed events at the time—a shrewd move, it must be said, because in 1986 my father, by then married to a petite blonde, a tragic widow named Carla, with two sweet blond daughters, Marcy and Steph, was elected to the Maine House of Representatives, 120th district. His wife bore him a son, Joe Junior. I baked him pound cake.

The cake was supposed to be a peace offering on my part, an apology for bringing shame on our family and a congratulations to my dad for his new, more successful life—although I'm sure to my father the act of baking was nothing more than further confirmation that I had never been cut out for a role in The Kennedy Plan. Anyway, I would never have cooked the thing had I known at the time what my brother told me in a bar many years later, that my father had in fact first met Carla all the way back in 1976—at the Democratic National Convention in New York City, at which time Carla's husband was very much alive. Apparently, shortly after the party nominated Jimmy Carter for president, my father and Carla made their way to a midtown hotel, where I imagine they discussed Ford v. Carter at great length.

For the next six years Dad and Carla continued their affair at various political functions across the Northeast—a meeting of minds, my father told Sean, my mom never having been the world's most enthusiastic party foot soldier—until, with his seat in New York seemingly lost, wouldn't you know it, we upped sticks and moved to a house less than a mile from the home of my father's mistress.

But for almost seventeen years I would continue to believe that the reason for our move, and my parents' subsequent divorce, was all because of something I'd done—or hadn't done, I suppose you could say.

———

MOM WAS ADAMANT THAT SHE didn't want her boys moving school again, so we stayed put in our neat house, a family home fit for a modest politician on the rise. Wanting to avoid the black mark of a messy divorce, mainly for the sake of my father's political ambitions, my parents agreed financial arrangements between them without resorting to a court. But either Mom was too sheepish to ask for much, or Dad was too skilled a negotiator to offer a comfortable monthly sum, which meant that, struggling to pay the mortgage and bills on a house slightly larger than we needed, my now-single mother had to find work. And so, having nothing recent or of note on her résumé other than homemaker, she took various cleaning jobs in private homes and dental practices, car dealerships and real estate offices. And when she wasn't cleaning, even if she was at home around dinnertime, she was always too tired to prepare food, so instead of home-cooked meals, we ate sterile TV dinners from segmented foil trays. One day my brother, his Salisbury steak only half-eaten, dropped his tray to the floor and said, Mom, this crap tastes like death.

Grateful for my brother's bluntness, I was about to toss my tray as well when I saw that Mom had started to cry.

I cooked my first ever meal the next day from a recipe I found on the side of a pasta box. Our mom still gave us an allowance, even though she never had anything to spend on herself, and so I had enough money to buy vegetables, canned tomatoes and ricotta. We already had some ground beef in the freezer and although I couldn't afford Parmesan and mozzarella, I knew there was some waxy orange cheddar in the fridge, so I used that instead.

I think that lasagna turned out pretty well. My brother said it wasn't bad and when my mom finished her last forkful, she cried for the second night running.

Gradually I became quite the home economist. Mom would tell me how much money we had to spend on food each week and I would budget. I bought secondhand cookbooks and learned how to make mac and cheese, sloppy joes with ground turkey, and spaghetti and meatballs. I found a meat grinder that cost almost nothing at a yard sale. Grinding my own beef cut down on the cost of making lasagna, meat loaf, homemade hamburgers and chili. When we had almost nothing to spend I cooked up a large pot of red lentil soup, which my brother called stupid hippie food, but he still finished his bowl every time, and if we had a little extra cash come Friday, I roasted a chicken on the weekend, making stock from the carcass and using up the leftover meat during the following week. I could turn one chicken into three meals for three, which made me realize what good value that bird had been, and we started eating roast chicken every Sunday, our new family triangle experiencing something like happiness as we shared our weekends at that dinner table. I learned how to bake bread, each loaf costing me only a few cents to make, and then figured out that adding milk to my dough kept the bread softer for longer and started using it to make toast for breakfast and sandwiches to take to school. My brother refused to give up his morning cereal and that was a big dent in my budget—until he left for college, that is, although whenever he came home I had to make sure we had his damn Cheerios in the pantry—but mostly I'd say that my brother supported me. He could have called me a little fag for liking to cook (his favorite term of abuse back then) but he never did.

I loved every second I spent in that kitchen—almost three years, from the age of fifteen until shortly after my eighteenth birthday when I left for college as well.

When you cook you can silence your mind for a while. You never feel sad or down when the heat starts to rise in front of a busy stove. I suppose that somehow I had stumbled upon exactly what I needed, the ability to unplug from life for a while—and not only the small world outside but also the larger world spinning twice as fast in my head.

Another thing I loved was the sense of transformation. I would line up my ingredients on the kitchen counter and draw a picture in my head of what these different elements were about to become. Sure, maybe I'd never get all the way to that picture, but I always got somewhere, the journey ended with a reward every time.

But what I liked most of all about cooking was simple. I had learned to make people happy. I'd discovered that food does not have to be only sustenance, food can be love.

WHICH IS ALL PERFECTLY WONDERFUL—I'm sure everyone needs to escape from the world sometimes and perhaps I'd found the best way to buy myself a few hours' silence each day, which was something I desperately needed because, every moment since it had happened, the story of that hot yellow day had been playing on loop in my mind, reeling away at the back of my skull like a home movie being projected in Technicolor over and over.

Baked orange bicycles, bright rocks and blue skies, black rat snake, Red Ryder BB gun . . .

Even when I wasn't consciously thinking about it, I was aware of the story whirling away, mindful of the background noise of my shame, the sound like the buzz of a neighbor's television set coming through the walls. When I did think about it, watching the events unfold behind my eyes, reliving that day again, the story would stick to the very same script every time—but only up to a point, because then, as the story neared its factual climax, it would take on a fictional twist. Yes, whenever I told the tale to myself, the ending would be different, a new sting in the tail each time. Patch running at Matthew and crushing his skull with a rock, Patch leaping in front of the forty-ninth bullet, Patch finding a splintered branch and driving it deep into Matthew's chest, Patch fetching the slingshot from under the tarp and firing a perfect shot into Matthew's left eye . . .

And I told it again. And I told it again.

Look, Dr. Rosenstock, I know what you would say if you read this, that when my imagination conjured up these changes to the end of the tale, I was coming to terms with what had happened. That by turning myself into the hero of the piece, I was finding a way to forgive myself.

Only, that wouldn't be true, Doctor, not even close. Because I'm certain beyond a doubt that this and only this is the message I was sending myself—

That there must have been a thousand and one different ways I could have saved her that day. But what did I do? I did nothing.

And I tell it again. And I tell it again.

So that now even the act of making food, an act of love, is something that has begun to catch and darken at the edges. Every day in the kitchen, every day with my thoughts—how would it feel? The crushing and cracking of things. The searing heat of a pan. The feel of the blade as it slices through flesh.

Because now it seems to me I have the chance to write my own ending. Now I can truly become the hero of the piece. Only this time around, I can make it the truth.

NEW YORK, 2008

Patrick ascends toward the world's number one restaurant on an escalator, its scrolling steps heavy with tourists, inside the marbled shopping mall of the Time Warner Center.

The tourists wear bright rucksacks, windbreakers and sneakers. Patrick has on a lightweight charcoal suit but no tie, because an hour earlier, when he received confirmation of the lunch, he went through his closet examining the necks of his shirts and discovered all of them frayed where recently he de-collared each one of them with kitchen shears. He picked out a blue-and-white Bengal stripe and tidied the loose threads with nail scissors.

Breathing slowly through his nose, he tries to untangle his thoughts and worries he will mistime his dismount from the escalator. When he sees the restaurant door across the narrow space of the fourth-floor gallery, he worries that he doesn't know under which name the reservation is held. And then he worries that these minor worries are only a distraction from what he should be worrying about most of all. That this meeting is probably a sham, not a life-changing event at all. That in all likelihood TribecaM is someone in PR who wants Red Moose Barn to promote spray cheese.

As he nears the restaurant, the mall is transformed into an avenue of orchids and bay trees and when he enters through the heavy antique door (shipped over from Jean-Jacques Rougerie's village of Crain, he has read), he is greeted by a man in a black suit standing at a slender lectern.

Mr. McConnell, welcome to Le Crainois. Mr. . . . *uh* . . . your dining companion is seated already. Is there anything you'd like me to take for you?

Patrick pats his pockets. No, thank you, he says, looking at his greeter's black silk tie, feeling the absence around his own neck.

Another man appears. Good afternoon, Mr. McConnell. My name is Frédéric, I'm the maître d' at Le Crainois. Would you like me to show you straight to your table?

They move down the corridor, through a beige bar, on toward the dining room. Patrick has noticed a unique rate of ambulation among the staff in the world's finest dining establishments—the precise velocity at which a koi carp drifts from sunlight to shadow.

Frédéric says something in a friendly tone that Patrick fails to take in as he tries to spot TribecaM in the dining room ahead. *What does he look like?* Patrick wonders, having already felt a small sense of disappointment when the man at the lectern revealed the gender of his lunch companion.

How did you know my name? Patrick asks the maître d'. The man at the front knew it as well, he says.

Sometimes images are available, says Frédéric. Whenever that's the case, we like to familiarize ourselves with our guests before they arrive.

Images available? says Patrick.

Online, for example, says Frédéric. And then he adds, Your photo of the sorrel soup was mouthwatering.

There are only a dozen tables in the dining room, its color scheme of browns and creams peppered with tubs of greenery and sculptural twigs. Patrick follows Frédéric past a long window that forms one side of the room, several floors above Columbus Circle, the statue of Columbus on his pedestal dominating the view, surprisingly paunchy when seen at eye level. Central Park fans out beyond the statue, its paths and trees overfringed with a hazy line of tall buildings.

Frédéric leads them around a pillar. Patrick doesn't know how he will be able to eat, feeling as if the contents of his breakfast are lodged up against his breastbone. He tries to shift the obstruction, swallowing hard as he arrives at a secluded table set in its own glade with its own private stretch of window, the face of the man seated at the table obscured by the wine list, a leather book as big as an atlas, Patrick almost starting to laugh as the mounting sense of this lunch-tease begins to feel preposterous.

And then the wine list is lowered, unveiling a face that Patrick recognizes in an instant, even though it has been twenty-six years, the eyes as insistent as the last time he saw him. Columbus, Central Park, New York—everything beyond the window a haze at the end of a vertiginous drop. There is only his face, Matthew, and the air smelling faintly of pine.

INTO THE BLUE

When I saw you again it was the late springtime of 2003, exactly a week after I'd swallowed too many painkillers, or perhaps not enough. I was gazing down from the balcony, early for my Bronxville-bound train, a blue puddle of light soaking into the pink marble concourse of Grand Central Station.

I was thirty-three years old and up to that point in my life I'd tried three times to kill myself. There's never been a fourth attempt. And naturally it was all because of you that I stopped at number three. I always wanted to save you, Hannah, but of course it was you who saved me.

I've never told you about those times I tried to end things, I never will, and I don't know if that's because I didn't want to burden you or whether it's because I was worried you might think me less of a man.

Anyway, more than two decades had passed. My last memory of you was your chin on my shoulder, the two of us together on my bike and a feeling of faintness. I had no idea that you were living in Manhattan. It was a Saturday morning, hundreds of city visitors spilling onto the station concourse, a small crowd massed around the famous meeting-spot clock, awaiting their loved ones, their friends, maybe even their futures. That's when I saw you.

I remember the reflection of your legs in the blue-splashed marble, the way you moved unassumingly like someone trying not to be picked out in a crowd. I kept on watching you, twenty steps, thirty, unable to look away, something about you. And then an impulsive urge propelled me down the steps, two at a time. A few moments later I was standing directly behind you in the ticket line, even though I'd bought my ticket ten minutes earlier.

I studied the winglike shape of your shoulder blades through your raincoat, listening in on your conversation.

I assumed you were talking about a movie or TV show because you were saying something about torture and someone taped to a chair. And then you said, *They chopped off his thumbs with a bolt cutter. I know, right? Left them standing in a tub of . . . oh damn, how can I forget the name? The Greek dip . . . No, not hummus . . . You know, cucumber and . . . Dammit . . .*

Tzatziki, I said.

You turned around.

Yes, tzatziki, you said into the phone, smiling warily at me before turning back.

I was already smitten.

You were at the front of the line now and soon the ticket counter came free. *Wait,* you said, *I'll have to call you back.*

I strained to overhear your destination. *Yonkers, round trip.*

Not one of the stops on my line. I remember the quick surge of my disappointment and then a second impulsive idea.

As soon as you moved away from the window, I rushed straight up to the counter and said loudly, *Yonkers, please.*

You stopped and turned around.

Round trip? came the question from behind the window.

Sure, I said.

I was facing the counter but all my attention was on you. I sensed your quizzical look. *Sure?*

Scooping up my ticket, I waved it like a kid going to his first ever ball game, you looking at me as if figuring me out harder with one eye than the other. *Maybe we're going to the same party,* I said.

Never in my life had I done anything like this.

No, you said, *you're probably going to one of those fancy cheese and tzatziki parties I keep reading so much about.*

Sorry, I said, *I couldn't help but . . .*

Were you eavesdropping on my private phone conversation?

Eavesdropping? I said. *No, it was impossible not to hear . . .*

Oh, so now you're accusing me of speaking too loudly?

Either that or the trains pull into Grand Central too softly.

I went over what I'd just said, certain I'd blown it. But you laughed. It was the most perfect laugh I've ever heard. *I'm Hannah,* you said, offering me your hand to shake, the movement of one hand making me think to look at the other. No ring. That's the only place my brain went in that moment, not making the connection, your name.

I shook your hand. *Patrick,* I said. *But my friends call me Patch.*

And then something happened that I didn't understand at the time. It felt as if I'd unwittingly detonated a bomb. The look on your face changed and I saw you more clearly, your eyes widening, two minutely different shades of the same fierce blue.

A moment later you were running—not toward any platform, but out of the station.

Hannah. *Hannah.*

I SAT ON THE TRAIN to Bronxville thinking about you, staring at the carriage's reflection in the dark window, my ears popping as the train burst clear of the tunnel, blue light crashing over me like a wave. I'd thought about you so many times since that day but in my thoughts you'd never aged. Were you beautiful back then as well? At twelve years old, thirteen? Yes, you were, this became suddenly obvious to me. I'd been too young to notice.

I was on my way to my brother's house, his first yard party of the year. I'd long been banned from making food for these events, or even helping out with the grilling. *We don't need all that fancy shit, bro!* And whenever I asked what I should bring my brother always responded, *Any hot secretaries at your place?*

All afternoon I drank keg beer, wondering how I would ever

find you again in such a vast city. Wiener jokes flew around the backyard while Sean and his colleagues talked law and sports. And as the light faded to its deep blue of dusk, my brother, drunk and boasting about his youthful prowess as a high school wrestler, pinned me to the ground and whispered, *Spin me over, bro—Annie's looking, she likes you, man.*

And I liked Annie but I didn't spin him over. No, you win, Sean, I said, tapping out.

Annie offered to clean a grass stain from my white shirt and I said not to worry, taking the train back to Grand Central Station a half hour later, alone.

SUNDAY MORNING I WENT OUT to get coffee, landing on a street strewn with the debris of another Saturday night in Partyland. Pizza crusts, chicken bones, crushed plastic cups. It had rained overnight and the remnants of a sodden newspaper were pasted to the sidewalk. The cover photo was the face of a man smiling up from the blue waters of a swimming pool. But something made me look down at the newspaper a second time.

MILLIONAIRE MURDERED FOR PEANUTS trumpeted the headline. And then, CASINO HEIR TORTURED AND SLAIN IN HIS HOME. I unstuck the few sheets from the ground. On the front page there were only two or three lines on the story, followed by the words SEE PAGE 5. I pulled the damp newsprint apart. Three, four, five . . .

And there you were, Hannah Jensen, your photo next to the byline.

Thumbs . . . bolt cutter . . . tzatziki.

I'd found you. The *New York Mail.*

I looked up at the sky in a gesture of gratitude. And it was so blue overhead, the morning so perfect, I knew right away what it was I would do.

PART II

PART II

HANNAH

I met Rachel at a party, alongside the buffet, the two of us bumping hands as we both tried to snatch up the last *gougère*. (I don't always see rapidly moving objects coming from my left. Close one of your eyes for several minutes and you might be surprised at the constant and obtrusive presence of your nose.) After the clash, the two of us shared a joke about how many of the devilish little cheese bombs we'd devoured already, while a furtive, hirsute gentleman brushed past us and popped the final prize whole in his mouth.

Probably for the best, my buffet neighbor whispered to me. Although the thing is, she added, I've been trying really hard to convince myself they're 70 percent air and that makes them diet food.

Cheesy puffs, I said. I tell myself the same lie about cheesy puffs, I confessed, and we both watched as Mr. Hirsute pushed several miniature cupcakes in his mouth, before piling his plate high with undipped crudités and heading back to his wife.

I'm Rachel, said the woman, offering me her hand, and then we started to chat—how we knew the hostess, who else at the party we were friends with, the location of our partners, Rachel's being the most attractive woman in the room, before landing eventually on the topic of what we both did for a living.

Rachel went first, telling me she worked as a literary agent, that she had both fiction and nonfiction clients writing in several different genres, but her main area of interest and great passion was true crime. Seeing my reaction, Rachel added quickly, Oh, please don't judge me. I mean, sure, I take an unhealthy interest in the most gruesome details of the lives of serial killers and the murders they commit, but . . .

Wait, I said, that's amazing.

It is? said Rachel. Oh, good, I was hoping you were one of the dark ones.

I'm a crime reporter, I said. For the *New York Mail.*

Get out of town, said Rachel.

We chatted away for an hour or more, quickly realizing that one of my former colleagues was a client of Rachel's—Mike Tucker, who wrote a *New York Times* bestseller about the Gotham Ripper, in which I stake out a spot in the acknowledgments—and then discovering that we both loved the same authors, the TV series *The Wire,* had both read Truman Capote's *In Cold Blood* as teenagers (under the bedcovers with a flashlight, in my case), and both came from small towns that no one has ever heard of. Eventually Rachel uttered the fateful words, So, have you ever thought about writing a book, Hannah?

We went over several of the stories I'd covered and Rachel said she'd love me to get something to her, just a couple of sample chapters and an outline would do for the time being, it shouldn't take ever so long.

That was four years ago.

I'm sorry about all those missed deadlines, Rachel. Also, I'm sorry if this tale didn't end up being quite the thing you had in mind.

For the next several weeks after meeting Rachel, I went back over my notes and stories concerning several of the murders I'd worked on in depth for the *New York Mail.* There were at least two or three I thought might warrant a lengthier telling, but every time I tried to get down the first page, my spirit crumpled before I hit the second paragraph.

For some time I tried to ignore the issue, but it soon became clear what the problem was. Evidently there was only one story that could be my first, the only true crime with which I was intimately familiar, an incident that took place up in the Swangum Mountains in the year 1982.

Once I accepted this, I knew I had to write it all down—the story of a girl and a boy and a BB gun—and then, upon finishing, I would lock all of the pages in a drawer, never letting anyone see what I'd written. After that I hoped I might be able to move on to something less personal.

At some point toward the end of 2007 (around the same time my husband, Patch, lost his job), I began. Which means that when I started writing this, I had no idea of the great secret our marriage was harboring. (For a short while I would have said that our marriage was based on a lie, but my opinion has softened a hell of a lot since then.) And of course I knew nothing of what was coming in 2008, had no idea how everything would end later that year. This also means that, when I started working on Grist Mill Road, the story existed within the bounds of only a single year. All I wanted to do was explain, as best I could, everything that led up to Matthew Weaver shooting my eye out in August 1982.

My favorite book, one that I've read more than a dozen times, is the greatest true crime book ever written, the same one I'd discussed with Rachel at the party—*In Cold Blood* by Truman Capote. Capote's *In Cold Blood* tells the story of the murder of four members of the Clutter family in 1959, each one of them bound and gagged and shot in the head, the quadruple homicide taking place in their home, a farmhouse on the high wheat plains of Kansas.

When most people write about crime, they write thrillers. But Truman Capote didn't write a thriller—Capote wrote his story as a tragedy. (He gives the reader a little wink at the end of his very first paragraph, comparing the image of distant grain elevators in Kansas to the appearance of temples in ancient Greece.) One of the most pathos-invoking elements of Capote's tragedy is that he makes the crime seem both brutally unique and yet, at the same time, disturbingly everyday. The opening of the book feels eerily familiar, scenes from small-town America, quaint details that might describe ten thousand different places across the land. Reading about the ordinary day-to-day lives of the residents of Holcomb, Kansas, feels a little like flicking through hundreds of postcards, small illustrations depicting the wholesomeness of daily American life at the geographical and spiritual heart of the nation. There's the farmer, Herb Clutter, clanging his milk pails. Oh look, do you see the postmistress in denim and cowboy boots? Now here comes the farmer's daughter, Nancy, arriving home late from her date with the school basketball star, Bobby. (Herb will have a few things to say to young Nancy.) And yet, while you're reading this, you understand that at some point as you flick through these pretty snapshots, you're going to get to the blood and that, when you do, this will be the worst thing you've ever had to read in your life.

It all makes tragedy feel both horribly average and terribly inevitable—and I think that's something I certainly believe myself.

When I started writing my own story, I suppose somewhere back in my mind I must have been thinking about *In Cold Blood*. I too was writing a small-town tragedy, a story that began very small, its ingredients the familiar details of American life. In my case those everyday ingredients were school hallways and lockers, sleepovers, boy crushes, and mean girls. All I was trying to do in my opening chapters was tell the story of a twelve-year-old girl, a few months shy of thirteen, who was just as selfish as children that age tend to be and just as myopic (I shudder to use that word now), but also just as innocent and naive and keen to learn about life, a bright-eyed girl wondering what the world would look like in adulthood, how she would turn out, what she would do and who she might love and settle down with one day.

So that's where I began, writing the opening lines a few weeks before Christmas 2007, obviously unable to see the story for what it was truly, the seed of a tragedy far greater than mine alone, the beginning of everything that's happened since the day when I first sat down and typed out the words, *I grew up ninety miles north and half a decade away from New York City.* Because just as with my favorite book, *In Cold Blood,* this story you're reading once started out as a perfectly ordinary, everyday tale. Until, very suddenly, it wasn't.

This is how it went.

I GREW UP NINETY MILES north and half a decade away from New York City in a big parchment-colored home standing right at the bend on Grist Mill Road, just before the junction with Earhart Place. Three miles east of our family abode, Grist Mill Road reaches its romantic end at a parking lot, having swept back and forth up into the Swangum Mountains, a legendary area for rock climbers, so I've heard, but famous also for their ice caves, a day-trip I'd recommend highly to anyone who finds regular caves just a little too cozy and dry.

From the front windows of our house we could gaze up at the Swangum Ridge, a rock face presenting itself majestically across the horizon like a vast lower jaw, a set of uneven teeth in a yellow-ish shade I believe to be known as *British White.*

While I was growing up on Grist Mill Road, my father's favorite joke while greeting any new visitor out front was to point up at the ridge and then the street sign beyond the bend, before an-nouncing to his guest, with a jovial clap on the shoulder, We live between a rock and Earhart Place. OK, so you had to fudge the pronunciation of Earhart and, strictly speaking, the Swangum Ridge isn't a single rock, of course, it's actually an intricate layer cake of various mineral strata, but still, my dad knocked it out of the park every time.

My mother, meanwhile, liked to say we were blessed to be living in the shadow of God's beauty.

I have a feeling I got my sense of humor from my dad.

Roseborn is not a large town and certainly not in any way fa-mous. However, you might be familiar with its name if, like me, you happen to be an aficionado of cement. (Perhaps you heard mention of it at a cheese and cement party, or in one of the better cement boutiques of Fifth Avenue.) Otherwise, you may have heard of Roseborn if . . . let me think . . .

No, Roseborn is pretty much famous only for its excellent once-famous cement.

You might eventually conclude that any lack of romantic feelings I hold toward the town in which I was born and raised has something to do with a little incident that took place nearby in the Swangum Mountains one Wednesday in August 1982, when a fourteen-year-old boy, Matthew Weaver, tied me to a tree and shot me thirty-seven times with a Red Ryder BB gun, the final shot piercing my eye—and there may be some truth to this, my hometown certainly looked different to me after I lost my left eye. And yes, I do like to say that I *lost* it, even if this doesn't adequately convey the horror of having one's eye irreparably damaged by a steel pellet and surgically removed by Dr. David P. Schwab. (For all you word lovers out there, the technical name of this hospital procedure is *enucleation,* so I guess you could say my eye got nuked.)

Incidentally, I have visions, half-visions in my case, of Dr. Schwab talking about the enucleation procedure to his shocked plaid-sporting buddies, maybe as they awaited their tee shots on the tenth, and using the golf ball in his hand and the tip of his red plastic tee to illustrate the tale.

This was big news in Roseborn.

Anyway, certainly in one sense of the word I did *lose* my eye, because two days after its removal, I asked where it was and no one could tell me.

What follows is one of the conversations I had on Friday, Thursday having been consumed by tears and whys and police, more tears and finally a platter of jelly beans that preceded a wildly psychedelic sixteen-hour sleep. (Although thinking about this twenty-five years on, perhaps those weren't actually jelly beans.)

But *where* is it? I asked my bedside parents.

My mom decided to take the lead on this topic. It's nowhere, honey, she said.

It's not nowhere, I said. It has to be somewhere. It didn't vanish into thin air. (In fact it probably did vanish into thin air. Most likely it would have been burned with a whole pile of other medical waste.)

Oh, Hannah. I don't know, the things you come out with.

Can I keep it? I want to keep it.

What? Are you serious?

It's *my* eye, Mom.

Next there followed a short silence as my mom covered her face and pretended to cry, one of the many child-rearing methods at which she excelled.

I can ask the doctor, Hanny Bee, said my dad.

My mom threw her shocked hands from her streakless face.

We are not asking the doctor, she gasped. What sort of people would ask a doctor a thing like that?

So that was that, we didn't ask. Which to my mind means that somewhere along the line, my eye was in fact lost.

IS IT JUST ME OR do Hannah's eyes look double-psycho today?

This is Christie Laing and you may have detected in her words just the faintest whiff of animosity toward me. It's January 1982, our first day back after Christmas break, and I have seven more months of blissfully biocular life ahead of me.

Yet things could have been so different between us. I was a pretty brunette girl, Christie was a pretty blond girl, if only I'd been prepared to play along, taunting the less attractive girls and mocking the quieter boys, we could have formed a great-hair superpower in Roseborn Middle School, strutting the hallways together like ABBA, me brunette Anni-Frid, Christie as platinum Agnetha.

I wish I could say it was a sense of decency that prevented me from joining forces with Christie, but really I think it was a kind of uncomprehending indifference. What would have been the point? As early as the age of eleven, I knew I wanted to stride out into the wide world to explore everything that existed beyond

Roseborn. (For years I was obsessed with Japan because I considered it the strangest place I could visit that didn't require space travel. Then again, I had not, until my early twenties, experienced New Jersey.) But knowing this didn't make me immune to Christie's torture campaign and so, as a child and then teenager, I fretted constantly about my too bright eyes, my too full lips, my impossibly thin legs, my excessively skinny ass . . . Oh yes, there was no doubt about it, I was *cursed*.

Christie wasn't done with me yet. My what big eyes you have, Hannah, she said in a singsongy fairy-tale voice, before adding, with a generous pinch of wicked witch—All the better to *bite me* with.

Christie's grasp of the dialogue of *Little Red Riding Hood* may have been seriously sub-kindergarten, but I didn't interrupt because I could see that Sandy Delillo was brewing up a zinger, and when Sandy Delillo switched to zinger mode, the world stopped to listen.

Hey everyone, her eyes look exactly like toilet cleaner.

Excellent work, Sandy. (Sandy would go on to own Roseborn's only hair salon, Curl Up & Dye. Because what better way to attract customers to your business than with a pun referencing the crippling effects of Parkinson's disease?)

Now Tammy Frankowski was ready to jump in, but it was too late because Christie was ready with the kicker.

That's why she sucks so much shit!

Pow! What a fine start to the first school day of 1982. Yes, Christie had been short of opportunities to mock me for nearly two whole weeks, not having noticed my presence at Jonny Spinoza's birthday party on New Year's Day.

That night, all of the boys had brought sleeping bags with them, the plan being for Jonny the Spin's party to end with a guys-only sleepover. I'd been keeping a lookout for Christie all night, trying to avoid another one of her verbal assaults, so when she wriggled down into the bag of Jonny the Spin's older brother, Benny Spinoza, a sophisticated sixteen-year-old, I observed everything that followed.

First of all Benny's shoulder started to move, as if he were trying to retrieve something from the lower reaches of his bag, and next Christie's face went all funny—first a blink, then a flash, and finally a quick shudder. While Jonny the Spin's brother resumed his conversation with Ted Benson about Phil Simms being the reason why the Giants hadn't made the playoffs, Christie turned her head away and started nibbling her nails.

Now, I was no expert in the chivalrous world of teenage boys and their gallant wooing techniques, but I was pretty certain I knew what Benny was up to, two feet under, in his red nylon sleeping pouch, and I wasn't going to let this opportunity pass, now that Christie had kicked off '82's hallway banter with such an elegant display of her wit.

I crossed my arms, paused a beat, and said, You know, Christie, Jonny the Spin's brother was letting every boy at the party smell his fingers after you left. I heard Ted Benson reckons you stink like dead skunk.

Christie's crew didn't dare react to my barb, but two boys nearby started to snicker like drunken trolls.

Now, as far as I knew, Benny Spinoza had said nothing about his between-the-zipper activities on that first night of 1982, but the look on Christie's face when I called her out in the hallway suggested my suspicion was correct and, pretty soon, the quality of Christie's comeback confirmed this.

Nobody likes you, bitch. (This happened not to be true, I just didn't have my own posse of gum-blowing joke machines.)

We were on our way to math, my class walking down the hallway, Matthew and Patch's class heading the other way, and there they were, hip-by-hip as always, Matthew looking like he was five years older than anyone else in middle school, Patch looking nearly the same number of years younger. Meanwhile, the trolls were still snickering, so Matthew stopped and asked them what was so funny.

Hannah says Benny Spinoza fingered Christie at his party.

Christie was already fading away down the corridor. She turned to scowl and flip the bird at the trolls.

A split second later, Matthew called out to her, Hey, Christabel, we don't actually need to know which finger he used.

The laughter everywhere was of the violent body-creasing kind, but Matthew stood tall as the hallway doubled up all around him. He couldn't have played it straighter if you'd frozen all the blood in his veins.

I believe that was the exact moment, right there in the hallway, when I decided I liked him.

WHEN I CAST MY EYE back over my twelve-year-old self, I can see that I wasn't exactly mature for a girl on the brink of becoming a teenager—and I was certainly no Christie Laing, who seemed ten shades of adolescence older than any other girl in seventh grade.

In the early stages, I honestly believed my feelings toward Matthew Weaver were nothing more than curiosity. I had always been fascinated by anything that felt different from my life in Roseborn, hence my obsession with Japan. Matthew had grown up in New York City. What was that like? Also, not only did Matthew possess Big Apple glam, but he was also older than most of us in seventh grade, having been held back a year sometime before he moved to Roseborn, and everyone in school knew that the left-back kids were the serious badasses of the world.

Yes, there was definitely something pulling me toward Matthew, but I suppose that, to begin with, Matthew must have seemed something like the concept of eating raw fish—an idea that intrigued me, but an activity I probably wouldn't be able to enjoy until my mid-twenties.

But then, after two days of quiet reflection upon Matthew's otherness, I felt everything start to speed up. I remember lying in bed trying to imagine what Matthew's mom was like (everyone knew about his dad, the town drunk), wondering what posters Matthew had on his walls and what TV shows Matthew watched before going to bed. Wait, was Matthew even in bed? Maybe

Matthew's mom was cooler than mine and he could stay up past ten o'clock at night. Damn that lucky son of a bitch.

Even after several days of obsessing over Matthew, it didn't occur to me that this might be a crush, because although I understood the mechanics of what had been going on in Benny Spinoza's sleeping bag, I really didn't understand the impulse. Around that time, Olivia Newton-John's *Physical* had gone to number one in the charts and although in her hit single the Neutron Bomb panted away about *getting animal* and *bodies talking horizontally*, it wasn't until I heard the song again in college that I realized the lyrics were about something other than dance aerobics. So whenever the track came on the radio in my childhood bedroom, I would bounce along to the beat in front of the mirror wearing a sweatband on my head, which lent me a certain John McEnroe chic. I'm guessing now that this must have been the reason why I incorporated both the serve and two-handed backhand into my carefully self-choreographed dance routine.

This wasn't exactly the behavior of a femme fatale in the making.

No, instead of fantasies of getting animal with Matthew, I dreamed about the fascinating conversations we would have, drew up a list of places that he and I would enjoy going together (the movies, the mall, Tokyo), and practiced my signature over and over with his surname in place of my own—*Hannah Weaver Hannah Weaver Hannah Weaver*—only I didn't like the way it flowed and decided he would have to take my name. Matthew Jensen. Nonnegotiable.

Obviously I didn't actually do anything to make any of this happen. What was I supposed to do, just walk up to Matthew and start talking to him? Impossible! I mean, it's not as if I were some sort of creature with two functioning legs and a fully operational voice box.

However, ten days or so after Matthew's already legendary finger joke, he strode straight up to me after I got off the school bus one morning.

Hey Hannah, stop a moment. You do know Christie's just jealous of you, right?

Why?

Come on, Hannah, you know why.

What?

Maybe there should be a club. I don't understand why everyone lets the Christies of the world take charge when there are so many of *us*.

Who?

The non-Christies. The anti-Christies. I just don't get it. Anyway, maybe we should hang out. You wanna hang out sometime?

Well . . .

Me and Tricky—I mean Patch—we don't do anything interesting, so . . . ?

When? (Thus far, you may have observed that my side of this conversation has proceeded as follows—Why? What? Who? Well. When? Was I *actually* an episode of *Sesame Street* brought to you by the letter *W*?)

No idea, said Matthew. How about tonight?

Where? (You see, this illustrates why I love my work in newspapers. From a very young age I clearly had an innate feel for the five *W*'s of journalism—who, what, when, where, why.)

You have a bike? I ride over to Tricky's most days after school. Oh, but I'm the only one calls him Tricky by the way, just so you know. Anyway, you only live a few streets from him, right? But maybe it would be good if we all had bikes.

Sure, I have a bike, but . . .

How about you, Jen, you have a bike?

(Sorry, I haven't until now mentioned the presence of my very best friend, Jen Snell, in this scene because, ever since Matthew strode up to us, she hasn't said anything, hasn't moved, hasn't taken even one solitary sip of the world's readily available oxygen.)

Jen's words came out in one rapid spew. *Ihavetoaskmymom.*

You have to ask your mom if you have a bike?

Ihaveabike.

Great, then everything's arranged. Tell your moms you're

going over to Joe McConnell's. But don't mention me, just say Patrick needs some help stapling leaflets or making ticker tape or something else *mind-blowing*. They'll dig that. See you tonight, then, Hannah.

Matthew turned and headed toward the school doors, taking the first few steps at walking pace and then broke into a run.

I stared wide-eyed at Jen. Jen stared wide-eyed at me.

Wow!

WHY DO YOU THINK HE runs everywhere? said Jen.

It was a good question. Now that I thought about it, I realized that whenever Matthew wasn't with Patrick, he was running—down the hallway, off the school bus, or fast up the school steps, taking them two and three at a time.

I don't know, I said. Maybe going to some place or another is just the stuff that happens in between, I don't know . . . better . . . stuff?

You mean like a sandwich?

Sure. But the other way round.

You mean cheese on the outside and bread for the filling? I made that for lunch one time.

Was it good?

No, it was seriously gross.

Yes, it was with witty conversations like this that were going to captivate the most dangerously thrilling seventh grader in Roseborn.

We started walking again, making our way toward school, a squat redbrick building that looked like it might have been designed using a Lego starter kit to achieve its wildly inspiring look.

So do you think we should go? said Jen.

I wanted to scream at her—*Should we go? Of course we should go. If we don't we'll regret it for the rest of our lives. We will die old and lonely in a house stinking of washcloth and cat feces.*

Maybe, I said.

Yeah, maybe, said Jen.

So that was a yes from us both.

I SPENT THE WHOLE DAY thinking about our postschool rendezvous, rehearsing conversations with Matthew in my head, being admonished by teachers for inattentiveness, talking to Jen between lessons about how weird Matthew was—majorly weird, we agreed, the word thrilling me each time we used it—and absently doodling on pages torn out of my schoolbooks. I scrawled various things on those scraps of paper, different configurations of the letters *HJWA* (Hannah Jensen Matthew Weaver), pictures of a stick boy and stick girl in stick Tokyo (some of those doodles including stick chopsticks), and bunches of flowers that may or may not have been wedding bouquets. However, at no point while I was doing any of this did I think of myself as being pressed down on by the all-consuming millstone of my life's first ever crush.

No, Matthew was a weird but interesting boy, that was all. The letters *HJWA* were no more romantic than a chemical formula. Those flowers I'd drawn in huge bunches were simply the blooms of intellectual curiosity.

Meanwhile, the feeling of having to wait for my dangerous liaison caused schooltime to virtually freeze, the day's lessons moving forward at a crawl. When finally the bell rang for the end of the day, I felt as if I'd been imprisoned for a lifetime, but now I was free, the light beyond the school doors beckoning me and the gray air clumping around our sputtering school buses a heady perfume.

Sitting next to each other on the ride home, as we always did, the bus inching its way through Roseborn, Jen and I made our plans (meet at Jen's, ride our bikes over to Patch's house, talk about *The Dukes of Hazzard* only if backed into a corner), and when finally the odyssey to the end of Grist Mill Road was complete, I exploded out of the bus doors onto my driveway as if a trigger had been pulled somewhere inside me—although, had anyone asked me, I still would have denied, vigorously and perfectly innocently, that my behavior bore all the hallmarks of a crush.

But Matthew Weaver, oh Matthew Weaver. I can admit it now, I was in love.

THINKING OF NOTHING BUT MATTHEW, my kindred spirit to be, I skipped up the short stretch of drive toward our gates, which were always open, passing through the stone gateposts topped with twin models of the Brooklyn Bridge arches. Erected by an earlier Jensen, the model arches were a nod to the nature of our family business, Roseborn's once-famous export, the powder behind the power—cement. OK, I'll grant you that it's not the most glamorous product in the world, but I can assure you that cement was once gray gold in them thar hills.

Yes, I was born into a rich family, there's no point in hiding it, and while it didn't seem to be a factor in my life when I was twelve, I wasn't thinking ever so deeply about such things back then. In fact, rather than being kindred spirits, there were actually many differences between myself and Matthew Weaver, differences that my twelve-year-old self never stopped to consider. I suppose I was aware that Matthew was a rough kid, an older kid, and an out-of-towner, but I probably never stopped to think how different my life was from his. The Jensens had been resident in Roseborn for more than a century and a half, and after I passed through those gateposts, the view that greeted me was of a large parchment-colored home, a three-car garage, a set of stables, and the vast acreage of our expertly landscaped grounds. And while the grounds were currently covered in snow, in a few months time we would have the greenest lawn, the wildest flowerbeds, and the trimmest hedges in town. Matthew, meanwhile, lived under very different circumstances, as I would find out for myself later on.

The upturn in our family's fortunes—which was also the upturn in sleepy Roseborn's fortunes—had come early in the nineteenth century when workers blasting out the bed of the Delaware and Hudson Canal discovered the snout end of a thirty-square-mile belt of high-grade limestone near Roseborn, New York, a large portion of which turned out to be buried beneath land owned by a farmer and recent immigrant from Denmark named Jens Henrik Jensen.

Every time we ate dinner in my childhood home, I got spooked by the oil painting of Jens Henrik that hung at the end of our dining table, the great Dane leering at me, pale faced and sharp boned, a dark mop of hair falling over his brow, almost all the way down to his lurid blue eyes. Noticing the eyes of this long-dead forebear as they followed me around the dining room—eyes that were clearly my eyes as well—I was filled every time with a dread sense of doom.

Prior to the discovery of Roseborn's powdered gold, Jens Henrik Jensen had owned and operated a grist mill (hence the name of our road), but shrewdly converted this to a cement grinding mill soon after the limestone's unearthing. Thereafter, production of Roseborn cement would quickly become the bedrock of our family business, a company known to this day by anyone who works in the construction industry, The Jensen Royal Cement Company. (Jens Henrik inserted the *Royal* both for the sake of gravitas and to honor Denmark's King Frederik VI.)

Apparently this ultra-high-grade limestone was some seriously good blow, good enough that our humble town rapidly gave birth to fifteen cement companies and lent its name to a whole new breed of cement . . . drumroll . . . Roseborn cement! And who in the world *does not* know that Roseborn cement was used for the Grand Central Terminal, the piers of the Brooklyn Bridge, New York's earliest skyscrapers, and the pedestal of the Statue of Liberty?

Shame on you.

From its discovery to present day, Roseborn cement experienced many ups and downs—our natural cement is formidably strong once it sets, but frustratingly it takes an incredibly long time to do so. Yes, tough but stupidly slow, Roseborn cement is the Sylvester Stallone of the construction world.

OK, let's pause there for a moment while I admit to employing humor to hide the fact that I am, truth be told, an enormous cement nerd. I find all this stuff fascinating, and even as a young girl, cement intrigued me. The Society for the Preservation of Historical Cements (a real thing, I kid you not) would hold its meetings at our house, and I would sit at the back of the room trying to take it all in—my father was a high-ranking official in the society and anything my father did fascinated me. The gatherings were hosted by a man named Pete whose face must have been carved from a rock, with a beard that looked like it was dusted with cement powder. Pete worked for the Conservancy and seemed to be the local expert on anything and everything, coming to our school sometimes to give talks on glaciers or the flora and fauna of the Swangums, but while glaciers left me cold and pine needles didn't spike my interest, there was something about the topic of cement that lit me up like gunpowder.

Anyway, by the end of the nineteenth century, Roseborn's fifteen competing cement plants were producing 42 percent of the nation's cement. However, there was trouble in store for our heroic local product because a foreign interloper had entered the market as well, a vile and inferior slurry known as Portland cement.

An early-nineteenth-century concoction, Portland cement was a man-made product cooked up by a bricklayer in Leeds, England. Yes, that's right, Lady Liberty's patriotic foundation, Roseborn cement, was being threatened by nothing other than limey limestone.

King Kong v. Godzilla, pah! You ain't seen nothing until you've seen two cements facing off. The war was hard fought, but there could be only one winner. Unfortunately, the long curing time of Roseborn cement made it unpopular in the hurried post–World War One construction boom with its vast road- and bridge-building programs, and so the winner was, alas, Portland cement.

However, as it happened, this egregious injustice turned out to be hugely advantageous to our family, the reason for which we will come to mercifully soon.

So, thanks to Portland cement, Roseborn cement fell on hard times, and I'm afraid it ain't pretty when a strain of natural cement lets itself go. Crapulent plants lay in disarray on the outskirts of Roseborn like broken men, their glory days behind them, until finally only one was left standing—Jensen Royal Cement. But although our family's business survived, it now ran unprofitably, staying open only because the cement business was so beloved by my grandfather, William Jensen, a shrewd operator who'd made money from investments in the 1920s and then, according to family legend, having been warned of the Wall Street crash in a dream by Jens Henrik Jensen, shifted all his profits away from shares and into movies and property just before the lower-rear hole was ripped from the stock market.

The Jensen Royal Cement Company returned slowly to profitability watched over by William Jensen and then, despite more hard times ahead, under the stewardship of my father, Walt Jensen.

Finally our family business flourished anew, and soon we did more than flourish—beginning with an inspirational act of diversification, we grew rich. A fact of which my mother was supremely proud.

Laura Jensen, née Snedecker, was a most august concrete baroness, and as a wife and mother she was much devoted to her husband, my father Walt Jensen, and her two sons, Bobby and Pauly. She was well known in Roseborn for her conspicuous wealth, her huge financial support of the Republican Party, and her jaw-dropping, eye-shutting bluntness. My mom had a mysterious ability to identify a person's weak points and proceed to ask the question that least wanted asking in any given social situation. For example—

My daughter says you're good with the boys. Not so much with the girls. Is there a reason for that, Mr. Bocelli? This question was asked right in front of me, to my teacher in tenth grade. Now, firstly, I had said no such thing, my mom had simply intuited it from several completely innocent statements. Secondly, and even worse, it was absolutely true. And finally, God help us all,

Mr. Bocelli was secretly, but quite obviously, gay—or *a fag,* as he would have been termed back then. Please don't judge me for my use of this word, or at the very least, hold fire for now, because we'll return to this later on. It's just a fact that, in the early 1980s, and in the place I grew up, for reasons I suppose I never thought about at the time, a faggot was one of the worst things you could be. Look, I'm a reporter, I am only reporting the facts.

Anyway, then there was the time after church when we were saying our goodbyes to the Snells, my best friend Jen's dad having just told us how his mother had recently died in a car accident resulting from a failure to stop at a set of rail crossing lights, at which point my mother said, Oh, that's too terrible for words, and not at all a nice way to go. (Always, immediately before one of my mom's gaffes, there came a pause, at which point my stomach would drop to my pelvic floor.) *Sooo,* she continued, a genuine note of curiosity in her voice, do they think it might have been because of the drinking?

As you might imagine, it was tact and sensitivity such as this that would turn the forthcoming monocular portion of my childhood into one never-ending party.

Only here's the thing about my mother's forensic ability to sniff out the awkward question and then go ahead and ask it. While in social situations such behavior is generally considered, at the very least, gauche, in the world of news reporting, awkward question–asking is something that's actually considered a skill. In fact, you might even say that awkward question–asking is the chief requirement of the job, which means that the very quality that made me squirm so often as a child, the quality in my mother that upset me the most as an adolescent, would in fact turn out to be her gift to me when, years later, I would discover that although my eyes and sense of humor had been passed down to me from the Jensen side of the family, my ability to perform in my job was 100 percent Snedecker. But despite my visible discomfort, my mother would continue until the day that she died to float through life blissfully unaware she was considered by the local populace to be the foot-in-mouth queen of Roseborn.

Besides, my mother occupied another position, and this was one of which she was both proud and very much aware, because according to family legend, Laura Snedecker had once saved the life of Jensen Royal Cement, and therefore was absolutely entitled to sit every day on the luxurious upholstery of the family throne. And how did my mother earn her crown? Well, despite the fact that Jensen Royal Cement had emerged as Roseborn's only survivor in its battle with Portland cement, the keeping of the business afloat remained a daily struggle. Roseborn cement was very much a niche product, and the prospect of financial ruin still loomed large. It's true that the business needed the kiss of life, and legend has it that one day, while they were courting, my mother heard that her beau Walter had come down with a bad case of the flu. Pulling on her boots double-quick, she then sped around to his house with a can of soup to find my father sweaty and delirious, but nursed him back to health with hand-fed spoonfuls of Campbell's Condensed Cream of Mushroom. As my father emerged from his fevered dreams, he saw the empty soup can and the word *mushroom* glowing as if lit up like a neon sign, and that's when the idea struck him.

You see, the extraction of vast quantities of limestone from the ground leaves behind dirty great holes, which means that on our land, a short trot behind the stables, we had ourselves a fine thirty-acre cave. (That's almost twenty-three football fields.)

Delirium, delirium, Laura, can, soup, mushroom, cave . . . wait . . . *mushroom cave* . . .

Bingo!

Within a year my parents had wed and the thirty-acre cave beneath the Jensen estate was producing five tons of mushrooms every day. From 1955 to 1969, Jensen Royal Cement's cave was the almost sole supplier of mushrooms to the Campbell Soup Company, which means that, in 1962, when Andy Warhol exhibited his thirty-two cans of Campbell's soup, one of those cans would theoretically have been full of Jensen-cave-grown mushrooms. Which is why my mother hung a copy of the Warhol painting right next to the oil of the great Dane, Jens Henrik Jensen.

Meanwhile my dad, an intensely quiet man, never spoke up about his role in keeping the business afloat, and no one in our family ever publicly questioned the details of the story, although personally I have always wondered about the likelihood of my mother's choice of condensed cream of mushroom as medicine—because isn't there a reason why chicken noodle soup is known as Jewish penicillin? Who on earth would take a flu patient condensed cream of mushroom soup as opposed to chicken noodle? But enough of my awkward questions. However it came about, Jensen Royal Cement's slim profits were now being fattened up on sweet fungo-dollars, and although the Campbell Soup Company would eventually find itself an even cheaper source of mushrooms, our family business had had a good run and my father had never been one to tread water. In fact, it was time to further diversify. At the beginning of 1969, the Jensen Royal Cement Company started to produce . . . I can hardly bear to say it, but here it comes, the vile twist in the tale . . . *Portland cement.*

Back in the 1930s, it had been noticed that if you added just a little sip of Roseborn cement to its Portland nemesis, the result was a considerably stronger cement, and by the end of the 1960s, thanks to advancing technology, it became possible to create this construction dream team without having to manually combine the two products.

All of which means that, while it was mushrooms that had kept our family business afloat, it was the enemy cement that led to Jensen's 1970s boom, a dramatic rise in profits led by sales of a new miracle product, a mixture of Roseborn and Portland cements, King Kong *and* Godzilla, sold under the proprietary name, Roseport Cement.

The money was about to start rolling in. A new cement had been born to the world, and, some three months later, so was I.

AND NOW HERE I WAS, teetering on the brink of adolescence, walking up our expensively paved driveway, between low walls of plowed snow, toward our large ancestral home, thinking about

Matthew Weaver (and yet not really thinking about the real Matthew Weaver), slowing down slightly when I noticed my dad's truck hurriedly parked close to the front door, two of its wheels buried in the snow just off the driveway, a half-grassed job.

Which meant that clearly something was wrong, because my father performed even the smallest of life's tasks with pinpoint precision. Right away I felt sick, my first thought being that maybe something terrible had happened to one of my brothers (who both lived out their lives neck-deep in dangerous vices), and I started to run to the front door.

In fact the worst thing in the world hadn't yet happened. The worst thing in the world was actually about to happen, and it was going to happen to me—or so it foolishly felt at the time.

Twelve years old, what did I know about anything? The world has taught me a lot since then.

OPENING THE FRONT DOOR AND seeing my brothers in the front room, very much alive, I felt a surge of relief. There was Bobby feet-up in the recliner, TV remote in one hand, fresh vodka-tonic in the other (if you ever asked what he was drinking, his response was 7UP), and there was Pauly, the younger of my two brothers, who preferred hash to hooch, stretched out on the sofa with a forearm draped over his forehead, looking like a Victorian lady recovering from a bout of the vapors.

Hey, little sis, said Bobby.

What's going on? I said.

You'd better go see for yourself, said Bobby, making an upward gesture with his drink.

Pauly dragged his eyes over to me. Yo, Hannah Solo, he said. You know, I think it might actually have been my fault. I kinda thought it through and I think, yeah, so don't worry, I'll tell her later some time.

I had no idea what Pauly was talking about, which wasn't unusual.

And then I heard Mom call out my name from the floor above, loud at first and then whiny. Han-*aaah*! *Haaa*-nah!

Now I wanted to run outside, jump on my bike, and pedal as fast as I could away from that place.

Coming, Mom, I called out, moving without any obvious haste.

MY BROTHERS WERE TEN AND twelve years old when I was born (something of an unplanned blip), and by the time I entered the world, bawling and bright-eyed, my mom had been sitting on the family throne for years. She spent her days enjoying a regal portion of Jensen Royal Cement's profits (she had a wardrobe straight out of *Charlie's Angels* and an eye for antiques), employing and firing a succession of housemaids and gardeners, and doting on her sons.

My mom had successfully constructed for herself the world in which she wished to live—the large house, the hired help, the stoic and protective husband, all of these things earned, to her mind, by her womanly wiles, and now she was free to sit back and enjoy a lifetime of restful days. But unfortunately in her idlesse she became a role model to Bobby and Pauly, my two sweet brothers, who to me seemed as innocent as a pair of toy bears, all goofy smiles and plump bellies, stuffed to the seams every day with the fillings of their choice.

Bobby, the eldest, had been drinking for as long as I could remember. Not that he was an angry or violent drunk, just more like an overgrown kid who had discovered an endless supply of his favorite candy and spent his days constantly on the edge of a sugar coma. Meanwhile Pauly, who was two years younger, was the mellowest dude in the county, popular at school, even more popular at parties, and much in demand among the sort of girls who hated sunlight and loved listening to obscure British bands. But really I think there was, hidden deep down inside, a little of my father in both of my brothers, a faint voice fighting hard to be heard, a longing to strive for something more in their lives.

Unfortunately, the tragedy of Bobby and Pauly was that they had both found the remote control that could turn down life's noise. The remote control was free and it was good and the more often you pressed the button, the better the haze and the dimmer the voice nagging at you to do things you didn't want to do, or rather didn't need to do, which ended up amounting to the very same thing.

My brothers both had immensely sad eyes, which flipped over to kindness whenever they looked at me, even when they teased me, which they loved to do and did so lovingly, and I loved them back very much. However, in truth, I wanted to be nothing like them at all, neither my brothers nor my mother. Not that this impulse to be something different was intended as an act of rebellion—it was just the way I was built, I was my father's little girl all the way through, my father the feminist, who wanted me to be an engineer, an astronaut, or even president of the United States. My father was a hero who toiled without complaint in powdery monochrome, his cement plant an airless moonscape, and even when he wasn't working, he was busy, helping out fixing the church roof, painting a fence with a buddy, or picking up groceries for elderly members of the parish, and I was my father's more-than-willing little helper whenever I was allowed.

So if I reacted badly to my mother sometimes, it wasn't that I simply wanted to defy her. No, what I wanted was the chance to be me (or my father, perhaps). Not my brothers. And not her, I'm afraid.

If I was less than loving toward my mother sometimes, then I'm sorry now. It seems to me that if we'd ever had the chance, we might have become the kind of mother-daughter who share friendly hugs at Thanksgiving and leave each other thoughtful presents under the Christmas tree. However, throughout my childhood my mother took my desire to go in the direction of my own personality as criticism of her character, her sedentary ways, and I suppose there might have been a little of that, but what good had it done my brothers, trying to be like her? So if I mouthed off to her sometimes, then let's not forget that I was a girl on the verge of that awkward transition to womanhood, and after the shooting, when things were at their worst between us, I was a self-conscious, hormonal teenager with only one eye. What chance did we stand?

HANNAH, WHERE ARE YOU, WHAT'S taking so long? yelled my mom from upstairs.

Mom was an epic summoner. Throughout the day she liked to bellow my name from some part of the house, most often her bedroom, and I would be expected to come running. Upon my arrival, she would then tell me she was exhausted (she was always exhausted), and I needed to go find something for her—a cup of coffee, her *Good Housekeeping* magazine, a small bowl of fancy mixed nuts.

Coming, Mom, I called out again, wearily this time.

Reaching the top of the stairs, I was greeted by the familiar smell of death, which was ever present in the top story of our home, an old house with a roof always in need of repair (even my industrious dad couldn't keep up), and with numerous chimneys and crooked attics. Somehow squirrels or chipmunks or bats would find their way into our home, wedge themselves into an unfindable space, and then promptly lose the will to live.

(*Han-aaaaah!* Walt, what is wrong with that girl?)

I knew how they felt.

There was always a bag of lavender hanging from a hook at the top of the stairs. I held it to my face and took a deep breath before turning right toward my parents' bedroom, and when I reached the open door, the first thing I saw was my father sitting on the corner of the bed, motioning me to hurry up. Moving into the room, I saw my mom lying on top of the bedcovers, her leg swathed in a thick protective cast and raised up on a stack of several pillows. It made me think right away of *The Princess and the Pea*.

Look, honey, I broke my leg, said Mom, sounding perfectly tranquil. And then she performed her sad-face pout, but I could tell that what she really wanted to do was burst into song—

I broke my leg
I broke my leg
Everyone has to do what I say
Everyone has to answer my call
For six weeks at least
Or maybe eight
With any luck
I broke my leg

Mom patted at a spot beside her on the bed. I went and sat down while my dad put his hands on my shoulders.

Oh, Hannah, it's not your fault, said my mother.

My father squeezed me tenderly while I made a confused face.

It was your tea-party table, she said, you left it out in the den and I tripped and fell. But don't blame yourself, honey.

Now I remembered what Pauly had said about something being his fault, and I knew for a fact that I hadn't left any miniature tables in the den. I might not have been in the full flush of puberty, but I was a long way from make-believe tea parties. Pauly often used that table as a convenient joint-rolling surface, it being just the right height, like one of those trays with legs for eating breakfast in bed.

We're all going to have to help your mom around the house a little more for a while, said my dad.

Which made me think instantly, Not all of us, Dad. *You and I.*

Mom gave me a look suggesting she was hurt on my behalf and then said, You don't blame yourself too much, do you, Hannah?

I responded with a series of hard blinks and then a hard *No!*

My mom look horribly aggrieved. But you did leave that table right where I could trip over it, Hannah, she said.

What was I supposed to say? I wasn't about to throw my brother under the bus, and anyway, there wouldn't have been any point, my brothers' vices were something completely ignored in our household, as if my mother had been hypnotized into not seeing the signs right in front of her—Bobby's slurred speech and stumbles, the smell of weed that leached from Pauly's room when he forgot to blow his smoke out the window.

Sorry, Mom, I said, without much enthusiasm.

My father squeezed my shoulders some more. It's not your fault, Hanny Bee, but let's be a little more careful in future. And for a while, your mom's going to need a lot more help around the house. Can you do that for me?

Yes, Dad, I said, half-turning to look up at him beaming at me like he'd never been prouder, the same look I got from my father a dozen times every day.

Good girl, Hanny Bee. Wanna help me make dinner tonight?

Sure, I said, but I promised Jen that I'd go over to her house. It's only an hour. Can I help when I come back?

At which point my father's smile started turning to a wince as I heard my mom say, Oh, that is absolutely not happening, Hannah.

I turned back to face her, my mother looking breathless with irritation. How could I think to suggest such a thing at a time like this?

And not just today, she continued. While I'm in this cast, I need you to come straight home from school every day. No more going around to Jen Snell's for a while.

No, I cried out, you have to let me go to Jen's today, you have to, it's all arranged.

It's out of the question, Hannah.

Please, Mom, *pleeease*, I pleaded.

Jeesh, said my mom, you and that vapid little girl sit on the school bus together every single day. You have classes together. What more is there to talk about? No, I can't spare you, Hannah, it's settled.

But Cathy can help. (Cathy was our latest maid.)

Cathy finishes at three, she has her own family to worry about.

No, it's not fair, I said, my voice getting louder. It's like I'm being grounded and I didn't even do anything wrong.

Nothing *wrong*? said my mom, her voice rising as she peered meaningfully down at her leg. This is ridiculous, Hannah, don't act like you're being punished. *Puh-leeze.*

That's exactly what's happening, I shouted, close to tears, I am being punished.

Then my mom shouted back, her voice a bitter rasp at the back of her throat. If helping around the house is such a punishment, then I get punished every single damn day of my life, Hannah.

There was nowhere else for my rage to escape, I had to spit it out and I yelled furiously back at her—I wish you'd broken your stupid damn neck!

There was a shocked pause, a moment of silence as if a clock had just stopped, and then my mom reached out and slapped me hard in the face.

In some sense the slap came as a relief because now I could cry, everything that had been building up could have its release, and my tears burst forth with a furious speed, my body stiffening with the sting of unfairness.

I got up from the bed and ran from the room, my father shouting after me, Hannah, you come back right now and apologize.

No, let her go, I heard my mom call out. Ungrateful *wretch.*

By the time I threw myself, wailing, onto my bed, I was certain that my life was absolutely over, that nothing in the world could be more painful than this and that now, thanks to my mother, I would never get close to Matthew Weaver.

And yet, on all three counts, I was wrong.

MIGHT EVERYTHING HAVE TURNED OUT differently if my mother hadn't broken her leg that day? My guess is that, had I gone with Jen to Patch's house that afternoon, had I got to know Matthew much earlier in 1982, the four of us would have become friends and surely then, however naive I was, I would have discovered at a much more leisurely pace that the Matthew I had invented in my head was not the Matthew that existed in real life.

Instead of this I would be kept at arm's length from my fantasy for another eight weeks while my mother's leg gradually

healed. Eight more weeks in which I could paint an even more intricate Matthew inside my head, eight weeks of an intense burning
at the unfairness of life as my brothers remained free to sink into
their evening fogs after their days *hard at work learning the family
business,* to use my mom's frequently whipped-out phrase.

Really? However much I loved them, Bobby and Pauly were
learning the family business about as much as I was learning the
secret ways of the ninja. Only very rarely did either of them spend
more than a couple of hours at the cement plant, although Pauly
sometimes put in a longer shift if he was having trouble locating
a new pot dealer, my dad having a long-held policy of quietly ush-
ering out a steady string of his suppliers.

So instead of getting to know Matthew and Patrick, I had to
endure eight weeks in the role of Cinderella, performing household
chores each day while pining for my prince, making and carrying
drinks for my mom and cooking dinner each night with my dad,
a series of Mom's classics, such as French onion soup meat loaf
(the *soup* coming in dehydrated form from a packet), tuna noodle
casserole (sprinkled with crushed cheddar Goldfish crackers), and
my brothers' all-time favorite, chili con wieners.

For the next eight weeks, I talked it through obsessively with
Jen every day at school. Had Matthew just made eye contact with
me when we passed in the hallway? What did his look mean?
Did he run his fingers through his hair a lot when I was around
or did he just run his fingers through his hair a lot? Was his decision to wear denim that day some kind of secret sign?

Yes, for eight weeks everything built and built inside me until
finally the cast came off my mother's leg and that same day, Jen
sauntered over to Matthew and Patrick between lessons, while I
hung back in awe of my best friend's astonishing possession of two
functioning legs and a fully operational voice box while she fixed
up a new liaison at the McConnell household for the following
evening. Once the arrangements were made, Matthew waved at
me and let out a kindly chuckle when I waved back with all the
vigor of a fainting damsel.

The next morning I could barely contain the feeling gushing

through my body as I stepped off the school bus with Jen, my eyes scooting around for a glimpse of him, oh Matthew, my gaze running fast up the school steps, taking them two and three at a time, and yes, there he was.

Only wait, because there *she* was, there *they were.*

Matthew, Matthew and Christie, Matthew and Christie *kissing.*

I remember that was the moment, for the first time in my life (although certainly not the last), I felt the very physical sense of my heart being broken.

NEW YORK, 2008

Patrick only blinks, twelve years old again, a small boy staring at a scene just out of reach.

How can it be him? But it is, Matthew, seated at a restaurant table, twenty-six years older, his dark hair swept back and faintly receding. Matthew in a suit and tie, although somehow he looks casually dressed, diagonal stripes in the tie, plaid shirt underneath, tiny polka dots peppering his pocket square.

Running at him and crushing his skull with a rock, leaping in front of the forty-ninth bullet . . .

Patrick looks down at the table. Glass, fork, knife.

. . . finding a splintered branch and driving it deep into his chest, fetching the slingshot from under the tarp and firing a perfect shot . . .

None of this makes any sense. And now Matthew is speaking. I'm sorry, Tricky, he says, I honestly thought there was no other way.

The name makes him dizzier still but Patrick manages to find some strength in his voice. Don't you *ever* call me by that name again, he says.

Of course not, says Matthew, loosening the knot of his tie. Patrick, I'm sorry.

Sorry for what? For shooting Hannah? Half-blinding her? For leaving her for dead?

Of course I'm sorry about that, says Matthew. But wherever Hannah is in the world, I doubt she'd want to meet me for lunch so that I can apologize to her in person.

Wait, he doesn't know that we're married?

Patrick presses the heel of his hand to the bridge of his nose. So why did you trick me into meeting you here? he says.

I just wanted to get back in touch, says Matthew. But look, I can see already that I've made a huge mistake, he says. I knew this could prove awkward, only I thought you might sit down. And then we might talk.

Just walk away, Patch. You don't have to do anything but turn around and leave.

He looks over his shoulder, the smooth flow of good service, plates floating in and out of view.

Wait, please wait, says Matthew. Patrick, look, I know this arrangement may have been stupidly clumsy of me but I promise it wasn't a trick. He reaches inside his jacket, pulls out a business card and pushes it across the table.

Matthew Denby, Proprietor
St. Lawrence Supplies

We work with only the very best restaurants, says Matthew. St. Lawrence Supplies sources the finest lobster, mushrooms, lamb, oysters.

The business card is thick, plush, it rests between them on the table like a small pillow, the padding inside a ring box.

You changed your name, says Patrick.

Matthew's smile twitches. Only half of it, he says.

A silent moment. And then Patrick pulls the business card toward him, flips it over. Printed address, phone number, fax. But also Matthew has written something in blue ink, the address of an apartment in Tribeca. How did you find me? he says.

I have an assistant who sends me things, says Matthew. Newspaper clippings, links to websites, the menus of new restaurants, that sort of thing. I try to keep my finger on the pulse of where food is headed, what ingredients might be in vogue in six months' time. Food is like fashion, it gets carried along by certain whims, certain styles. She sent me a link to your website. I haven't lied to you, Patrick, I genuinely enjoy what you do. Matthew locks his fingers, resting his hands on the tablecloth. Are you sure you won't sit down? he says. One minute, I promise. The business proposal—it was a lure, yes, but it wasn't a lie.

Patrick drops the card into a pocket. I've seen your delivery trucks all over the city, he says.

Good, says Matthew, we get around.

St. Lawrence Supplies, says Patrick, speaking the words in a contemptuous drawl.

Yes, I named it for the patron saint of—

Cooks, says Patrick.

That's right, says Matthew, running his hand through his hair, a stray curl breaking loose, dropping over his brow and hanging there like a meat hook. He taps at the menu, his forefinger hitting the gold curlicues of Le Crainois. Jean-Jacques is one of our best customers, he says. He and I have become very close friends. I'd really like to introduce you.

This *proposal,* says Patrick. Whatever it is, it's impossible.

Impossible? says Matthew. Why?

Perhaps he really doesn't know, thinks Patrick. *No, there are no photos of Hannah on the website. I never use her name. All I need to do is turn around and leave, there is nothing else to be done.*

He leans heavily on the table. Listen very carefully, says Patrick. Don't ever try to contact me again, you understand?

Matthew folds his hands in his lap. Of course, Patrick, he says. And once again, apologies for my misjudgment. I promise to keep my distance.

This is his cue to leave. And yet Patrick hesitates. Perhaps he wants to see if there are signs of rejection on Matthew's face—Patrick doesn't remember ever turning him down as a child. And now Matthew's expression does seem to suggest some mild degree of disappointment.

Patrick looks down at him a moment longer, Matthew's hair

with a rich shine, his stubble dark, his eyes green. And then Patrick realizes something that startles him—Matthew is good-looking, perhaps even exceptionally so. The revelation unsettles him, as if somewhere a tale has taken a surprising twist.

And then at last he turns around.

But please, says Matthew, promise me you'll think it through. You have my card. I just want a chance to talk everything through, Patrick.

He walks away.

RUN! PATRICK FEELS AS IF a spear is pointing at his back. Out through the sculptural twigs, past the bar and the greeter, who bids him goodbye, out into the mall, hard to breathe, trying to loosen a tie that's not there, stepping onto the escalator.

Why didn't I attack him?

No, you did the right thing, Patch. You didn't listen to his proposal. You walked away.

But these are just words, only words, and the body knows better, Patrick's muscles stiff and alert, an empty, sick feeling in the place where he carries his shame, a place he knows well, like a mole knows his tunnels. What did Matthew want? What was his proposal?

A second escalator. A third. And then Patrick hears his name, a voice calling out to him from above.

Monsieur McConnell? Monsieur McConnell, please.

He turns and sees the plastic-clad tourists moving to one side of the steps. Pushing his way past them is Frédéric, the maître d' from Le Crainois.

Monsieur McConnell, stop, please stop.

At the bottom of the escalator, Patrick hangs back and waits.

Thank you, Monsieur McConnell, says Frédéric when he reaches him. Please, this is something very important. Chef would like to speak to you.

That's impossible, says Patrick. I'm not coming back.

I see, but this is not impossible, says Frédéric. I brought something, he says, raising his left hand, which is carrying a tablet computer, like a thin hardcover book.

Frédéric leads Patrick by the elbow to a viewing point that overlooks the gleaming atrium and spinning entrance doors. Please, says Frédéric, just give me a few seconds. He presses a button on the device, which lights up, and taps the screen a few times. Chef, excuse me, I have Monsieur McConnell now, says Frédéric, speaking into the tablet and then turning the screen to face Patrick.

On-screen, Patrick can see the chef standing in his kitchen, Jean-Jacques Rougerie, whom he recognizes from the newspapers and magazines, from the photos in his book, *La Cuisine Précise*. The chef is bent over a plate of morel mushrooms, inspecting them. He nods, the plates are whisked away and Jean-Jacques Rougerie looks up.

Welcome to my kitchen, Monsieur McConnell, he says. May I call you Patrick?

Yes, Chef, says Patrick, slightly starstruck.

You like my video linkup, Patrick? This way I can be in my restaurant in Paris and my restaurant in New York at the same time. Remarkable, no?

Yes, Chef, says Patrick.

Please, I am Jean-Jacques to you, Patrick, always Jean-Jacques for my friends. The chef turns and speaks firmly to someone off-screen. Not glossy enough, more butter, he says. And then, looking back up, he says, Now, Patrick, I cannot say what happened just now and why you leave so fast. But Mathieu is a good friend of mine. And I think it is true that everything can be made better with good food and excellent wine, yes? And we have prepared a surprise for you, a meal that is truly unique. We have some ingredients from Mathieu. His *morilles* right now? Excellent. And we use some of your own recipe ideas that I see on your website, Patrick, we mix them with a few ideas of our own, I think we have something exceptional. Perhaps you can return, eat and then I show you around my kitchen. You think it is possible?

Thank you, Chef, but no, another time, perhaps.

I cannot change your mind? You see, I wanted maybe to invest. And also to help out if I can.

Invest? Invest in what?

In this business of yours with Mathieu, of course. Your Red Moose Barn, no? First I see there being one restaurant but then many more. I read your recipes online, see your ideas, I think this is something exciting. Old but new. This is a very modern idea, I think.

Red Moose Barn?

Of course. And Mathieu says the two of you grow up together. This is the best way, the strongest. Like brothers, you know? Because you must fight, always fight in this business. For a restaurant not to die you need courage and strength. And this is why Mathieu's company is called St. Lawrence, I think. St. Lawrence for courage and strength. You know the story of this saint, Patrick?

I do.

To the left, Frédéric, I have only half a face, says Jean-Jacques.

Frédéric tilts the screen.

Better, says Jean-Jacques with a sigh. Now, St. Lawrence, he says, yes, this is a story about heart, about faith. And in Rome, of course, they kill St. Lawrence for his faith. They cook him alive on *un . . . un uh . . .* how do you say, like in the American football?

A gridiron, says Patrick.

Gridiron, yes. They roast St. Lawrence alive on a gridiron over hot coals. But as he was dying, still he showed them his courage and strength to the end.

Patrick starts to laugh.

Jean-Jacques Rougerie smiles up at him. Of course, he says, this legend is so grotesque all we can do is laugh. It is truly something terrible that we cannot imagine.

No, says Patrick, I'm laughing because I remember how the story ends.

The end? says Jean-Jacques. But this part is the most grotesque of all. I think perhaps you have a darkness in you, Patrick, no?

What else can Patrick do but laugh? He is standing in a shopping mall talking to the world's most famous chef via a small screen held by a man called Frédéric. Tourists pass by and stare at the curious scene. And, remembering how the story ends, Patrick snorts and covers his mouth to hold back the laughter. But the laughter will not be held back. Still, Patrick tries to speak, the words coming out in short bursts. St. Lawrence said . . . He told them . . . (Patrick wipes a gathering dampness away from his eyes.) He said, *Turn me over . . . Turn me over . . . I'm done on this side.*

And then Patrick laughs so hard that Jean-Jacques, whose arms are now folded at his chest, starts laughing as well. The two men stand there at either end of a video link laughing together, ten seconds, twenty, and now they are both laughing too hard, their howls and tears feeding each other, so that when the laughter is ready to die it is rekindled by the other man's laughter.

Now Frédéric is laughing as well, a low chuckle that causes the screen to shake. Several passersby stare at them, this curious scene being played out, some of the passersby being affected by the contagion of the laughter as well.

Patrick bends his knees and holds his thighs, unable to see the shaky screen until he wipes away more tears. And then at last, when this feast of laughter is almost over, Patrick waves at Jean-Jacques Rougerie, the gesture sapped of its strength, so much has he been laughing. The chef tries to say something but the words are caught up in the last gasps of his laughter and before he can get them out, Patrick walks away, rubbing his sides.

Turn me over, I'm done on this side. And as he steps on the escalator, Patrick turns to see Frédéric switching off the screen, smiling to himself at the increasingly endearing strangeness of the world, of New York. And especially *les Américains*.

THE SUMMER IS AS HOT and slow as the pre-Maine summers of his childhood, the air with a watery quality, Patrick feeling submerged in the city whenever he steps outside of his building to shop for groceries or follow Don Trevino, the only two activities he can bear in the life-sapping heat. Outside of the apartment he feels himself becoming attuned to all the anger in the world, as if New York is soaking into him, wave after wave, horn after horn, voices everywhere screaming obscenities into their phones, the city infecting him with a fever that gets worse by the day.

Soon Patrick can feel himself getting more and more angry about incidents that don't quite happen. A cyclist who thinks about running a red light as he's crossing the street. A woman leaning past him in the greenmarket, almost snatching the bunch of dinosaur kale he's considering. So much potential for conflict in the city, like a tray of metal balls being rattled together, and after each near miss Patrick replays the event in his head but with a twist, as if the incident *has* actually happened, the collision, the theft, hearing himself yelling abuse, seeing himself throwing punches . . .

It is as if his mind is readying him for the moment when he will be called upon. Something is going to happen, he can feel it.

Every week he sits in Dr. Rosenstock's office telling him none of this. And he doesn't tell Dr. Rosenstock about Matthew, Red Moose Barn, or Jean-Jacques Rougerie, because what if his therapist begins to suspect him of something? What if he feels duty bound to report him to some kind of authorities?

Or what if Dr. Rosenstock is part of the plot?

And it has to be some kind of a plot, doesn't it? The offer to make Red Moose Barn a reality coming from the one person in the world whose offer Patrick can never accept? What other tortures does life hold up its sleeve? And how can this be an accident? No, the world has turned against him. First Trevino, then Matthew. And who else might be in on this? Who next? A taxi driver failing to yield at a crossing? A skateboarder careening across the sidewalk? Or Hannah? Might Hannah be next?

No, Hannah loves me, he thinks.

Sure, because you're quite the catch, Paddyboy. Bed-maker, laundry boy, food blogger.

June, July, August.

It happens slowly, piece by piece, day by day, like with the growth of a child. You look away for a few months and when you turn back it seems as if a new person has entered the room.

Patrick can feel some kind of structure being gradually built up around him, the scaffolding rising pole upon pole. And soon there are panes of frosted glass being erected, the panels of a structure whose purpose is to keep him from the world, to keep the world from him, Patrick bound in a foggy kind of prison.

At home he still cooks, slogging his way through the recipes and techniques of Jean-Jacques Rougerie, refining the menu of Red Moose Barn, calibrating the ingredients in his breads and biscuits and waffles. He must keep himself busy busy busy, because if he stops moving, everything will be over. Only on the weekends can he relax, making breakfasts that he and Hannah eat in bed before settling down with the newspaper or a book. Slow mornings, idle time. To be in a room with another person doing nothing feels like meditation, to be idle in a room all alone feels like disease.

Now the depression seems even worse than it had been in his late teens, then twice in his twenties. But can that be true? This time around he doesn't want to hurt himself—he wouldn't want Hannah to find him. This is just one of the ways in which his wife saves him, over and over, every day of his life.

And yet something is fading between them, so that the night of their wedding anniversary has begun to feel like one last great fling, their midnight hours on the table reminding Patrick of his late twenties, the end of an eight-month relationship with a woman called Nina. The breakup, the bedroom floor, Nina packing her bags the next morning.

Why doesn't Hannah ever ask him what he's doing with his time? Why doesn't she ask what's going on with him?

Perhaps she doesn't want to know.

Well of course she doesn't want to know. Who wants to know that everything in the world is not fine? No one—his wife especially, perhaps. And so he must stay behind his panes of frosted glass, living in the half-light, only half alive in the world, looking on as the glass thickens.

Becoming a ghost. That's how he feels. Patrick is slowly turning into a ghost.

IT HAS BEEN SIX WEEKS since the aborted lunch date at Le Crainois and what has he done apart from shop, cook, blog and record his steadying obsession with Don Trevino, his gradually diminishing sex life?

Answer. He has learned how to stabilize the emulsion of salad dressings with soy lecithin. He has become a master of the dark arts of pressure caramelization. He can make a chocolate ganache so pliable you can tie it in a knot.

You the man, Paddyboy.

And then one afternoon, before leaving the apartment, he pulls one of his kitchen knives from its wooden block, the knife a present from Hannah, bought when they were on vacation in Japan from a place in an alleyway near Tsukiji Fish Market. He selects it because it fits snugly into the pocket of his cargo pants, where it will remain, hidden up against his thigh, until it is time.

The pain of doing nothing for so long has to be released. Patrick has to do something.

In the elevator a neighbor smiles, says hi and asks how it's going, as his neighbors still do. The frosted glass structure being built around him must be almost complete, because apparently no one can see the storm pounding and raging inside him.

Patrick steps into the lobby where Jorgé is on duty at the front desk. Funny how Jorgé always greets him when he's leaving the building and says farewell whenever he arrives.

Hello, gentleman, says Jorgé.

Goodbye, Jorgé, he says.

IT IS ONE OF THOSE late summer afternoons in New York when the sunlight falls like dust and even the traffic seems sapped by the long burn of the season, cars and SUVs bumper-to-bumper, the summer Friday crawl, Manhattan packing up early, heading off to second homes in the Hamptons, upstate, New Jersey, the Berkshires . . . It feels to Patrick like an appropriate day for what he has planned, a Friday-ish sort of activity. Knife, stroll, action. Nine months ago, when Trevino had fired him, that had taken place on a Friday as well. It is all coming together.

The lights are kind to him as he walks toward Forty-Seventh, thinking it through, just as he has thought it through a hundred times before, a thousand, more.

Was there something else he could have done in Trevino's office that day? Was there any other way he could have played it? Did it even matter what answer he gave?

Nine months have passed and he can't stop thinking it through, reconstructing it, debating it all over again. He supposed that eventually it would get better, that time would soften his bitter recollection, but it only got worse.

Don Trevino's office, dress-down Friday, Trevino's tie patterned with little Donald Ducks.

Take a seat, Patrick, says Trevino from behind his desk, his hands laced together, fingers moving gleefully, forming a steeple, bird, roof. I'll get straight to the point, I've called you in to ask you a question, the same one I'm going to ask Clark in a minute. So here's the thing, Patrick, we all know the latest financial weather forecast—tornadoes with a 50 percent chance of Apocalypse. It gives me no pleasure to say this but I have to lose someone. Idos Investments simply can't maintain its current staffing levels. So here's the question. Who should I let go? You or Clark? One-word answer.

Patrick crosses Sixth Avenue, thinking that Clark Anderson is sitting in the offices of Idos Investments right now, in the same chair two cubicles along from where he used to sit, Data Acquisition, their department sandwiched between Risk Team and Programming.

What? Don . . . Mr. Trevino, you can't . . .

Come on, it's a simple question. You or Clark?

On Trevino's desk there is a birthday card with a yellow sticky note attached and on the note the words, *Your son's birthday, 16yo, Sunday.*

Every time that Patrick gets to this part, recalling the next three, five seconds, every time he thinks it through again, he tries to remember his reasoning. What was it that led him to his answer?

Trevino, no longer even looking at him, has reached for his computer mouse and is clicking away at something on-screen.

Me, says Patrick.

Me. The word remains lodged in his head like shrapnel.

Good, says Trevino, still not looking at him. Good, you can go now then, Patrick. Send in Clark when you get back to your desk. I'll let you know my decision by the end of the day.

Me? What was it that led him to say this?

Was it because Clark Anderson is a father of three with a mortgage and a stay-at-home wife? *Sure, wouldn't you like to be the hero just once in your life, Paddyboy.* Or had he actually thought that this was the correct answer, that this would save his job? Because after an answer like that, Trevino would have to see that he was a good guy, the kind of solid, decent human being you should want to hold on to, right? Or had it simply been a trick all along? Had it mattered at all what answer he gave? If he'd said *Clark,* wouldn't Trevino have claimed that he wasn't a team player? Surely it was a trick.

When Clark Anderson came back from Trevino's office, Patrick asked him what he had said.

Clark looked offended at the question. What do you think I said, Patrick? What in the hell did *you say*?

Trevino called a meeting five minutes later. Everyone had been summoned, asset managers, developers, risk engineers, programmers . . .

Trevino gave a speech about the precarious state of the economy, dropping in the same phrase he had used in his office, *tornadoes with a 50 percent chance of Apocalypse.* And then Trevino had said, More than ever I need people who believe in themselves, people who stand up for themselves. I need my employees with some fight in them. This is the toughest challenge our business has ever faced.

Patrick knew what was coming. He should have run at him right then, he should have knocked Trevino on his back, pinned him down. They should have had to pull Patrick off him, yelling, punching, screaming.

Trevino told the room exactly what had happened, Patrick's answer, Clark's answer. McConnell, you're outta here! he said. I'm not going to believe in a man who doesn't believe in himself. Sorry, gotta let you go, pack up your things, back to work everyone. You could tell right away that the room got the message—behold the sacrificial lamb and work harder, or you're next.

No one in the room would look at him. It felt to Patrick as if he were invisible, the world moving around him, unaware of his presence—and perhaps this was the precursor to how he feels now, a ghost. Or maybe this was the precise moment he began to fade from the earth.

And what did he do? What did Patrick actually do? Nothing. *Not true, Paddyboy. I do believe you packed up your shit.*

He crosses Forty-Fifth Street, Forty-Sixth, knowing what he has to do. Trevino will say sorry, has to say sorry. Patrick wants to see the look in his eyes as he holds the knife to Trevino's throat. He wants to see the fear, feel him shaking.

And then Trevino will apologize. He needs to know what it feels like to be treated like something small and worthless, to feel so powerless. Yes, Don Trevino will be sorry.

HE SIDLES UP TO HIS usual spot on the sidewalk. Patrick has already scouted the street and made a tentative plan—a delivery entrance to a building farther along Forty-Seventh, Trevino has to pass it on the way to his lunchtime sandwich spot, Patrick will push him inside and show him the knife. Quiet now, Don, *shhhh.*

He has to wait only twenty minutes before he sees him, the elevator doors opening, Trevino stepping out in a white seersucker suit and exchanging a few genial words with security. Patrick raises his map to half cover his face. Never in his life has he felt this ready.

But when Trevino exits the building, he steps to the curb and waves his arm, a taxi pulling up beside him on the street.

What to do? Should he postpone the plan?

No, his iron is hot right now. He must strike before it cools. The taxi pulls away and Patrick starts to run.

The traffic is heavy on Forty-Seventh and he doesn't have to run fast. But then the taxi turns right on Sixth Avenue, stopping at the next light—and when the signal changes, the cab will have a clear run all the way north to the park, so he starts running faster, passing the taxi, crossing Forty-Eighth.

As the lights change the traffic surges up Sixth Avenue, Trevino's taxi speeding past him (47851, he tries to remember the number). And then, attempting to keep the taxi in view, Patrick runs suddenly into an oversize tourist who has stopped moving for no good reason at all, the man's gallon-size drink flying from his hand, ice spilling over the sidewalk. But the sound of complaints fades away as Patrick keeps running and running, feeling like a child again, his lungs sparkling with life.

However, the collision has distracted him enough such that he can no longer see Trevino's taxi. The crossing light is red at the next junction, pedestrians crowding the street corner as traffic starts to move. Patrick pushes through anyway, voices yelling at him, a van driver seeing him and blasting his horn. But everything is clear to him now, as if he can see out through the frosted glass for the first time in weeks, a path of light shining in front of him and Patrick sprints hard, hearing brakes screech, more horns, and yet he makes it over unscathed, the crowd on the other side of the street parting for him.

Central Park is only two blocks away now. What if Trevino's taxi made a turn before it reached the southern edge of the park? But he keeps running anyway until he reaches Fifty-Ninth, looking frantically, his senses wildly alive. Left or right?

Right, he gambles, eyes searching the traffic, so many taxis. A four followed by a seven is all he can remember. He sees horses pulling tourists in carriages, one of them fouling the street without breaking stride, a cyclist shouting obscenities at a bus. But no four-seven anything.

And then, pushing his way past a line of paired schoolchildren being waved along by a teacher, convinced of his failure, Patrick feels a flash of euphoria as he spots the shimmering white seersucker no more than fifty yards up ahead.

Trevino turns right into a building, a hotel doorman tipping his cap as he passes. Patrick can feel the sweat running down his back, even his legs. And then he notices a pain in his thigh, a bruise perhaps, his collision with the tourist, or did that van perhaps clip him? But no time to stop, he pushes his loose shirttails back into his pants.

Perhaps the world is not entirely against him. Or maybe its conspiracy is unraveling at last. He hurries toward the hotel.

TREVINO STRIDES THROUGH THE DIM lobby in his radiant seersucker, smoothing his silver hair, fussing with the knot of his tie.

Patrick has started to limp. But it doesn't matter about the pain in his leg, he feels nothing but the steel of his resolve. Trevino moves on past the front desk toward the hotel restaurant and Patrick pauses by a sofa, picking up *Cosmopolitan* from a coffee table, leafing through its pages while keeping his eye on Trevino. Trevino is speaking to the restaurant greeter now, the woman laughing as she touches the screen of her terminal and passing Trevino on to a waiter who leads him away.

Patrick thinks about how best it would work. Yes, at some point Trevino will have to use the restroom. Patrick will follow him there. Quiet now, Don.

He looks down at the magazine, 27 SURPRISING WAYS TO TELL IF HE'S MR. RIGHT, drops it on the table and walks across the lobby. The restaurant greeter's head is down over her screen but she lifts it when Patrick is only a few steps away.

Good afternoon, sir.

He spots him right away, Trevino sitting down at a two-top, another man at the table already.

Good afternoon, says Patrick. I wonder if you have . . . He feels a stab of pain in his leg . . . Do you have any tables available this evening for . . . He reaches down to touch the leg where it hurts and the woman's eyes follow the movement, down to his thigh where he feels the shape of the knife handle.

The woman throws her hands to her cheeks. Oh, sir, your leg! You're . . . Let me call someone to help you right away.

He feels it before he sees it. Blood. More blood is running down his leg. He looks down and sees that his pants have turned almost black from his thigh to his knee and blood is running into his shoe, darkly staining the sand-colored suede.

No, it's nothing, he says, grabbing the knife handle, pulling.

The woman sees the knife, its blade covered in blood, and screams.

No, he says, attempting to conceal the weapon behind his back.

He has a knife, she shouts.

Panic ripples through the restaurant, heads spinning around, hands grabbing for cell phones. Don Trevino is reaching inside his jacket where he keeps his bifocals. The other man at his table is turning.

And it doesn't make sense to Patrick for as long as a second or two—the other man, hair swept back and faintly receding, dark stubble, green eyes. This isn't where he should be, he left him somewhere else. And yet it is him, undeniably him.

Matthew.

Matthew?

Well, that changes everything, Paddyboy.

HANNAH

Recalling that kiss was as far as I got.

Matthew and Christie, their lips pressed together at the top of the school steps, would be the last thing I wrote for several years, because everything in 2008 was about to start speeding up. A Friday afternoon at my desk in The Shack, a phone call from Detective Mike McCluskey—how could I have known that everything would be over before the weekend was out?

Which means that Matthew and Christie's gaudy display now seems immensely trivial to me, insignificant almost compared to everything that took place later on, both in 1982 and 2008.

Although, when it happened that kiss was everything, all four walls of my existence. Christie had displayed impeccably malicious timing, she couldn't have chosen a worse moment at which to smash my glass slipper to pieces. For days, weeks, I felt as if I were still rooted to that spot watching them kiss, the world spinning on without me, a sense of heartbreak giving birth to jealousy, and then jealousy spawning my rage.

I think Christie had fallen for some version of Matthew almost as much as I had fallen for my fantasy version. Why do I think that? Because she left me alone. For as long as they were together, Christie Laing kept her barbs to herself. (Don't worry, she would return to spectacular form not long after I lost my eye.)

And how much did this put me off Matthew? Not one inch. From the black seed of my rage there grew an even deeper sense of yearning for him, the world conspiring to keep us apart until the school year was over. I had turned thirteen years old, I was flowering inside, and if my adolescent desire hadn't built to such a fever pitch by the time summer vacation started, maybe I would have been able to see everything that happened later much more clearly.

I'VE JUST REMEMBERED SOMETHING PATCH once said to me in the early days when we were dating. He said you could line up a hundred cooks and give them all the same ingredients, that those hundred cooks could prepare each one of those ingredients in the same proportions and by the same method, but not one of the finished meals would taste the same.

I think that's how I feel about this story. How am I supposed to know what made the difference anymore?

For example, should I have noticed what was happening to my husband before that Friday afternoon? Maybe I was suffering from self-hypnosis, just as my mother had somehow hypnotized herself into turning a blind eye to everything concerning my brothers. Or did I think that because we had money, because Patrick didn't absolutely have to find another job, that everything would simply work itself out in the end?

How foolish of me to have seen so clearly, even from a young age, how money had distorted my immediate family, but to have failed to notice it affecting my own life.

Oh, the money—gray gold—yes, I suppose if we're listing all the ingredients, I really should tell you about that.

TOWARD THE END OF 1992, little more than a year after completing my journalism degree at Northwestern, I was living in New Jersey, working at the *Star-Ledger* in Newark where I wrote mostly about the least serious of reportable local crimes—domestic burglary, spates of car thefts, minor assaults.

On December 12 that year, my mother, father, and brothers set off together on a family vacation to Clearwater, Florida—even in their thirties Bobby and Pauly were living at home and vacationing with our parents. They had chartered a small aircraft, my mother being not fond of flying commercial, and somewhere off the coast of Delaware they encountered a thunderstorm of such violence that the wings were torn clean off the plane's fuselage, the remaining trunk then dropping from the sky, straight down into the Delaware Bay, leaving no survivors.

I heard the news of the air crash when I was called back to the office urgently from a story, the coach at a local high school having been accused of supplying his students with alcohol, the juiciest story I'd been assigned up to that point.

Until that day, I had always believed my first editor, Max Reagan, to be a man with no discernible heart, very much of the old school, grizzled by years of hard news, and fond of shouting his very public and scathing rebukes. (Among other things, we called him Old Yeller.) Max was the kind of boss who kept Scotch in his bottom drawer, because somewhere in the newsroom there was always a fire in need of extra fuel.

I suppose that before I was nervously ushered into his office, Max's newshound nose had sniffed the story out of the police officers, who had come to find me at work, and he'd offered to be the one to sit me down and tell me of the accident and no survivors, his furious yell replaced that day by an avuncular growl, the police officers looking on and filling in details when asked, strong and official, the room solemnly darkened by their uniforms.

That day the editor of the *Star-Ledger* and I finished a bottle of whiskey in less time than it takes a good journalist to track down the free drinks at a party. Later on he told me that it was the worst news story he'd ever had to break.

So, early in 1993, the sole surviving beneficiary of my parents' will, I sold the stables, the cave, the house, everything. I also sold

Jensen Royal Cement, which turned out to be worth unfathomably more than I could have imagined.

I wanted to use the money well, and for a long time I thought that I did, looking upon my inheritance as nothing more than security, something that could steer my life in the direction I wanted to go. The money allowed me to stay in a poorly paid job that I loved, meaning that I never had to move away from the streets, up to the higher-salaried echelons of editing or management. No, I could remain where I felt safest, felt best, on the beat, surrounded by the police in their uniforms, in their blousy fitting suits, while I told the stories of the victims—the victims who want to be listened to, who want to be heard almost as much as they want justice. That's all I ever wanted to put down on the page, the tales of crimes solved, cases closed, and criminals punished.

Or that's what I thought the money might allow—and I hope there's some degree to which this has been the case—but perhaps another effect of the money was that I became partially blinded to what was happening in the world around me.

Despite 1993's windfall, I remained at the Newark *Star-Ledger* for another three years (Max Reagan becoming something of a father figure to me in that time), and after the funeral I wouldn't return to Roseborn for the next fifteen years.

When Max told me the news of the accident, me sitting in his editor's chair, I can clearly remember my very first thoughts.

No, that can't be true, not my dad. Please not my dad. Please, anyone but my dad.

Guilt is a terrible thing. I mourned my father first and hardest, I still do, and when I remember my family, I cry for him most of all, seeing his face the clearest when I close my eye. But what am I supposed to do? I can't rewire my thoughts, unthink them or ignore them. And the thoughts refuse to go away, words that whisper themselves to me over and over, feelings of guilt like a bad neighbor I will have to live next to for the rest of my life.

The only thing that dims those thoughts is my work. *Work work work* has become my mantra, the only drug that has any effect.

Of course I didn't want to neglect my husband, my wonderful Patch, but when he was in pain, more pain than I could see, the burden was too much for me to share. I had to keep on going, keep on working, my job not so different from Bobby's vodka or Pauly's pot.

Obviously I miss my brothers too. And I wish I'd gotten the chance to know my mother, to properly understand her. Perhaps one day Mom would have gotten to know me as well. It is one thing to miss a father and brothers you loved, and another thing to miss a mother you never quite had.

But in the hierarchy of my guilt, all of this now forms only the midsection of the pyramid. A Friday afternoon at my desk in The Shack, a phone call from Detective Mike McCluskey—it was time to start building that pyramid higher.

NEW YORK, 2008

Jen has tried her cell three times already, each call unanswered, Hannah working a police brutality story that is currently blowing up, two female cops, great angle, maced and pistol-whipped a van driver, great story, and now there's a witness, Good Samaritan telling the investigating officers how one of the cops pointed a gun in his face and . . . Hannah's phone makes a sound—Not now, Jen. But then she looks at the screen, not Jen's number, and she answers.

I'm pretty busy here, McCluskey.

Sure, but look, something has come up. You and I, we need to talk.

We're talking. So talk.

Nah, I have to show you.

I'm trying to get this witness—

Trust me, this is more important, Hannah.

OK. Where are you?

At my desk. But not here.

Coffee and a sugary repast?

Come on, Hannah, it's Friday. Paddy Finn's, thirty minutes.

WHEN SHE GETS THERE MCCLUSKEY is at the bar looking like a large scoop of vanilla with a cherry on top, acres of white shirting damp from the single-block trek, his round face reddened by exertion.

Georgie is pouring the drinks today, he greets her like family, McCluskey twisting on his barstool. He closes the copy of the *New York Mail* he's been thumbing through, calls out to her, Hey, Aitch. And then, This one's on me, Georgie, McCluskey's big finger chalking it up in the air.

Ginger ale, Georgie.

Put something Russian in it, Georgie. Twice! And then seeing Hannah's expression, he adds, What? Don't make me drink on my own here, Aitch.

Hannah studies the liquid in McCluskey's glass, which looks suspiciously unlike a beer, and steals a sip, seltzer water. Drink? she says. That's not a drink. What's going on, McCluskey?

Jeesh, OK, Lindy's got me on this diet, he says, no alcohol for six weeks. And she makes me these smoothies for breakfast. This is about the only thing I've drunk for a week that isn't green. Every morning's like St. Paddy's Day for fuckin vegans.

But for some reason I need two shots of vodka? Come on, Mike, you're scaring me.

McCluskey looks up at one of the giant flat-screens decorating the bar, the baseball highlight reel jumping from city to city. You believe this guy? barks McCluskey, spreading his arms up at the TV. This bozo gets paid fifteen mil a year to swing at that junk? The pitcher smacks his fist triumphantly into his glove. Oh and you can talk, shouts McCluskey, you serve up homers like an all-you-can-eat buffet.

Behind the bar, Georgie finds a glass to wipe clean.

Sorry, Aitch, says McCluskey, turning back to her. This whole green diet thing is making me angry.

Everything makes you angry, McCluskey.

That's true, says McCluskey, taking a sip from his seltzer on ice, his body bobbing back-and-forth in affirmation. But Lindy says it's to be expected now, he says. She tells me I'm something called *hangry,* which dumbass me had no idea is a combination of hungry and—

I know what it is.

Right. Well, you know what else makes me angry?

The word *hangry*?

Fuckin A, Aitch. McCluskey sighs so heavily his newspaper ripples on the bar.

And then he points to Hannah's drink and she drinks and says to him, Is there a reason we're not getting to the point here, McCluskey?

Yeah, number one, because I haven't eaten anything that doesn't look like Astroturf for a week and, number two, because I don't want to be the one who shows you this. McCluskey slides a piece of paper out from beneath his *Mail*. But before you turn it over, Aitch, remember a month ago? Fatal stabbing in that restaurant on Mott, perp still at large?

Of course. I suggested RED SAUCE JOINT for the headline, but apparently that kind of thing's considered insensitive.

Fuckin clowns, Hannah. Anyway, so today, some guy was waving a knife outside the restaurant in the Park Square Hotel. Long story short, it ain't my guy. Today's guy must've been carrying the knife in his pants pocket and somehow managed to stab himself. Staff sees the blood, guy waves the knife around . . . Anyway, they grabbed some stills from the security cameras and sent them to me, just in case. Finish your drink before you turn it over.

The instruction seems odd, but she drinks anyway, the alcohol doing its job, her thoughts softening at the edges, McCluskey has turned up something juicy perhaps, someone famous, but then why the preparatory drink? And she turns the piece of paper over, an image time-stamped in the corner, colors faded, a man holding a magazine but not reading . . . McCluskey towels his face with his hand, she can hear the sound his fingers make scraping the bristles on his neck . . . And she sees the man in the image, not just some guy, but then unsees him, no, ridiculous.

I'm sorry, Aitch, says McCluskey.

No, she says, it can't be.

McCluskey swallows, waits.

Why the hell are you showing me this, Mike?

Aitch, look, I'm trying to help.

There must be an explanation. Patch wouldn't do anything like this.

You sure, Aitch? The guy's still out of work, right? You said he was having a hard time. He ever wave a knife in your direction? So help me, Hannah, he ever so much as touches you, *I swear to God . . .*

No, Mike, come on. I told you, he's not like this, this isn't . . . And she's about to say *this isn't him,* but she looks down again at the piece of paper, tilting her head, trying to see it another way as Georgie pushes another drink across the bar, and she reaches down and touches him in the image, Patch, so small and all alone. Whatever could make him do a thing like this?

And then everything starts to blur, McCluskey clambering off his barstool and clamping his arms around her so that Hannah can conceal her tears between them, crying into his shoulder not just for what Patch might have done, or what he might have been going to do, but for everything, the last nine months, the sick feeling that although she still loves him, something has faded, that when she should be strong, she is elsewhere, that when she should be there, she is here, or on the streets that she thrills to, in the job that she needs and she loves, wrapped up in the lights and the tape and the badges, in the place where things are resolved, not always, but bad people are caught and punished and everything has a strange sort of order, a logic, the crimes always the same, the hunt always the same, and the resolution happens or doesn't happen. But is always the same.

She pushes McCluskey away, patting him gratefully, smearing her eyes dry. What will you do? she says.

You and me are the only two people who know who this is, Aitch.

Do you have to arrest him?

That was something I wanted your opinion on. But if you say he's kept his hands off you . . .

I swear it, McCluskey. He gets sad sometimes. He doesn't do angry.

Right, the kind that bottles it up and then *boom*. McCluskey slaps his big hands down on the bar, Hannah flinching, looking at the printout of her husband again. Sorry, Aitch, says McCluskey. Hey, do me a favor will you? Look over this list. McCluskey pulls a second piece of paper from beneath the *Mail*. These are all the people who made reservations at the restaurant that lunchtime, he says.

Alvarez, Bachman, Denby . . . Kim, McManus, Nathan . . . Samson, Suarez, Villanova . . .

No, nothing, she says.

McCluskey rubs at his thin white covering of hair. Aitch, I gotta let you make the call, he says. You want me to talk to him? Let me talk to him. I don't have to bring him in.

I'll talk to him, Mike.

Yeah, I was worried you'd say that. But I gotta get involved at some point, unless you can swear to me nothing else will ever happen.

She looks down at her husband again, as if this time it might not be him. Right, she says, distractedly, thinking about whether this might somehow be her fault.

Goddam, this makes me nervous as hell, says McCluskey, his leg jiggling against the bar. Aitch, you're the person I'm most worried about right now, he says. If you talk to him, you gotta be careful how you put the questions.

I know how to talk to people, Mike. I know how to talk to my husband.

Yeah, but you have to make him think like talking's his idea, like he wants to open up to you.

Mike, I know how to do this.

Right, right. But whatever you do, you don't wanna corner the guy, Aitch.

I do this for a living too, Mike.

I know, I know. But handling a witness is a whole different ball game from handling a suspect.

He's not a suspect, McCluskey, he's my husband.

Not a suspect? Dammit, Aitch, I never won any gold stars for sensitivity, but there were other images I could've shown you.

Mike, you know I appreciate this, right?

Sure, this whole thing makes me nervous, says McCluskey, rubbing the back of his neck. You know, if I could just have one . . . Georgie, you got any of that green Guinness left over from last Paddy's Day?

Georgie leans on the bar in front of them. It's just food coloring, Mikey, I can knock some up for you, he says, whipping the bar with his towel as he makes to move.

Nah, says McCluskey, ignore me, I'm like that Greek guy tied to a mast.

Odysseus, says Hannah.

Right, I'm like Odysseus, Georgie, no matter how much I ask you for a real drink, you gotta ignore me, OK? I made a promise to Lindy. Here's to promises, he says, raising his glass, and then, after swallowing a sip of seltzer, McCluskey makes a face like a kid after cough syrup. Jesus, Aitch, he says, you know the only thing in the world worse than fizzy water is green smoothies. You know why? Every time I get handed one I can't help thinking of that joke—What's green and goes round at a hundred miles an hour?

Go on then, McCluskey, if you have to.

Kermit in a blender. I'm tellin you, Aitch, frog purée would taste a thousand times better.

Georgie taps the bar. That reminds me of one—what's green and smells of pork?

Hey, Georgie, not now, says McCluskey, his voice turning sharp. Can't you see we're trying to have a serious conversation? He raises his hands in confused disbelief as Georgie skulks away, and then McCluskey turns back to Hannah. Look, Aitch, he says, Patrick's head's gotta be going in ten different directions at once right now. Let's just let him calm down, you go home when you normally go home. McCluskey takes Hannah's hand and stares hard at her. Aitch, you call me and tell me when you're getting there, right? I'll be in the lobby and you lock yourself in the goddam bathroom and call me if he even breathes at you funny, you hear?

She squeezes his hand. I love you, Mike.

Terrific. And you know what I love? says McCluskey. Three words, *retirement full pension,* he says, using a hand to block out the words in the air. Because if anyone finds out I knew who this was and kept quiet . . . So you gotta promise me, Hannah, this is the right way to play this.

On my soul, says Hannah, pulling her hand away, placing it over her chest.

McCluskey gives her a dubious look before dropping some notes on the bar. Hey, Georgie, he says, sorry about cutting you off like that, apparently I'm *hangry.*

No problem, big fella, says Georgie.

Come on, Aitch, says McCluskey. I'll hail you a cab.

As they climb from their barstools, Hannah puts her hand to her mouth and stage-whispers it over the bar. Kermit's finger, she says, Georgie seeing her off with a wink.

SHE WISHES THE CAB COULD drive around forever, Hannah like a child in the backseat being soothed by the motion, nodding off perhaps, the way she always did when returning home from family trips and vacations as a young girl, and if she could only fall asleep today might she wake up to discover that none of this was real? The taxi lurches urgently downtown, the concrete city speeding by, not unlike her thoughts, nothing settling in one place, nothing that can quite be grasped or held on to, her husband brandishing a knife, the evidence clear, but also making no sense at all. And she wishes they could just keep driving round and round in circles, and when she has looped past the same thought a fifth or seventh or thirteenth time, maybe she could pluck it from the crowded sidewalk, maybe she could hear its words clearly, *this is what it means, Hannah, and this is what you have to do.* And then they hit a red light, the taxicab coming to a halt alongside Union Square, and if they pulled forward just another few feet she would be able to see the exact spot where they first kissed, five years ago, she and Patch, and before their lips touched she already knew he was the one, the one she felt safest with, the one who would give purpose and direction to her future, and what does all of this mean right now? That she was wrong?

Moving again, Broadway, movie theater, bookstore, McCluskey, Patch, The Shack, but how can she think of work at a time like this? And soon, back at her desk, all she can concentrate on is the waiting, pretending to work until the moment when she will go home, Hannah carrying something too huge in her chest, who, what, when, where, she has all these pieces, her husband, a knife, this lunchtime, a hotel, which means there is only one more thing she needs for the story, and she can hear herself asking it over and over.

Why?

SITTING ON A PADDED BENCH with his newspaper, McCluskey nods at her from behind its pages as Hannah crosses the lobby, steps into the elevator, and then, too distracted to find keys in her bag, rings the doorbell when she reaches their apartment.

When Patch opens the door, she pauses, as if waiting to be invited in, her husband giving her a look as if she is the one behaving oddly, the sadness that recently has been worrying away at his eyes still there, but nothing more she can detect, nothing new, he kisses her cheek.

Is anything wrong? he says.

No, of course not, she says, shaking her head as if coming out of a work fog, and then stepping inside.

Sorry, he says, it's just pretty basic pasta for dinner tonight. I didn't get around to buying anything special. I'll go get everything started, he says, smiling weakly, turning around, and then, with a faint limp, heading into the kitchen.

Hannah touches her lips when she sees the limp. Why did she need confirmation? Hadn't the photo been conclusive enough?

And then she thinks, *How did he seem? Normal?* But at some point in the last year, Hannah might have lost her sense of his normal.

The apartment looks neat and clean, always neat and clean when she returns home, maybe this is how Patch hides his secrets, concealed beneath order, buried in tidiness, she imagines him making a mess of the place every day, the evidence of his hidden life strewn across the room, and then scrupulously packing everything away at night, just before she comes home.

Hannah moves through the orderly space and steps into the bedroom where she takes off her shoes, pulls her sweater over her head, and thinks, *I don't know him at all. Have I ever known him at all?*

After a minute, Patch comes to the bedroom door, rubbing his hands on a dish towel. Any crimes of the century I should know about? he asks, Hannah looking at the thigh of his pants as if expecting to see blood. But of course he is wearing a different pair from the ones she saw on McCluskey's piece of paper.

What's that? Sorry, what type of pasta did you say you were making?

Just some spaghetti, he says, spaghetti and red sauce, ready in ten. Patrick drapes the dish towel over his shoulder and heads back to the kitchen.

She takes out her phone and thumbs out a message.

> Everything normal. No need to worry, McC.

> OK. Stay in touch, H. Guess I'm skipping Astroturf Smoothie Night. Tragic.

SHE SITS AT THE DINNER table, waiting for him to come out of the kitchen, wondering how to speak to him, wondering whether to tell him that she once did something terrible too, perhaps she should know how he feels, but she has no idea.

Patrick comes into the room, places two bowls on the table, kisses the top of her head, and picks up the Parmesan, grating it over her food, stopping when she says *thank you,* touching his leg softly, feeling something through the fabric, the edge of a bandage.

So tell me what you got up to today, she says.

The usual, he says, grating cheese over his own bowl, sitting down.

I think I lost track of what *the usual* is, she says.

He picks up his fork, puts it down again.

What is it, Patch?

I don't know, he says, I feel like I'm running out of words, Hannah. What could I tell you? You come home and you've been to a murder scene, or you know the inside details of the latest robbery that's all over the news, or you can tell me what the police are saying off the record about a drug bust on Wall Street. Those are stories, Hannah, those are real talking points, things the world finds genuinely interesting. Me? I could tell you about my latest trip to the laundry room—two loads, Hannah, normal and delicates. *A two-load day, Patch? Fascinating.* Or I could talk to you about having the same conversations I always have with our neighbors in the elevator—the weather, and here's your headline, IT'S STILL HOT—or that the grocery store was inconveniently out of blueberries. *Really? No blueberries, hold the front page.* So excuse me for saying nothing about nothing. Why don't you just do all the talking for both of us, Hannah? he says, out of breath when he finishes, as if he has returned from a run.

Did something happen, Patch? she says to him. What's wrong?

No, Hannah, nothing ever happens, that's what I'm trying to tell you, nothing happens.

And there it is, she sees it in his eyes, the crack in her husband's look, the concealment of something with a neat truth, *but whatever you do, you don't wanna corner the guy, Aitch.*

Do you remember how much we used to talk? she says.

Yes, I remember, he says, his body sinking.

We'd talk about books, or thoughts, what made us happy, what made us angry. But I think I lost track of you somewhere, Patch. So you don't have to tell me about your days, you can say anything you want to me, you know that, right?

He covers his eyes with one hand, drops his fork from the other, and she can see that he's crying, she takes his empty hand in hers, Patrick squeezing it, but still keeping his hand over his face until the tears have slowed enough to be wiped away. And finally, after a few gasps and sniffs, he manages to talk. I'm sorry, Hannah, it's just, I don't know, I think I'm unwinding, he says. And I don't think anything can help me, or anyone. And I'm sorry, I don't want to unwind. I don't want to, I'm sorry.

She stands up and holds his head to her belly. Please talk to me, she says. Patch, please let me know what's happening. I haven't been very good, but I'm going to be better. Please, if you let me inside . . .

I just want it to be over, he says.

Want what to be over?

I don't know. Nothing.

Patch, you're scaring me.

No, it's all right. I'm going to tell you everything, I promise.

I want you to, please, she says, rubbing his head.

I will, Hannah, I promise. But not tonight, not like this. Is that OK?

OK. But when?

Tomorrow. Tomorrow, I promise.

And you'll tell me everything, everything you're feeling? Everything that's going on in your life?

Everything, he says, I promise, Hannah. But tonight can we just drink wine and watch something crappy on TV, and you can make jokes about it, and I'll fall asleep on the sofa. He pulls his head from her belly and looks up at her.

I'd like that, says Hannah, sitting back down. Apart from the last part. You always refuse to admit you were ever asleep when I wake you up thirty minutes after you start snoring.

You never have any evidence, he says.

I'm going to get you on video one day, she says.

And Patrick doesn't seem to notice Hannah's small catch of breath as she realizes what she's just said. Well, he says, until then I remain innocent of all charges.

She glances down at the table.

How about I make something special for dinner, tomorrow? says Patrick. And then we can sit down and properly talk.

Good, she says, picking up her fork, good, something special.

I'll get up early and go buy what I need, he says.

Great, she says, that's really great. Hannah sinks her fork down into the bowl of pasta. And Patch? she says.

Yes?

Don't forget the honey, sweetheart.

SHE TAPS OUT ANOTHER MESSAGE after dinner, but McCluskey refuses to go home, so when Patrick falls asleep on the couch, she heads to the bathroom, switches on her electric toothbrush, sets it on a shelf by the door, and then turns on the faucet before making the call.

Still alive then, Aitch.

What, you think he was going to bake me into a pie?

It sounds like he's sawing you up into pieces right now. What the hell is that?

Toothbrush.

You got a lawn mower engine in that thing?

Don't think of grass, McCluskey, it'll only make you *hangry*.

Fuckin A, Aitch. Anyway, what's the climate like up there?

We're going to talk tomorrow, he promised me.

Right. When?

After dinner.

Great. Another night in your lobby? And how is he?

He's sad.

Sad? Or batshit fuckin dangerous?

Just sad. Very, very sad.

Gotcha. Sorry, Aitch.

Go back to Lindy now, McCluskey. There's nothing to worry about here.

Right. Sure.

You're not going to sleep outside in your car.

Nah, I'm getting too old for the Homicide Hilton.

Just think of all those full-pension retirement cruises.

I spew chunks even looking at pictures of boats. Listen, Hannah. Tomorrow, I want you to send me a message every hour, you got that?

Yes, sir.

I want to know where you are, what you're doing, and how Paddy McKnife-Edge is behaving himself.

Yes, sir.

Because if for any reason I don't hear from you, I'm showing up with my gun in my hand, you understand?

Understood, sir.

OK, then. Stay safe, Hannah.

Permission to go to bed, sir.

Good night, Aitch.

Sleep tight, Mike.

HANNAH'S BODY FORMS TWO SILENT curves beneath the covers.

He gets up and dresses with barely a sound and yet as he is tiptoeing out of the room she stirs. Patch? she calls out. Patch, where are you going?

To the market, he says, something special for dinner tonight. Remember?

Right, she says, sleepily. And then we were going to talk about everything.

That's right.

Tonight, she says, stretching and rolling over.

Yes, tonight, he says.

As he steps out of the bedroom she calls out again, Oh, and Patch?

Patch, don't forget the . . . make sure to buy some . . . And then she sighs. Never mind, she says. Never mind, I don't remember.

THE SUBWAY CAR IS ALMOST empty, rattling through tunnel-dark, *click clack click,* metallic sounds filling the vacant space.

Patrick sits on the edge of the bench, wearing a backpack, wiping the sleep from his eyes. *So they are in it together,* he thinks, Matthew and Trevino conspiring.

And at least this makes sense. *Who should I let go? You or Clark?*

Don Trevino's question had been a trap all along. And now Patrick understands why. Matthew is trying to get to Hannah through him, it's the only thing that makes sense.

Not if I get to you first, Matthew, he thinks.

The doors open onto Canal and soon he is climbing the stairs, up into the early sunlight of an August morning, the air already filling up with heat, Patrick heading toward an address he has memorized.

When he gets there, the building looks like an old factory or warehouse. Iron-framed, six floors, the sky hazy with papery cloud. He presses the buzzer and waits for almost a minute, presses the buzzer again. And soon Patrick hears the sound of a chain spooling, a window sliding. He steps back to the curb, looks up and sees a man in his twenties with dark cropped hair squinting at him through the bars of the third-floor fire escape. The man calls down to him, If it's a package, I'll buzz you in and you can dump it in the elevator, right?

I'm looking for Matthew . . . Matthew Denby, says Patrick.

Sorry, no one by that name here, the man calls down, Patrick noticing an accent, like one of those British Shakespeareans who play all the bad guys in the movies. The dark-haired man begins to retreat back inside the window.

Wait, says Patrick, Matthew Denby does live at this address, right? From a pocket he pulls out a business card and waves it, the card Matthew handed him at Le Crainois.

Oh, Christ, says the man, glancing up and down the empty sidewalk. Listen, love, he hisses angrily, I really don't give a shit which seedy little khazi you blew 'im in. It didn't mean a thing, OK? He's not fucking interested.

I'm sorry, but I don't know what any of that means.

It means he's already taken, lover boy. Cheerio.

I really think you must be mixing me up with someone else. My name's Patrick McConnell, I knew Matthew twenty-odd years ago, from school, Roseborn Middle School.

Roseborn? says the man. Wait, I think he just bought a house there. Nice of him to tell me why. Bloody typical, actually.

Patrick shades his eyes. Is there any chance I could wait up there for him? he asks.

How well did you know him at school? Do you have any stories?

We were best friends.

Even from three floors below, Patrick notices a sense of curiosity slipping into the man's eyes. Oh fine, he says. But I have literally no idea when he'll be home.

PATRICK STANDS IN THE LOBBY, waiting for the elevator, which is slowly descending with a series of loud *ding*s as it passes each floor.

He wishes he could have told her last night. But what if Hannah had tried to stop him coming here today to challenge Matthew? And he has to do something. For just one day in his life he has to do something.

He takes off the backpack and checks the front pocket, as if the knife might not still be there. But the knife is there and also, inside the bag, a change of clothes.

Finally the elevator arrives and opens. He gets inside and it starts to rise, stopping at the third floor, bouncing and settling like old-fashioned kitchen scales. The doors open up straight onto the apartment. But when Patrick steps out there is no sign of the man who spoke to him from the window.

It is a huge, high-ceilinged loft, one whole floor of the building, seven cast-iron pillars running down the center of the space.

And then Patrick hears a voice coming from the far corner, from behind the only walls in the place—Out in a second, just putting on some clothes, make yourself comfortable.

He sits down on a long, cream sofa and looks around, the space scattered with furniture, colorful Persian rugs, African masks, abstract artwork on the walls and rocks everywhere, on almost every surface—crystalline, smooth, sparkling, colorful.

Then something peculiar catches his eye, nearby on a bookshelf, a framed photograph of a man, gray-haired and gray-bearded, and something clicks in Patrick's memory, the photo reminding him of the old guy in the Conservancy, *no fishing in the lake, boys,* having to carry around a sketch of Jakobskill Falls.

He is about to go and take a closer look at the photograph when the man from the window emerges, pulling down on the hem of his sweater as he begins the long trek up the apartment toward Patrick. Do you drink tea? he calls out.

You have coffee? Patrick calls back, almost having to shout.

Oh, bollocks to coffee, I don't know how to work his stupid machine, the man says.

Patrick looks across at the kitchen area and sees the bright hulk of metal being indicated.

The man turns into the open kitchen and pours water from the faucet into a kettle. The only people who know how to use *that* monstrosity are Matthew and the ten most pretentious baristas in the world. Mind you, I'm not really sure you could narrow it down to ten, could you?

Tea's fine, says Patrick.

Good, says the man, leaning against a kitchen counter. I'm Andrew by the way.

Patrick, says Patrick.

OK, Patrick. Well, let me get these teas going and then I want to hear all about his majesty's schoolboy years. Andrew gives him a wink.

THE BACKPACK IS NEXT TO his feet. Patrick could reach down to its pocket in less than a second. But what will he do if Matthew walks in through the elevator doors right now?

The way he had pictured it, Matthew would have been alone when he pulled the knife on him, *Stay away from my wife or I'll kill you.* Although now something seems wrong with that picture—something much more than the presence of a witness.

How do you scare Matthew? He could never have scared him in the past. Has Matthew changed? How do you threaten him? It is possible that it cannot be done.

And what if he says no, he won't stay away?

Andrew moves around the kitchen humming something poppy. Patrick wonders how old he is. Early twenties? Twenty-five at most, dark eyes with long lashes and a face that tapers sharply down from its cheekbones.

On the coffee table in front of Patrick there sits another rock, faintly red, glossy and smooth. He reaches out to pick it up but Andrew sees him and calls out, Wait, don't touch his precious gastrolift or whatever it's called.

What is it? says Patrick.

God knows, I can't remember exactly, something disgusting I seem to recall. He calls it his dinosaur rock. The way he treats it you'd think it was the skull of his dead father.

Patrick notices a small gesture, a motion of Andrew's head toward the photo on the bookshelf. I doubt that, says Patrick. Matthew hated his father.

Great, that's all I need, says Andrew. Another one with daddy issues. You can see where Matthew gets his looks from though, can't you.

Patrick looks across at the photo again, the old guy from the Conservancy does possess a certain rugged presence, he supposes.

Andrew brings the drinks from the kitchen, handing Patrick a mug painted with the Union Jack. Sorry, he says, last of the clean ones. That's the sort of crap people send you when you move abroad, like you want constant reminders of the place. And then he pulls a chair from beneath a long farmhouse table, dragging it over and sitting down a few feet from Patrick. Right then, he says, now comes the price of admission. I get to ask you all sorts of questions about Matthew back in . . . Wait, how long ago did you say it was?

The last time I saw him was 1982?

1982? Oh Christ! And you were how old?

Twelve. Nearly thirteen.

Bloody hell, says Andrew, then that makes him . . . He starts to move his fingers.

Actually Matthew was a year older than me.

So he's . . .

I suppose he turned forty this year, says Patrick.

Forty? squeals Andrew. Well, that explains everything. That's why the bastard hasn't once celebrated his birthday with me. He takes a sip from his mug and then makes a face as if the tea tastes bitter. God, now I feel like a victim of child abuse.

So what did you want to ask me about him? says Patrick.

There's not much point now, says Andrew. I can't get over the fact that he's forty.

Then can I ask you something? says Patrick.

Go on then, says Andrew, feigning a bored look.

So is Matthew . . . (Patrick can't think how to phrase it) . . . Is he . . . ?

Go ahead, says Andrew, spit it out. You got yourself into this pickle, I'm not bailing you out.

Is Matthew . . . Patrick half whispers the word . . . *gay*?

Andrew laughs so hard he has to put his mug down on the floor. No, Patrick, he says, Matthew is not *gay*. And even if he was *gay*, gay is a label and Matthew doesn't do labels. Labels are for soup cans, apparently. Why don't you ask him all about it next time you see him. That'll be two hours of your life you'll never get back.

But, sorry, I got the impression that you're . . . ?

That I'm what? His boyfriend? His *loverrr*?

Right.

Well of course I am. Bit slow on the uptake, are we? Look, it's simple enough, our mutual friend Matthew is . . . OK, I'm trying to think of a way to say it that he'd find almost palatable. Let's just say that Matthew . . . Yes, he's kind of a surf-and-turf guy, if you catch my drift.

Bisexual?

God, no! *Severe* label alert! Don't say that to him either. You'll get the bonus feature, another ninety-minute monologue. Here's a word to the wise—don't try to define Matthew. Matthew does whatever the bloody hell Matthew likes and *whoever* the hell he likes. Although I told him right from the start, you can have all the boys you want, as long as it's nothing serious. But you go anywhere near a bloody woman while you're with me, I'm straight out that fucking door.

And he hasn't . . . ?

No! He was with some *female* before I showed up. Actress. Pretty, I suppose. Bit haggy, mind you. But wait, it's my turn now. So you said you were best friends, right?

We were.

Oh God and I bet you were impossibly drawn to him.

Not in the sense of . . .

Don't worry, I can tell men aren't your flavor, Patrick. But how did you and Matthew become friends?

I suppose it happened after . . . I was twelve, I was being bullied by an older boy called Ryan.

Oh shit, says Andrew, I know where this story is headed. He bloody well jumped in and saved you, didn't he. God, that's classic Matthew. OK, so you were twelve, something juicy must've happened between then and the time you left school. Come on, spill.

Matthew didn't make it to the end of school, he didn't tell you?

As I explained, he tells me *nuh*-thing. It might be a problem if he weren't so . . . you know . . . Anyway, what happened, was he expelled for nefarious activity with a schoolmaster?

Andrew seems to be finding everything funny, his leg starting to jiggle, the sight of it making Patrick feel sick.

You don't know? he says, the sick feeling rising from stomach to head, the loft floating around him as if being swirled with the past. He shot someone, says Patrick. Matthew shot a thirteen-year-old girl.

What? No.

When he was fourteen, August 1982, Matthew tied a girl to a tree and shot her thirty-seven times with a BB gun. The girl's name was Hannah. The final shot hit her in the eye, an innocent teenage girl. She lost the eye.

Bloody hell, says Andrew quietly, his voice stripped of humor. Wait, you're kidding me, right? he says, half whispering now.

Her left eye, says Patrick, spearing his forefinger toward his face.

No, you're making this up, says Andrew, shaking his head uncertainly. Why on earth would he do something like that?

He told the police he felt like it. Pleaded guilty. And that was it.

Andrew looks away, all of the excitement having drained from his leg. No! he says. No, he's not like that, you're a nasty fucking liar.

I'm sure you can find old newspapers online or in the library. Try the *Roseborn Gazette,* anything printed after August 18, 1982. The coverage went on for some time, you can't miss it.

She must have done something horrible to him, says Andrew.

She didn't do anything, says Patrick. And then, seeing Andrew pressed back in his seat, he can feel in the back of his throat that he has been shouting, perhaps for some time. Andrew covers his face and now Patrick realizes he is on his feet, standing over him.

I want you to leave now, says Andrew, sliding to the edge of his chair. Please, just go, right away. If you don't, I'm going to call the police. He scoots up from the seat and moves quickly to the kitchen where he stands by the knife block.

Patrick wipes his face, can hear the air-conditioning whirring, buzzing against the window frame, and yet still it feels as if he has been struck by a wave of heat. Ask him about it when you see him, he says, picking up his backpack, undoing a shirt button as he heads to the elevator, the doors opening up right away when he presses CALL.

Hannah Jensen, he calls over his shoulder, that's her name. Write it down so you won't forget. And then Patrick steps inside, hitting the *L* hard with his fist, the elevator bouncing and beginning its descent.

HANNAH

This is as far as I go. I would have told the rest of it myself, the story of everything that led up to that day in 1982, and I would have told the truth as best I could, right up until the final shot. However, three months after the terrible events of August 2008, a letter came into my possession via one of the investigating officers, a friend of a friend of Detective Mike McCluskey, and instead of admitting to the world the rest of what happened in my own words, I will soon be handing over to the only other person intimately familiar with the story. It's time to let Matthew explain to you what really happened in 1982.

I wonder if I would have come out of it any better in my own words?

I suppose it doesn't matter now. I don't dispute anything Matthew has to say—what reason would he have to lie while writing such a letter? Which means that what I believed for a very long time to be the truth wasn't quite what it seemed.

How does the phrase go? *Seeing is believing.* Not true. Your eyes can deceive you.

One thing I'd like to make clear before Matthew begins—when you read the whole truth about everything that happened in 1982, please understand that I didn't lie back then. *Seeing is believing,* I was thirteen years old, a confused teenager, and I certainly didn't act with any sort of malice. Only now it would seem that I got everything horribly wrong.

Which is something you could also say about the events of August 2008, when what might have remained the story of a single year became something much bigger, a tale that begins with a toy gun and ends with the real thing.

INTO THE BLUE

An early summer burst onto New York City like a wave, the skies so clear they shone with a kind of reckless abandon, the city framed golden and blue.

After seeing you at Grand Central and finding your byline in the newspaper, I waited a week before trying to contact you, not wanting to seem like some kind of stalker, even though I'd quickly worked out how easy it would be to get in touch, what with every one of the email addresses at your workplace being of the same format—firstinitial.surname@newyorkmail.com.

I don't even remember what I wrote to you that first time. Something bland.

. . . so good to run into you . . . and then my family whisked me off to Maine and we never got to talk . . . would really like to sit down and catch up . . . coffee, perhaps?

I didn't think there was a chance in hell you'd get back to me. Why would you speak to someone who stood there and watched while his best friend shot out your eye? And yet, two days later, you replied.

. . . sorry for my reaction in Grand Central, Patrick, when I realized who you were . . . a lot of baggage . . . I did always wonder what happened to you after your family moved away . . . the other day I saw your father interviewed on the television about gun control . . .

please understand that I don't like to talk about that day, I just DON'T talk about that day . . . but if you would like to meet up . . .

I tried to calculate the precise amount of time I should wait before I sent a reply, one of life's great imponderables. Three hours and I couldn't wait any longer. I hammered out a long message about life in Maine, how I came to New York to major in economics at Columbia and never left, that I worked an incredibly boring job in the Data Acquisition department at Idos Investments, that I had a tiny apartment on St. Mark's Place, in which I liked to home-cure my own bacon and smoke it on the roof, that I owned a blowtorch for completely nonmasculine reasons and was thinking of starting a food blog.

You replied that East Village fume-smoked bacon sounded delicious, that you were a crime reporter for the *New York Mail* and lived on bodega bagels and stale coffee, had an apartment in Chelsea and that your idea of a culinary treat was to buy the slightly more expensive tub of hummus. Your office was a place called The Shack (I had to look it up) and you said you'd love to grab a cup of stale coffee sometime.

I'd seen you for no more than a minute, we'd exchanged only two messages and yet somehow I already knew you would change my life, Hannah. Somehow I knew that with you beside me I would become a better version of myself and that therefore I would do anything to be with you.

It was all true. How did I know?

I suggested lunch at The Odeon, quietly proud of myself for thinking of it. Firstly, it was close to your workplace and, secondly, what with you being employed as a wordsmith, I thought I might impress you by mentioning the restaurant's appearance in *Bright Lights, Big City.* Furthermore, I would bowl you over with my ability to correctly pronounce Jay McInerney's name. No sir, I wasn't any old run-of-the-mill Data Acquisition employee. I cooked, I read books, I could pronounce the names of famous people after having looked up how to pronounce their names on the internet.

I waited for you outside One Police Plaza, where I thought we'd arranged to meet, but when you came out, you were speaking on your cell phone. I stepped toward you, vaguely waving my hand, but you didn't see me.

Sorry, Jen, I'm in a hurry, running late . . . No, not as usual—as sometimes, Jen, as occasionally . . .

And now it felt awkward to interrupt, which means that I wouldn't describe what happened next as *following*, as me *tailing* you. I walked in the same direction, that's all.

OK, OK, but listen, guess who I'm meeting for lunch . . . No . . . No . . . How about I just tell you, Jen? . . . Patrick McConnell . . . He sent me a sweet message, suggested coffee, but instead we're meeting at The Odeon, I'm on my way now . . . Come on, Jen, it's not like he actually did anything wrong . . . OK, so he was sort of there. But look, Jen, you know I'm not really going to talk about this, however the point is he wasn't actually THERE there when Matthew was . . .

What? My whole body lurched, the city seeming almost to swing halfway around me. I couldn't believe this. Could I possibly have heard you correctly?

Right, but how could he do anything to stop it? Matthew sent him away, clearly Patrick didn't know anything . . . I'm sure he would've done if he'd been right there when it happened . . . I know, Jen, but being friends in seventh grade isn't exactly the crime of the century . . . Come on, if it wasn't for Patrick I might still be tied to that tree. He actually saved me, if you think about it . . . Of course I'll be careful . . . It's a lunch, that's all . . . No, it's very sweet that you're worried about me . . . I promise, Jen, the second I leave . . .

That's when I stopped moving in the same direction as you, ran off to the street, hailed a cab and sped away to the restaurant, thinking about what I'd just heard, picturing it all over again, August 1982, me looking on like a spectator at courtside, the way Matthew had tied one of the ropes around your neck, your head pointlessly twisting after Matthew's final shot.

Of course you hadn't seen me there.

He actually saved me.

That changes everything, I thought.

And obviously I feel terrible to have kept this a secret from you, Hannah. But how could I ever, since that moment outside One

Police Plaza, have told you that I witnessed what happened to you and did nothing? What would have been the appropriate moment? Over dinner? After the theater? In postcoital whispers?

We never spoke about that day. Never, not once. Because, Hannah, quite understandably, you never wanted to. And does this mean that in some way I deceived you, that I lied to you?

Wait, if I'd never even overheard your conversation with Jen, it's perfectly possible that everything between us would have gone exactly the same way that it actually did. So does that really mean that our love is based on a lie?

I hope you don't really believe that, Hannah, because I certainly don't.

Anyway, you know what? It doesn't matter, I don't care. And if I am a liar, so be it, because I would happily lie all over again. I would lie twice as hard and a thousand times more just to be with you, Hannah. To have spent part of my life, any part of my life, with you, my beautiful wife, I would have done anything.

An absence of action? A small act of silence? These are as nothing compared to all the things I would have done for you, Hannah, you who have been the one happiness in my life. You must know that I would do anything for you, anything. Lie, steal, cheat, kill . . .

The cab dropped me off and I rushed into The Odeon, getting to work on my innocent face while I waited. When you stepped into the restaurant, I stood up. I was in a blue suit, you in a blue dress, everything about you a hundred times brighter than anything else in the room. You offered me your hand to shake and we sat down, me noticing right away that I'd forgotten the wild blue of your eyes—forgotten not only from childhood but even from a few weeks earlier. And did I notice at the time how one of those eyes roved less than the other? I suppose if I did then that's not my main recollection of our first lunchtime meeting. I also don't remember what we ate, what we drank, anything about the waitstaff or anyone sitting around us. I remember you, only you, Hannah.

We didn't talk about your eye that first time. We didn't talk about Roseborn or school or anything else to do with your childhood. You asked a lot of questions, that's mostly what I remember, and I also recall trying to keep my answers short because I didn't want to talk about me, I wanted only to hear about you.

I managed to turn the conversation to books, asking you what you liked to read, you surprising me by saying that you liked novels full of blood, the gorier the better, you told me, which meant that you ended up reading a lot of crime fiction, you said. I asked if that was also because of your job and your reply has always puzzled me. *Maybe it's that,* you said with a hint of doubt in your voice. And then you told me that right now you were reading something by an English writer whose name I forget. Literary gore, you called it, the plot centering on the dismemberment of a body.

Sounds like fun, I said.

How about you? you asked me.

I just finished a book by Jay McInerney, I said, pronouncing the name with perfect aplomb and pulling *Bright Lights, Big City* from my briefcase. *Actually, this is what made me think of this place,* I said, pointing to the book jacket, a picture of the restaurant in which we were sitting on the cover, *ODEON* spelled out in red neon.

Oh, look at that.

Please, why don't you borrow it, Hannah.

Is there any blood? you said.

Not really. But there's cocaine, I said. *I mean, there's a ton of cocaine.*

That'll have to do then, you said, thanking me and dropping the book in your purse.

Next I asked about your work—your work, which has always been as fascinating as mine has been dull (although you forced me to talk about it, even managing to appear interested). And before I knew it, coffee arrived. *Not stale enough,* you joked.

I could have spent the whole afternoon talking to you. But then your cell phone made a sound. *Oh shoot,* you said, looking at it, *I really have to go, it's something urgent.*

Damn, I was really enjoying this, I said. *And please, Hannah, let me get the check, lunch here was my idea. Any chance you might want to meet up again sometime?*

Well, I have to return your book, you said. And then after a meaningful pause, you added, *Isn't that why you wanted me to borrow it?*

Guilty as charged, I replied, blushing. *I hope you're a fast reader, Hannah,* I said.

I remember your smile and the gleam of your eyes as you kissed one of my flushed cheeks. I was already in love with you. And then you turned and headed out of the restaurant, out into the wide blue of the city.

THE SECOND TIME WE MET, at a restaurant called Blue Water Grill, was the first time I saw you wearing an eyepatch. We agreed to hook up for dinner and again I arrived first, standing to greet you, noticing how you seemed strangely timid as the waiter showed you to the table. This time we didn't shake hands but kissed each other's cheeks.

After a little small talk, I asked you if something was wrong. You indicated the eyepatch. *You don't have to pretend you didn't notice,* you said.

Of course I noticed, I replied. *It looks great on you, Hannah,* I said.

So stupid, you said.

Stupid? What do you mean?

OK, you said, *so here's the thing about prosthetics. You're supposed to get a new one every five or ten years. However, I left mine for eleven. Just like everyone else in this town—work work work!*

A prosthetic? I said. *Is that the same thing as a glass eye?*

Yes, you said, *although they're mostly not glass. They used to be— but unfortunately the Germans had all the best glass. So during World War Two, they had to come up with something else. And then the U.S. Army Dental Corps worked out how to make prosthetic eyes from dental acrylic. False teeth, false eyes, same thing. I hope you're finding this conversation thoroughly appetizing.*

It's fascinating, Hannah, I want to know everything. Anyway, nothing in the world can put me off food.

Careful, or I'll take you up on that challenge, you said, gently prying your patch from your face. *So anyway,* you continued, *silly me had been wearing the same prosthesis for eleven years, which is way too long. And as a result, last week I developed conjunctivitis. Mmm, isn't this the tastiest start to a meal you've ever enjoyed? Con-junc-ti-vi-tis!*

I'm ravenous, Hannah.

Right, that's sweet of you. Anyway, the punch line is that I'm having another prosthetic eye made. But until it's ready, unless I want to scare small children, I have to wear this monstrosity, you said, lightly snapping your eyepatch elastic.

Wait, I said, *if you don't have your acrylic eye, then what's under the patch?*

Aha, you said, *now we come to it. So you're probably one of those people who think there's something like a cave back here when I take out the prosthetic.*

I hadn't thought it through. But maybe I would have thought something like that.

And you also probably imagine that an artificial eye looks like a little Ping-Pong ball, right?

Prob-ab-ly. Although I'm beginning to suspect that maybe it doesn't.

Correct, it's more like a seashell.

Seashell? Seashell sounds good.

Precisely. So this is how it works. After an enucleation, which is the technical term for the surgical removal of an eye, most people, me included, receive an ocular implant, which actually is like a little ball. The implant helps the empty eye socket keep its shape. Also, they attach the ocular implant to four muscles behind the socket to provide movement so that the artificial eye, which sits on the little ball like a seashell-shaped contact lens, looks real. However, that's where I got unlucky. The muscles behind my eye socket were so badly damaged that I have hardly any movement. All of which adds up to the fact that I have a kind of dead fish stare on one side, which I can assure you I feel very self-conscious about. And if you dare tell me you didn't notice it when we met, I'm walking straight out of this restaurant.

In which case, I'm saying nothing at all.

Look, there are some people who wear prosthetics and you might go your entire life without ever noticing that one of their eyes isn't real. The acrylic eyes they make these days are works of art—and if they move like a real eye, they can be really hard to spot. But that's the problem, my prosthetic doesn't move like a real eye. Which means that it freaks some people out.

No, come on.

Absolutely. Have you heard of the uncanny valley?

Is it somewhere near San Francisco?

Ha, nice try! But no, the uncanny valley refers to the dip on a graph charting a person's feelings of comfort when faced with various likenesses of human beings. So let's say that at one end of the graph you have metal robots—C-3PO from Star Wars, *for example. And that's not too bad because he looks sort of like a human but clearly he's not a human. Meanwhile, at the other end of the chart you have a real, actual human, which doesn't freak anyone out, unless it's Michael Jackson, perhaps. Following me?*

Don't forget, I'm in Data Acquisition, Hannah. Charts are kind of my thing.

Good. So anyway, there's a point on the graph, somewhere in the middle, where the line dives down before rising again, which indicates the cases in which people are freaked the hell out. The uncanny valley. It's what happens in the case of an android, say, that looks almost like a real person—skin, eyes, features—and yet there's something wrong with this android, it's very humanlike and yet perceptibly not human. And that's exactly what makes people feel uneasy. The same thing happens with almost-realistic humans in computer games, ventriloquists' dummies and puppets. Oh, and clowns, clowns do it for me.

Clowns are freaky as hell.

Exactly, right? So that's the very same problem that some people have with my prosthetic eye and its lack of movement. It looks real but there's something a little bit wrong, just a tiny bit off. Which means that for some people there's something troubling about me, even if those people can't put their finger on it. I'm just a tiny bit off.

So wear the patch, I said. *It looks great on you, Hannah.*

Right! And get called pirate hundreds of times every week—which is mostly little kids, admittedly, but not exclusively. You'd be surprised.

What's wrong with being a pirate?

OK, that's a fair question. And the answer is, it reminds me of being thirteen years old again. You'd left for Maine by this point, Patrick, but at school, waiting for everything to heal and then for my first eye to be made, I had to wear an eyepatch for months. Do you remember Christie Laing?

Unfortunately, yes.

Let's just say that my injury was a gift to Christie. And she didn't waste a single ounce.

At this point the waiter, who had been hovering for a while, apologized for interrupting and asked us if we were ready to order. We dutifully opened our menus and quickly found something, anything. Again, I don't remember what we ate or drank, I just remember that I'd never met anyone so easy to talk to, that our conversation carried on without a second's pause for the entire duration of the meal. But when I try to remember the rest of the evening, my memory starts to get hazy. Or not hazy perhaps. Was there something strange about that night? Am I imagining it or did this really happen, Hannah?

Everything began to turn blue at the edges.

Maybe it was a trick of the light in the restaurant . . . But wait, was it really the Blue Water Grill in which we met or have I only imagined our second date there? Because now when I see it again everything looks to be filling up with a pale film of water. And as night fell outside, the walls in the room began shifting to a darker shade, almost as if they were turning from bright lake to deep ocean.

I remember how your dress matched your eye and we were both wearing blue.

Really? Could that possibly be true?

Or perhaps this is just how it works, how the mind holds on to the memory of falling in love—a feeling of passing deeper and deeper into the brightest waters you've ever seen.

One thing I know for certain, I was falling more and more in love with you, Hannah, that night and every night ever since. And then it would take less than a summer to fall so far in love with you that the rest of the world trailed away. Soon there would be you, only you. I remember that summer as luminous. I remember a season of infinite blue.

PART III

PART III

MATTHEW

Where should I start?

Perhaps by saying this is a letter I wish I'd written in my cell, a letter I should have sent twenty-three years ago, after the final time you came to visit me, when at last I understood how much it hurt you that I seemed to have no reason for what I did to Hannah Jensen. Of course, if you were able to read this letter now, you might still decide I had no reason, or insufficient reason, at least, and certainly that's true.

The first time you came, sitting across that jail table from me with the visitation show going on all around us, you asked me why I did it and I said there wasn't any particular explanation. I'm sorry, that was a lie. The truth is I didn't want you to know everything that happened, not at the time, and the awful thing is, now that I do want you to know, you won't understand—the kernel of you that remains seems unable to comprehend anything anymore, not even on the good days, which are becoming rarer and rarer with each one that passes.

I wish I could cure you, reverse the erosion. I wish I could bring you back.

You were the first person I truly loved. I don't find meaning in most things, but this means something to me. I love you and I always will.

However, you know only half of what I did. If you'd known the rest of it, if you'd known what I'm about to tell you, what would you have thought? What would you have done? Would you have stuck by me? Because knowing there was someone on the outside who was still in my corner was what kept the fight burning inside me those first two tough years, and you needed the fight in that place.

The only other person who knows the whole thing is Hannah.

There you go. There is more to this story than meets the eye.

But I want to make one thing clear from the start. This letter isn't any kind of defense. I'm not attempting in the slightest to excuse or mitigate what I did to Hannah Jensen in 1982. What I did that day was wrong, there is no gray.

However, the reality is there are more than two sides to most stories. Truth is seldom a lens, truth is a kaleidoscope, and I have my truth too.

There's something else as well—another reason to write this letter now, the explanation for why I first came looking for you after not having seen you for twenty-three years. I'm getting married. Or at least, I think so, I haven't actually posed the question or even bought the ring, because speaking to you seemed like the right thing to do first of all. I suppose I was hoping that, as well as listening to my confession, you might offer me your blessing. I thought if I told you everything, you might give me permission to find a second person in the world to love.

Anyway, now I will tell you the story as if you were never a part of it, as if you were never there, because the way you are now, your mind irreversibly lost in a fog, I suppose in some sense that's true.

HERE'S MY FIRST TRUTH—MY daddy beat me, that's just a fact. Oh, but this isn't one of those lines from the courtroom—*Your Honor, I only done what I done because my daddy done beat me.* No, this truth is just one of the colorful beads in the tube.

If I was lucky it was strap and nothing but strap, but sometimes the buckle snuck in. Occasionally the buckle was the whole point. Or sometimes my daddy, his liquored fingers finding nothing under his belt loops, would curl up his hands and make fists. Although saying all this, having a father who hit you wasn't exactly uncommon back then.

Attitudes change. My daddy was born in 1948 in the great state of Texas—remnants of state pride being the reason why he insisted we call him *Daddy*, even though people laughed at us openly for doing so. He grew up in the city of Beaumont, living in an age when everyone chewed tobacco, smoked unfiltered, and merrily lit up their small boys' behinds. Bred for a lifetime of poverty, he was raised among swamp and oil and knowing the back of his old man's hand. Only my daddy's life took a sharp turn when, fourteen years old, his momma died, hospitalized for tuberculosis before succumbing to pneumonia. This would've been 1962, the year my daddy was bused more than fifteen hundred miles northeast to live with an aunt, his momma's sister, in Queens, New York, and although his geographical influences may have shifted, my father's credo remained forever stuck in that swamp.

He didn't do well in New York, left school at sixteen and worked for a while fixing roofs and digging clams before, aged eighteen, he decided to join the army. He always spun you the American hero version, that he was a patriot who signed up to do what was right. However, if you listen to my mom, who enjoys talking about him now that he's long dead, she'll tell you my daddy was classic draft bait—blue collar, single, and poor. If he hadn't signed up they'd have pulled him in anyway. Better to stick up your hand.

She also likes to say she fell for his Texas charms—before laughing and throwing back another Beam.

Anyway, whatever the reason my daddy signed up for the army, sign up he did. He received his orders to report to Fort Dix, where he was put through sixteen weeks of training, which were followed by a few weeks leave, including at least one night in the company of my mom, it's safe to conclude. Next, the army packed him off on a boat for *a month-long ride to hell,* as he always told it. However, my daddy's hell ended up being no more than a seven-week stopover. After months of training and those thirty-one nights on a military transport ship, exactly fifty days after he arrived, late June 1967, he was medevacked out of Vietnam with a gut shredded by shrapnel and a wild dose of the Saigon clap.

At this point, I must've been steadily unfolding in my mom's belly for eleven weeks or so, not that she had any idea I was there, mistaking her first bouts of morning sickness for fears concerning her boyfriend's well-being. Later bouts of nausea, she supposed to have been triggered by news of his injuries.

So, a little further down the line, I was born, January 2, 1968, the first of two sons, my brother, William, arriving twenty months later—on the very same day that Ho Chi Minh died, September 2, 1969, as it happened. I do believe this was the achievement in life my daddy was proudest of, the propitious timing and flourishing of his second seed. Henceforth, my brother's birthdays became a kind of double celebration, the day always prompting misty retellings of my daddy's war stories. His favorite tale was all about the time he shot a Viet Cong while *the goddam gook was crouched down hopin to enjoy his mornin shit*. Whenever he told the story, he took great delight mimicking the look on the Viet Cong's face as he strained to move his bowels, exaggerating the eyes by stretching them out with his fingers, while exhaling in an apparently Asiatic manner—*Aaaah-sole, aaah-sole, aaah . . .* —and then he'd break off halfway through the third iteration, making a gun-shape with his hand and slamming down his thumb with a loud exclamation of *bang*! After that he'd spit something out like, *Now we gonna see if you can shit metal, Charlie*. Funny guy.

Anyway, because this was the only war story my daddy told with such cartoon levels of grotesquerie, I'm more than a little convinced this was the only Viet Cong he ever actually killed.

At any rate, however many men my daddy killed, and in whatever state of grace he found them, something had left him unsated. Or maybe his brief stint in Vietnam just turned him into a guy who went looking for trouble and found it in all the predictable places—a nose for whiskey and fistfights, he spent his nights downing Four Roses and throwing his knuckles around. If he couldn't find a man to fight? Well . . .

You might have thought that, what with my having a baby brother, the burden of my daddy's mood swings might eventually have been shared. However, little Billy was, to use the word the doctors employed when informing my parents of their baby's condition, a *mongoloid*. I remember how, growing up in the 1970s, gradually the terms *mongolism* and *mongoloid* would be heard less and less and the term Down syndrome used more and more, but human niceties and linguistic fashions were something to which my daddy never subscribed. However, he did have principles—little Billy was disabled, and he never laid a serious finger on the son he referred to as The Pug.

Anyway, none of this felt unnatural to me, I wasn't unlucky or mistreated, this was just the way the world turned.

I spent the first ten years of my life growing up in a narrow green-painted apartment in Woodside, Queens, our walls being pretty much the only greenery I'd ever experienced until, not long before my eleventh birthday, we moved upstate to Roseborn, Ulster County. I don't remember which of my daddy's short-term jobs was the stated reason. No doubt he didn't last long in it because every brief period of employment in Roseborn came to an end after some kind of trouble. He worked in body shops, fixed farm machinery, built fences, plowed drives, painted houses . . . He was good with his hands. Hilarious, huh? Anyway, when my daddy wasn't working, he got into even more fistfights than usual. You know that phrase, *the apple doesn't fall far from the tree*? The townspeople of Roseborn looked at me like I was trouble a long time before I was anything like it.

The nicest thing my daddy ever did for me was steal a bicycle. He told me it was salvaged. Anyway, that bike got me out of the house plenty, as far away from my daddy as I could pedal for as long as possible. Win-win.

I liked living in Roseborn. Although Queens was a much bigger place, it felt somehow smaller, everything squeezed down to neighborhoods from which you never broke free, but in Roseborn I could ride my bike anywhere on the streets, along the dirt trails outside of town and all the way up to the Swangum Ridge. It was wide open country, a place where a child could have secrets and fantasies, a place for building hidden forts. You could shape your own world up there in the mountains, even if there were only two of you doing the dreaming—me and Tricky.

Tricky's real name was Patrick McConnell. (I think you met him only a couple of times.) I suppose I gave him that nickname because part of me must have realized there was something dark and evasive about Tricky. Most of the kids at school used the innocent moniker Patch for him, but I guess they didn't see in Patrick what I saw, that he might have seemed like a quiet kid, only that was all just a front. I could always tell there were secret wheels turning inside his head. Patrick didn't keep his own counsel because he had nothing to say; quite the opposite, it was because he didn't want anyone to know what he was thinking. However, everyone went for the misdirection, the quiet kid act, and to my mind at least, that was his trick.

Anyway, the truth about me and Tricky is the first reason I wanted to be his friend was jealousy, and it might sound stupid, but this is absolutely true—I was envious of the way he rolled up his shirtsleeves.

My first day of school in Roseborn was the start of sixth grade. I was the new kid in town, so no one spoke to me, but that was fine, it gave me time to size everything up, a chance to identify who I might want to befriend.

Everyone came to school in hoodies, sports jerseys, sweaters, or T-shirts, but Patrick McConnell came to school in clean white shirts, button-downs that were as bright as the teeth in whitening advertisements, clean cotton as crisp as hotel linen, and every day, Patrick had the sleeves of those shirts rolled up just past his elbow. Now this might not sound like much to be jealous of, I'll admit, but something about the way those cuffs were folded spoke to me about everything missing from my life, because this wasn't a technique you were born with, someone had to show you how to roll and fold something so neatly, so crease-free. Hell, maybe you even needed a special kind of shirt designed for sleeve-rolling. I spent a few quiet weeks just breathing him in, marveling at those revelatory shirtsleeves.

Our mom was vaguely Catholic, taking me and little Billy to Mass maybe once a month (although we knew our place, we weren't good enough to go to Sacred Heart, where the McConnell family prayed alongside the more important burghers of Roseborn), and I had one good white churchgoing shirt in my closet. Getting home from school one afternoon, a little way into the first term, I took that shirt from my closet and snuck off to the bathroom, the only room in our house with a mirror, pulled off my tee, buttoned up the shirt, and proceeded to fold and roll the sleeves. Only, by the time I'd flipped the cuffs twice it was already creased as hell. I started again, but the result was the same. While Patrick's folded shirtsleeves were as smooth as a priest's collar, whenever I tried to roll up my own sleeves, after a few turns it seemed some wrinkle was already there and there was nothing I could do but repeat it.

The next day, while we were all sitting in English class waiting for the teacher to show, I turned to Patrick and said, Hey, Patch, I like your shirt.

Patch looked at Jonny the Spin, Jonny the Spin looked at Patch. No one said anything. I could tell they were trying to figure out whether I was being sarcastic or just plain weird. I was used to that.

Christie Laing, a few seats farther behind, said, Hey, did you hear that everyone? Weird Matt is a faggot for Patch.

My name's Matthew, I said to her.

Fag-hew, said Christie, her goons letting out a squeal.

Matthew, I said a bit harder. She didn't come back from that. I've never found a situation where a clever line worked better than firm intent.

How'd you do the sleeves? I asked Patch.

His axis of glances with Jonny the Spin tilted back and forth a little more.

Rolled them up. He shrugged.

Nice, I said.

The teacher came in.

I'VE NEVER KNOWN HOW TO make friends. Sometimes it happens and sometimes it doesn't. In the end, my friendship with Patrick McConnell came down to dumb luck.

Christie Laing had a cousin, a boy in eighth grade called Ryan McMahan, who was known to most people at school as Ryan McMeathead, the football team's one-man wrecking ball. By the age of fourteen Ryan had developed a linebacker's neck and immense puffed-up arms. The Laings and McMahans were the northern equivalent of my daddy's side of our family, purebred hicks and Republican down to the bone.

So what with Patch being smart and neatly presented and having a lawyer Democrat for a father, he quickly became a target for Ryan McMeathead who had this fun game he liked to play where he'd fold and fold pieces of paper into thin strips, about three inches long, bend them into U-shapes, wet their ends, and let them dry out on a radiator until they turned hard as rock. Between lessons he'd sneak up on his victims with a rubber band stretched between thumb and forefinger, slip one of those hard U-shaped pellets over the band, draw the thing back and snap!

Patrick was one of his prime victims. The seat of his pants, *crack*! The cartilage at the back of his ear, *thwack*! His neck right above his shirt collar, *blam*! That time he snapped Patch on the neck, the welt stayed there in furious red for three whole days.

Like I said, I always thought there was more to Tricky than mere shyness, and what happened next made me want to become Patrick's friend even more, because goddammit if the button-down boy didn't go away and make his own pellets.

I guess McMeathead had driven him so mad, he didn't even think it all the way through, he just snuck up on McMeathead in the hallway and loosened his pellet so hard against the back of his skull, *smack*, you could've heard the hollow thud from several miles away. McMeathead screamed and started running around like a balloon losing air while Patch stood there in shock, unsure what to do until McMeathead stopped yelping and dancing and turned on him—

You are a motherfucking dead man, McConnell.

At which point, Patch ran. He ran straight down the hallway and then out the school doors, *zoom*, pursued by McMeathead and his cohorts—Meatbrowski, Meatchini, O'Meatneck—but Patch was a lightning bolt compared to the lumbering meat-pack and they never got close to him. Round and round the sports fields they ran until Patch pulled a spin move and sprinted straight back to school, out of breath and trembling slightly when he sat down for geography.

It seemed like the whole room was in shock.

Way to go, Patch, I said, though he didn't acknowledge me.

Unfortunately, however, that wasn't the end of the McMeathead story. The world tells you to punch a bully on the nose and he'll leave you alone, and isn't that precisely what Patrick had done? The world knows less than shit.

Patch did a pretty good job of sneaking around for the rest of the day, avoiding the pack, staying well away from their meat lockers, but in homeroom, the day after his act of defiance, Christie Laing handed him a note. I didn't see the words, but everyone in the room knew what it said. Day, time, place.

Patch went pale and started to shrink like a sack of grain with a hole slashed in its belly, and then word got around between lessons. Behind the bleachers, lunchtime.

I could pretend that I came up with a plan right away, but the truth is I never made one.

A few hours later, I followed the small group of boys that ushered Patrick toward his fate, the large crowd that had gathered parting to let Patch into its ring.

I was pretty tall for my age, plus I was thirteen years old already, having been held back a year at school in Woodside, so it wasn't hard to find a spot from which I could see. I stood at the back of the crowd watching McMeathead in front of his pack, moving his fat head in circles. Ten yards away stood Patch, a kid two years Ryan's junior and weighing in at a hundred pounds less. How was any of this fair? Patrick had chalked up a solitary act of retaliation in return for how many provocations? Nine, ten? A dozen?

You ready to settle this one on one? said McMeathead.

One on one? Patch was half the guy's size and shaking in terror. He moved his lips, but nothing audible came out.

McMeathead put his hand to his ear and laughed. This here was The Ryan McMeathead Show. In daily conversation he employed the vocabulary of a coloring book, and yet when it came to fighting talk, McMeathead was fluent.

Hey, kid, you know what? he said. I'll make you a promise. I won't go easy on you.

The pack snorted.

Patrick's arms went stiff, his fingers spread wide at the ends of his hands. Look, he said, I'm really sorry, OK?

Correction, said McMeathead, you will be. Now, you want some more time to piss your little pants or are they all good and pissed? At which point McMeathead started his slow lumber forward, flexing his fists in front of his huge barrel chest.

Like I said, I never came up with a plan, but there was a sense of anger running through me that began somewhere in my gut and then started to grow. As the anger got closer to my skin, it turned to rage, and the rage was electric, the rage needed to burst out from within.

I don't remember much about what happened next, just a few flashes of flesh and a humming in my ears that changed pitch whenever McMeathead landed a blow. In every fight I've had, and I've had my share, it's as if you move into a shadow world, a bubble forming around you, a place in which all of life becomes simplified, existence reduced to a single question—

How far are you prepared to go?

I've always known my answer to that question.

How far am I prepared to go? I will go further than you. However many weapons you're willing to bring, I will bring more. However low you go, you will never dig deeper than me. I will

win, because what this will cost me in pain, I will pay. My re-
sources are limitless, I will always outbid you and I will never back
down.

As soon as your opponent understands this, you have him de-
feated.

No one held me back, no one pulled me off. I don't remember
much. At the end I was standing and Ryan McMeathead was
down.

I WENT TO A RESTROOM to wash his blood from my hands
along with some of McMeathead's skin, which was stuck under
my fingernails. Every now and then, someone would open the
door, perform a rapid one-eighty, and the door would close again.

When recess was over, I headed back to class, but Patch wasn't
there. I found out later he went to see the nurse, threw up in front
of her, and got himself sent home for the afternoon. As for the
other kids in our class, no one was looking straight at me, as if it
were one of those schoolyard games, because every time I turned
my head the children in that part of the room froze like statues. I
won't pretend I didn't enjoy the sense of power, the feeling of respect. Now everyone knew my potential.

Only potential isn't worth all that much when five of them
come at you from behind. It happened right after I stepped out of
the doors at the end of the school day. They dragged me off to the
side of the building, up against the wall, four-fifths of the meat-
pack pinning each of my limbs to the brickwork, leaving Ryan
McMeathead free to do whatever he wanted, his fat hands making
fists, his arms swinging and swinging.

I closed my eyes and waited for it to end.

IT WASN'T THE WORST BEATING I've ever had, some bruising and swelling, nothing broken, although bad enough I would
have to take the next day off school.

It was only me and Billy when I got home, me being my

brother's de facto babysitter much of the time. Little Billy cried when he saw me and tried to stroke my bruises better, the way he often did. Several hours later, when I saw headlights swinging over the broken blinds of the living room, our mom being dropped off after her workday at the Blue Moon diner, I snuck off to bed.

Fortunately my daddy was passing through one of his brief phases of employment, so I didn't have to see him the next day. Three days later, when he noticed my faded wounds, I was able to say to him, Yeah, but you should see the other guy.

He liked that and chuckled.

But when my mom saw me the morning after it happened, she gasped. Oh, Matthew, she said. Oh, baby, this is the last time, I swear it, I promise. (How many times had it been the last?)

No, it wasn't him, Mom, I said, just some dumb kids at school.

Mom looked relieved and then fussed over me all morning, seeming to enjoy the chance to tend to some wounds, my daddy never letting her touch him after one of his brawls. *It's nothing, Lucille, lucky fuckin shot, that's all.* She heated tomato soup and fed it to me, wiping my chin while I struggled to swallow, and kept bringing me ice wrapped in a dishcloth while we watched her daytime shows. When she left for her shift at the diner in the afternoon, I fell asleep on the couch.

I was woken up by a knocking at the door. When I looked out the window and saw it was Patch, my first thought was not to answer, embarrassed to see him standing outside our run-down shack of a home, barely better than a trailer, Patch looking church-neat in his shirtsleeves.

I opened up, Patch looking at me, horrified and confused.

Fucking cowards, I said. Jumped me from behind, needed five of them.

Oh, shoot, he said. You OK?

I will be, I said. How about you?

Me? he said, sounding shocked. I mean, good, but . . . Look, the reason I came here, about what happened, I just wanted to say—

Hey, I said, interrupting as fast as I could, you wanna come in?

Sure, he said, nodding uncertainly. When Patch stepped inside, you could see he was looking for some kind of doormat on which to wipe his feet, but then, finding nothing, he crouched down and started untying his laces.

Don't worry about it, I said.

Patch pulled off his shoes anyway. That was the start of it all.

NEW YORK, 2008

Matthew, Patrick McConnell here.
Want to meet up and discuss your
business proposal?

Patrick? This is a surprise. Definitely,
yes. Where are you?

Outside your apartment.

Interesting. I'm out of town. But I could
be there in two hours.

2 hrs won't work. Monday?

Sure. But if we're going to meet I'd
love to show you something. It's a two
hour drive from the city. I could pick
you up. 11am say?

11am good. But I'll drive myself.
Where you want to meet up?

How about Palisades Parkway? After the first exit heading north there's a parking area, Rockefeller Lookout. You can follow me from there. Good?

Works fine. By the way, I just met your boyfriend. Don't think he liked me much.

Andrew? Don't worry. Andrew's harmless.

Monday then, 11am.

Monday, great. Look forward to it.

MATTHEW

I loved it in the Swangums, the summer of '81 one of the best of my life, me and Tricky spinning up the hill together and gazing down at shadows, the clouds in the sky painting dark lakes on the earth and our friendship growing little by little as we played our own games, turning life into a daily adventure. When the heat rose, we'd jump into the cool waters of Lake Swangum or spread-eagle ourselves against the damp flanks of the ice caves. We plunked cans, built forts, ate wild blueberries, showered beneath waterfalls . . .

Adventure was the opposite of school, adventure was a real education.

However, we were boys and often there was an edge to our fun. Sometimes I'd hide in our fort and let Tricky attack with a slingshot to see if it could withstand a raid. Other times we'd roughhouse a little, which I thought might be a learning experience for Tricky, useful if he ever found himself embroiled with another McMeathead. There was also the time we made a spear and I threw it at Tricky, grazing his leg, and then told him to throw it at me, only Tricky seemed upset and wouldn't do it.

Nothing scared me. To this day nothing does. I thought I might grow up to be a stunt man or a fighter pilot. I liked jumping between the outcrops at Steeple Rocks, Tricky telling me to stop because it made him feel sick just watching me, which was something I never understood at all. Every time I'd just laugh and find a larger gap to launch myself across. When we'd play Tarzan, swinging across the stream, Tricky always wanted to pick a spot by some deep water, but I wanted to go where the rocks were sharp. I loved the thrill. I've always felt a supreme sense that nothing will ever go wrong.

If anyone was to hold a gun to my head, for example, I wouldn't be scared because I wouldn't believe they had any intention to pull the trigger, even though I understand that they might—I'm not stupid.

That's just how I feel. That's how everything feels.

Eventually winter intruded on the games of '81 with its inevitable snowfalls, each new layer of crust building on the next beneath the air's deep freeze, and being snowbound made me feel itchy, although at least we could hang out at Tricky's place shooting tanks or flying biplanes on his Atari and watching shows the McConnells had taped off TV, *The Dukes of Hazzard*, *Fantasy Island*. But still, I couldn't wait for the thaw, glancing hopefully out of my bedroom window each morning, about to begin another turgid day, school always rolling so slowly, the same changeless routine every day—move from point A to point B, wait forty minutes, go to point C, wait forty minutes, D, E, F . . . How was it that no one else could see this? We were all being trained as drones, everyone just waiting to be dropped into the appropriate box. The whole thing made me restless, my agitation with school often getting me in trouble, although mostly for nothing more than mouthing off or not doing homework. I didn't get into any more fights—didn't need to.

Only then something happened that shook up those school days a little.

The two most attractive girls in our year were Hannah Jensen and Christie Laing. Hannah Jensen was sweet and seemed smart and was pretty as hell—although she came across kind of young for her age. Christie Laing, on the other hand, wasn't sweet. Christie Laing was a nasty piece of work, the kind of girl who brought out the worst in others. Normally I stayed away from people like her if I could, but the problem was, Christie was hot, a hot blonde, and then one day, she kissed me.

In my defense, although I might not have liked Christie at all, theoretically speaking, I was a pubescent boy, fourteen years old. What was I supposed to do? At a certain age, most boys would fuck a bucket if you gave it long hair and a girl's name. Well, I was definitely at a certain age—and also the only boy in seventh grade who had reached that age, as far as I could tell, more than a year older and foot taller than almost any other kid in my year, seventh grade being a particularly strange stage of growing up anyway, what with the fact that half the girls in our year were taller than two-thirds of the boys. Some of those boys were still doing all the same things they'd been doing since five years of age, happy just playing with plastic trucks or toy soldiers or *Star Wars* action figures.

I'm pretty sure that at this point in our lives there were only two people in seventh grade prepared to make a fully fledged commitment to their puberty. So you could say that when it came to Christie and me, it was nothing more than a coupling of convenience.

It didn't take long for it to go beyond kissing and groping. One day during recess, Christie slunk up to me. (We never made a show of being together—which was fine with me, by the way—because Christie didn't want her cousin Ryan to know. This was probably the most sensitive thing she'd ever done in her life.) In a half-whisper, she then went on to tell me that her house would be empty after school that afternoon. Did I want to come for some fun?

That was my very first time with a girl, with anyone in fact, up in Christie's bedroom, me concentrating on performing the role properly while two posters stared down at us from above the headboard, one from the movie *Grease,* the other of Michael Jackson looking sultry in purple silk, the shirt open to his waist, his skin darker and nose fuller than in later years.

While Christie was wiggling beneath me, considerably more

adept at playing her part than I was, I looked up at the *Grease* poster. There was Sandy (Olivia Newton-John) pictured after her transformation in the movie from sweet Sandy to slutty Sandy, a hot tousled blonde with big hair. Down beneath me was Christie, a hot tousled blonde with big hair.

Up, down, up, down, up, down . . .

Sandy from *Grease* had her arms around Danny (John Travolta). I looked at his hair, dark and slick, his eyes twinkling twice as blue as Sandy's. His lips were fuller than hers as well and he was coming across as both masculine and vulnerable at the same time.

Sandy, Danny, Sandy, Danny, Sandy, Danny . . .

That's when John Travolta broke character and launched into one of those trademark smirks of his. That's right, John Travolta was looking at me like he knew where I'd rather be—and with whom.

I thrust a little harder. Christie gasped, her nails digging into my back.

The second time we had sex beneath Christie's posters, it was Michael Jackson who volunteered himself to my gaze.

OK, so this was getting complicated, and there was an odd feeling inside of me, possibly something a little like fear. Although wasn't I bored of life with its pointlessly black-and-white rules? And hadn't the world shaken things up for me?

Only life was about to get even more complicated than posters of John Travolta and Michael Jackson.

NEW YORK, 2008

She is sitting at Patrick's desk in the corner of their bedroom when her cell phone rings, and she sees who it is, and she answers.

Morning, Mike.

Jesus, Aitch! You were supposed to call me. Confirmation of a little something called breathing, no?

Too loud, McCluskey. Did someone wake up on the wrong side of the bed?

I tip the scales at two-eighty, Aitch, I wake up on both sides of the bed. Now come on, give me some help here, I'm trying to look out for you.

Sorry, Mike. Busy. Lost track.

Well, at least not being slain is keeping you occupied.

I'm going though all his stuff. Closet, drawers, computer.

Who said journalistic ethics were dead?

He's my husband.

Then it's kosher.

Exactly.

I figure this means Chef Death isn't there with you, then.

Wow! What's with all the names, McCluskey?

Gallows humor, Aitch.

He's out. Grocery shopping.

Oh snap! That's exactly what I always have a hankering for after a day of public disturbance and self-mutilation.

Not now, Jen . . . Sorry, Mike, I have this friend trying to call me, that's the second time this morning. Where were we?

I believe you were somewhere on the moral high ground. You locate anything useful up there?

Not yet. Wait, what's this? There's a document tucked away on his computer here labeled, *For Dr. Rosenstock*. That's the name of his therapist. You think it might be like a diary?

Sure, only probably a thousand times more personal if it's for his shrink.

You think I should open it?

I think . . . I guess you . . . Dammit, I'm not Dr. Phil, Hannah. I can't tell you what the hell to do.

OK, you're right. I should wait. He said he'd tell me everything tonight.

Then again, of course, it could describe his fantasies about buying groceries Saturday morning and turning his wife into chopped liver for dinner.

Come on, McCluskey. Whatever Patch was doing, there's no way it had anything to do with me.

So don't open it.

On the other hand . . .

So open it.

That's all I needed to hear, Mike.

She double-clicks, the document opening on the desktop, her eye moving down . . .

I remember the gunshots made a wet sort of sound, phssh phssh phssh, *and each time he hit her she screamed. Do the math and the whole thing probably went on for as long as ten minutes. I just stood there and watched.*

MATTHEW

With the revelation that I was able to find both men and women equally attractive, 1982 had already ambushed me once, but the year was far from done with surprises. The next thing to jump out at me would be the saga of Randy McCloud.

Randy McCloud lived all alone in an inherited house in the center of town. He was a big, harmless bear-man with an overgrown red mustache and a particular fondness for two things in life—White Russian cocktails and strolling around Roseborn looking to shoot the breeze with little kids. Only, to be fair to Randy, the reason he liked talking to kids wasn't because he was some kind of sick creep but because kid talk was the highest level of conversation Randy was ever likely to achieve.

Predictably enough, this led to all manner of rumors being spread about Randy. Parents warned their children to stay well away from him, or had angry words with the police, or shouted names at Randy across the street, but when the time came for the newspapers to sift through the details of Randy's life, there would never emerge even one shred of evidence that he was anything other than a genial lummox.

I don't know for how long Randy McCloud's existence had been a philosophical challenge to my father, but the incident I myself witnessed happened back in December of 1981.

It was a Saturday evening and me and little Billy were in the back of the car on the way to pick up our mom from her job at the Blue Moon diner when my daddy stopped by the drugstore to buy himself a carton of Larks. While we were waiting, Randy happened to come walking by, and seeing us sitting in the backseat, he stopped, bent at the knees and gave us a wave.

Little Billy waved back, wound down the window and started jabbering away about this action figure Ewok he'd named Danny and why Danny didn't like cinnamon gum and what Danny really liked was Hershey's Kisses. Randy was utterly entranced.

That's when my daddy came out of the drugstore, yelled something obscene and broke into the only sprint I ever saw him work himself up to. Now he was right up in the poor guy's face, pushing him around, Randy looking hurt and confused as he bumped and bounced from my daddy's hands like a pinball.

Little Billy was getting upset because Randy had been laughing at everything he'd said despite the fact that the funniest thing my brother had said was *cinnamon gum.* So just before Randy could get himself shoved all the way out of view, Billy waved goodbye to him and Randy waved back, giving Billy one of those gleeful little wiggle-your-fingers farewells.

That wave wasn't the brightest idea Randy ever had in his life—my daddy saw it from the corner of his eye and, lickety-split, Randy was down on the ground, holding his nose, blood spilling onto his overshirt.

After spending a few moments shaking the hurt from his knuckles, my daddy crouched down over Randy, and I don't know what he said, but I doubt it was useful information on the topic of stain removal. After imparting his advice, he spat on the ground, came back to the car, slammed the door and, seeing little Billy crying, cuffed his ear for it. Don't you ever speak to that fat fuckin faggot again, he yelled. You hear me boy?

Now forward-wind to a Friday night, early April 1982, and although no one knows precisely how the whole thing unfolded, here's how I imagine it went—

My daddy sitting on a barstool, kitty-corner from Randy,

stewing over the roof repairing job he'd just lost, throwing stares at the bear-man enjoying his effeminate cocktail. Randy taking dainty sips of his drink. My daddy noticing some cream from Randy's White Russian clinging to the bottom of his red mustache . . .

That probably would've done it.

However, O'Sullivan's wasn't short of potential suspects that night, and by the time Randy left shortly before midnight everyone's eyes were swimming and there wasn't a single witness who could (or would) say who left O'Sullivan's Dive Inn around the same time as Randy McCloud.

Whoever it was, within a mile they'd forced him off the road, Randy swerving and his truck ending up snagged between the trees of an apple orchard.

Perhaps his attacker didn't even mean to kill him. Randy was found dead outside his vehicle, killed by a single blow to the head, probably something like a tire iron, said the *Roseborn Gazette,* quoting the police.

No one living nearby heard or saw anything of the brief but deadly encounter, although several of them were awoken soon after its conclusion by a loud bang, opening their eyes only to see the flames of the explosion lighting their bedroom ceilings.

Randy died at forty-three years of age, unmarried, and never having hurt a fly. In a few months' time his story, which was covered in depth by the *Roseborn Gazette,* a newspaper that was used to splashing big on temporary bridge closures and local planning meetings, would be relegated to only the second biggest news item of 1982. My daddy was the catalyst for both.

TWO DAYS LATER, SUNDAY AFTERNOON, the police arrived to take my daddy in for some friendly questioning, saying that it was nothing more than wanting to speak to everyone who'd been in O'Sullivan's that night, but our mom got herself into a state of high panic and, an hour after my daddy was whisked away, she drove down to the station house with me and little Billy and told us to stay in the car.

A few minutes later, inspiration having struck, she came out, grabbed me by the arm, pulled me into the station house, and handed me some change as she told me to call Tricky's house from the pay phone and ask to speak to his dad. I did what she asked and when Tricky's dad came on the line, he explained that, as the potential prosecutor should anything go to trial, it wouldn't be at all appropriate for him to get directly involved, but he also said he had a friend who could stop by and make sure everything went by the book.

By the time the friend arrived in his weekend slacks and blue Oxford, our mom had calmed down a little. The lawyer convinced her to take me and my brother home and he'd make sure everything was taken care of.

My daddy came home a few hours later, all puffed up with smugness, just in time to see the Knicks-Pistons game. Waving a can of Genesee Cream Ale, half an eye on the basketball, he did a lot of bragging about *the smooth streak of piss* who'd shown up and sat in on his questioning, but never in his life, he continued, had he needed any help *runnin rings in a pigpen*. Also, he proclaimed, if he'd been the one to kill Randy McCloud, the cops would've had no trouble finding the murder weapon, because they would have had to pull the thing out of Randy's *fat faggot ass*.

WHEN I GOT HOME FROM school the next day, I was about to head over to Tricky's when my daddy told me he was driving into town to pick up some Larks and maybe I'd like to hop in, take the ride with him. This was an odd request and my face must've said so.

What, I can't take my firstborn for a drive and some man talk? he said.

We took the road away from town, window down, my daddy's arm catching the afternoon sun and not a word passing between us. He turned right before the bridge and, a mile or two farther on, after a lot of glancing in his mirrors, he pulled to the side of the road, stopping close to the river. Getting out, he went back to the trunk, lifted out a blanket, and started wiping something down. After surveying the pastoral scene one more time, my daddy drew a tire iron clear of the blanket and launched it as far as he could, javelin-style, out into the Jakobskill River.

When he got back in the driver's seat, he didn't even look at me, just turned the key, gunned the engine, and spun out through the gravel onto the road, and we drove back just the same way we got there, in silence, all the way home.

NEW YORK/
NEW JERSEY, 2008

He pulls up, lights flashing red-white-and-blue, and Hannah hurries into the front seat, McCluskey wrapping his big arms around her, his jacket several yards of cheap cloth smelling of chewing gum, smoke, and baby powder, and as they head out of the city, lights no longer flashing, she starts telling him the story of 1982, only the second time she's told it to anyone, her former editor Max Reagan the first time, a Newark bar thick with smoke, and now she's telling McCluskey about Matthew Weaver in the half-light of the Lincoln Tunnel, taillights bouncing from white tiles, their glow like red flares sailing over the ceiling and walls, and when she reaches the part about the tree and the rope, they emerge from the darkness, soaring into the widening New Jersey sky, the story building to its finale, that Red Ryder BB gun, the sting of the pellets over and over, a pain like being punched in the eye, and then darkness.

And though she doesn't tell him everything, doesn't tell him what she did that day and weeks before, she tells him enough, McCluskey driving in silence, his knuckles whitening on the black steering wheel.

Goddammit, Aitch, why didn't you say something? he shouts, hitting the dash, and quickly apologizing, Sorry, Hannah, sorry, I'm not yelling at you, I'm not, it's just, this damn fuckin world.

Why would I have told you? she says. What difference would it have made?

McCluskey doesn't say anything, doesn't know what to say.

Then she starts talking about Patrick, Patch the twelve-year-old boy, Matthew's buddy, how she thought he wasn't there, not *right* there, how she thought he had saved her, only saved her, and then she tells McCluskey what she just saw on her husband's computer screen, and that she didn't read everything, but she read enough, enough to know he was there . . . *only half a scream . . . the way her head twisted despite the rope tied around her neck . . .* more than enough to know he could have stopped it all, and that their marriage, their entire life together, is based on a lie.

Back in their apartment, she had made sure to leave it open on his computer, *For Dr. Rosenstock,* one line highlighted . . . *Hannah's eye socket looked like it was housing a dark smashed plum . . .* so he will see it when he gets home.

She could look at the thing now, she could read everything Patch had to say for himself on her phone, because almost an hour ago, when she read more than she could bear, after crying a little more with every word, she had copied it, the whole thing, fingers shaking, command A, command C, and sent it to herself, her work email, all of the words (how much did he write?), before running out of the apartment, running to the café across Seventh Avenue, and waiting for him to arrive, flashing red-white-and-blue, red-white-and-blue.

And they reach Pulaski Skyway, and there's nothing more she wants to tell.

Aitch, I'm sorry, that's the worst fuckin thing I ever heard in my life.

Nah, McCluskey, you're a cop. I mean, it's not like anyone died or anything, she says, and then shudders as she realizes this isn't true, so that when her phone starts to ring, the sound startles her.

Is it him? says McCluskey.

No, she says, feeling a sense of relief as she looks at the screen. Just Jen again, she says, turning the phone over, dropping it into her lap. Not now, Jen, she whispers, letting the call drop to voice mail.

Christ, I don't know what to say, Aitch. I don't know what to say about any of it. Like, this Matthew, what happened to that sick little fuck?

They locked him up, she says. After that, who knows?

And your husband—how old you say he was when this happened?

Thirteen. No, wait, I was thirteen. I guess he was twelve.

But still. Just standing there? Doing nothing at all?

Right.

And meanwhile he's telling his therapist all about it, for crying out loud.

Looks that way.

Fuckin asshole. Sorry, Aitch, sorry, it's not my place . . .

And then Hannah's phone makes a sound, a new message.

> Home now, Han. Where are you? Px

> Go take a look at your computer.

And knowing he will try to call her in thirty seconds, a minute max, she taps out another message . . .

> I never want to see you again.

. . . presses SEND, powers off.

MATTHEW

The year 1982 did, however, have something other than unpleasant surprises in store for me, because amid all the horror surrounding Randy McCloud's death, the first green shoots of something wonderful had sprung into being—and that something wonderful was you.

It all began outside Roseborn Police Department, my mom inside about to have her moment of inspiration—that I would enlist Tricky's dad to our cause—me still outside, hands in my pockets, kicking stones to pass the time and little Billy sitting snot-nosed and whiny in our car. That's when a green pickup truck pulled into the parking lot, and I went to sit down on a bench.

As the truck parked, I noticed the markings on its side, a gold maple leaf set in a gold triangle, the logo for the Swangum Conservancy. I also recognized the driver when he jumped out.

It was you, you who used to wave at us whenever you saw us in the mountains, you who had stopped us one time to tell us no fishing in the lake when we had Tricky's Red Ryder hidden in one of the fishing rod bags.

I'm sorry we lied to you about that.

You headed toward the station house, pausing by the bench to say hi to me. I responded in kind, and then you said, Hey, aren't you one of the boys who likes drawing water up in the mountains?

Yes, sir, I said. But it's Patch who's the artist, not me.

That's right, now I remember. So what do you do while he's sketching?

Look at the rocks, I guess. (I don't know why I said that, I never really cared much about rocks before I met you.)

Really? you said. And you know what's interesting about those rocks, right?

There's one shaped like a space invader? I shrugged.

You laughed, but in a kindly way. If you're interested in rocks, you said, I could tell you a few things about them sometime. For example, did you know there used to be a glacier right over the top of the Swangums?

What's a glacier?

You laughed again. Wow, there's a lot for you to learn . . . Sorry, I don't think I know your name.

Matthew, I said.

Pleased to meet you, Matthew. And you don't need to call me sir. I'm Pete, just plain old Pete.

Yes, sir.

Yes, *Pete*.

Sorry, I laughed. We both laughed.

How about it? You want to learn about the rocks and the glacier sometime?

Yes, sir . . . *Pete*, I said.

Sir Pete? Hell, he sounds like one of the knights from King Arthur's round table. You know the story about King Arthur?

No. I shook my head.

Well, that's another story about rocks for some other time. Probably we should stick to glaciers for now. Maybe the next time you and your friend Patch head up there?

The snow had recently melted, and Tricky and I were riding our bikes up there as often as we could, but I think I sensed something right at that moment, that I wanted to learn something Tricky didn't know anything about—just as I knew nothing about rolling up shirtsleeves. I suppose I thought I might impress him one day.

Next Sunday? I suggested. (Tricky always had to take part in something the McConnells called *Family Sundays,* a concept that seemed totally alien to me.)

Next Sunday? you said. That's great, just great. I knew you two were a pair of fine young boys when I saw you the first time.

Yeah, but Patrick can't do Sundays, I said. But that's OK, he mostly just likes sketching water.

Well, that's great too, you said. But once you learn about the glacier you'll change his mind, he'll want to do rocks as well. So how about I meet you at noon next Sunday? You happen to know the swim-hole at the edge of Lake Swangum?

Yeah, I know that spot. Tricky and me—sorry, that's my nickname for Patrick—we call it the beach.

The beach? I like that.

Uh-huh. But I guess it's just a slab of rock.

There's no such thing as *just* a slab of rock, you said, you'll see. So the beach it is then. Midday next Sunday?

I nodded.

That's when Mom came flying out of the station house to haul me inside so that I could make that phone call to Joe McConnell.

You nodded politely farewell, turned, and headed back to your truck.

NEW JERSEY/
NEW YORK, 2008

Lindy, it's been too long, says Hannah as they hug on the porch, Lindy pulling her closer with a maternal squeeze.

I know, babe, says Lindy, and what's Mikey been saying about me in the meantime?

That you still have the patience of a saint. Well, to be honest, I deduced that myself.

No kidding, right? You're a better detective than he is.

Hey, I'm standing right here, says McCluskey, holding up Hannah's small bag. I got ears, OK? And a little something called feelings.

Hannah and Lindy exchange looks, and then laughter.

Everything all right, hun? says Lindy, Hannah responding by squeezing her eye shut, hunching her shoulders.

Don't worry, says Lindy, swiping the air. You can tell me everything later, babe. We got vodka.

Lindy, who has a head of gray curls, is as trim as McCluskey is huge, used to date Mikey back in high school, so the story goes, gave him the heave, took him back seven years later when he'd done some growing up (*not much, mind*), and weighed in at one-eighty, looked good in his uniform, McCluskey's coda to the tale always the same, *twice the man she married*.

She beckons Hannah inside, Let's get you settled, she says,

taking the bag from her husband who heads to the kitchen. Straight up there, first on the left. Hey, Mikey, she calls out, make yourself useful, Bloody Marys for the ladies.

And what about me?

There's a Green Goddess in the fridge, special kale flavor.

Goddammit, Lindy, it's the freakin weekend.

Exactly, it's the only time I can keep you in line. You know the choices, it's this or we plug in that treadmill in the basement. Sorry, Hannah, you think when your kids leave home your work's done, only that's when you notice you're living with *an overgrown toddler*. Lindy turns up the volume on the last three words, and then adds, dial still set to ten, *I know exactly what's in the fridge, Mikey, right down to the last slice of cheese.*

SHE UNPACKS HER THINGS AND sits on the bed for a while, thinking about turning on her phone, the compulsion strong, but what could he say that would make her feel better?

Yes, I was there, and I lied to you, but . . .

She heads downstairs, out onto the deck, where Lindy has arranged a spread on a low frosted-glass table, cheese and crackers, fruit plate, shrimp with a dipping bowl of cocktail sauce, and they sit in the shade of a canvas awning, Hannah managing only a few berries, Lindy allowing McCluskey *something for the weekend*, three pieces of shrimp, husband and wife bickering enjoyably as Hannah lets the summer heat mingle with her numbness, and then a second Bloody Mary, a third, and after that she switches to wine, and when Lindy starts to light candles, Hannah pulls out her phone, turns it on.

Sure you're ready, Aitch?

No, she says. But can you take a look, Mike, tell me what he says?

No problem, Hannah.

Lindy begins clearing the table as McCluskey takes the phone and starts thumbing through its screens. Thirteen new voice mails, Aitch . . . Seven emails, all from him . . . Twenty-one texts . . .

Start with those, she says.

OK, here we are. He's sorry . . . sorry, he loves you . . . he loves you . . . please forgive him . . . he didn't know what to do . . . always wanted to make up for it . . . He didn't lie to you, he just didn't tell you everything—yeah, I've heard that a few times in my life, buddy boy . . . can't live without you . . . same . . . same . . . you make him a better version of himself—nice, I might steal that myself sometime . . . OK, and here's the last one, it says he's going to prove how much he loves you, says he loves you again, he needs you, yada yada.

Hannah feels as if Patrick has stolen part of her away, something missing now, nothing to stop the cold winds.

You want the emails as well? says McCluskey.

Sure, why not? she says. But only if he has anything new to say.

Oh, wait, says McCluskey, I just noticed the words *extremely urgent* in a message from someone called Jen. She's the one that was calling you, right?

OK, I'll take a look, she sighs, McCluskey handing over the phone.

> Extremely urgent we talk H. Keep trying but no answer. Just heard someone bought your old house on GMR. Only want u to hear this from me. Call right away. Pls pls PLEASE xxx

Hannah stands up. Just need to make a quick call, Mike, she says, stepping to the edge of the deck, the trees at the back of the property starting to blend together as the woodland fades into darkness, Hannah pressing the button to return Jen's call.

Jen answers right away—Hannah, thank God.

What's up, Jen?

Are you OK, Han? You sound odd. Is something going on?

Just tired, Jen. No, that's not true. But you go first.

Oh, Hannah, if there's anything wrong, I'm not sure . . .

Please, Jen, just . . . So what is it, they're going to knock down my old house and build a Target? Robert De Niro just moved in? What's so important?

A pause. And then Jen says to her, Oh, Hannah, please don't flip out. But Matthew Weaver bought it.

. . .

Hannah? Are you still there, Han?

. . .

Oh, Hannah? Please say something, honey.

What? Matthew? No!

It's true, Han, I'm so sorry. He changed his last name but it's definitely, definitely him.

. . .

Hannah?

Uh-huh.

Is Patch there? Are you with someone?

Patch? No. No, I've left him, Jen.

What? Oh my God, Hannah, what the hell happened?

He was there.

What? He was where?

Oh, sorry, I'll explain later. Sorry, I think I have to go now, Jen.

Hannah, I'm heading down to be with you as soon as I can. I can drop the girls at my mom's, I'll be on the bus in an hour.

No, Jen, don't.

Come on, Han, I'm your best friend.

I know, Jen, that's why I'm coming up to see you.

What? You haven't set foot in Roseborn since your family's funeral.

Then it's long overdue, right? Look, I'll get back to you, I have to go.

Oh, Hannah, I'm sorry, but I had to tell you.

I know you did, I know. See you soon, Jen.

———

MCCLUSKEY IS SMOKING A CIGARETTE, holding it between drags under the frosted-glass table like a schoolboy afraid of being caught by his parents.

I need you to take me to a car rental place, Mike.

He blows the smoke over his shoulder. What? he says. Are you fucking nuts, Aitch? Did something happen I don't know about?

Just take me, Mike, now. I'll tell you on the way.

Aitch, listen, you've been drinking like it's an Irish wake. Sit down, tell me about it and we'll work something out.

Then take me to the train station. Or call me a cab. I need to leave now, can you just fucking do it?

Whoa, whoa, Hannah, what's up? McCluskey hurriedly stubs out his cigarette and gets to his feet, but when he moves close, Hannah gestures for him to stay back.

Fine, take it easy, Aitch, all right? But you go anywhere, you got me for company, you understand?

OK then, OK, says Hannah, crossing her arms impatiently. But you need to bring your gun, Mike, she says.

Wait, was that your husband on the phone? says McCluskey. Did he threaten you, Aitch? McCluskey's body straightens as somewhere deep down his muscles start gathering.

No, nothing to do with him, Mike. Patch hasn't threatened me at all. It was an old friend. Can we just get moving?

McCluskey closes one eye and squints through the other. You're gonna have to help me out a bit more here, Aitch, he says, you know I'm a bit slow on the uptake.

Hannah starts raising her hand. We have to go and see the man who did this to me, she says, and when she points to her face, Hannah's finger is shaking.

And then Lindy comes out of the house, the noise of a sliding door puncturing the scene. Anyone for coffee? she says. Or we got Scotch if you wanna go in the other direction. Lindy turns quiet for a moment as she takes in the scene. Sorry, guys, she says, but did I miss something here?

———

SHOCK JOLTS HER AWAKE FROM the dream, Hannah opening her eye, not knowing where she is, what she's doing, her body fighting a rope, something pinning her down, someone . . . and McCluskey places his hand on her thigh. Aitch, hey, Hannah, it's OK, you fell asleep, we just turned off the thruway, you're safe, everything's all right, he says.

The seat belt is bunched in her fist as she looks out of the windshield, confused blinks gradually subsiding, the sunlight at a morning slant, and now Hannah remembers McCluskey and Lindy talking her out of doing anything last night, waking up with a hangover in New Jersey, can still feel it now, like a hot wire being fed into her brain, the pain spearing itself deeper, and then ebbing away.

The road looks vaguely familiar, the shades of green skirting it, the styles of the houses. Are we there? she says.

Not far, says McCluskey, maybe . . . the voice on his GPS interrupting him with an instruction to turn right . . . A couple more miles, he says. Sure I can't talk you out of this?

Which part, McCluskey, the bit where I confront him or the bit where you play chaperone? Because part two is negotiable.

Jesus, Aitch, I'm not fuckin happy about this.

Me neither, Mike. But maybe you can redirect your anger at the man who shot out my eye and just moved into my childhood home.

Now that she's fully awake, Hannah warms to the sense of being glassed in, the air from the vents blowing cool, the morning sunlight etching the road with sharp shadows, wires strung overhead between wooden poles casting skipping rope patterns, a series of arcs strung together at the edge of the asphalt.

And now she knows exactly where they are, although the bridge over the river looks different, Hannah remembering it being an aqueous shade of blue, sun-faded, rust-spotted, but now the bridge looks warm, repainted an autumnal red, and just before they cross it, she sees a sign has been erected, WELCOME TO ROSEBORN EST. 1843.

McCluskey drives slowly past a strip mall of newly built stores, the GPS again telling him where to turn, Hannah remembering the last time she was here, sixteen years ago, four holes and four coffins, the Swangum Ridge beaming miserably over the scene, Jen holding her up on one side, Max Reagan on the other.

OK, Aitch, says McCluskey, here are my conditions.

You don't get to make any conditions, Mike. You're the one who insisted on coming with me.

Hey, he says, louder, I'm going to say this in the nicest way possible. Fuck you, Aitch. Now listen up, because these are the *nonnegotiable* conditions.

Go on, then.

Numero uno, I'm the one talks to him. And numero two-oh, you stay inside the car.

No way, Mike, I have to be there, I have to hear what he says.

Goddammit, Aitch. Fine. Fine, then you stay at least ten feet behind me at all times, you understand?

Sure, Mike, she says.

Sure, Aitch? What does *sure* mean? Tell me one more time, so I believe you.

When we get there, I'm saying nothing, you do all the talking.

Praise be.

And then you're going to shoot him in the eye.

Jeez, Aitch, are you fuckin kidding me here?

Right, it's a joke, Mike. I'm displaying my awesome ability to retain a sense of humor despite a difficult situation.

McCluskey forms the stiffest smile he can muster. That's funny, Aitch. You're a regular clown.

Make a left up here, she says, reaching over the dash to turn off the GPS.

And they swing past O'Sullivan's Dive Inn, Hannah surprised that it's still standing, the car coasting down Grist Mill Road, the last quarter mile of the hill, and she points to the driveway. It's this one, she says, the models of the Brooklyn Bridge arches gone from the gateposts, new paving on the driveway, her parchment-colored home newly pale blue, and a large millstone leaning next to the front door, right where her dad used to sit in his rocker.

This is where you grew up? says McCluskey, almost whistling.

It looks a lot different now, she says.

Right, says McCluskey, so you weren't raised in a nineteenth-century mansion set in its own park?

That's right, Mike, I've led a charmed life, she says.

And McCluskey feels it, a change in the air like a small crack in the windshield, he turns to see Hannah staring straight ahead, and all he can see is her eyepatch.

Fuck, Aitch, he says. Look, I'm sorry. Lindy's always telling me I gotta turn it off sometimes.

That's OK, Mike, she says, you can leave it on around me.

And then Hannah notices the car parked on the far side of the house, black Mercedes, McCluskey turning the wheel sharply as they reach the end of the drive, the car pulling up with his side of the vehicle facing the house.

Don't forget, I do all the talking, you stay behind, says McCluskey, reaching under the driver's seat for his shoulder holster, slipping it on outside the car before taking his jacket from the backseat, and pulling it on while he examines the house, window by window.

MATTHEW

On Sunday, six days after that circus ride with my daddy to the banks of the Jakobskill River, I got on my bike a little after eleven in the morning and pedaled up to the Swangums. It felt odd without Tricky, no one to race up the hill, the climb twice as hard.

I left the bike behind Split Rock, walked the short distance to the parking lot and took the red-blazed trail that led down to Lake Swangum.

When I arrived at the place we'd arranged to meet, you were already there, perched on a rock looking out over the view. Before then I'd only ever seen you in your Conservancy gear, tan slacks and green shirt, but that day you were kitted out in red corduroy shorts and a cream cable-knit sweater. You had on old leather hiking boots and gray camp socks with blue stripes at the top. I remember every detail.

I was about to say hello when you put your finger to your lips (although I couldn't really see them through your beard), and then made a gesture to close my eyes, which I did.

Listen! you whispered to me.

It took me a while to retune myself, but then, piece by piece, I started to hear the world. Lake water sloshing, the drift of the breeze—a sound similar to my breath—a woodpecker hammering somewhere far off. Then I noticed something else, an odd-seeming sound as if rain were falling, even though I could feel sunlight on my face and was certain the sky had been scattered with nothing more than a few wisps of cloud when I closed my eyes.

What do you hear, Matthew? you said.

Sounds like raindrops, I said, opening my eyes.

You smiled and pointed over our heads. It's a cottonwood, you said.

I looked up at the tree, its leaves clattering like paddles, and then you said, Cottonwood's the only tree that makes that sound, turns the air into water. But that's trees and you're interested in rocks and glaciers, right?

I don't mind learning all sorts of stuff, I said.

Really? You must enjoy school then.

No, not much, I said.

Me neither, you said, never did. That kind of learning doesn't suit everyone.

Not me, I said.

Well, why would it? you said, starting to get animated. You sit on the same school bus every day so that you can enter through the same door into the same box. They tell you where you'll be every minute, even give you a buzzer that trains you like a dog with a dinner bell. You take the same path between the same boxes. How's that supposed to teach you anything beyond how to walk along a painted line? You think your brain enjoys that? Your brain that evolved out on the wild plains of Africa learning how to cheat death every day? Not mine, no thank you.

This all sounded like it might be true, but I didn't know what to say right away and when you saw me dumbstruck, you let out a huge laugh. Those were the only times I'd see your teeth through your beard, when you laughed, and the perfect flash of them always felt like a secret reward.

I remember your beard being mostly dark apart from a few gray hairs, and your hair was brown without showing any age at all. You were a few years older than my daddy, but anyone would have put the two of you the other way round. You had a glow to you, not just the outdoorsman tan but a wilderness energy as well.

(I have a friend, Andrew, who saw a photo of you taken when you were older and he claims you're the spit of the actor Lee Marvin. He even made me watch *Paint Your Wagon* to prove his point.)

You pulled something out of your backpack, a brown paper bag, and shook it at me. It's trail mix, you said. Homemade. You want some?

What's trail mix? I said.

You don't know what trail mix is? It's for energy. Nuts and raisins. I like to put in some dried coconut as well.

Shit no, I said. Sounds disgusting.

You let out another huge laugh. Don't worry, you said, I'll add M&M's next time.

Sure, I said, and take out all the other shit.

You gave me a look like I was as remarkable as the cottonwood tree. OK then, you said, rocks and glaciers, that's why we're here, right? Let's get started. But first, I have a question for you, Matthew. And remember, there are no wrong answers here. Now, what would you call the thing I'm sitting on here? you said, giving the rock beneath you a hard rap with your knuckles.

This felt like one of those trick questions where the obvious answer is *a rock* and by saying it I would have fallen for the trick. Well, I wasn't planning to go along with any tricks so I said, If there are no wrong answers, then that there's a motorcycle.

You actually looked pleased at my sass, I couldn't believe it. Very well, you said, let's just go with that. How about if I told you that this rock did in fact ride over here, just like a motorcycle might, from miles and miles away? I mean, look around you, how else did it get here, Matthew? We're almost at the highest point in the Swangums. There are no peaks nearby that this rock could have rolled down from. So how on earth do you think it might have traveled here?

Maybe by glacier? I said.

You gave me a look of astonishment. Hell's bells, you said, that's exactly right. And how did the glacier get it here?

Honestly, I said, I don't even know what a glacier is. But you mentioned rocks and glaciers, so . . .

So you deduced it, you said, beaming at me so hard I felt like I'd performed a complicated feat of algebra. Look, you said, a glacier's just a river of ice. And twenty-one thousand years ago, during the time we call the Ice Age, there was a glacier right over our heads. Now, you said, how far from the edge of town would you say we are?

Maybe a mile, I said.

Sounds about right, you said. And that's about how high the ice would've been over your head back then. Imagine a mile-deep river of ice pressing down on you.

Sounds like sitting through math, I said.

Exactly, you said, or being made to play football.

But I don't get the bit about the river, I said. A glacier sounds more like the North Pole than a river.

Right, you said, because of ice being solid. So you'd think it doesn't move much. But oh, it was a river all right, there's just a difference in the speed of flow. See, a glacier's so heavy it can't help but move. The weight of the thing, gravity, keeps that huge pile of ice chugging along—but slowly, of course. Most glaciers creep forward maybe three to five feet each day, although some can move up to a hundred feet. Can you imagine living in Roseborn with a mile-high river of ice bearing down on you?

Five feet a day? I said. I think I could probably outrun it. But a river of ice does sound cool.

Pleased to hear it, you said. So let's get back to this motorcycle I'm sitting on. This here Harley-Davidson of a rock was picked up by the glacier, probably ripped clean off the edge of a mountain, and carried along until one day, about sixteen thousand years ago, all the ice that was above us finally melted and this rock was dropped, literally like a stone, right here, miles away from home. And what if I told you this rock came from somewhere yonder in that direction? you said, pointing over your shoulder where I could see the distant humps of the Catskill Mountains. How do you think I might have deduced that?

I had a quick think and couldn't work out the answer, so instead I tried out a joke I'd often heard people in town making about the folks who lived in the Catskills. Maybe you heard it married its sister, I said. (If I'd said anything like this in school it was called mouthing off and I'd land in detention.)

You cracked a smile and said, Well, who knows, maybe it did marry its sister, although that sounds like an odd thing for a motorcycle, no? I think you might be mixing your metaphors just a little. But take a look around, Matthew, perhaps there's another clue somewhere around here. Hey, tell me, what's that down there between your legs? you said, before quickly adding, Now don't get all clever with me this time, I mean down on the ground right under your feet.

I grinned and looked down. There was a line in the rock there. It's a big crack, I said, making myself snigger.

No, look again, you said, trying not to laugh along with me.

OK, a huge scratch? I said, laughing again, although I'm not sure what was funny about that.

Exactly, you said, recovering yourself, that's a scratch. And, from where you're standing, where does that scratch point? Let's try and be serious for a moment.

The same direction you were pointing, I said.

So what if I told you that the glacier made that scratch? you said. How do you think that might have happened?

Fingernails? I said, trying to be funny again.

Well, actually that's not completely wrong, you said. The glacier did sort of have thousands and thousands of fingernails, sharp objects that made scratches like the one at your feet. And now you've seen one, you'll start noticing them everywhere up here. Some people call them scars, although personally I like footprints. But the proper name for them is striations.

Stri-ay-shuns, I repeated.

And what made those striations weren't nails exactly, they were something called cobbles, which is just a fancy technical name for a size of rock. A cobble's between about this big and this big, you said. When you placed your index fingers about three inches apart, and then widened the gap to an impressive ten, I couldn't help it, I started laughing all over again.

You looked down at the space between your fingers and started to shake your head, even though I could tell you were amused. Now how am I supposed to teach you anything when you're just being lewd? you said.

Look, I said, I get it. The cobble's like a fingernail, the glacier's a hand and this rock under my feet's like a table that got all scratched up.

Couldn't have put it any better myself, you said, looking proud of me. I shrugged like it was nothing, despite the warmth spreading inside me, and then you said, See how smooth the bedrock looks down there around your feet?

The rock did look smooth, sunlight glittering from its glassy surface. Right, it's kind of shiny, I said.

Remember you told me you call this place the beach? you said. Well, that's an interesting name, because it's sand made that rock shiny. As well as hauling off boulders and dragging cobbles there's a lot of sandy stuff at the bottom of a glacier. So as it passed over this place, the glacier kept on rubbing at the rock here, like it was buffing it up with very fine grit sandpaper. That's known as glacial polishing. And this boulder I'm sitting on right here has a fancy technical name as well—besides Harley the Motorcycle. This rock is known as an *erratic*—that's a boulder that's been carried from one place to someplace else by a glacier. Pretty impressive, huh? But this boulder right here is nothing. Do you want to see a properly large glacial erratic?

I nodded.

Shall we take the trails, you said, or would you rather go the cool way?

The cool way, I said.

You jumped down from the rock. I don't know, you said shaking your paper bag at me, I'm not sure you have enough energy in you to handle the cool way.

I rolled my eyes, took a handful of the trail mix, and popped it in my mouth.

The cool way's a rock scramble, you said, pushing up the

sleeves of your sweater. So what do you think then? you said, shaking your bag of trail mix again.

I closed one of my eyes like I was giving my answer some serious thought. Yep, I said, really does taste like shit.

AS WE WALKED THE MILE or so to the start of the rock scramble, you told me more stories about the glacier and asked me all about my life. When I told you I'd grown up in Queens, you got excited and told me that Long Island didn't even exist until the glacier started melting and left behind a big pile of sand and rocks at its snout end—that pile was Long Island.

The place where you grew up, you said, is nothing more than glacial nosebleed.

Then you told me how you could see the same kind of striations down in New York City, Central Park, same glacier, same footprints. Had I ever been?

Manhattan? Hell no. My daddy had come back from Times Square one time and said it was *nothin but hookers and skin flicks*.

Finally we got to a cliff with a mess of rocks piled up high against its face. It must have been a hundred feet or more, the cliff cresting darkly against the pale sky, and you told me that technically it wasn't a cliff at all but an escarpment, before pointing to the summit. Now we go up, you said.

How? I asked.

That's the great thing, you said, there's no correct way. No straight lines either, you added, you have to figure it out for yourself.

I paused for just a moment, as if faced with an impossible problem, and with that you were gone, bounding up the rocks with so much vigor it looked as though someone had taken a movie of a ball bouncing down some stairs and then played the tape backward.

I followed as fast as I could, uncertainly at first, not being able to figure out the best place for my feet, but soon I started to get the hang of it. Sometimes you pushed with your legs, sometimes you pulled with your arms, the rocks meshed together like a giant puzzle, like nature had set you a perfect challenge.

Halfway up, you were sitting on a flat-topped boulder, munching away on your trail mix. You good to keep going? you said.

I was drenched in sweat and had scraped half the skin off an elbow, but still I gave you a look like your question didn't even make sense, springing past the flank of your rock to take the lead.

That lasted about thirty seconds. Your cable-knit sweater swept past me in a blur.

When I got to the top, panting like a dog, you looked like you were ready to do the whole thing over again. You were standing by a tree, peeling the bark from a twig.

Smell that, you said, handing me the twig.

I gave it a good sniff. Smells like mint, I said.

It's black birch, you said, nodding at the tree. What you're smelling there is the same thing that gives chewing gum and Listerine their flavor.

Cottonwood and black birch, glaciers and striations, if they'd told me any of this stuff at school I couldn't have cared less.

So how do you feel now? you said.

Out of breath, I said, but also . . . I paused, trying to map out my feelings. I wasn't sure I could put it into words, I just started to smile.

Feels good, doesn't it? you said. Kind of like all the lights just got turned on in your brain.

It feels amazing, I said. It feels nearly as good as . . .

Whoa! you said. You say anything lewd, young man, and I'm knocking you straight back down to the bottom of the cliff.

I looked over my shoulder, not quite believing how far I'd climbed, and then said, in my best wiseass voice, I think you'll find that technically it's called an escarpment.

Your beard cracked wide open.

I can't think of a time in my life when I ever felt better than that.

ROSEBORN, NEW YORK, 2008

McCluskey is sweating even before he reaches the front door.

Stepping onto the porch, he mops the back of his neck with a handkerchief, and he sees the doorbell but reaches for the knocker anyway, swinging it hard three times before taking two steps back, angling his body, gun-bearing side nearest the house.

The temperature is rising by the second, Hannah's dress already starting to cling to her body, the mounting heat reminding her of another day in August, twenty-six years ago, and when the door opens up, it swings wide, as if thrown open by her father to welcome family or guests, *between a rock and Earhart Place.*

And there he is, Matthew.

The air rushes into her chest, Matthew Weaver, Matthew dressed as if he is about to head off to church, a fresh white shirt tucked into blue pants, his shirtsleeves rolled up past his elbows, *just like Patch,* she thinks briefly, and then Matthew glances at her, nothing more than half a look, but he knows who she is, no hint of surprise, almost as if he's been waiting for her.

McCluskey gives him a few moments to take in the scene, and then a few more, let the suspect be the one to start talking, judge the guy by his first move, but Matthew says nothing, and everyone just stands there, as if waiting for the heat of the sunshine to kindle the conversation, Hannah feeling as if she might burst into flames on the spot.

Eventually McCluskey lets out a brief snort, an amused admission of defeat, and begins. Matthew Weaver?

Used to be, says Matthew.

Oh yeah? says McCluskey. And I used to be a tight end. So what?

It's Denby now.

McCluskey sniffs disinterestedly. OK then Matthew Who-Gives-a-Fuck, my name's Detective McCluskey, he says, taking his badge from an inside pocket, holding it steady and a little too close to Matthew's face, Matthew not altering the track of his gaze, still staring straight at McCluskey.

You can put away the badge, Detective, says Matthew. I know what police look like.

Yeah, I heard you spent some quality time with a few colleagues.

That was many, many years ago, says Matthew.

We don't change all that much, says McCluskey. Anyway, I'm just saying who I am so you know who you're dealing with. This visit isn't exactly official.

Matthew folds his arms, and leans on the doorframe. So you're telling me I could close the door right now and you'd have to go away?

Whistling a merry fuckin tune, says McCluskey.

I don't mind talking to you, says Matthew.

That's great, says McCluskey, I never did learn how to whistle.

Matthew leans forward and laughs. What is this, Detective? The preamble? The softening-up period?

Nah, says McCluskey, this is the bit where I'm assessing your character using my many years of experience dealing with dangerous criminals.

And?

It ain't good news.

Because?

Because unfortunately I don't think I can scare you, says McCluskey. You don't seem like the nervous type.

And why would that be bad news?

Usually you just frighten someone and you don't have to shoot them.

Shooting me would be an issue, Detective?

Yeah, unfortunately. Unless you'd be good enough to come at me with a weapon—see, I only ever shot this one guy and he'd just killed his wife and baby boy and then came charging at me, head down, with a bloody machete.

I guess kills don't come much cleaner, Detective.

Right. Luck of the Irish.

So you never had cause to shoot anyone innocent?

Not so far. Bad for the pension. In most cases.

Then I'll take my chances with you, Detective McCluskey.

McCluskey tucks his fingers into the front pockets of his pants and starts tapping a foot. You understand why I'm here, of course, right?

Matthew purses his lips, bobs his head. I'd say I could probably guess.

Yeah, well this ain't *Family Feud*, so I'm thinking I should spell it out, just in case.

I can do it for you, Detective. *H-A-N-N-A-H*.

Fuckin A, Matthew Weaver. Now just add the words *stay away from* and we're good to go.

Matthew unfolds his arms and puts one of his hands in a pocket. And yet there she is, he says. On my lawn.

McCluskey blows out hard, running a hand over his mouth, as if fighting to keep something down. Your lawn? he says. That's what you said, no? *Your? Lawn?*

That's right, Detective. Legally speaking, it's my lawn.

Right, and I'm legally speaking's biggest fan, fuckin trust me. However, you can see how it comes across, your choice of property, right? You know, bearing in mind your criminal record.

Matthew raises a hand, holds it over his heart. Detective McCluskey, he says, you have my word that I will stay away from Hannah Jensen.

McCluskey claps his palm to the back of his neck as if swatting an insect, can already feel the sting of the heat. And I should believe you exactly why? he says.

Because otherwise you'll shoot me, says Matthew. I thought we'd already reached an understanding on that front.

We did? says McCluskey. Well, that's just great. You see, sometimes I say things and people don't listen, and I got this foul fuckin temper.

I don't want to upset you, Detective.

Considerate guy. Who knew this would be so easy?

Matthew lowers his chin, drops his gaze to the ground, and then, looking quickly back up again, says, But if Hannah ever wants to come to see me, of course . . . He lets the sentence trail away, punctuating its end with a shrug.

McCluskey can feel the heat stirring inside of him now as the sunlight pierces his suit, penetrates his skin, McCluskey feeling like there's something swarming inside, his voice rising quickly to threat level, Now you listen to me, fuck-hole, I know exactly what's happening here . . .

I doubt that very much, Detective.

. . . no more fuckin games, he warns. I've dealt with your type—psychopaths, bullies, whack jobs, lowlifes—every type of fuckin type, you understand? And I win, Matthew Weaver. I always win. And you know why?

But Matthew doesn't answer, doesn't even seem to be listening, just starts to move his head, turning it to look at her, McCluskey slapping the doorframe . . . *Eyes back on me, get your eyes the fuck back on me* . . . turning his head to meet her eye for a second, two seconds . . . *Or so help me, I'll fuckin drop you right now* . . . and having held her gaze, having taken her in, he opens his mouth, and he says to her, Hannah, I'm sorry.

The words seem to shatter something unseen in the air.

McCluskey stops, everything stops, there is only the chirring of insects.

And then, when Hannah opens her mouth, the words come out loud. Shoot him, she cries, why don't you shoot him? And then she is running, her anger aflame and unquenchable, running for McCluskey, not knowing why, not even wondering why, and when she gets within reach, McCluskey catches her, wrapping her up in his arms, Hannah struggling against the mass of his flesh, but she can fight for only a moment, and soon she surrenders, nothing left, only McCluskey saying her name over and over, hoisting her into his arms and carrying her off, nothing left.

MATTHEW

Hannah's thirteenth birthday was on a Thursday, four days after I'd met you down by Lake Swangum. How is it I remember the exact day so well? It's because that was the day Hannah kissed me. I imagine you thought the giving and receiving of birthday kisses was supposed to take place the other way around. Me too.

I'd almost befriended Hannah a few months earlier, and I can't remember exactly what happened, but it hadn't worked out. I don't recall feeling spurned, it was just one of those things, but perhaps in trying to make friends with her, I'd planted some kind of seed. Certainly Hannah wanting to kiss me came as a complete surprise at the time.

The first thing that happened was that Jen, Hannah's friend, got Tricky out of the way. It was nearly the end of the school day and Tricky was dumping books in his locker when Jen approached us, Hannah half a step behind, and said she wanted to talk to Patch. After that, Jen led him away by the hand—*by the hand!* I can still picture the way Tricky trudged away down the hallway, all stiff-armed and stiff-legged, his ears lit up like taillights.

Hi, Matthew, said Hannah.

Hannah, what's up?

It's my birthday today.

Happy birthday. I didn't get you anything.

That's OK, don't worry about it.

Why would I worry about it?

At this point, Hannah glanced off into the distance, where I'm fairly certain she saw one of Christie's cohorts, Tammy whatever-her-name-was. Hey, come with me, she said, walking off down the hallway.

I hesitated a moment—not because I wasn't intrigued, but because I didn't like being told what to do. Finally intrigue won the battle and I went after her, Hannah twenty steps ahead and flashing me coy over-the-shoulder looks. She stopped at the front doors to school, checked to see if there were any teachers around, and slipped outside.

When I followed her out, Hannah was on the top step, right next to the doors. Her back was against the wall and she was inviting me closer with a come-hither finger. For once I did exactly as I was told and Hannah reached up to pull me down, a look of shock on her face as if she couldn't believe what she was doing, and we kissed.

It was interesting. Kissing Hannah wasn't at all like kissing Christie—drier, but not too dry, and with less of the mouth-circling and tongue-thrusting that formed the basis of Christie's washing-machine-like technique. I liked the innocence of Hannah's kiss, I liked the way it was slow and yet keen, nervous and gentle. I opened my eyes for a moment as our lips remained pressed, Hannah's face a picture of beauty—but at the same time there was a complete innocence to her allure, Hannah having no idea of her feminine power. The look on her face was one of wanting only to please, and also a kind of focus, as if Hannah were desperate not to make a mistake, as if this kiss were nothing but giving. I closed my eyes again and enjoyed every second.

When we emerged from the fog of that kiss, Tammy whatever-her-name-was was standing close by, openmouthed, her shock exposing a pink wad of bubble gum wedged between her gums and her teeth. Oh my God, she said, when I tell her about this, Christie's gonna shit!

I frowned at her. That would be an odd reaction, I said.

You total, total dick, Matthew, said Tammy, scurrying back through the doors.

I turned to Hannah, who looked amused, although I didn't realize I'd said anything funny. *An odd reaction?* she said, bursting out laughing.

I liked the way she looked, laughing like that, and I wanted to kiss her again. Hurting Hannah was the thing furthest from my mind in that moment, but still, that's exactly what happened, because when Hannah stopped laughing, she said to me, So, Matthew, does this mean you're my boyfriend now? And instead of simply saying yes, a response that would have led to the most preferable outcome, unfortunately I hesitated. In fact, more than that, I'm fairly certain my body made some kind of recoiling-in-disgust motion.

I felt bad right away, I wasn't actually hesitating at the idea of spending more time with Hannah, romantically, and I wish I could have explained that to her at the time. Only the trouble was, I didn't understand it myself, that what was in fact causing me to recoil was something bound up in the abstract concept of language, because now that I'm older, I can see very clearly what the problem was—the word *boyfriend*.

Boyfriend, what an unappealing and sickeningly childish label, no? Labels in general have always made me feel queasy—it's just like I remember you saying to me one time, Pete, labels are for soup cans—but when it comes to the language of dating (*date* is another word that jabs at my gag reflex) the naming of things starts to become especially sickening. *Boyfriend, girlfriend, going steady, going out with, sweethearts, wooing, courtship* . . . Did someone come up with these belittling terms while they were in kindergarten? Shouldn't they be written in crayon?

However, the extreme discomfort I feel when it comes to the infantilizing language of . . . *dating* . . . has nothing to do with a fear of commitment. Think about the words we use for the committed. *Husband* and *wife*. And we talk about *marriage, wedlock, ceremony, union*. These might be labels, but at least they're strong words, the sort of language appropriate for adults. None of these terms make me want to throw up in the nearest trash can. (Although I will admit the word *nuptials* does strange things to my stomach.) Perhaps in that moment if Hannah had asked me to marry her, although I might not have said yes, at least I would have given the question some serious thought.

Only I couldn't have explained any of this to Hannah at the time. I just knew there was something about the word *boyfriend* that made me flinch. So when she said it, I hesitated, and then recoiled—it's also not completely impossible that I looked repulsed.

Hannah marched straight past me, looking ashamed, hurt, and confused.

Hey, Hannah, come back, I called out.

She threw open the doors and ran back into school.

I FELT BAD ABOUT THAT, I truly did. I kept thinking about the look on Hannah's face and being the cause of her pain made me feel uncomfortable, so the next day at school I decided to swallow my distaste for the word. I would walk up to Hannah the moment she got off the school bus, take a deep, fortifying breath, and offer to be her *boyfriend*.

Which was a perfectly good plan, except for the fact that when Hannah's school bus disgorged its morning contents, I saw Jen skipping down its steps but no Hannah.

Hey, Jen, where's Hannah?

You're disgusting, Matthew Weaver.

What?

You're a filthy old snake, said Jen.

Jen, I have no idea what you're talking about.

She's sick at home. She has mono.

So?

The kissing disease!

What's that got to do with me?

You kissed her.

I didn't kiss Hannah, she kissed me. And anyway, I haven't got mono.

You're a rat, a weasel. A pig!

OK, Jen. Any other animals you'd like to add to the list?

Creep!

I shrugged and headed off to find Tricky.

MEANWHILE, CHRISTIE'S RESPONSE TO THE news of my cheating lips had been, first of all, to instantly banish me from her affections—*so dumped* was the actual phrase, the message coming via a couple of her best shrews—and, secondly, to spread word around school that I was a fag.

However, there was nothing in any way insightful about Christie's choice of rumor, this was just one of the fashionable insults back then, *fag, dick, pussy, wimp, wuss, suck shit, bite me* . . . I never even understood what the last of those means. Not that anyone dared call me a fag to my face, but for a few weeks at school I could sense the word on everyone's lips. It really didn't trouble me at all.

Soon it became increasingly clear that mono had hit Hannah pretty hard because she was away from school for four whole weeks, and while I wouldn't say that Hannah and that kiss vanished completely from my thoughts during that time, my feelings about her certainly started to fade, because the better I got to know you, Pete, seeing you up there in the Swangums, surrounded by the evidence of things that had happened tens of thousands of years ago, the older and more out of place I felt around people who were supposedly of a similar age to me.

It started to feel as if the other children at school, already young-seeming anyway, were getting older only in single-year increments, while I was aging in geological aeons, and although I remained friends with Tricky, he seemed even less ready to bloom into the world than Hannah. However, on Saturdays he and I would still head up to the Swangums on our bikes together. For a while I tried to teach him about rocks and glaciers, only Tricky, it quickly became clear, wasn't at all interested in the deeper meaning of rocks, no matter how hard I tried to educate him. He still wanted to play all the childish games we'd invented, Tarzan, Houdini, and Deer Patrol.

It was my Sundays that now meant everything to me, those Sundays when you and I would meet up at the beach, you already occupying your spot when I arrived, perched up on that glacial erratic, which we'd taken to calling Harley—*Harley at noon? Sure, Harley's good. See you at Harley.* Every time we met you'd ask me, with an amused grin, How was school this week? To which I'd answer, I got named Scholar of the Week, or, I aced the history test, or something like that, and then you'd jump off the rock, chuckling, and offer me some trail mix, and the first few times I rooted around your paper bag, eyed my pickings suspiciously and then, without eating so much as a peanut, heaved the whole fistful out into the lake. Eventually you stopped offering and just gave me an amused grin every time as you fished around in the bag for a small fistful of food, and after that we'd hike and scramble and you'd teach me about everything we saw, mountain spleenwort, hemlock trees, yellowthroats, bunchberry, the name of the nubbly rock up there, Swangum conglomerate, quartz and more quartz, tougher than granite.

I remember you pointing to a deep gouge off the trail, a quarry, you told me, explaining that Swangum conglomerate, tougher than granite, was perfect for making millstones back in the day. All of the millstones for hundreds of miles around had been carved from those rocks, but now they were only good for yard ornaments or marking the entrance of the park in town, those two stones having been taken from a mill that once sat at the end of Grist Mill Road. This is before the cement industry came along, you told me.

A few days ago, driving over to New Paltz, I saw one of those millstones being used as a yard ornament, just like you'd said twenty-six years ago. I stopped the car, knocked on the door, and offered the man who lived there five hundred dollars on the spot. I know it was foolish to think that the sight of a millstone might cure you, or at least provide a jolt that would start to bring everything back, but right now I'd try anything to have you the way you once were.

I remember the day we scrambled down Devil's Ladder by Jakobskill Falls to the place where the water thundered down into the plunge pool, and you told me how you could make rainbows dance over the wet rocks by moving your head around. Nature's disco club, you said, and I laughed at you. Disco club? When's the last time you went for a night out, Pete, 1975? And you said, What? That's only seven years ago. And I said, Right, that's exactly what an old man would say.

You flashed your teeth at me. You always liked it when I teased you.

For those first few months we spent together, I suppose I thought of you as something like a teacher—although I respected you, so perhaps *guide* or *mentor* might be the better word. I certainly had a sense that, whenever you taught me something, whenever we hiked through the mountains, or especially when we scrambled the rocks, you were helping me to find my own path in life, enabling me to blaze a trail that school would never reveal to me, something I could never have learned from my parents. This was my awakening into the world, my becoming an adult, or maybe just becoming myself. After that first rock scramble you'd noticed the look of wonder on my face, how it was like lights turning on in my brain, and that's how it was every week, every Sunday, new flashes and clusters, little galaxies of existence bursting to life.

What was becoming clear to me was that I didn't have to be like everybody else, and that was the best lesson you taught me, I was just fine as myself.

WE WERE SITTING ON A boulder downstream of the falls, you munching your trail mix, me breathing the good air, when I realized how you always asked questions about me, but I didn't know much about you. So I said to you, Pete, are you married?

Not up to this point, you said.

What do you do when you're not here? I said. Watch TV? Go
to the movies?

Mostly read, you said. I like learning on my own, I like books.
Magazines as well, *National Geographic, Time*. Read the Bible
every day.

The Bible?

Sure, that surprises you? You're not from a religious family?

Mom takes us to church sometimes. But not much.

And how do you like church?

About zero percent.

Well, church can be a whole lot like school. There's nothing
wrong with learning, it's just that most of the teachers fail their
subjects. But that's just my two cents.

You don't go to church?

No, sir.

That felt funny, you calling me sir. Funny but I liked it.

You thought things over for a while, staring off into the falls,
and eventually you said to me, Pews are just more of life's boxes,
Matthew, and then there's an aisle, so you have two sets of boxes
divided by a straight line. My parents were Quakers, but even the
most informal meetings never sat well with me. So now I wouldn't
know which church to go to—Catholic, Episcopalian, Method-
ist, Lutheran . . . What's the point? Labels are for soup cans, Matthew. But I do read the Bible and I believe in God, even though
I'm not sure the God I believe in is the one I'm reading about.
But it's a wise book, for sure. I like to think the Bible gets most
things right—I let it guide me, although I wouldn't say I let it rule
me. So I read, I think about what I've read, I come up here, and
here's where I hear God's word, beneath the tall sky. I never heard
a single utterance of God anyplace with a roof. But maybe that's
just me and it doesn't matter what I think. What do you think,
Matthew?

I don't believe in God. And church is a crock.

That's a valid opinion as well.

You don't want to talk me into it?

Nope.

We looked at the rainbows some more and I put my hand in your paper bag, which you'd left beside us on a rock. When I pulled out a small handful of trail mix it was studded brightly with M&M's. Hey, I said, you never told me.

You never asked, kid.

It tasted way better with chocolate. After I'd munched through a couple of fistfuls, I told you it had given me enough energy to scramble back up Devil's Ladder. Boosted by candy, I climbed twice as fast, but you still beat me to the top, and then we agreed—same time, same place, next week.

One day later, Hannah hopped off the school bus, all fresh-faced and peppy, six weeks of school left to go, six weeks before Hannah would tip my life over the edge, sending me to a place where there could be only one way, one choice of direction—down.

ROSEBORN,
NEW YORK, 2008

Hannah is beside him in the front seat, her meltdown somewhere in the post-thermonuclear phase now, McCluskey wondering which way he should turn at the end of the driveway, left or right?

Yeah, shit couldn't have gone any better than that, Mikey, he thinks.

He heads left, back the way they came in, seeing O'Sullivan's bar at the top of the hill, pulling into the parking lot, lights off inside, neon unlit, the clock on the dash reading 9:09, several hours until opening, shame, Hannah could do with something. Shit, he could do with something. Temperature on the dash already reads eighty-five.

He puts his hand on her shoulder, Hannah having reached the deep-breathing stage, just about ready to talk.

Hey, Aitch, he says, giving her shoulder a squeeze. What happened back there—don't worry about it, OK?

One final breath, her head tilting back. Sorry, Mike, she says, I'm sorry, I just lost it.

Nah, I seen a lot worse at closing time, he says.

She wipes her face. Yeah, well no one forced you to live in New Jersey, she says, letting out a wet snort at the end.

Laughing at your own jokes, Aitch, he says, patting her shoulder three times. I guess you're all fuckin better then.

King of the world, Mike, she says, putting her hand on top of his. And by the way, McCluskey, you have my permission to run a million miles now. Just drop me off at my friend's and don't ever look back, OK?

Nah, he says, don't worry. I'm Team Aitch all the way.

SHE CALLS HER FRIEND TO let her know they're en route, and directs him through town, the place full of climbers with colorful ropes, belts heavy with clips, morning coffees in hand, stark ridge in the distance.

As they pull up beside the house, two girls come running out the front door. The big one's Katie and the little one's Lizzy, says Hannah, unbuckling her belt, getting out of the car, and then squatting to receive the girls' greetings as they fling themselves around her like horseshoes, the girls' mother standing in the doorway, beaming at the scene.

Say it, Aunt Hannah, squeals Katie, say it, say it.

Say it, *pleeease*, says Lizzy.

OK then, says Hannah, snapping the elastic of her eyepatch, and then whispering it conspiratorially, Why are pirates called pirates?

And then they all shriek the punch line together.

Because they *arrrr*.

Arrrr, repeats Hannah.

Arrrr, the girls growl, making pirate arms as each of them covers a tiny left eye with a tiny left hand.

Who's that man, Aunt Hannah? says Katie, pointing at the car, McCluskey still in the driver's seat, lowering the window.

He's a police detective from New York City.

Are you in trouble? says Lizzy.

Nooo, you know I'm a good pirate, right?

I have an arrest warrant, says McCluskey, leaning out of the car. The suspects are about yay high and yay high, he says, his hand jumping Lizzy-tall to Katie-height.

Oh no, says Hannah. Wanted dead or alive! A pair of salty sea dogs.

I'm not salty, says Lizzy, I'm sweet.

I'm not a dog, I'm a cat, says Katie, making kitten paws.

Are these suspects dangerous, Detective McCluskey? Hannah calls over her shoulder.

Yeah, exceedingly, says McCluskey. I gotta handcuff them immediately, he growls.

The girls look at each other, Katie tagging her little sister on the arm and squealing, This one's chief pirate, as she starts running away, and then they are both running, running and screaming back to their mother.

Hannah stands up and turns to him. Are you leaving, Mike? she says. I told you it's OK, you can go. Jen'll look after me.

Nah, I'm coming back, says McCluskey. There's just this one thing I gotta do, he says, scratching his ear.

I'll see you soon then, says Hannah.

Yeah, soonish, he says, winding up the window.

HE DRIVES BACK THROUGH TOWN, Roseborn seeming like a pretty nice hood, decent place to raise a family, nature and shit. McCluskey scratches his ear again, because he can't scratch the voice, the voice that doesn't give half a crap about the town, couldn't care less about family-friendly, because all the voice is concerned with is *the right thing to do.*

He lowers the window, pulls out a cigarette from the packet in the cup holder and lights it.

Yeah, *the right thing to do,* that's a good one, almost as funny as *I got your back.*

Oh right, you got my back? Doesn't that imply I'm going in first, then? You know what? How about you got my front here? Or maybe just one of my sides? No, better still, how about I stay here, drink a coffee with my feet up on the desk, and you can take care of whatever kinda shit's going down?

Only here's the problemo. That wouldn't be *the right thing to do.*

Jesus, he hates that whiny-assed voice.

Makes a left at the turn, maybe O'Sullivan's might be charitable enough to be open next time he passes, because what McCluskey has somehow stumbled upon here is one hell of a setup, or what might be known as a five-alarm shitstorm.

And yet the voice is still there. *You're Team Aitch, you stand by her. It's a little something called loyalty, buddy boy.*

When he arrives this time, he leaves his gun under the seat before stepping out of the car, no need for a jacket to cover his holster a second time, and he ditches the thing on the driver's seat.

Matthew is cleaning dirt from the millstone on the porch, brushing its furrows with a dish towel. Detective McCluskey, he calls out. Welcome back, he says, standing up, wiping his hands on the towel. Come in, come in, Detective, says Matthew, beckoning. Celeste is making pancakes. You like pancakes?

MATTHEW

Straight off the school bus, Hannah's first day back after her mono-enforced absence, Jen gave me a threatening look, while Hannah flashed me a tentative smile. This didn't happen often, but at that moment I was paralyzed by indecision because, not knowing when Hannah would be back, I hadn't formulated a plan for this scenario.

I called out to her—something bland like, *Hey, Hannah, glad to see you're all better*—then turned and ran up the steps into school. It was just a delaying tactic, I've never been much of a liar. A good lie has to be premeditated—my first instinct is always to say what I think.

I suppose at that point I must have had some sense I was falling for you, Pete, because I knew that I wanted to keep Hannah at arm's length—and yet I didn't want to reject her completely. Not only did I still feel bad about what had happened in the aftermath of our kiss, I was also, let's not forget, a pubescent boy bursting with hormones. However, not pushing Hannah away, while not inviting her closer, seemed like an impossible task.

It was Hannah who provided the solution. When I went to my locker at lunchtime, I found that a note had been slipped inside, a message from Hannah signed off with only her name and no kisses, the words as tentative as her earlier smile, something banal about being happy to be back at school—evidently we weren't meant to be together—and thanking me for saying I was glad she was better. Clearly, Hannah was waiting for me to make the next move.

I nudged one of my pieces carefully forward, replying to her note with one of my own. Something like, *Hi Hannah, sorry you were sick, I was really happy to get your message.* (No word of a lie.)

And so it began, the trading of secret messages back and forth, Hannah leaving notes in my locker, slips of paper adorned with drawings of flowers, birds, and bumblebees (but never love hearts). Some of the messages would recount to me the travails of her difficult teenage life (older brothers, an annoying mother, boohoo), never mentioning the great hardship of being from the richest family in town. Others told me about her desire to escape Roseborn and her longing to visit exotic places like Japan.

In return I wrote her about my adventures with Tricky in the mountains and she replied that she'd been up to the Swangums only once, that her mother had spotted a suspected patch of poison ivy and ran screaming back to the car. Next I switched to family stuff, writing about how my mom was an Italian-American from Corona, Queens, and that she worked at the Blue Moon diner. I even told her my daddy's favorite war tale, and then when I ran out of adolescent chatter, I told her about the process of Wisconsinan glaciation, the formation of Long Island, terminal moraines, striations . . . In retrospect I realize this isn't exactly the stuff of secret missives and dangerous liaisons, but increasingly this was what mattered most to me now. Every week, Pete, you taught me a little bit more, and I sucked it down like a milkshake.

Even the most technical geological musings didn't discourage Hannah from continuing our correspondence, however. I think she was in love with the mystery, a sense of conversations in the dark, of playing out her fantasy life without all the messy business of bare flesh and body parts. In truth, I even started to enjoy the sharing of notes and the telling of tales. I liked the knowing looks she gave me in the hallway.

However, more and more I was coming closer to understanding that what I truly loved lay somewhere else, because that's what I spent most of my time thinking about. You in the sunlight, you breathing the good air. You, Pete, beneath the tall sky.

IT WAS THE SUNDAY IMMEDIATELY before the last few days of school. You led us on a hike you'd been promising me for a while, along Sunset Ridge to see Dinosaur Rock, a glacial erratic as big as a school bus.

When we reached the erratic, the pleasing illusion of a dinosaur's head was unmistakable, craggy rock giving a sense of reptilian scales and a crack running half the length of it forming the mouth. It even had teeth, jagged stones lining its jaw, although you told me people had added those in to complete the look. Perhaps most remarkably of all, however, the huge rock was balanced on the edge of the escarpment.

Just think, you said, if the glacier had dropped this rock a foot farther west, it would have toppled straight down into the valley. Some kind of miracle.

Next, you pointed out carvings in the bedrock all around our feet. V.H. MORRIS 1866. ELLENVILLE BAND 1883. T.A.S. CONKLIN 1890.

There used to be a huge hotel nearby, you said, five hundred rooms. Burned down sixty years ago. The Victorians would come up here by horse-drawn carriage, three presidents stayed, Oscar Wilde, all the famous people of the age. As you can see, they liked to leave their mark, and people think graffiti's something new. There's nothing new, you said. Then you pointed down at the barrens below us, nothing but dwarf pines as far as the eye could see. I like to call that place the pine orchard, you said, but perhaps that's just me, an old man's foolish whimsy.

I didn't think it was foolish at all, and I didn't think of you as old anymore, either.

You started fishing around in your backpack. I'd like to give you something, you said. This here is to commemorate your first trip to Dinosaur Rock. You pulled out a stone and handed it to me. It looked like a red potato, and when I took it in my hand it was smooth as glass.

That there is a gastrolith, you said, *gastro* for stomach and *lith* for stone. A stomach stone. Did you ever hear about why chickens need grit?

Is it so they can cross the road? I said, grinning.

Enough of your sass, kid, said Pete. Now listen, chickens like pecking up grit because they can't chew. No teeth, see. So they swallow the grit and it sits in their gizzards. When the food mixes around with the grit it gets broken down. That there in your hand is something similar, you said.

I looked down at the rock covering most of my palm. Must've been one helluva chicken, I said.

Certainly was, you said, laughing. That was a chicken the size of a Greyhound bus, maybe bigger. That rock you're holding once sat in the gut of a dinosaur. Sure enough, those were some pretty big chickens.

My body started to tingle as I rubbed the rock in my hand. Feels like soap, I said.

Doesn't it just, you said. That stone got tumbled and tumbled around in the cement mixer of the dinosaur's belly, wore the thing smooth. But anyway, you said, I guess as well as using the word *gastrolith,* you could also say that what you're holding there is a *dinosaur rock.*

I loved the proper names for everything you taught me, *bedrock, striations* and *chatter marks, cobbles, boulders* and *glacial erratics* . . . but right up to this day, I have always thought of that gastrolith as my dinosaur rock.

The tingling in my body increased as I felt an intense connection to the world, from its smallest grains to its tallest mountains. However, what I was also feeling was a connection to you, and all of a sudden I became overwhelmed by emotion. I knew I was going to cry, but certainly didn't want you to see, so I threw my arms around your neck.

Hey now, whoa, you said, not knowing what to do with your

hands for a moment, a heavy pause in the air, before eventually you thought to ruffle the hair at the back of my head. Well, I guess that means you like it, you said.

My arms holding on, your cable-knit sweater drying my eyes—that was the precise moment I fell in love with you, Pete.

ROSEBORN,

NEW YORK, 2008

Matthew doesn't wait to see if he's following, just turns and steps inside the house.

McCluskey stands on the drive, hands on hips, the heat battering him as the voice says it again. *You gotta hear the guy out.*

Fuck you, Mikey, he whispers, heading down the path to the porch, then through the front door, closing it behind him.

We're all in here, Detective, he hears Matthew call out from a room beyond the end of the hallway, where McCluskey can see a kitchen counter and a bunch of black metal skillets hanging from hooks.

He enters the kitchen, Matthew and a black woman standing at the stove, their backs to him, the room smelling of bacon grease. At a large kitchen table sits an old man in a billowing nightshirt, three-quarters bald but with long cirrus wisps of hair sprouting from his crown and the sides of his head.

Matthew reaches across the stovetop for a piece of bacon that hisses away on a griddle, and just as his fingers pinch the end of a slice, the woman slaps his hand with a spatula, Matthew yelping, turning to McCluskey.

Take a seat, Detective, he says. Coffee?

Nah, says McCluskey, I'm bitter enough already.

He sits down at the end of the table, and then Matthew heads over, cup of coffee in hand, and takes the seat opposite the old man, who looks like he's about to fall asleep. Matthew picks up the old man's hand, and says, Look, Pete, we have a visitor. But the old man's sagging head doesn't move, and Matthew speaks to him louder this time, Pete, Pete, this is Detective McCluskey.

And not looking up, the old man says, Do I know him?

No, you've never known him, says Matthew.

The old man sighs, hunching farther down in his seat.

Please, Detective McCluskey, says Matthew. You can speak freely, Pete's not going to remember anything you say to me.

McCluskey glances toward the stove.

Celeste, Matthew calls over his shoulder, will everything keep in the oven for a few minutes? This shouldn't take long.

Is he here to arrest you or me? says Pete to the table.

McCluskey twists in his seat. What was that, sir? he says. Arrest someone? Why would I want to arrest anyone? Has Matthew done something wrong?

Pete is opening and closing his eyes, one then the other, looking confused and upset, as if someone is deliberately misconstruing his words. Matthew squeezes his hand encouragingly.

He shot her in the eye, Pete snorts.

Celeste, who has finished stowing breakfast in the oven, starts to leave the kitchen. Shout when you ready, Mr. Matthew, she says, McCluskey noticing a Caribbean accent. I be in my room till you need me, she calls out, her voice fading away down the hallway before her feet hit the stairs.

Pete, they already arrested me for that, says Matthew. I went to prison, remember? You came to visit me every month for two years. Every single month without fail.

The old man looks annoyed at the latest misunderstanding, and slaps the table. I could never have done it, he says, becoming quickly upset. I could never have gone through with it. And then his fingers start to trace lines following the grain of the wood, as if something is written there, but when he can't find any words, he shakes his head and closes his eyes. Matthew eighteen? he says, No, Matthew . . . A moment later, Pete sighs, and starts to breathe deeply, McCluskey hearing that he is already asleep, the air catching in the old man's throat now and again, before exiting with a low whistle.

Matthew drops Pete's hand gently to the table, stirs his coffee a few turns, and looks across at McCluskey. Pete gets easily confused these days, Detective, he says.

McCluskey runs a hand down his cheek, feeling the scrape of his missed morning shave. Your father has Alzheimer's, right? he says.

Matthew nods. Yes, he says, only Pete's not my father. Pete's a friend.

McCluskey feels like he's being played, and yet he's not sure the guy's playing him. Yeah, he says, you know, my grandfather had the same thing, the Alzheimer's. Me and my little sis, we were just kids, right, so we thought it was funny. He'd put stuff on back-to-front, like this wifebeater he always wore down to breakfast, so you could see all the white hair on his back, then he'd get lost buying the newspaper, knock on the wrong houses coming home, accuse the people opening their own doors of being burglars. And after that he'd yell the whole street down and my dad would have to come running. Me and my little sis thought it was this funny kind of joke, right? Just a couple of dumbass kids, what did we know? Anyway, I guess I get it now, now that it's too late. So I'm sorry about your friend, Matthew.

Thank you, Detective, says Matthew, running his finger around the rim of his coffee cup, looking first at Pete, then down at the cup.

The bacon smell still hangs in the air, like some kind of Abu Ghraib fuckin torture, McCluskey glancing out of the kitchen windows to the back of the property, large lake with a rowboat, and what must be a hundred-plus trees. He scratches his ear. You know what, Matthew? he says. I guess things got a little heated this morning, so thank you for inviting me in. And in return, I'll level with you. I got two questions, that's all. Then I swear I'm out of here. Do you mind?

Ask me anything, Detective.

Appreciate it, says McCluskey. So, not to waste anyone's time here, straight on to the first one. This morning, right? Why'd you say sorry to Hannah?

Matthew smiles, cocking his head, as if McCluskey has wasted one of his questions. I said sorry because I'm sorry about what I did to her, Detective.

McCluskey turns away, as if there's something unpleasant in the air. Yeah, he says, that's what I was worried you'd say.

Worried, Detective? Why?

Because it makes the answer to question number two a lot more complicated.

And question two is?

McCluskey shrugs. If you're so fuckin sorry, he says, why'd you go and buy Hannah's house?

Matthew takes a sip of coffee. That is complicated, he says.

Fuckin A, says McCluskey. Because the way it looks to me sitting here, you buying the house of someone whose eye you shot out? I gotta say, that seems like a provocative act, you know? Not exactly some kind of *so fuckin sorry* behavior.

Provocative? I can see that, Detective.

So was it?

Matthew blinks, once, twice. Yes, Detective, I suppose that it was, he says.

Now McCluskey wants to hit the fuckin guy, not for anything he's said exactly, but just because throwing a punch would make him feel a whole lot better. You wanted to provoke her why? he says. Because maybe you wanted her to come see you?

I suppose, says Matthew. Or to make contact by some other means, perhaps. I'm not sure I really self-analyzed the whole thing at the time, Detective.

McCluskey makes his hand into a fist, bounces it three times on his thigh, like he's playing rock, paper, scissors. So what was the angle? he says. What did you want from this contact with Hannah?

Matthew keeps his eyes fixed on McCluskey as he thinks it through, like being stared at by one of the big cats in the zoo, and then finally he speaks. Detective, I'm not really interested in psychotherapy, he says, but perhaps some part of me wants Hannah to acknowledge what she did.

Acknowledge? says McCluskey. What she did?

That's right.

And you wanna tell me in your own words what Hannah did?

Not really.

No? You mean she didn't tie her fuckin self to the tree?

Matthew crosses his arms. Detective, he says, the problem for you here is that you're swimming in the waters of a story you don't understand.

McCluskey laughs. Nah, he says, that's not a problem. Most days of the week that's the top line of my job description. And then he stares at Matthew, because if he's being played, the guy's good, and Matthew just gives him that cat-on-the-prowl stare again.

But then Matthew's cell phone, on the kitchen counter beneath all the hanging black skillets, interrupts the staring match with a bleep, McCluskey leaning back in his seat as Matthew reaches over his shoulder, picks up the phone, and glances down at the screen. Could you give me a moment, Detective? he says. I have to reply to this. He looks up at a clock on the wall, peers at it thoughtfully, and then pecks away at the cell phone one-fingered.

Sorry, says Matthew, placing the phone facedown to the table. Where were we?

You have someplace you need to be? says McCluskey.

I can spare a few more minutes, says Matthew. And look, he says, there's something important I need to add, Detective. You see, I didn't buy this house solely to provoke Hannah Jensen. That might not even have been the main reason I bought it. Does anyone really know why they do all the things they do? But you asked me a question and I answered it as honestly as I could, provocation was an element in the decision, I suppose. However, also I had the money to buy this place, Detective, and it's arguably the finest house in the area. I wanted somewhere for Pete to live that would be big enough for a caregiver as well—Celeste looks after him full-time when I'm not here. I wanted Pete to stay in Rose-born, near the Swangums, where he's lived all his life. He loves the mountains, Detective, he spent years working up there. You can see the escarpment ridge from all of the windows at the front of the house—I suppose I hoped it might jog something. But I didn't actively come looking for this house, Detective, I was work-ing with a real estate agent on finding a place in the area and suddenly this property came on the market. And there's some-thing else important, maybe more important than anything else. I first saw this house when I was fourteen years old. Did you ever see something when you were a child, Detective—a friend's clothes, their mother's jewelry, their father's tie—and realize there existed an entirely different world from the one in which you'd been growing up?

And McCluskey knows this is it, he's got all he's going to get. Yeah, he says, Benny Fazio's record player. Big, beautiful beast, red leatherette. You could stack five records and play them one after the other. First time I ever heard The Beatles was in Ben-ny's bedroom, his parents were out somewhere and he pounded *I Wanna Hold Your Hand* through these speakers half the fuckin size of my bedroom.

Matthew nods encouragingly. Right, he says, and if you saw a record player just like it in a store tomorrow, maybe even the very same one, might you not be tempted to buy it?

And he waits a few beats before giving the answer. *Nahhh,* says McCluskey, milking the exhale. Thing is, Matthew Weaver, I'm a CD guy. Switched over my whole collection years ago—Huey Lewis and the News, that was the first disc I ever bought. Oh, you know what? That was probably around the same time you were tying a girl to a tree and shooting out her eye. Early eight-ies, right?

Fair enough, Detective, says Matthew, glancing up at the clock. Have I answered both your questions now?

Sure, deal's a deal, says McCluskey. But before I go, do I need to run through my whole stay-the-fuck-away shtick again?

I already gave you my word, Detective. But if you need me to say it again, I promise you I won't go anywhere near Hannah Jensen.

McCluskey stands up with an uneasy sense of believing the guy means what he says, the legs of his chair scraping the floorboards, the noise waking Pete, who comes to with a snort.

Pete, our visitor's leaving now, says Matthew. Would you like to say goodbye?

But still Pete doesn't lift his eyes from the table as he speaks. No, I could never have done it, says Pete, his fingers tracing the wood again. Better to have . . . better *for him* to have a large millstone hung around his neck and to be drowned in the depths . . . Pete hesitates, starting to sound doubtful . . . How does it go? To be drowned in the depths . . . to be drowned in the depths of . . . ? What comes next? Pete asks, looking up at Matthew. To be drowned in the depths . . . of the ocean? says Pete, quickly becoming upset, his fingers stiffening on the table. No, that's not it, he says, looking back down at the table, that's not what it says, those aren't the right words.

Matthew gets up and walks around the table. He crouches down beside Pete and puts a hand on his shoulder. Do you mind seeing yourself out, Detective, he says.

No problemo, says McCluskey.

Detective? says Pete, his fingers starting to tremble. Detective you say? Is he here to arrest me?

No, Pete, says Matthew, taking Pete's hand and rubbing his shoulder. No one's arresting you, not today, not ever. The detective was only here to see me, but he's going now. I know you can't remember but it was a long time ago. And I promise, Pete, I promise, you didn't do anything wrong.

Pete squints at the table. Yes, he says, with a relieved sigh. Matthew eighteen, he nods, Matthew eighteen.

MATTHEW

Yes, I had fallen in love with you, Pete, and yet, on the last day of school before summer vacation, 1982, I signed off my final note to Hannah with the little crossed swords of a kiss, placing the piece of paper in her locker so that she would find it toward the end of the day. It wasn't an especially gallant act, I'll admit, considering the feelings I'd developed elsewhere, but I wish the world good luck ever finding a teenage boy whose body is exploding with honorable hormones.

Just before she climbed onto her school bus for the last time in seventh grade, Hannah turned, her eyes locating me alongside Tricky. The look she gave me was something I hadn't seen from her before, as if that kiss at the end of my note had prompted something. There was nothing glacial about this change—while Hannah's kiss a few months earlier had been innocent, the look in her eyes on my last ever day of school certainly was not. What a look, and oh how it thrilled me—considerably more than anything Christie Laing had ever done. Hannah's burning blue eyes made me feel breathless with a deep and powerful sense of lust.

———

AS FAR AS I WAS concerned, there was nothing wrong with wanting both you and Hannah at the same time. I still feel that way to this day.

When I lay in bed at night, having the same thoughts I'm sure most teenage boys do, I would think about you both and picture you both—not at the same time, but sometimes both on the same night—and while the feelings might have been different, the biological response was exactly the same.

For Hannah, I felt a kind of urgent rush of desire. Thinking about her as I lay beneath my bedcovers was an intense multisensory experience. Those bright eyes, the way she laughed, the feel of her lips. I swear I could even smell her scent in the darkness of my bedroom, a kind of female musk that drove me wild and left me feeling short of breath, my lust for her so fierce I could taste it. I wanted my skin on her skin, my mouth against hers, our bodies joined together as one.

However, the feelings I had for you, Pete, were deeper. When it came to you, it felt as if it were not just the weakness in my flesh that desired you, but the strength inside my bones. You were something of the soul, filling a hollow place inside of me. I didn't only crave you like a drug, I needed you like air, like a fish needs water.

I know what most people would think if they were ever to read these words. They would say that you were a father figure, that my feelings were misplaced because my desire for your love bloomed from the fact that my own father didn't love me, didn't like me, wanted even to hurt me, but I don't care what people think. I always loved you for you, Pete, and if you happened to fill a father-size hole in my life, if that made me love you even more, then so be it.

You see, it isn't always this way around when it comes to who I love in the world—the urgent lust for women, the deep longing for men. I've craved men in that same feverish way I yearned for Hannah as a teenage boy, and I've loved women deep down in my bones, in the place that makes me worship another human being for their heart, for their mind, for the sense of something magical in their soul.

So let no one ever call you a father figure, Pete. Labels are for soup cans, just like you said. I won't ever let another human being label me.

I love who I love, that's all there is to it. Don't we all? Why should something like that need a word? I can't see why people find this so hard to understand.

Perhaps they're afraid. Afraid of what? I was never afraid.

THE NEXT DAY, TRICKY'S PARENTS took us out for breakfast to celebrate the end of school, me and Tricky, Tricky's brother Sean, and Sean's best friend and next-door neighbor, a boy named Kyle.

Tricky's dad offered to pick me up from home, but I didn't want the McConnells seeing the dump in which I lived, so I rode my bike over to theirs instead, and then we headed out, four boys in the back of a blue Chevy Impala, just about sitting in each other's laps, my face smooshed up against a window. The route took us along a few streets in town I hadn't been down before. There were kids shooting hoops on their drives, sprinklers sprinkling lawns, all the usual, and then, on a street called Tall Pines Road, before we made the turn onto Main Street, I saw something that made me look twice—it was parked in a driveway, a green truck with a large decal of a gold maple leaf set in a gold triangle adorning its side. It was your Swangum Conservancy truck, Pete.

I was still making sure I'd remember the location when Tricky's dad turned onto Main Street and parked up. Hey, look at that, he said, so pleased with himself you'd have thought he'd just won the election. The perfect spot, he said, right across the street.

Even with my face smooshed up against the wrong window, I knew what was behind me, right across the street.

Everyone squeezed out of the car, and then I stood there, just staring over the road at the Blue Moon diner with a feeling like there was a rock lodged in my gut.

It was Tricky's mom who noticed me hanging back.

What's wrong, Matthew?

Nothing, Mrs. McConnell. Just . . . my mom works here, that's all.

Oh, she said, turning to Tricky's dad, everyone else hovering by the crosswalk. Joe, she called out, her voice half an octave higher than it needed to be, did you know Matthew's mom works at the Blue Moon?

Joe McConnell was fingering his car keys. Well, we don't have to, I mean . . .

It's fine, I said, no, it's good. She wants to meet you, Joe . . . sorry, Mr. McConnell. She said she's thinking of voting for you.

Well, that's nice, said Joe. Isn't that nice, Carrie?

In the diner, I sat at one end of the moon-blue banquette next to Tricky. Opposite us, Sean and Kyle were playing some childish game they'd come up with, blowing paper sleeves from straws as far as they could, and then everything proceeded to go as badly as I'd imagined it would, my mom spotting us and hurrying over, fixing her hair and her apron, and then becoming all deferential to Tricky's parents, while Tricky's parents acted like the three of them were old buddies from college. At some point, Sean O'Connell asked my mom if it was true that waitresses spat in the drinks of customers they didn't like, and when the time came to order food, Kyle asked for a club sandwich and then sent it back because he didn't know there was tomato in a club sandwich. All the while, my mom, a nervous smile nailed to her face, fussed around us like she was proud of me—not for anything about me as a human being, mind, but simply for having made it into the company of such esteemed Roseborn royalty. Then Kyle sent back his sandwich a second time because all they did was pull out the tomato and he said he could still taste it, but worst of all, as my mom was clearing away the plates, Carrie McConnell said to her, Listen, Patricia . . . *Please, call me Pat.* . . . Oh isn't that nice. Well, Pat, we'd love to have you and your husband over to dinner sometime, what with our sons being such good friends. What do you think?

Sure, said my mom, in her broadest Queens, we'd love to have dinner with the both of you. We'll bring the liquor and make a proper party of it. Hey, Matthew, here's my pen, write down our number on a napkin for Mrs. O'Connell while I clear the table. Settle up when you like, Joe, no hurry.

I did as I was told, looking up from the napkin to see Joe McConnell throwing down singles one by one, making a slow, ostentatious show of leaving a generous tip, and then at last we got the hell out of that place.

As for that dinner party? Well, praise be to God, Pete, that such an enchanting soirée would never actually happen, which was just one of many good things to result from the fact that my daddy had only a short time left on this planet. Amen!

I NOTICED YOUR TRUCK WAS no longer outside your house when we drove back to the McConnells along Tall Pines Road. Tricky and his family were headed down to Westchester to visit relatives later that day. I thought about riding up to the Swangums and trying to find you, but I knew you'd be working and it didn't seem right, so I just headed home.

After that painful hour in the diner, home looked twice as ugly as before, a huge array of crap in the front yard that any visitor would have to wade through before they could get to the front door. Hubcaps and I beams and oil drums, a whole bunch of lumber, an old rumble seat, half a tractor . . .

There were two tall piles of old broken pallets leaning against one side of the house, and whenever I was worried about whether my daddy was home, I'd make sure to take a quick peek behind them to see if his car was parked there. Only at that point in our lives, my daddy had actually been enjoying a period of unbroken work, his latest job, something at the Jensen Royal Cement plant, getting close to setting an all-time record—seven or eight weeks and he hadn't been fired. Life was considerably easier to bear whenever my daddy was working, employment cooling his moods a notch or two.

So I didn't see his car behind the pallet piles. If I had I would have gotten right back on my bike. As I opened the door, still thinking of the horror show back at the diner, finally I laughed at the whole thing, especially the way Joe McConnell had laid down his tip, most of the adults in the world seeming ridiculous to me back then, and that's when I saw him, my daddy waiting for me on the couch.

What you laughin at, Chuckles? he said.

Nothing, I said.

How bout you set yourself down and tell me all about all this nothin?

I took the armchair farthest away from him.

You hungry? he said.

No, sir.

What? You mean you've eaten already?

Yes, sir.

Anythin interestin?

Blueberry pancakes.

Blueberry pancakes? And where'd you go for these *blueberry pancakes*? he said.

At this point I realized my daddy clearly knew where I'd been. My mom had never been the sort of person to let her brain get in the way of her mouth. My guess is she called him right after we stepped out the door of the diner to tell him the good news about the dinner invitation. God bless her, she probably even thought he'd be excited.

Now I had two choices. I could lie to my daddy and get whupped for being a liar, or I could tell him the truth. My immediate future right now was like a flow chart, this way or that, that way or the other, only this chart was all screwed up because everything ended up landing in the very same box.

So, talking fast and putting it all out there as if it couldn't possibly mean anything, I said, The McConnells took us to the Blue Moon, and I had pancakes there and Carrie, Mrs. McConnell had them too, and this other boy—

Wait, wait, wait. Blue Moon diner? Did you say Blue *Moon*?

Yes, sir.

You sayin you let your momma wait on you in front of a whole room of strangers, boy? You went and humiliated her in her place of work? Now wait one goddam minute. Do you think you're better than your momma, boy?

No, sir.

No, sir? Why, you piece of unholy shit. How'd you think that made your momma feel? All warm inside? You think because you hang around with those McConnells you're better than us, that it?

No, sir.

No, sir, that's damn as hell right, sir. Makin your momma wait on you. Probably thinkin like you're a man now, boy? Women waitin on you. Takes more than that. You wanna know what it feels like to be a man? A real man? You need to be punished, boy. And you gonna be.

I guess I can stop at this point because the precise to and fro won't add much. Or maybe I just can't face writing it all down. Besides, you saw the bruises yourself, Pete, how they ran down one side of my body because of the way I was curled up in the armchair.

Anyway, apart from small details, the way it went down that particular day wasn't much different from all the others.

I KEPT MY BRUISES HIDDEN from the eyes of the world, only occasionally wearing shorts, the flesh on my arms always concealed beneath long-sleeved T-shirts and sweatshirts. Even if I'd ever learned successfully to roll my shirtsleeves like Tricky, half the time I would have had to keep them buttoned up at the wrist.

My daddy always stayed away from my face, a level of calculation that made him all the more monstrous to my mind. At least there would have been something honest if he'd drunkenly given me a black eye once in a while. *Looky here, people, sometimes I hit my son when I'm all good and toasty.*

Why did I keep the bruises hidden? It certainly wasn't because I was ashamed of having been beaten. It takes a hell of a lot to shame me. No, I was ashamed of having a daddy who was a beater, that was the problem.

Right after it happened, I lay on my bed curled up on the side that wasn't hurting, trying to concentrate on the feel of the blueberry pancakes slipping their way into my stomach. Apparently I'd caused my daddy to be late for work, and as soon as it was over, he left the house, our front door sounding his continued fury, the wheels of his car screaming violently as he pulled onto the road.

A few moments later, little Billy came out of his room, pushed himself up against my back and held me by the shoulder. My daddy had only ever given little Billy a few light cuffs thus far in life. I don't know if this was because of his age or his Down syndrome. It was a strange relationship my daddy had with Billy's condition, if another man had ever called my brother Pug, I have little doubt my daddy would've propelled the guy to the ER in less than a flash.

Although I liked little Billy being there to comfort me, there was someone else I really wanted lying on my bed with me, only I knew you'd be at work the whole day.

I tried to imagine telling you what had happened, but when I pictured it the words were too hard to get out. Then I imagined me touching one of my sore ribs and me wincing hard enough that you'd notice, and then maybe you'd take me by the arm, concerned, and I'd wince again at your touch. Where else does it hurt? you'd ask me, and I'd start to point, here and here and here, all the way down one side of my body, then you'd lift up my T-shirt and see the first bruise, lift a little higher, another and another, and you'd have to pull the T-shirt all the way over my head to see every one. Finally, you'd kiss my bruises better, Pete, that's what I wanted you to do, and in return, I would have done anything to make you happy, anything at all.

THE NEXT DAY I'D ARRANGED to ride up to the Swangums with Tricky, both of us thinking this was the start of a whole summer ahead of us, not totally unlike the summer before, two boys adventuring in the mountains—although obviously on Sundays I was planning to be up there with someone else.

I was too distracted to really enjoy myself, not that Tricky would've noticed, but we stayed in the mountains until late afternoon anyway. I don't remember much of what we did that day, probably played a few of our games, Houdini, perhaps, which Tricky was better at, not only because he'd learned to tie various knots, but also because he was so much smaller than me, making it easier for him to wriggle free.

At some point in the late afternoon, we headed homeward and were coasting down Grist Mill Road, closing in on town, when your green truck drifted by with all the windows wound down. Have fun, boys, I heard you call out.

Tricky and I split up on Main Street, right after the turn by O'Sullivan's Dive Inn, but instead of heading home, I stopped and watched Tricky turn left and disappear from view. Knowing that you were probably home now, I decided to pay you a visit.

I REMEMBER THINKING THAT YOUR place on Tall Pines Road looked like the kind of cabin you might find in a fairy-tale forest, the wood stained brick red, your house with green-painted shutters and a green front door. I walked my bike over your trim lawn and left it by the porch steps. I was about to go up to your front door and knock when I saw a light breaking from under a shade that hadn't been pulled all the way down. There was a gap about as wide as a mail slot, and seeing it I had this feeling that I wanted to know what you did all alone in your home, so I knelt by the window and peeked under the shade and there you were, boots kicked off on the rug, lowering a glass of red wine onto a blanket chest placed like a coffee table in front of an armchair. I'd never seen a man with a glass of wine before. You were still wearing your dust-colored Conservancy work shirt.

Your home was only one room, but it wasn't small exactly, more like a kind of large open space. I could see an armchair, a couch, a pine dresser, your kitchen . . . I couldn't see any kind of bed, but then I noticed a ladder that led to a loft, so presumably it was up there. I imagined it all cozy, one side of your bed hugged by the pitch of the roof, and then, while I was marveling at everything, you started unbuttoning your shirt. I breathed in sharply, quickly becoming transfixed, every newly unfastened button spiking my excitement higher and higher. When you arched your spine, reaching back to pull the sleeves from your arms, the motion thrust your chest forward. It was a strong chest, not overdone like a bodybuilder's, and lightly forested with dark, wiry hair. You folded the shirt and took it over to the dresser, leaving it on top and taking something out of a drawer. All of your muscles were firm and compact. Then you pulled on a T-shirt, returned to the spot by the armchair, and picked up the wineglass, drinking from it and then tipping back your head before breathing out. Returning the glass to the surface of the blanket chest, you sat down in the armchair and picked up a copy of *National Geographic* from the floor, sinking back into the upholstery as you read, almost disappearing from view.

I stood up awkwardly, feeling breathless and faint. I had to wait almost a minute before I could knock on your door.

MATTHEW, YOU SAID, WITH NOTHING but delight in your voice.

I spotted your truck, I said.

Really? you said. And you tracked me down from that one clue alone? So which one of the Hardy boys are you?

Man, that's the worst show on TV, I said. My little brother loves it.

You're supposed to read the books, kid.

I pulled a goofy face, and then said in a dopey voice, But I can't read, sir. Got rocks in my head. Don't know who coulda put them there.

You leaned against the doorjamb and folded your arms. Remind me, you said, how was it I ended up with the freshest kid in town? Am I not keeping you from a more pressing engagement?

Nope, I said.

So you think I'm just going to invite you in?

Yep, I said.

You beckoned me forward. You've got more cheek than a chipmunk, you said as I passed.

Stepping inside your home, the first thing I noticed was the dense, overpowering presence of wood—and by wood I mean *real* wood. My own home was full of wood as well, only it was all just veneer, most of it curling away from the particleboard underneath. You could have peeled all the wood from our house like the skin from an orange.

When you turned on a lamp, the whole place glowed like a campfire. I noticed a cast-iron stove with split logs piled up below. At the edge of the room there was an old wooden workbench that you'd used for a sideboard, covering it with photos and candlesticks and vases full of cattails and pussy willow. All of the furniture was old and dented—there must have been a thousand stories carved into all that timber. The scent inside was heavenly.

What is this place? I said. A goddam museum?

You stepped past me, toward the armchair. I built it myself, you said. What do you think?

Everything feels so old in here, I said.

Appropriate for a sad old man then, you said, lowering yourself stiffly into your armchair for comic effect.

I sat down on the couch. You're not sad, I said.

You laughed. You're not rebutting my use of the word *old* then.

There's nothing wrong with old, I said. I'm old.

You gave me an odd look.

It's true, I said, I feel a hundred years older than everyone at school. I'm old as hell.

I started to look around at your walls, which were covered in art frames, but when I looked closer, I realized it wasn't art that you'd framed but a whole bunch of religious mottoes, lines from the Bible, all of them rendered in cross-stitch. The one nearest me read, *The Lord is my shepherd—Psalm 23*, and beneath the words stood a sheep embroidered in big boxy stitches like video

game pixels. It looked like the kind of thing you'd blast to smith-
ereens on Tricky's Atari.

There must have been ten or a dozen of those framed verses
on your walls. I got up and wandered around the room peering at
them.

God is Light, and in Him there is no darkness at all—1 John 1:5
(That one, I seem to remember, was illustrated with a stitched
lighthouse.) *For God so loved the world, that He gave His only begot-
ten Son—John 3:16* (The picture beneath was of a cross-stitched
cross.)

You watched me looking around and said, You've discovered
my collection of samplers then.

You collect this crap? I said, standing under the cross.

Not collect, exactly, you said. My grandmother, God bless her
soul, she sewed all of these. Mildred Mae, tough old bird, grew
up picking blueberries in the Swangums. And when they couldn't
make enough money from blueberries, they set fire to the moun-
tainside and got paid to help put out the blaze. The fires were
good for the blueberries as well, as it happens.

I went back to the couch and sat down.

Can I get you a drink? you said. I might have some 7UP in
the fridge.

I'll take some of that wine you're having, I said.

You shot me a look and said, suspiciously, I don't know, are
you sure you're eighteen?

Goddammit, I said, going by age is so stupid. Some kids are
older than other kids around the same age, I said. Like with
Tricky, right? I feel like I'm about fifty years of age whenever I'm
around him.

Tricky, he's the one who likes to sketch the water right, the boy
I saw you with cycling down Grist Mill Road just now?

I nodded. That's him, I said.

So Tricky's your little brother right, the one who likes the
Hardy boys?

Hell no, I said, Tricky and me are in the same class at school.

You narrowed your eyes. Wait, so you and he are . . . ? You

stopped to take in a sharp breath. My God, you said, how old are you, Matthew?

I'm fourteen, I said, sounding immensely proud of the number.

Fourteen?

I know, I said, not noticing the way you spoke my age, or how you were turning very pale. Everyone normally guesses maybe seventeen, sometimes eighteen.

You picked up the wineglass, and now I could see that your hand was shaking as you struggled to take a drink. It was still shaking as you put the glass back down on the blanket chest.

That's when inspiration struck. I snatched up the glass, took a healthy gulp, and then, very deliberately—although trying to make it look like an accident—spilled what was left of the wine down the front of my long-sleeved T-shirt.

Oops! I said.

Christ almighty, you said, your body starting to show signs of panic. Matthew, no, what are your parents going to think if they see this? You rushed up from the armchair and motioned me to raise my arms. Quick, you said, I'll throw it in the kitchen sink to soak.

I lifted my hands, ready to surrender myself completely, but there was nothing romantic about the way you removed my T-shirt, trying your best not to let your fingers brush so much as a square inch of my skin, pulling it over my head as quickly as you could. Yet still I felt a surge of pleasure, my heart burning for you, my body desperate for your touch. I looked up into your eyes, but you didn't look down into mine.

You were motionless, standing above me, staring down at the bruised half of my body.

Oh dear God, Matthew, you said. Oh dear God, who did this? Who did this, you poor, poor boy? You moved your trembling hand toward my side, but your fingers stopped short of touching me. I could see the tears forming in your eyes, a single streak falling down your cheek. Taking your hand away from me, you wiped your face and then, as if all the strength had been sucked from your body, you fell back into your chair. How sorely I felt the absence of your lips as you sat there, hands clutching the armrests, with a look of utter defeat on your face, and seeing you so desolate, so monumentally upset at what had happened to me, moved me intensely—moved me perhaps even more than your lips on my bruises might have done. That's when I felt something I hadn't experienced since kindergarten, tears welling up behind my eyes, an irresistible force. Soon I started to cry, an audible sob tumbling out of my throat.

Hearing my pain, your eyes shot up and, looking even more hurt, you said, Oh, my poor child, come here. Oh my poor Matthew, come here, come here, you poor child.

I stumbled over to you, your weakness feeling like my weakness now, and collapsed to my knees, my head falling into your lap as I started to cry harder than I'd ever cried in my life, my body shaking, my head shaking, all of my sadness and the hurt of every blow my daddy had ever inflicted on me coming out in one long torrent of tears. You stroked my head and made shushing sounds. Let it all out, you said, let it all out, Matthew. And then you stroked my head some more.

For how long did I continue to cry? Who knows? It was a long time, perhaps long enough to make up for all the tears I hadn't shed for years, and there wasn't a single tear left inside me by the time I was done.

When it was over, you lifted my head, held it, and looked into my eyes. Did your father do this to you? you said. When I nodded, you held my head tighter and said to me, You are the greatest of God's creatures, Matthew, don't you ever forget that.

It wasn't cold, but I remember I was shivering. You helped me back to the couch, took a blanket from the back of your armchair, and wrapped it around me. Crouching down in a kindly way, you put your hand on my knee, but then an awkwardness came over you and you took your hand away. This is a test, Matthew, you said. For both of us, you understand? *He* sent you to me, you said, pointing heavenward. I understand it all now, it makes perfect sense. *He* gave me a sign. You were nodding the way people do when the world suddenly comes to make sense to them. Wait here, Matthew, you said, patting my knee.

You picked up my T-shirt, walked over to the kitchen, dropped the tee in the sink, and turned on the faucet. Then you pulled out a box from under the sink and poured powder into the running water. When you turned off the faucet, you walked over to a bookcase and pulled out the Bible, then came back to sit in your armchair.

I guess I thought you were eighteen, you said. Or hoped, you added. Or perhaps not even eighteen exactly, you said, and I don't know what age would be right, I honestly don't, but for some reason that's what I had in my head. And now I see why, that's how I know this was a test, Matthew. This was God's test, you understand?

You opened your Bible and started flicking through the pages. Listen to this, Matthew, you said. This here is Jesus speaking to his disciples. And this is taken from Matthew eighteen, you said, tapping at a spot on the page, *Matthew eighteen*. Then you cleared your throat and started to read, your voice deepening as you spoke your holy words—

If anyone causes one of these little ones who believe in me to sin, it would be better for him to have a large millstone hung around his neck and to be drowned in the depths of the sea. Woe to the world because of the things that cause people to sin! Such things must come, but woe to the man through whom they come! If your hand or your foot causes you to sin, cut it off and throw it away. It is better for you to enter life maimed or crippled than to have two hands or two feet and be thrown into eternal fire. And if your eye causes you to sin, gouge it out and throw it away. It is better for you to enter life with one eye than to have two eyes and be thrown into the fire of hell . . . Matthew eighteen, you said, tapping at the spot on your Bible and breathing easier now, Matthew eighteen.

I felt a powerful presence in the room at that moment. I'm not going to call it God because I didn't experience the blinding light of conversion in that moment and never have since, but unholy wretch though I am, nonetheless I bless you, Pete, for what you did, for what you didn't do, and if I'm wrong, if there is a Lord above, I'm damned sure as hell that he blesses you too.

Woe to the world because of the things that cause people to sin. Who in the world can't offer an amen to that?

You closed your Bible, held it in your lap and smiled at me. You are the greatest of God's creatures, you said, and your father will be punished, Matthew, I promise you. I promise you that from the heart. By God's holy means, he will be punished.

I STAYED FOR ANOTHER FIFTEEN minutes or so. At some point it occurred to you that I was almost the same size as you, and you pulled a long-sleeved T-shirt from your dresser. It was only slightly loose on me. After that you started to usher me politely out of your cabin—surely it was my dinnertime soon, what if my poor mother was worried? Briefly there grew a sense of unease between us. Outside of my immediate family, you were now the only person who knew my shameful secret, the things my daddy could do with a belt buckle, and even though you thought you'd passed God's test, there was still a sense of apprehension behind your words and your movements.

Then, as I was heading out the front door, you made a face as if a thought had just come to you in a flash, and you said something about owing someone a favor, changing shifts with a guy at the Conservancy, meaning you wouldn't be able to see me on Sunday this week. That left me feeling hurt, and probably I was a little ashamed of you having witnessed my tears—I'd never cried like that before, not even when my daddy mustered his worst. So you ushered and I shuffled and you didn't linger at the door to wave goodbye when I left.

I rode my bike out of town and checked behind the pallets when I got home. My daddy's car wasn't there, he was out at O'Sullivan's, already in pre–July Fourth celebration mode, so I stepped into the house without having to tiptoe.

My mom didn't notice the T-shirt I was wearing wasn't my

own. She offered to microwave some dinner, spaghetti Bolognese.

The tray spun around in the oven as my mom spoke about her day at the diner. Little Billy was in the living room pretending a screwed-up piece of paper was a football and he was throwing touchdown after touchdown for the Giants. Then my mom said to me, Oh, wait, I nearly forgot, a girl came looking for you today, Matthew. Real cute and with these pretty blue eyes.

Oh yeah? I said. Sounds like Hannah. What did she want?

Hannah, that was it. Not much, asked if you were in. I told her no and she headed away on her bike. Now, honey, do I need to have the talk with you?

You already gave me the talk, Mom.

The microwave pinged. Yeah, well, I heard how she asked for you, all breathless and goo-goo eyes. Maybe you need the talk one more time. Mom opened the microwave and took out my dinner. Here you go, handsome, she said, sliding the tray of spaghetti toward me over the kitchen counter.

Right then, none of this meant very much to me. Hannah had come, Hannah had left, so what? For almost a whole day I would remain blissfully ignorant of the greater significance of this fact. That earlier in the afternoon, riding back home after failing to find me, Hannah had seen me in the distance waiting for Tricky to disappear from view, which also meant I had no idea that Hannah had followed me to Pete's, and that from the end of Tall Pines Road she'd even called out my name, that Hannah had seen me kneeling by a window, as if at an altar, an act that must have looked odd enough that she stopped in her tracks and just watched what I was doing. And I certainly had no idea that, after I went inside, Hannah had taken up the same kneeling spot as me.

What did she actually see? I can tell you she saw nothing because there was nothing to see, but only you and I know the truth, Pete, even if it's buried too deep for you to remember. Anything else is a lie.

Anyway, not knowing any of this, I went ahead and finished

my spaghetti, licking up the last of the sauce from the tray. After that, I caught a couple of touchdowns for little Billy. I'm not sure what I did for the rest of the night, only that I made it to bed well before my daddy came home, and probably slept well, usually did. I guess that was all about to come to an end.

ROCKEFELLER LOOKOUT, NEW JERSEY, 2008

Matthew arrives first at the parking area, gets out of his car, and heads across the trodden-down grass to take in the view over the Hudson River, has always liked looking down from high places, experiencing that sense of wonderment, the vastness of a planet. Off in the far distance, Manhattan is nothing more than a pale huddle of sticks, and he thinks it through again, how he doesn't understand, doesn't *exactly* understand, why it has come to him at this point in life, the urge to tell someone the complete story of 1982. Perhaps it has something to do with turning forty, although forty is nothing more than a number, another one of life's less interesting labels. More likely it has something to do with Pete. There is something life-changing about bearing witness to Pete's deterioration. When he came across Patrick's food blog three months ago, that was when it had struck him, that Pete would probably never be able to take any of it in, but Tricky was someone he could tell the whole truth to, someone who might hear his confession. Yes, maybe Tricky would understand.

He glances down at his watch, two minutes to twelve, two hours after Patrick's message.

> Matthew, something has come up, not sure meeting Monday will work. How about today instead? I can do any time. Same place?

> OK, let's meet midday. Same place. See you there.

Matthew's thoughts slip back to the morning, the police detective at his breakfast table, Hannah on his lawn, and then he thinks about the one thing that he didn't tell Detective McCluskey—that he knows about their marriage, he knows Hannah and Patrick are husband and wife.

How absurd.

Not that he knew they were together when he first contacted Patrick with his confessional urges, or even when he invited him to lunch to talk about his Red Moose Barn business proposal.

Tricky's odd reaction, the way he said no without even hearing the proposal, makes a lot more sense to him now. At the time, because of the strangeness of that brief meeting in Le Crainois, when he got back to his office that day, Matthew had asked his assistant to look into Patrick, see what she could find out about him. A few days later she had come back with little of interest, apart from something she'd printed out from the internet, a newspaper article that Patrick had linked to on one of those websites people use to share the minutiae of their lives—he has never seen the appeal—a travel piece that had appeared in the *New York Mail* about a married couple on vacation in Tokyo, where to go, what to eat, that sort of thing. He had to look twice at the photo of the couple outside a temple, husband and wife surrounded by Japanese schoolchildren making peace signs. Even then, it was only when he saw the byline he believed it. Hannah Jensen. Hannah and Patrick were married.

How absurd.

There is something about this marriage that isn't right. How can she forgive Tricky for being there and doing nothing—and more than forgive him, *marry him* no less?

Matthew swivels his foot back and forth in the grass. How many times has he acknowledged that what he did was wrong? To the police, his attorney, the court, the judge, the parole board, Pete . . . Guilty, guilty, guilty—and not only guilty, but sorry. That's the only reason he said as much to Hannah this morning. He said sorry because he is sorry.

What has she ever said to anyone? Did she ever tell *anyone* the whole story, the true story? Did she tell her best friend from school? (Fran? No, Jen.) Did she tell her mother, her father, a priest? Her *husband*? Anyone?

Matthew knew the answer to this question as soon as he saw her outside his house on the lawn this morning, standing twenty feet behind police detective McCluskey in the morning sunlight, her eye burning at him.

She has never told anyone.

Can it be right that she hasn't acknowledged what happened that day, what happened six weeks before that day? Because she might be guilty of nothing, but she isn't innocent of everything.

So let her come to him and talk and he will apologize all over again. Let her talk about what happened back then and he will sell the house, he will even sign it over to her. Yes, perhaps that would make her understand how genuinely sorry he is. What need is there for the house anyway? If Pete is lost in the world, does it matter anymore where they live? He thinks he would like to spend some time in Argentina, Patagonia perhaps, a land of high places, where he once saw the Perito Moreno glacier rupturing, vast shelves of blue ice calving off into the waters of Lake Argentino, a huge wave rushing forth.

Now, below him, the river sparkles, sunlight winking from its surface, and Matthew glances down at his watch, two hands in perfect alignment, and then hears a voice—

Matthew?

Turning around, he sees him, Patrick standing a dozen paces back, shielding his eyes from the sun.

Good to see you, Patrick, says Matthew, right on time, he says, tapping his watch.

So where is it you're taking me? says Patrick, lowering his hand.

It's a surprise, says Matthew. Are you sure you don't want to ride up in my car? he says. I thought by meeting you down here, it would give us some time to talk.

No, perhaps we'll talk later, says Patrick.

Matthew points to the parking area. Which one is yours? he says.

Blue Audi, says Patrick.

Great, says Matthew. Follow me, black Mercedes. I'll do my best not to lose you.

PATRICK SLIPS ONTO THE PALISADES PARKWAY behind Matthew, the same road he had driven up early that morning.

It surprised him how easy it was, the internet good for such a wild variety of things, so much more than food blogs, ingredients and recipes. Plugging his search into Google Maps he'd found plenty of places within easy reach of the city, many of them with pleasantly homey-sounding names—Bob's Guns, Dave's Sports, BJ's Gunworks—as if you might be heading over for coffee and some neighborly chat.

Bob's Guns was open on Sundays from six in the morning. At the end of the hour-long drive some light form-filling was required, followed by a quick phone call. The whole transaction took little more than ten minutes.

Even before they pull onto the thruway, Patrick can guess where they're headed. And then they begin the drive north, the rocks pushing steadily harder through the earth as they head upstate, passing road signs familiar from childhood—SLOATSBURG, SUFFERN, SCRANTON.

A little over an hour later they leave the thruway at the New Paltz exit and he thinks about the art supply store where he and

Matthew bought the plastic carry tube, their story about sketching the lake, the BB gun concealed in the other fishing rod bag.

Just before they head right to skirt town, he sees the ridge looming large on the horizon. And then they make the two turns that will take them all the way to Roseborn. He hasn't seen his hometown since he had just turned thirteen. He'd thought about heading up there once or twice but by the time he had a car, he was married to Hannah and he'd promised her they'd never even talk about *that place.*

They coast past apple orchards, the trees growing heavy with fruit, almost picking season now. The crowds from the city will be arriving soon, the sort of crowd he'd imagined for Red Moose Barn.

Good land up here, thinks Patrick, wondering if Roseborn has changed much, but before they reach its outskirts, Matthew pulls off the road onto a dusty spot beside an apple orchard.

Matthew's car looks no more than a year old and this makes Patrick angry all over again. How exactly does he deserve it? After what he did to Hannah, how does Matthew deserve any of it? The expensive car, the huge loft in Tribeca, friends with Jean-Jacques Rougerie?

He pulls up behind the black Mercedes, the conspiracy clear to him now. Obviously Matthew had Don Trevino fire him from his job at Idos. And why? Because Matthew is coming for Hannah, of course, coming after her because of some twisted sense of bitterness, resenting her for the time he spent in prison. And how has Matthew chosen to come for her? Through him. Matthew is coming for Hannah through him.

Not if I come for you first, Matthew, not if I get to you first.

Patrick looks up and down the road. Too much traffic here. But it doesn't matter, he will wait for his moment, everything prepared, the shotgun in the trunk already loaded and next to it a roll of duct tape, a hundred feet of rope and a kitchen knife, in case he needs to cut the rope, in case he needs to cut anything.

Conspiring with Trevino to have him fired from his job— surely this alone would deserve some sort of punishment. And yet there is so much more, motives piling higher and higher, compelling him, urging him forward. Justice, retribution, protection. And even greater than all of these reasons to act, this has become the only way to make up for what happened twenty-six years ago, to make up for what he didn't do. Because now Hannah has left him.

Go take a look at your computer.

Matthew steps out of his car, handsome smile, loose sense of ease.

Look at him. Exactly how has Matthew been punished for what he did? And even more than anything else, now this has become the only way to win back his wife, the only way to earn back Hannah's love.

I never want to see you again.

Patrick opens the car door and steps out onto the dusty shoulder at the side of the road, the sun pushing down on his back with the weighty insistence of great sheets of rock, compelling him, urging him forward. Because what other choice does he have?

Nothing. There is no other choice. There is only one way.

MATTHEW

It was a Friday, two days before the Fourth of July, my morning devoid of anything out of the ordinary. I met Tricky at the same spot as always and we spent several run-of-the-mill hours in the Swangums. When Tricky had to leave—earlier than usual for a dental appointment—I hung around on my own for a while, only it turned out shooting soda cans all alone was about as interesting as schoolwork.

Friday was one of my mom's days off from the diner. She and little Billy would probably be at the library sticking crap together with glue, hanging out at Joppenbergh pool or some other kind of summer activity, and I liked the idea of having the house to myself for a few hours, so I left the BB gun under the tarp and trekked back to Split Rock.

Heading back home on my bike, obviously I had no idea that while the start to my day had been perfectly uneventful, my daddy, meanwhile, had pulled off a Friday morning of truly epic proportions, displaying once more—but for the last time ever—his uncanny knack for fucking everything up.

SOME EIGHT WEEKS EARLIER, MY daddy had been sitting in O'Sullivan's Dive Inn, enjoying a few quiet beverages, when he'd noticed that the customer parked on the barstool beside him was showing some form. When my daddy was in a good mood he liked to order George Thorogoods—named for that song of his *One Bourbon, One Scotch, One Beer*—and once the bartender slid the three drinks over to him, my daddy would line up the glasses and offer to take on challengers to beat him in a race.

Well, that night early in May, my daddy's drinking neighbor turned out to be none other than Bobby Jensen, brother to Hannah Jensen, and the son of Walt Jensen, proprietor of Jensen Royal Cement, the last place in town still producing what had once been the lifeblood of Roseborn. So Bobby and my daddy proceeded to have some fun, downing their drinks while George Thorogood hollered away on the jukebox. They shot the breeze and breezed the shots, and then at some point they got to talking about the cement business, Bobby mentioning in passing that one of Jensen's employees, who happened to be his brother Pauly's regular pot dealer, had got hitched to a girl from Buffalo and moved up there to work in a steel mill.

To be fair to my daddy, even liquored up, he had enough smarts about him to recognize a potential lucky break when he saw one, and on the spot, he offered to supply as much pot to Pauly Jensen as he wanted if the brothers could swing the cement plant position his way.

I'd be surprised if my daddy had *drug dealer* on his résumé at that point, but whatever else he was, he was a hard bastard. I can imagine him making the short trip north in his car the very next day, rocking up to the seediest neighborhood in Kingston, and saying to the first local he came across, *Take me to your dealer.*

Anyway, just a few days later, my daddy would simultaneously embark upon two new careers, cement worker and dope pusher, managing to keep both jobs for as long as two whole months, Walt Jensen turning a blind eye to the pot dealing, as he always had by most accounts, and if my daddy had only stopped there, my humdrum Friday morning would have remained nothing more than the start of another unremarkable day.

However, at some point back in June, five or six weeks into the job, my daddy had got to thinking about the profits to be made from marijuana—low-cost, slow burn—versus the profits that might be made from cocaine—luxury product, gone in a sniff—and probably if Pauly liked one he'd be a good target audience for the other. Moreover, wasn't cocaine a stimulant that was popular with drinkers, a kind of symbiosis made in heaven? Every time he took on Bobby Jensen over another round of George Thorogoods, my daddy made him look slower than pond water, so maybe Bobby could do with a little help from the white lady. Sure, why support just one brother's lifestyle choice when he might support both?

No doubt it seemed like a capital idea, and one day in June, my daddy headed up for a business meeting with his new colleagues in Kingston. The time had come for a little diversification.

So now my daddy was working at an industrial plant producing large bags of gray powder while also pushing small bags of white powder, not only to two of his employers but also, by all accounts, to a number of coworkers.

Unfortunately this was one enterprise too far for Walt Jensen. Maybe he'd been hearing rumors and keeping an eye on my daddy, or maybe he just stumbled by accident upon the transaction. Either way, on the morning of Friday, July 2, Walt Jensen came across my daddy taking a sly cigarette break out back while, in his company, Walt's sons Bobby and Pauly were handing over the greenbacks for enough white powder to make their July Fourth weekend go off with one hell of a bang. At which point, the last remaining cement baron of Roseborn fired my daddy's ass on the spot.

I heard all of this from my mom many years later, who told it to me while sipping away at her third Beam of the afternoon, but my daddy's next few hours on earth are a part of the story gathered by the police and recounted in print by the *Roseborn Gazette*. Apparently, the first thing my daddy did after losing his job was drive over to O'Sullivan's Dive Inn, at which point normal service ensued. However, after starting a bar fight, he was kicked out sometime around two in the afternoon. Reportedly, not long after this he purchased a fifth of Four Roses at the liquor store over on the other side of town, where he was seen drinking straight from the bottle as he gunned out of the parking lot.

However, the police could find no one to tell them what happened after my daddy's first three jobless hours—or at any point up until the next morning, when his body was discovered by two hikers—but I could have told the police everything, such as where he went next, for example. After hitting the gas and necking his whiskey, he drove home.

AFTER THREE MONTHS OF HIS doubly gainful employment, I'd become almost accustomed to my daddy being at work until five at the very earliest, so when I arrived back from the Swangums, sometime around four, I didn't even check to see if his car was behind the pallet pile—which, of course, it was.

The house was quiet when I walked in, and although I suppose there might have been signs that my daddy had returned, I wasn't looking out for them. From the living room you could see my parents' bedroom, but you couldn't see their bed. I guess he was lying there passed out when I arrived.

Maybe I made myself a PB&J or ate some pickles from the jar or watched TV, I don't really remember, my day was still in its everyday phase. At some point I heard a knock on the door and went to answer it. When I opened the door, Hannah Jensen was standing there.

Damn, she looked cute—and actually I'd been thinking about Hannah ever since my mom had mentioned her visit the day before. I certainly wasn't going to give up having fantasies about you, Pete, or stop hoping those fantasies might come true, but in the short term this now seemed unlikely. Although I'm not going to say that Hannah had become my plan B—because in some sense, you were both my plan A.

Hey, Hannah, I heard you came looking for me yesterday, I said, before turning and jumping on the sofa. You wanna hang out? I said.

When Hannah stepped inside, I detected a look of disgust on

her face, but that didn't faze me. Sure, we lived in a crappy home full of crappy veneer and even crappier furniture—why wouldn't she be disgusted? Plus, I knew Hannah lived over in the rich part of town, everyone in Roseborn knew about the Jensen property, that place was supposed to be some kind of palace. So anyway, I didn't mind the disgust, even though it seemed pretty rude walking into someone's home with a look on your face like you wanted to gag.

Come on in, I said, sit down.

The only place left to sit was the armchair, which was bandaged up with duct tape to prevent the stuffing spilling out. Hannah walked over looking all prim, like she was afraid of catching cooties, and sat down in a way that left as little of her body in contact with the chair fabric as possible.

I found this cute as well.

Then it occurred to me that maybe she wasn't disgusted by the furniture. I gave her a second look, perched at the edge of the seat with her arms folded like she needed to keep herself warm. Wait, perhaps she was just nervous.

Hey, what's up, Hannah? I said.

You know it's not right, she said.

What's not right?

It's illegal.

Hannah saying *illegal* kind of turned me on—it meant she had come to my house for more than a kiss. Now wasn't that something to think about. I got off the couch and went over to her.

Hannah scooted back in the chair.

Still thinking she was just nervous, I knelt down and put my hands on the arms of the chair, leaning forward to kiss her, thinking that's what she wanted, the precursor to something excitingly illegal. So what happened next came as a complete shock.

Hannah screamed.

It's OK, it's OK, I said, trying to sound reassuring.

Her face was all twisted up, as if she couldn't decide whether to kiss me or spit in my eye. I didn't understand—at least, not for another few moments.

That's when she yelled it right in my face.

You're disgusting, Matthew. *Disgusting*! I saw what you did with that man!

What? I said, feeling something drain out me. What man? I said.

Now that Hannah had released this secret of hers, all of her words came flying out fast. I saw what you did, she screamed. You went to his house and I saw him undress you, I only came here yesterday because I thought you liked me and I thought I liked you, but I don't like you, Matthew, you're disgusting.

Wait, Hannah, I said, what are you talking about? It wasn't like that.

Liar, she said, her eyes flashing with fury. I saw you, she shouted, I saw you with my own eyes.

Really? I said, becoming angry myself now, leaning forward so that soon both of us were up in each other's faces. What did you see? What exactly did you see, Hannah? *What?*

How often since then have I tried to make sense of her answer, tried to imagine looking in from the outside, from Hannah's sliver of window? You pulling the T-shirt over my head and reaching for the bruises on the far side of my body, you falling back in your armchair, me burying my face in your lap and my head starting to move. How long did Hannah stay there before she ran from the window, her head full of fiction, and how many times did she think it through, the picture building and building overnight, her mind sketching in lines that her eyes hadn't seen, fueling the lie that would change our lives forever?

She screamed it loud.

I saw you take him in your mouth. I saw you give that disgusting old pervert a blow job!

That was the precise moment my daddy came out of the bedroom.

WHAT THE FUCK YOU SAY?

She twisted around as he teetered out, Hannah's body turning instantly stiff.

I said what the fuck you say, girl? My daddy was advancing on Hannah with a demeanor I knew only too well. I stood up to block his way, but a split second later I was staggering backward, struggling for breath, the recipient of an expertly placed punch to the middle of my torso.

My daddy took Hannah by the hair and damn near lifted her out of the armchair.

What the fuck you say about my boy? You say it again. Again.

Hannah's body was shaking, her lips trembling and her mouth sputtering. She couldn't say a word.

My shoulders were up against the wall and it was taking me a while to recover, but when finally I was able to breathe again, I sniffed hard, wiped my lips with the back of my hand, and ran at my daddy, a low growl coming from my throat.

He let go of Hannah, made a quick turn, and caught me by the neck with both hands, choked me a while and then kneed me in the groin before tossing me easily to the ground. I lay on the carpet moaning in agony and gasping for air.

Now Hannah was quivering as if she were being jabbed at with a cattle prod, tears streaming from her eyes, her knees clenched together. My daddy leaned in at her until the tip of his nose was almost touching her face and said, Little girl, did I actually just hear you accuse my firstborn of bein a homo? Is that what you said fore I came in the room? Did I hear *blow job*? Say it again, girl. Again.

Hannah closed her eyes and shook her head, a high and terrified sound coming out of her throat, and then suddenly my daddy leaped away from her, bounding over to me instead. Before I knew it, he was sitting on my thighs, pinning me down by the shoulders. Who is he? he yelled.

Fuck you, I said.

My daddy punched me in the ribs. Who the fuck is he?

Fuck you, I said.

This time he punched me on the other side, working my liver.

We repeated the procedure a few more times before my daddy got up and started pacing around the room, rubbing his face and running his hands through his hair. Hannah was curling herself tighter and tighter in the armchair, and then my daddy strode over to her and in a loud whisper said, Don't you dare move one goddam fuckin muscle, girl. I'll kill you both, that's God's word.

I started to claw my way across the floor toward Hannah, but I wasn't able to move all that fast. I could hear the sound of several drawers rattling and slamming, and soon a victorious cry, *There you are, bitch,* before my daddy came back in the room pushing a silver magazine into the heel of a black pistol I never even knew he owned.

I just assumed he was going to shoot me, and right then I was hurting and gasping so hard, it didn't seem like the worst idea in the world, but I caught my breath pretty fast when he went and stood beside the armchair, lifted the pistol, racked the slide, and pointed the gun straight at Hannah's head.

Hannah closed her eyes and started to make a really high-pitched sound, her body about ready to shake itself to pieces. My daddy just slapped her hard across the face, and she shut up right away.

I didn't even wait for him to ask me again. His name's Pete, I said.

Pete, said, my daddy. Sounds about right for a faggot. And what's this homo Pete's last name?

I don't know, I said.

My daddy gave Hannah's temple a little push with his gun, and then showed me three fingers, two fingers, one . . .

I don't know his last name, I yelled, waving my hands. I promise I don't know, I said, but he works for the Conservancy.

My daddy let the gun drop from Hannah's head. Well, in that case, he said, pushing it into the waistband of his jeans, you and I are about to go for a little ride, boy.

ROSEBORN, NEW YORK, 2008

Matthew crouches to tie a shoelace, twenty feet of gravel and dust between them, pausing to get a better look at Patrick, some indefinable air of sickness about him, as if the drive up has made him queasy. Does Patrick know where Hannah was this morning?

Maybe he shouldn't bring this up right now. Later, perhaps. He pulls the shoelace tight and thinks, *But before we go any further, I should level with him.* Matthew stands up, wiping his hands on his shirt. Patrick, there's something I need to tell you, he says.

What? says Patrick, looking somehow lost, as if their boyhood landscape is alien to him.

I know that you and Hannah are married, says Matthew.

Patrick's body turns stiff, Matthew raising his hands, as if to hold him back. But I promise you I had no idea when I first contacted you, he says. I found out later on, sometime after our brief meeting at Le Crainois. And I stuck to the promise I made you that day, I haven't tried to get in touch with you since. All I've done is reply to your messages.

A truck blows by headed east, a car going west. Patrick is toweling his face with sweeping hands.

There's something else, says Matthew. You remember Randy McCloud?

Sure, says Patrick, taking his hands from his face, looking immensely agitated, as if he might leave.

But Matthew keeps going, because everything can still be resolved, he truly believes that. This is where it happened, he says. This was the orchard where they found Randy dead next to his truck.

So what? says Patrick, the sense of agitation appearing in his voice now as well. What's the point of all this, Matthew?

The point is that the police never worked out who killed Randy, says Matthew. But I know who killed him. Matthew waits until Patrick looks him in the eye. It was my father, he says.

Something seems to drain out of Patrick as he looks down at the ground, then up again. OK, so you never shared your big childhood secret with me, he says.

Right, says Matthew. Well, it never came up.

A pickup drives by, and for a moment Matthew thinks he recognizes it, Pete's pickup truck, but it is just a green truck.

Why are we doing this now? says Patrick, squeezing his brow and closing his eyes for a moment.

You're right, you're right, says Matthew. I guess we're doing this now because I wanted to tell you everything, he says. But now I realize, I don't think I can.

Everything? says Patrick. Really? Why not?

Matthew wants to say, *Because you're married to the rest of it.* Only it feels like a bad idea to talk about Hannah again, something odd about the way Patrick reacted to her name. Matthew pushes his hands deep in his pockets. Look, he says, nodding sideways, I have something to show you, remember? And then we can talk after that if you like. You want to see what it is? he says, taking a few deliberate steps toward the orchard. The actual entrance is farther up the road, he says, but this is the best way to see it.

Patrick glances across at his car, then up at the orchard. Fine, he says. After you, then.

The orchard is set on a steep slope. Matthew heads up the hill, pulling an apple from a tree and taking a bite before throwing the fruit away. They need another week or two, he says, looking over his shoulder, Patrick keeping his distance.

The day is absent of breeze, the air troubled only by the sounds of insects and traffic, cicadas and car engines, the growl of a motorcycle. Matthew stops at the brow of the hill, putting his hands on his hips. When Patrick reaches him, standing almost alongside, Matthew points down into the valley.

This is what I wanted you to see, he says.

The land drops away before them, the Swangum Ridge blotting out the horizon, and in the valley below, in an apple-fringed clearing, paint peeling from its weathered boards, there stands an old red barn.

We completed a few months ago, says Matthew, but I decided to hold off for a while before starting work. I own the barn along with most of the land you can see on this side of the road, including this orchard. More than enough apples for several kitchens. And the soil is incredible, glacial till, you can grow just about anything here. Plus it's a great location. Look at that view of the Swangums, imagine sitting outside at a wooden picnic table, watching the sun set behind the ridge. Not much competition from other restaurants, plenty of city folk at the weekends—climbers, hikers, second-homers . . . Throughout fall you could pull in the apple pickers and the leaf-peeping crowd. Weekdays and off-season, there are enough locals with money to sustain the business, this whole area's much wealthier now than when we grew up here. What do you think?

When Matthew turns to look at him, Patrick pulls his hand quickly from his eyes. I didn't realize the food supply business was so lucrative, he says.

It's just an old barn, says Matthew.

Plus all the land, the orchard, the huge loft in Tribeca . . .

I've been lucky, says Matthew. Most of my money comes from investments rather than the business.

You should give me the name of your broker, says Patrick, his voice almost suggesting there is something to laugh about here.

I use a few different places, says Matthew. There's a great guy called Levine I could hook you up with. The returns are modest, but I like him—he has a country home in the Poconos where he cold-smokes his own salmon. But if you want something riskier with higher potential returns, the place I'd most recommend is called Idos Investments. Apart from having to deal with an asshole called Don Trevino, I have nothing but good things to say about them. Remind me when we're done here today and I'll put you directly in touch, the VIP treatment, you don't want to have to go through the minions.

Patrick only stares at him, his lips pale and stiff.

Is something wrong? says Matthew.

This was your plan? says Patrick. Just this?

I was in the middle of completing the purchase when I invited you to Le Crainois, says Matthew. I was going to bring you up here after our lunch. I only found out about Hannah later on, like I told you. Honest mistake.

Patrick doesn't say anything, just looks away from Matthew and stares down into the valley at the rickety barn.

Look, I know there's a lot we should talk about, says Matthew. And after this we'll go somewhere and talk everything through if you like, but why don't you just come take a look for now?

Matthew begins heading downhill, looking over his shoulder to see if Patrick is following. Patrick wipes his nose with the back of his hand and then starts to walk.

Work gets under way in a week, Matthew calls out over his shoulder. Some light landscaping to begin with, he says. We'll need a parking lot. The shell needs shoring up and eventually a new lick of paint. We basically need to gut the inside and renovate. We'll make everything from reclaimed barn wood—the bar, tables, flooring—and we need to build an addition at the rear for the kitchen.

They are close enough to the ridge to see the turkey vultures soaring over its sheer white face, sliding through the air, six or seven of them, like figure skaters tracing patterns in ice.

I know the right people to help out with the vegetable garden, says Matthew. We could be almost self-sufficient in a few years on that front. Also I know all the best cattle farms, who has great chickens and pigs. And there are some excellent local cheese makers as well. *Local,* that's one of the magic words in the business these days. Plus, Maine's only a few hours away—a ready supply of lobster, fresh fish delivered before lunchtime, straight off the Portland dayboats. This could be the first restaurant of many.

The ground has leveled out, they walk across a small meadow of wildflowers, the lush grass speckled purple and yellow, and then along the last of the dirt track that leads from road to barn.

I know why you think you can't say yes, Patrick, I do understand, but you don't have to say anything right now. Everything can be resolved, says Matthew. I really do believe that.

Matthew stops when he reaches the front of the barn, its double doors held shut by a large rock leaning into a crack where the doors don't quite meet. You recognize that? he says, pointing at the rock. It's from up there, Swangum conglomerate, harder than granite. He lifts the rock, moving it to one side and swinging open one of the doors. I'm afraid you'll have to use your imagination, says Matthew, glancing over his shoulder and seeing Patrick closer now, before turning back, stepping inside the barn and breathing in the smell of the wood as he enters.

Breathing the good air—he turns to see if Patrick is breathing it too, but there isn't time to do anything but flinch as the rock smashes into his skull.

MATTHEW

I was in the passenger seat holding his Four Roses, my daddy driving slow, but still barely able to stay on both lanes of the road, let alone one.

Hell, take a swig, boy? said my daddy, nodding at the jug. Maybe it'll cure you some.

No, thank you, I said.

No, thank you, he said, in a mockingly effeminate way. Now when did you stop calling me *sir,* boy?

When I lost all fucking respect for you.

My daddy found that funny. You're plenty brave for a faggot, he laughed.

I stared out of the window as if looking for an answer. It didn't happen, I said. Whatever you heard back there, she made it up.

Is that so? said my daddy. Is that so? I could see him checking his rearview mirror all cockeyed, so I turned to look over my shoulder. Hannah was a few hundred yards back, trying and almost failing to stay upright on her bicycle, leaving our driveway. But here's the thing, boy, said my daddy. Why would a pretty girl like that make up something so ugly, just the two of you in a room? You think I'm dumber than a box of rocks?

She got the wrong end of the stick, I said.

Ohhh, so there *was* a stick? said my daddy. Well, why don't you tell me about it, this *stick*?

I looked out my window again as my daddy chuckled away to himself.

Come on, said my daddy, isn't that what she said? Now that would be one helluva lie for a young thing like that, sayin my son took an old dick and put it in his mouth. And we ain't the kind of family for lettin stuff go. My daddy slowed to a halt and squinted into his rearview again. You really sayin that girl's nothin but a filthy liar, boy? Because slander like that deserves punishin, he said. Now you listen good. If that little girl's a goddam liar, I'll turn right around and me and my friend, we'll be havin a few words with her, he said, touching the pistol in his waistband. Otherwise, if she's tellin the truth, me and my friend, we'll be havin a word with old faggoty Pete. Either way, me and my friend, we got some serious fuckin talkin to do. So what'll it be? Is that girl a goddam liar? he said. Or are you a goddam faggot?

I looked him straight in the eyes and said nothing.

My daddy shrugged and spun the wheel sharply before braking so that the car straddled both lanes of the road, and then shifted from drive to reverse.

Stop! I said. Just . . . don't turn around, please.

OK, said my daddy, but I'm only gonna ask you one more time. He clamped his eyes hard on me and said, Are you . . . an old man . . . cocksuckin . . . faggot?

I looked straight back at him and nodded.

Say it, then, boy. Say *I am a faggot*. I won't hurt you. I'm your daddy, for chrissake.

The alcohol was already beginning to drip from his pores.

I'm a faggot, I said, refusing to mumble my words.

My daddy put his hand to his ear anyway. Little louder for your old man, he said.

I could see Hannah wobbling closer on her bike, pausing when she saw the car stopped up ahead in the road, and I shouted it hard in his face. *I am a faggot.*

Good boy, he said, patting my knee ever so gently. Good boy.

WE STOPPED IN THE CONSERVANCY parking lot, only a couple of other cars there, and headed out on the red-blazed trail. As we walked, my daddy hung back from me five or ten paces, smoking his Larks and drinking his whiskey. Whenever we'd hit a fork in the trail he'd ask which way we should go to find Pete, squinting hard at me as I answered, sometimes nodding OK, sometimes chuckling, calling me a sneaky little so-and-so and waving his pistol in the other direction, a regular dowser of truth. Not that any of this mattered—I couldn't have led him to you anyway, it's not as if you worked at a desk.

My daddy was mumbling to himself as we walked, a monologue about fighting and faggots and gooks, questions as to my true paternity, a conclusion that in all likelihood I couldn't be his, that probably I was the son of *some pillow-bitin sailor boy.*

After a mile or so, just as we were coming to another fork, I heard my daddy swear loudly. I turned around, hoping he'd stepped on a rattlesnake, but unfortunately the cause of annoyance was simply that he'd finished his Four Roses. My daddy put the bottle down on a rock, marched away ten paces and then spun around with his black pistol pointed at the offending vessel. When he pulled the trigger there were two sounds, and neither of them was breaking glass, only the gunshot rippling through the air and the sound of a ricochet, bullet glancing from rock.

My daddy shrugged. Sometimes chicken, sometimes feathers, he said, staggering toward the empty bottle and picking it up. Then he walked over to me, passed me the bottle, and motioned for me to start moving. Up against that tree, he said, I need incentive to shoot straight, that's all.

I gave him the most hateful look I could muster.

I said stand against the fuckin tree and put the fuckin bottle on your fuckin head, boy. I gotta be sure my aim's workin good when the time comes.

I did what he told me. I can't explain to you why I wasn't afraid, maybe it was just that I was overwhelmed by hatred, but I did close my eyes, I closed my eyes and thought about you, Pete, remembering the time you rushed up to me and Tricky one time to tell us the rules, no fishing in the lake, boys.

Then I thought about another rule—no hunting on Conservancy land—and imagined you hearing the gunshot. I could picture the way you'd hold your head trying to work out the direction the sound came from and how, if you found him, you'd walk up to my daddy all smiling and friendly.

That's when I heard a second shot and the smashing of glass. I waited a moment before opening my eyes. There was broken glass at my feet and my daddy was hands-on-knees laughing. Sometimes chicken, sometimes feathers, he hooted, I can't believe you fell for that, son, you shoulda seen yourself. Come on, boy, you know I was the best damn shot in my platoon. You don't remember? You fell for me missin that bottle from ten yards? I wish you coulda seen the look on your face, boy, *ooh hoo hoo*. That was a picture, that was a regular treat.

My daddy took another few seconds to recover himself and then waved his gun toward the fork on the right, still sniggering away. It was the path that led to Dinosaur Rock, there was a sign saying as much. Now come on, he said, let's keep moving. We still got us some faggot to hunt.

I CAUGHT SIGHT OF YOU about ten minutes later. We were up high on Sunset Ridge trail and you were down in the barrens, the place you called the pine orchard. Sunlight flashed from your binoculars as you glassed the ridge, searching for the source of the gunshot, but my daddy was too drunken-eyed to notice you off in the distance. You were on the very same trail as us. From where you were standing, it would carry you straight to the bottom of the ridge and then along its base a few hundred yards, before heading up steeply to join the section we were on now. I didn't know what to do. There weren't even any trail junctions where I could hope to get lucky or try and trick my daddy into picking the wrong route.

Sunset Ridge was nothing but rocks on rocks, large boulders you had to haul yourself over alongside smaller ones, football or softball-size. We came to a short rise with footholds like steps in the rock face, and when I clambered up, Dinosaur Rock was only a short distance away, big as a school bus, its jaw hanging over the edge of the escarpment. It looked to be the only place to hide from your binoculars for several hundred yards, so as I passed behind the dinosaur's tail, I faked a fall, letting my toe catch on a small fissure in the bedrock.

Well shit, laughed my daddy, who looks drunker'n a skunk now?

I rolled over and reached for my ankle. I think I twisted it, I said.

Walk it off, said my daddy. I had to make it through that jungle with guts drippin outta my fingers.

I touched my ankle and winced. My daddy pulled his Larks from his chest pocket and lit one. OK then, he said, five minutes, or I'm leaving you here for the buzzards. He sat down with his back against Dinosaur Rock to enjoy his Lark in the sun, closing his eyes against the dipping light and sucking peacefully on his cigarette.

I sat down and tried to think everything through. I pictured my daddy spotting you heading toward us on the trail. You wouldn't stand a chance—he had a gun, you didn't—and once he saw you, my daddy would whisper something like, You say a word, boy, I'll shoot you on the spot. Only there's no way I'd let that stop me, I'd yell, Run, Pete, run! Anything to give you more time. My daddy could go ahead and shoot me for all I cared, because if I didn't shout out a warning, I could picture exactly how that would go as well. My daddy would force you to get down on your knees and open your mouth, and then he'd make some kind of joke as he pushed the barrel of the gun between your lips.

I looked across at him in the goldening sunlight, a long husk of ash on his Lark. A moment later the husk dropped to his chest and my daddy didn't move, at which point a whistling sound came out of his nose.

The plan thudded into me in an instant, no need to think everything through. Right beside me was a football-size rock, Swangum conglomerate, tougher than granite. Picking it up, I moved over to him fast. It felt like nothing, bringing that rock down on my daddy's head. He didn't make a sound, just slumped over to one side, blunt force. There wasn't even much blood to talk about.

After that, I don't even remember it being that hard dragging my daddy over the polished bedrock, past all the names that had been carved there a hundred years ago. Once I got my daddy's limp body all the way to the edge, I stopped to look down at the pine orchard, bright green and tranquil and no sign of you. By now you must have been bounding up the steep rise to the ridge. You probably made it to the spot where my daddy smoked his last cigarette not long after it burned itself out.

I stood there for just a few moments enjoying the view, blue glimpses of skylake and cloud shadows drifting over the face of the valley. You can feel like a god in the mountains.

I knelt down beside my daddy, not so much wondering if I could do it, more wondering what it would feel like.

I saw his eyelids flicker, and I knew what he would say if he opened them, if he could see where he was.

You ain't got the balls to push me off this cliff, faggot.

I corrected him before he had the chance to say it.

It's called an escarpment, I said. And I pushed.

ROSEBORN,

NEW YORK, 2008

Patrick runs across the wildflower meadow and up to the orchard, moving as fast as he can through the crowds of apples, only starting to slow when he reaches his car.

After driving the short distance, he backs up until the trunk of the car is within a few feet of the barn doors. He gets out and looks around. With the car where it is, no one can see inside the barn, not even if they look carefully, blowing by at fifty-five.

He opens one of the barn doors and peers inside, Matthew still in the same spot where he fell, half sunlight, half shade, the heavy rock beside him. Patrick opens the trunk, takes out the rope and duct tape and tosses them onto the sunlit floorboards. He picks up the shotgun, carrying it inside and leaning it against the closed door. And then he stops and listens as an engine sound comes closer, but passes, and he goes back to the trunk, taking out the kitchen knife, the box of shotgun shells and a picnic blanket, quickly putting the shells in the backseat and covering them with the blanket, before heading back into the barn with the knife.

He walks over to Matthew and kicks his foot. Nothing. Patrick bends down, putting the back of his fingers to Matthew's nose. Breathing. And the blood has stopped running from his head.

After uncoiling some of the rope, he cuts it into several six-foot lengths. First he ties Matthew's hands behind him, next his legs and finally his hands again.

And then he sits down, leaning back against the wall next to the barn doors.

Perhaps it would be better to do it now, with Matthew unconscious. But how hard would it be to lift his body into the trunk? And probably impossible to drag him all the way to the spot where he wants them to find him.

Will I remember the right tree? he wonders.

Blades of sunlight slip inside the barn through one of its tumbledown sides. Elsewhere the light is gray, a smell like sawdust in the air.

Was it all just an act? Everything Matthew just said, was it really nothing but part of some revenge plot? Act innocent, fake some honesty. *I know that you and Hannah are married—but I promise you I had no idea when I first contacted you.* If Matthew's plan is to come for Hannah, wouldn't he deliberately try to confuse him? Wouldn't he make out as if telling Patrick the truth, offering up a confession? *The police never worked out who killed Randy. But I know who killed him.* And speaking so openly about investing with Idos as well, was this just another one of his tricks? *Apart from having to deal with an asshole called Don Trevino, I have nothing but good things to say about them.*

But what does it matter? Whether everything Matthew has said and done was some kind of an act or not, Patrick knows he has to burn these thoughts from his mind. Hannah has left him, there is only one way.

He takes out his phone and writes her a message, telling his wife how much he loves her, telling her what he is going to do, that he is doing it for her, because he loves her. After he presses SEND, Patrick closes his eyes and covers his face with his hands, sitting like this for a few moments, the darkness behind his eyelids interrupted only by an afterimage of the sunlight in the barn. And then, as that old light fades, Patrick's mind begins to slide as if from one world to another.

When he opens his eyes and drags his hands from his face, the sunlight in the barn seems to burn twice as bright. And that's when he can see it starting to form, the first shape appearing slowly in an empty spot close to where Matthew is lying unconscious. It is a wooden pulpit salvaged from an old church, the place where the diners are greeted in Red Moose Barn. He glances around as he begins to hear the sort of sounds that rattle through a happy restaurant. Cutlery, crockery, chatter. Now Patrick can see the bar forming, running down the far wall where the sunlight pours through, a stained glass window casting its red and green leaf-light on tobacco-colored floorboards. And there's the barman in blue chambray shirt and leather half-apron, pouring cocktails from a shaker into vintage glasses etched with cherries and leaf scrolls. The retired professors who live in the converted schoolhouse nearby pick up their Barnstormer cocktails, clink glasses, take a sip and nod with approval.

From somewhere at the other end of the darkness, music is playing. A live band, perhaps.

And look, table seven has ordered the cowboy steak for two. It arrives sizzling in a cast-iron skillet, earning a round of applause from table seven's diners, a young couple who look like they've come up from Brooklyn for a day of apple picking and cider donuts.

There is such a buzz in the place, motes of dust dappling the late-afternoon sunlight, the air full of laughter, an immense sense of good cheer.

And now, better than any of this, he starts to hear a voice, a woman's voice saying the same thing over and over as the guests wander up to the pulpit. Welcome to Red Moose Barn, she says. Welcome, welcome. And it makes him so happy to hear Hannah's voice in this place, Hannah who has quit her job at the newspaper and moved up here to support him. What a fine life they have together, living in the old farmhouse they fell in love with as soon as the real estate agent showed them around. At night, when their day at the barn is over, they sit together on their porch swing, sipping red wine, gazing up at the madly bright stars.

Welcome to Red Moose Barn, she says. Welcome, welcome. So good to see you again.

WHEN MATTHEW STARTS TO MOVE, Patrick looks down at his watch, a little after four o'clock, still plenty of light left in the day.

He picks up the duct tape and rolls Matthew onto his side, Matthew's eyes flickering, his body making small efforts to move as he tries to say something.

Shh shh, not yet, says Patrick. He tears a strip of tape and moves it close to Matthew's face, Matthew trying hard to turn his head away, Patrick pressing the tape to his mouth. And then he sits there on his haunches while Matthew slowly comes to.

The blades of sunlight have slipped all the way across the barn now, falling over an old sign that reads, U-PICK APPLES HERE.

A few minutes later, Matthew starts fighting the ropes.

There's no point, says Patrick. You never were any good at that game anyway.

But Matthew carries on fighting, knees bending and straightening, his arms struggling behind him.

Patrick heads over to the barn door, picks up the shotgun and moves back around to where Matthew can see him. Stop! he says. But Matthew keeps moving a few more seconds until Patrick cocks the hammer on the gun.

Good, says Patrick. Now listen, I'll make you a deal, Matthew. If you do what I say, go where I say, walk where I tell you to walk, if you do *everything* I say, then when we get where we're going, I'll take away the tape and you can tell me anything you want. Agreed?

Matthew doesn't move, just stares fiercely up at him, as if he imagines he might disarm a man with the strength of his gaze, snap rope with the power of thought.

Patrick waves the shotgun up and down. Move your head like this, he says, or else move it like this, he adds, waving the gun side to side. It has to be one or the other, Matthew, he says.

Matthew glares at him a moment longer and then nods.

Good, says Patrick. First I'm going to cut the rope at your legs. Your arms stay tied at all times. Then you're going to climb into the trunk of my car. Agreed?

Matthew nods.

Very good, says Patrick, picking up the knife. And don't worry, it won't be long now, he says. I'm really looking forward to hearing everything you have to say.

MATTHEW

I doubled back along Sunset Ridge to avoid you, not wanting you implicated in my daddy's death at all, thinking it better you weren't even aware of it, and then headed back toward town, taking the trail that ran down the North Mountain Gully, a route in and out of the Swangums that almost no one ever took, reaching the edge of Roseborn unseen by another human soul.

I knew the Jensens owned the last house on Grist Mill Road. There was a rail trail that ran alongside their land, so all I had to do was squeeze by a few bushes and there it was, Hannah's home.

Hours earlier, as my daddy had left the house waving his pistol, he'd threatened Hannah in the vilest terms imaginable against breathing a word to anyone. I just wanted her to know she was safe.

For a few moments, I stood there, looking across the grounds at the house. It was late in the evening, that moment of twilight when the trees lose all sense of depth, becoming nothing more than cutouts against a fading sky. The lights from within Hannah's house were burning amber, and I felt a sense of looking in on something pure, something I could never have, a happy family living in the perfect home.

Later on it would feel to me as if I'd taken a snapshot of that scene, that precise second of my life, and I pictured it often while

I was in prison, imagining myself growing up in those golden rooms, how differently everything might have turned out.

While I was breathing it all in, I noticed some movement behind one of the windows, Hannah pacing around a room, gripping herself by the shoulders. I headed across the lawn, picked up some gravel from the driveway, and threw it so that it clattered the glass.

Hannah came to the window, saw me, and clapped her hand to her mouth.

When she came out through the back door, she looked like she'd been shaking for the last several hours, Hannah's skin moonlight pale, her face marked by tears. She ran over to me gesturing to keep quiet before taking hold of my hand and leading me away past a pond, and then on toward a large outcrop of rock. Up ahead I could just about make out the opening of a cave. Hannah kept on pulling me silently until we were both inside and reached down to switch on a lantern, some of the cave lighting up, but the space so vast the lantern wasn't strong enough to illuminate its farthest reaches. Then Hannah turned to me, wrapping her arms around herself and said, in the most fearful voice I've ever heard, Is he dead?

I nodded at her, not realizing right away that she was talking about you, of course, Pete.

Oh God, said Hannah, her words little more than squeals, he's going to kill me, now he's going to kill me, she said, and then started to shake feverishly, tears coming out of her eyes.

Still with the same cold sense of calm I had up in the mountains, I grabbed hold of her by the shoulders. Hannah, stop, I said. No one's going to kill you.

I don't think she heard what I said, she wasn't even looking at me. I'm a witness, she said, her voice stuttering out through her tears. So he has to kill me, she said, he's going to kill me. Hannah started rubbing the spot on her head where my daddy had pushed the barrel of his gun.

Finally I caught on. Wait, Hannah, I said, he's not going to kill you, I promise. He's dead. It's my daddy who's dead.

Hannah started to blink. What? she said, her face tilting up at me, an edge of disbelief in her voice.

I promise you, Hannah, he's dead. You're safe. We're all safe. My daddy's dead.

Looking down at her, I could see Hannah trying to work it all out, everything changing inside her head, a different world. Was it him? she said. The old . . . ?

No, I said. No, Hannah, I killed him. It was me.

Hannah's eyes froze on my face, and then, a moment later, she threw her arms around me, pressing one of her cheeks to my chest. Oh God, she said, I'm sorry, Matthew, I'm sorry, I'm so sorry.

I lifted my hands to hold her, and in that moment, it felt to me that the two of us would be forever bound by this secret. For minutes our bodies were locked together as Hannah's tears soaked into my T-shirt, and I stroked her head, the two of us bound in each other's arms, bound by the knowledge we now shared.

WE SAT IN THAT CAVE for an hour, its cool breath lapping over us as I told Hannah everything that had happened since my daddy climbed out of his car for the very last time.

When I reached the part about picking up the rock and bringing it down on my daddy's skull, Hannah placed a hand on my knee to comfort me. You had to, Matthew, she said, you didn't have any choice.

It felt so good to be understood, Hannah's hand on my knee like a candle in the dark.

Someone will probably find him tomorrow, I said. There's a trail right under the spot where I . . . And I guess there'll be police. And a funeral. So I don't know when I'll get to see you again. Will you be all right, Hannah?

She nodded and leaned over and kissed me on the cheek. Thank you, Matthew, she said.

I should probably get home, I said.

When I stood up, Hannah got to her feet as well, giving me a look as if she understood me, as if she knew everything I was and wanted to tell me that everything inside me was OK—no labels, no judgments, only compassion.

Standing there in that dimly lit cave, I think I trusted her look, I really did believe Hannah was capable of understanding me. Which is not to say that she deliberately tricked me, I don't think that's what happened at all, but perhaps the person Hannah was deceiving at that moment, at that moment and for the next several weeks, was herself.

TWO HIKERS CAME ACROSS THE body the next morning.

My mom had barely noticed my daddy's absence from their bed—often he would sleep in the car after one of his special Friday nights—and after a perfectly normal breakfast, Tricky and I pounded our way up Grist Mill Road on our bikes as if it were any other Saturday morning, but before we could reach the parking lot, a police officer, his car blocking the road, turned us away without telling us why. The officer didn't even pay me any special heed, so I guess he hadn't realized whose son I was—because even if they couldn't identify the body right away, my daddy's car would've been the only one left in the parking lot overnight.

The police didn't take long to come to the conclusion that my daddy's death was unsuspicious. There seemed to be a simple explanation—the day my daddy died he'd lost his job, gotten steaming drunk, and had been shooting his mouth off in O'Sullivan's and his gun in the mountains. Probably the only issue the police stopped to consider was whether my daddy had drunkenly slipped or drunkenly thrown himself from the polished bedrock of Sunset Ridge. Perhaps the detectives who suspected him of killing Randy McCloud thought he'd suffered an overwhelming attack of guilt, that's the sort of thing you might have thought if you didn't know him.

Anyway, whatever the police suspected, when they came to find my mom at our house Saturday night, the word they used was *accident*. I heard them clearly through the thin walls of my bedroom, Mom having sent me and little Billy packing when she saw uniforms approaching our front door, and after the officers told her what the result of that *accident* was, I heard a little shock come out of my mom, but not ever so much in the way of tears.

In the days that followed, I wouldn't say we were buried beneath an avalanche of bereavement cards. Those we did receive were all covered in sick-looking flowers, and it seemed to me that the messages written inside had about as much feeling behind them as scientific formulae, the same phrases repeated over and over.

There was only one card I cared about. It arrived with my name on the envelope and no return address. My mom handed it over numbly, not even watching to see me open it, so I took it to my room. The card inside was plain and white, and in your elegant hand were written the words—

If it is by the Spirit of God that I drive out demons, then the kingdom of God has come upon you

A year later, it occurred to me to search for those words in the Bible. It didn't take me long to find them, the first place I turned was the book of Matthew, and there they were.

For years I've been wondering the same thing over and over. If Hannah had known the truth—that I loved you, but nothing had happened, and that you loved me, but nothing had happened— would it have made any difference? Would Hannah have accepted me for who I was, or would things still have gone the same way, several weeks later, up in the mountains?

IN THE MIDDLE OF THE night, several hours after my daddy's funeral, something hit me like a blunt object, thudding into my thoughts while I was asleep, a nightmare in which I had a cold feeling of certainty that my daddy was alive, only I couldn't see him, that my daddy was speaking to me, but I couldn't hear him, that his belt buckle was ready, he was everywhere, waiting for me, and I would never escape.

For the first few minutes of wakefulness, the feeling of being trapped by something I would never shake was all-consuming, and yet that single nightmare would turn out to be the closest I ever came to feeling any sense of guilt for what happened on that Friday, July 1982. If I've ever dreamed about my daddy since that night, I certainly don't remember. I knew then, almost as strongly as I know now, that what I did that day was right. My daddy had already murdered Randy McCloud. How many other people might he have killed if I hadn't pushed him off Sunset Ridge? However, waking up that morning after the funeral, my bedcovers soaked through with sweat, I did begin to feel an urgent need to talk to someone. The previous week had seemed to move at an agonizing pace, having to keep everything locked inside while soaking up little Billy's tears and listening to my mother's complaints about the unfairness of life.

How I wish it were you that I'd gone to that morning, Pete, your cabin I'd chosen as a place of refuge—I should have realized I could spill out a thousand words to a hundred other human beings, and not one of them would understand me nearly as well as you, who understood even my blinks—but instead I left my bike in a patch of bushes by a rail trail and, reaching the house, picked up a handful of gravel. When Hannah came to her window, I was already walking toward the cave. It was eleven in the morning, tiny purple flowers in the grass winking at me, the air wet through with threats of thunderstorms.

When Hannah got there, I was already sitting on the ground with my back pressed to the cave wall. Hannah sat down as well and nestled up to me. I guess I was still feeling the aftershocks of my nightmare, because the first words I said to her were, I killed him, Hannah. My daddy, I murdered him.

Hannah rested her head on my shoulder. That's not what I think, she said. I think you saved me, she said. And you saved that man as well.

He's called Pete, Hannah.

OK, she said, but I don't want to talk about him. I only want to talk about you from now on, she said.

That's how we began.

I've never much seen the appeal of talking about myself. Even as a child, the idea of confession at church seemed like an essentially selfish act—selfish on both sides of the box—but back in that cave, never switching on the lantern in the daytime, something about the half-light that surrounded us made it easy to talk, as if darkness had the power to drag words out of me. Or maybe it was nothing to do with that cave, maybe it was Hannah who was in possession of that power. Just a few days ago, Pete, I found out that she became a journalist. Hannah Jensen is a crime reporter for the *New York Mail*. How many words has she dragged out of how many people?

We would meet in that cave every two or three days, and when we did, I would tell Hannah stories about growing up in Queens, our thin cramped apartment, the airplanes roaring over our heads as they slipped down to LaGuardia, and how I thought if you stood on top of the tallest rooftop and jumped as high as you could, you might be able to reach up and touch one of those jet planes right under its belly. I told her about moving upstate and seeing Roseborn for the first time—on the drive up, I fell asleep in the back of the car and, not having been told where we were moving, simply assumed my daddy had taken us all the way back to Texas.

I told her about rattlesnakes, skylakes, and ice caves, I told her about Tricky and our games, Tarzan, Houdini, and Deer Patrol. I don't know how we filled all those hours, our lives so barely lived at that age, and the more I told Hannah about myself, the more my feelings for her deepened.

I remember thinking that Hannah was feeling the same way toward me—and who knows, perhaps she was—but although we might have been together in that cave, I realize now that we were actually hundreds of miles apart, not only at different stages of life, but also different people altogether.

Anyway, it felt immensely easy talking with Hannah. Somehow she managed to convey a sense that she was interested in everything I had to say, as if my words were sustenance, and she a hungry soul in need of saving.

As July drained away and summer neared its peak, that dark cave became somewhere to retreat not only from recent events, but also from the fierce temperatures outside. Sitting with our backs to its cool stone flanks, I remember that one day I was telling Hannah all about the good air in the mountains, how you could make rainbows dance over the wet rocks and that you could swim in the lake and dry off in the sunlight. That's the moment when the feeling came to me that I wanted to share the mountains with Hannah. Hey, why don't we go up there tomorrow? I said. It'll be great, I can show you around.

Perhaps Hannah sensed that I had more than one motive for wanting to be with her in the Swangums—for a while I'd been thinking about kissing her again, only somehow it would have felt wrong in that cave, a place that was meant only for talking.

OK, she replied, hesitantly, but you should invite Patrick as well.

Why? I said.

Because he's your best friend, said Hannah.

Maybe you're my best friend now.

He'll be upset if he finds out you went back to your secret place without him.

So what?

Hannah looked down, not saying anything, so I relented, figuring it wouldn't be so hard to find some time alone with her up in the mountains.

A few hours later I telephoned Tricky, and pretty soon everything was arranged.

ROSEBORN, NEW YORK, 2008

It is late afternoon when they leave, Lizzy and Katie running after the car, still *arrrrr*ing and waving as it pulls out the drive, McCluskey *arrrrr*ing as well, having spent the last five hours in the role of Captain Blackbeard.

But you don't have a beard and your hair is all white.

Arrrrr, but fat beardless old guy is just my disguise. For I be a pirate with a price on his head, girls.

Hannah had been sitting at the kitchen table all the while, talking to Jen, drinking wine as the swashbuckling games spun around her.

Now she waves a final goodbye and winds up the window. Thanks for playing along, Mike, says Hannah.

No problemo, Aitch. But Christ, do those girls love a treasure hunt or what?

I thought you were going to keel over at the end of the fourth hour.

Nah, that's nothing compared to having three boys. Plus, you know, with boys you gotta beat them at everything as well.

What?

Sure. You ever need to know the darker arts of winning Uno every time, I'm your man.

You cheated your own children at cards?

Fuckin A, Aitch. How else do you think those boys got their cojones of steel?

Their what? Tommy teaches pre-K.

Right, but he rules those four-year-olds with an iron fist.

Hannah tries to hide her laughter from McCluskey, turning to look out the window, the Swangums a white band on the horizon like a cloud bank that has sunk from the sky, the ridge seeming such an unlikely setting for nightmares right now, and then they drive past the park entrance with its twin millstones, on toward Main Street, and she turns back to McCluskey.

So, now that you no longer have to play Captain Blackbeard, tell me what happened with Matthew, she says.

McCluskey rubs his nose back and forth, and performs a long shrug. The guy offered me pancakes, he says, not dropping his shoulders until he's done speaking.

Pancakes? says Hannah. Anything else?

Sure, says McCluskey. You know, it's complicated, Aitch.

Mike, come on, you're stalling. Just say it.

McCluskey starts to act like he's interested in reading all the store signs they're passing, finally speaking at the end of another long shrug. So there was this old guy in the house, he says, and the guy was just a friend of his, right? Only it turns out this friend has Alzheimer's, and Matthew's paying a nurse to look after him full-time.

Hannah sighs. What was the old guy's name? she says.

I dunno, says McCluskey. Pete—something like that.

Hannah crosses her arms, hugging herself at the ribs, feeling herself beginning to burn at the memory, her body tensing up.

What's wrong? says McCluskey, glancing across at her. You know this guy? Pete?

Something like that, says Hannah. Anyway, what's your point, Mike?

I dunno, says McCluskey, gripping the wheel tighter and taking a few heavy breaths. Look, he says, don't forget I'm Team fuckin Aitch all the way, right?

Just tell me.

And remember, this Matthew comes anywhere near you, I'll drop him on the spot, I swear.

But . . . ?

McCluskey starts checking his mirrors, rearview, side view, and scratching his ear as he says to her, Look, I think when the guy apologized to you this morning, Aitch, I just think, you know, maybe he was being kinda genuine, that's all. And then McCluskey's voice rises halfway to anger. Goddammit, he says, I didn't want to have to fuckin say that, OK? And he glances across again, Hannah making herself small in the passenger seat. You mad at me, Aitch?

No, I'm not mad, she says. But just give me a minute, Mike, can you?

McCluskey swallows hard, and keeps on driving, until at the end of Main Street they join a line of traffic, everyone waiting to make the turn toward the bridge, while Hannah hugs herself as she remembers, picturing it all over again and wondering all the while, *What did I really see through that window?*

Because sometimes when she thinks about it, she can see it one way, through the eyes of a thirteen-year-old girl feeling crushed, and there he is, the boy who on the last day of school put three kisses at the end of his note to her, now with his head bobbing in the lap of the man who chairs cement meetings at her family's home, or gives nature talks at their school, and seeing is believing, isn't that how the phrase goes, and she believed what she saw. Only sometimes she can picture it differently, because what if the phrase can be flipped around, what if you believe something strongly enough, and you make yourself see it, an optical illusion, a trick of the mind?

Soon they are crossing the bridge, the traffic starting to flow faster as they pass through the outskirts of Roseborn, the road carrying them up from the floodplain, and whatever she saw or didn't see, she couldn't have known Matthew's father would overhear her, and didn't she try to make things right later on? Or at least she tried to make everything a little less wrong, because when she woke up in that hospital bed, the left side of her face covered in bandage and gauze, she could have told the police right then that Matthew was guilty of more than one crime, and years later when she thought about it, she couldn't remember if she didn't tell because she was scared of being guilty of something as well, guilty of concealing a murder, or whether she didn't tell the police anything because whatever Matthew did to her while she was tied to that tree, he had killed his own father because of something she'd said, it was all because of her, whether she meant for it to happen or not. It was her fault.

Whatever she said to Matthew when his father was listening in, and whatever she said to him later on, just a few moments before he tied her to that tree, after she thought she could go through with it, thinking that she owed him *something*, but was just too young for *that thing*, and of course she regrets saying it, is ashamed of what she said, the memory of that word still burning her cheeks, and whatever she said, nothing can justify what Matthew did to her that day. Nothing.

For years she has wanted to tell someone the whole story, but maybe she thought she still had to keep Matthew's secret, or maybe it was because of the burning shame of what she said to him that day, August 18, 1982, and whatever the reason, she has never told anyone, the guilty feeling coming to her sometimes after she wakes with a scream, another one of the nightmares, pistols and rifles, airplanes falling out of the sky, the darkness that will be with her forever, the left side of her world always in shadow, and she has never told anyone what happened that day. Never.

Now they are passing through open farmland, past grain silos and barns, driving away from the ridge, and she knows it is time to admit what she did, to admit it to someone, let go of the burden, so she uncrosses her arms, and she takes a deep breath. Hey, McCluskey, she says, there's something I want to tell you, something that happened before Matthew did what he did to me.

McCluskey looks alarmed. Aitch, wait now, you know you don't have to tell me anything, I'm Team fuckin Aitch no matter what.

She stares distantly out through the windshield, a red barn in a wildflower meadow, a car about to turn from the end of a dirt track onto the road. No, she says, I want to, Mike, I think I need to . . . but something about that car, a blue car, stops her from finishing the sentence as it pulls onto the other side of the road, turning toward Roseborn, its driver obscured by sunlight, Hannah staring hard at the license plate as they pass.

Wait, she says. McCluskey, wait, that's our car, the blue Audi that just went by, it's ours.

McCluskey looks in his mirror. What? he says. You sure?

Positive, she says. It must be Patch. What's he doing up here?

McCluskey has to wait for a farm truck to pass before he can pull off the road, spinning the wheel hard to turn around, stopping at the dusty edge of an orchard right behind where another car is parked, but pausing before he shifts to reverse. Aitch, you recognize that? he says, pointing at the black Mercedes.

Wait, is it Matthew's? she says.

Fuckin A it is, Aitch. I made a mental note of the plates so I could check a few things later on. McCluskey squints into the distance, the blue car already out of sight. You get any more messages from your husband? he says.

A few, says Hannah. But none that I've opened.

Yeah? says McCluskey. Well, maybe you wanna take a look now.

MATTHEW

You won't remember the final time you came to visit me in jail, Pete. A few days earlier, out on patrol in the Swangums, you'd heard reports of an illegal campfire via your walkie-talkie. Seeing the smoke, you headed into the woods, dousing the flames when you reached the spot, the culprits already having fled. You hadn't ever been in that small clearing before, the place where it happened, but after radioing in a report, you looked around, and once you realized the significance of where you were standing, you closed your eyes for a few minutes and prayed for Hannah.

There were tears in your eyes as you told me this. I asked if you prayed for me as well and you shook your head. Not in that place, you said. I've prayed for you, Matthew, but not when I came upon that place. You told me that forgiveness was now a matter between me and God, because when you stood in that clearing with your eyes closed, thinking about Hannah, thinking about the pain she must have suffered, you realized that you had to stop visiting me. God might find it in his heart to forgive me but you couldn't do it anymore. Forgiveness simply wasn't in your power, you told me.

I wouldn't see you again for more than two decades.

When I drove up to Roseborn six months ago, hoping to find you still living in your cabin, it was because finally I had met the one person in the world other than you I've ever wanted to spend my life with. I was thinking of proposing, marrying him in Massachusetts, and I wanted your blessing—his name is Andrew, I'm sure you'd like him, Pete, he'd make you laugh. However, I think there was another reason I wanted to see you, and possibly I was even deceiving myself about the whole marriage thing, because even more than your blessing, perhaps what I really needed was your forgiveness. Maybe I did eventually come to think of you as a father figure, Pete.

When I pulled up to your home, I saw a FOR SALE sign out front. A neighbor checking his mailbox told me you'd gone to live with your brother, Bob, in New Paltz, and I had my assistant track down the address. When Bob opened the door, I wasn't sure how he might react. I said that you and I had once been *friends,* your brother seeming to understand what I meant by this, his reaction not unduly negative. Bob warned me about your condition and invited me in. There was just enough of you left to remember my name, and you smiled when Bob brought me into your room. I would drive up to see you eight or nine times over the next few months. Your brother could tell how happy you were when I visited—and meanwhile, I could see the great strain on Bob's marriage that caring for you was causing. I think it came as a great relief to your brother when I offered to look after you for the rest of your life.

Now that your mind has slipped almost completely from the world, if you were to tell me you've forgiven me, would it even mean anything?

That's why I wish I'd written this letter twenty-three years ago, and I did think about writing it back then, even drafted a first page several times. But on the one hand, I was angry at you for praying for Hannah and not me, and on the other, I was worried it might hurt you, finding out the whole story. I knew you would feel somehow to blame for everything that happened, guilty for having stopped to talk to me outside the station house, wicked for befriending me, damned for loving me.

Now my confession feels like too little, too late. Although just writing everything down has brought some sort of comfort.

So anyway, this is where it ends, Pete, the final part of a letter I'll never send.

August 18, 1982. The clearing. The truth.

HANNAH ACTED THE WHOLE TIME like she and I hadn't recently been sharing all those hours of quiet intimacy in a cave. Not that she would've needed to put on much of an act to keep Tricky in the dark, but I played along, anyway.

We plunked some soda cans and inspected the fort, which was in need of repairs, the old fence uprights moldering, Tricky doing his best to act like a girl being around wasn't weirding him out. After twenty minutes or so, I got rid of him, sending him off to look for deer or something. He seemed relieved.

After Tricky left, Hannah looked nervous at being alone with me, but her edginess just felt like part of the game. I wondered how far I could lead her.

Hey, Hannah, I said, remember I told you about Houdini and you said it sounded like fun?

Mm hmm.

You want to play?

You mean you tie me up and I have to escape?

You don't *have to* escape, I said. Only if you want to.

Hannah shrugged sweetly. Sure, she said, but don't make it too difficult.

I went to fetch the rope from under the tarp. When I returned Hannah was leaning back against the fallen tree, the one where we lined up soda cans whenever we played Rifle Range. First I tied her ankles, then Hannah offered me her wrists. No, put them behind you, I said. I didn't pull the rope so tight it might hurt, but I made sure the knots were firm.

Now what? she said.

Now you try to escape.

Hannah started to writhe against the fallen trunk, giggling as she struggled, the rope barely coming loose. I remember she was wearing ink-dark jeans and a pink T-shirt with an ice-cream cone on the front. I remember how much it excited me, watching her wriggle around like that.

This is too hard, Matthew, she said after a minute or so. Can you help me?

Sure, I said, I can help. But you know there's a charge.

What's the *charge*? she said in a playful voice.

You have to kiss me.

Hannah rolled her eyes. OK then, she said, her voice not matching the gesture.

I walked toward her, Hannah trying to focus, looking as if she were in the school gym preparing for some kind of difficult gymnastic stunt. When I moved my face close, she shut her eyes.

I kissed Hannah hard.

After a few seconds, she pulled away and I smiled down at her, Hannah blinking back at me. So then I knelt down to loosen the knot at her ankles, but while I was on my knees, I put my hand between Hannah's legs, quickly stroking the inside of her thigh, her body shivering before I pulled my hand away and stood up. Taking a few steps back, I said to her, That's all you get for half a kiss. Give it another try, I said, pointing at her feet.

Hannah started wiggling her legs. The rope was a lot slacker now, but she was struggling to work the back of the loop past the heels of her sneakers. Let me know if you need any more help, I said. Of course, it'll cost you something more next time.

Not long after that, Hannah looked up and said, OK, then. How much more?

I want to see it, I said.

See what?

You know what, Hannah, I said. Do you want to see mine?

She thought about it a while, and then nodded, hesitantly. OK, she said. But only if you go first.

I unbuttoned, unzipped, and lowered my pants and underwear—not far, but far enough. I enjoyed the look on Hannah's face as she glanced quickly down and back up again.

Your turn, I said, pulling my pants up and zipping them shut.

Untie me then, she said.

I gave Hannah a disappointed look. You haven't earned it yet, I said, stepping toward her. Then I reached out slowly, staring at Hannah all the while. I could see she was nervous, so I tried to do everything without any hurry, undoing her dark jeans, exposing her white underwear and then easing the elastic toward me.

After only a moment or two, Hannah said, That's long enough. I waited another half-second, letting the elastic snap back into place, then rebuttoned her jeans, my blood pumping hard with desire. Kneeling down again, I untied the knot behind her ankles and threw the rope to one side. Then I stood up, our bodies just a few inches apart. Would you like me to untie your hands? I said, whispering the words into Hannah's ear.

Yes, she said softly.

But there's one more thing I want to do first. Is that OK?

Hannah didn't say anything.

I whispered again. You know what I mean by that, Hannah, right?

Yes, she said.

Yes? I said.

Hannah nodded.

I felt a surge of lust and a taste in my mouth like I'd eaten something sweet. As I pulled my pants and underwear halfway down my thighs, Hannah looked down and swallowed. Then, just as before, without moving too fast, I reached out to unbutton Hannah's jeans, her breath starting to quicken.

My fingers were just an inch away when Hannah spoke again. Wait, she said, firmly—and then louder as I grasped the button on her waistband. Wait, Matthew, no!

It's OK, Hannah, I said, pulling my hands away. I promise I'll be gentle.

No, she said, I can't do it.

Why? I said.

I thought I could but I can't, I just can't.

Why not?

The next few seconds moved slowly. The air was so hot that day it clung to me like damp tissue paper, all the hair at the back of my neck wet through, and after her efforts to free herself from the ropes, Hannah's pink T-shirt was damp with sweat as well, almost crimson in places. I noticed how there seemed to be a dark smile at her belly, two eyes over her barely formed breasts. I remember thinking how cute she looked in that moment, the ice-cream cone forming a nose.

I cocked my head, confused for a moment, but then something about the expression on Hannah's face made me ask her again, my tone becoming more insistent. Wait, I said. Come on, *why not?*

Hannah looked like she was trying to find the right words, her tongue wetting her lips, her eyes scanning something within, and then she said, as if it were a statement so obvious it made her angry even having to say it. Because . . . she said, hesitating as she screwed up her face with a sense of distaste . . . Because you're a faggot, she said.

I could almost hear the snapping of leather in the air as that final word hit me hard as a belt buckle. It might have been Hannah calling me faggot but it was my daddy's voice I heard saying the word.

What did you call me? I said.

Wait, I'm sorry, she said.

No, what did you call me? I repeated, spitting the words out so loud it made Hannah jump.

I'm sorry, it's just the word.

Just *the* word? I said. Say it again.

I can't, Hannah whimpered, I'm sorry.

You're a liar, I yelled.

But I saw you with that man, said Hannah, half turning away from me, as if she thought I was going to hit her.

I looked down, noticing my hands were clenched into fists.

Liar! I said, my voice flashing with rage. Nothing happened, Hannah, I said, the rage making me shake now, my anger so blinding, I'm not even sure who I thought I was yelling at, Hannah or my daddy. *You're plenty brave for a faggot, boy.*

Hannah's hands were still tied behind her. I don't remember pulling her over to that tree, finding more rope, tying more knots.

You need to be punished—that's something my daddy used to tell me, and I could still hear him saying it. I think at some point I probably even shouted the same words at Hannah.

What was I planning to do? I don't know. Wasn't punishing Hannah going to be something like my daddy teaching me a lesson with his belt? You feel the sting, you endure, and finally it ends. I'm not sure I was thinking of this being more than that, because I've never been afraid of anything in life. I understand danger, but I don't think about consequences. How could I imagine what Hannah might feel?

I could hear my daddy just like he was in the clearing, standing right behind me. *Is that girl a goddam liar or are you a faggot?* Hell, hadn't I saved her? Wait, more than that, hadn't everything happened only because of Hannah? And now I was the one being accused of something? Now I was the one being despised, labeled, betrayed? Faggot? When I looked down at her, I thought I saw Hannah's eyes ablaze with that word, condemning me over and over again.

I don't remember her putting up much of a fight. I suppose she thought that by complying, by playing along, she might bring me down from my rage.

I know how that goes, I've been in that dark place myself, but there was no bringing me down, my daddy somewhere nearby, whispering in my ear, whipping my rage ever higher.

Are you . . . an old man . . . cocksuckin . . . faggot?

How dare Hannah condemn me. How dare she betray me with my daddy's own words.

You ain't got the balls to push me off this cliff, faggot.

He was an evil son of a bitch. Maybe killing my daddy once hadn't been enough.

I picked up the BB gun.

ROSEBORN, NEW YORK, 2008

She sees their blue car half concealed by pine trees, parked in front of a split rock, remembering them leaving their bicycles in the same spot twenty-six years ago, but no sign of her husband now, McCluskey stopping the car, getting out fast, a lone trail leading away from the road, McCluskey pushing his gun into its holster as they head out together on the path she remembers, and even if McCluskey were to keep quiet, someone will think to suspect Patch if he goes through with what he wrote, someone will find the message he sent her this morning. What was he thinking? She prays they will not be too late.

McCluskey is surprisingly fast over the ground, Hannah working hard to keep up, the story jumping through her mind in fragments, like cards being flashed in front of her eye, McCluskey pausing to help her over the rocks, Hannah tiring now, and again she can feel the sense of that pistol being pressed to her head, the same spot on her temple where the nightmares fire up in the dark, the dreams in which she remembers the smell of his teeth, *say it again,* and then suddenly she is tied to a tree, feeling the sting of those pellets on her skin, a pain like being punched in the eye, never a harder punch in the world, and then darkness, dark like a cave, her eye like a cave.

The trail carries them over hollows choked with tree roots,

across the heat-baked earth, the ground studded with half-buried rocks, the path coming to a fork.

Which way, Aitch? You remember?

She thinks about Patch and a red bandana soaked in water.

There was a stream, she says, panting, out of breath, McCluskey nodding and pulling her along the path that heads down into a shallow valley, and the closer she gets to that place, the more she can hear it, like moving toward a waterfall, the sound starting out like a whisper, building up to a roar, as she remembers her words. *Because you're a faggot.*

The scree on the steep trail makes the path almost slick, Hannah trying not to fall as she remembers how the words came out of her, not even thinking what she would say before she spoke it out loud, especially not that final word, something she heard at school a hundred times a week, the confusion of a young girl, a different kind of world, twenty-six years ago, another century.

There are other words. What if she'd used another word? Would it have made any difference?

They cross the stream, and she knows they must be nearing the place, remembering the way Patch had moved that red bandana toward her, holding it up to what was left of her eye, and the look on his face, that's when she realized how bad it was, Patch's cheeks turning pale, a sense of him wanting to recoil.

The trail starts to rise, sheer rock face on one side, the other thick with mountain laurel, McCluskey turning to help her, another shelf of rocks, but Hannah gesturing to stop as she remembers pushing through bushes, and she points off through the branches toward a place she will never forget.

Stay here, Aitch, he whispers, but when McCluskey turns off the trail, she follows him into the brushwood and dried leaves, the undergrowth brown like butcher's paper, and then into the thicket of glossy leaves, the tangle of branches, stepping carefully, quietly.

Until suddenly McCluskey halts, throwing his hand back to stop her as he reaches for the gun beneath his jacket, but Hannah takes another step, a twig snapping underfoot, and she can see past his shoulder, into the clearing.

There it is.

She remembers the tree, the same tree, only this time it is Matthew tied to that tree.

And Patrick is holding the gun.

HE STANDS BACK, EXAMINING THE ropes and the knots, the shotgun hanging in his right hand. Matthew appears groggy but with a look in his eyes as if he still believes he can talk his way out of this. And Patrick supposes he did promise to remove the tape from his mouth. Besides, what harm can it do now?

He is about to step forward when a sound comes from the bushes and Patrick raises the shotgun, steadying it with his other hand as he swings around, turning and seeing a man at the edge of the clearing. The man reaches under his jacket.

Patrick lifts the shotgun to his shoulder, cocking the hammer. He is about to shoot when he notices someone else and his finger loosens its tension on the trigger.

Hannah?

And now the man in the bushes has a gun pointed at him. Patrick, hey, it's Mike McCluskey, the man shouts. We met one time, right? Detective McCluskey. Look, will you do me a favor? Can you lower your weapon?

Hannah? he calls out.

Patch, it's me, she says. Patch, listen, everything's OK.

Mike McCluskey? Yes, Patrick does know the name, Detective McCluskey, he always passes on the best details to Hannah. The detective waves his hand. Patrick, keep your eyes on me, buddy, just me, he says. Remember, you made brisket? Best damn brisket I ever had. So how about you put down the gun, Patrick? Come on, we can talk about this.

Hannah! he says, everything starting to become clear as the detective shouts something else. But Patrick isn't listening to the words, noticing only how the birds in the treetops haven't stopped singing and then hearing the sound of his own breath in his head, his breath and his thoughts swirling together, everything falling into place now. There is only one path, nothing can be undone and Patrick can see his own path like a light, how could anything else matter, how could he ever have thought himself lost if this is where the path was leading him? Now he sees Hannah more clearly than ever before, understands her better than he's ever understood anything, seeing her as she sees him, the distance between them nothing but air, a space so empty he can hear what she's thinking, what she wants him to do, what she has always wanted him to do, the look in her eye perfectly clear.

Life has always been sending him back here. It feels so inevitable now, this ending, a sense of purpose at last.

Patrick, please, I need you to drop the weapon *now*!

He turns and pulls the trigger.

A KIND OF DARKNESS STARTS to fade and Patrick opens his eyes, a weight pressing down on him, as if rocks have been piled high on his chest. And then he hears a voice as everything starts to turn softly blue. Hannah's voice, a warm sound. Patch? Patch? Oh God, Patch.

That's it, keep the pressure on, right there, Aitch. I got no fuckin signal in this place, I'll go and get help.

Patrick is looking up at the sky, its darkening blue. But then he sees Hannah. This is everything, there is nothing else in his world.

He is lying on his back, wondering how he got there. And now he remembers, feeling again the kick of the shotgun in his hands, a prickling in his fingers.

Her eye is wet. He tries to speak, tries to say her name, *Hah*, and she hushes him but he has to speak, he has to, *Hah* . . . What happened, Hannah? Am I shot?

Yes, Patch. Yes you are. But someone's going to come and help you. Very soon, I promise.

Matthew?

He's dead, Patch, Matthew's dead.

Did I save you?

Yes, you saved me, Patch, of course you did. I always knew you would.

He was coming after you. I had to stop him this time.

Yes! Yes, he was coming after me, Patch.

Had me fired. Him and Trevino. Together.

Oh, Patch.

I was never on his side. I was always with you, Hannah.

I know, Patch, I'm so sorry.

No, it's like an escape.

An escape from what, Patch?

What? I don't know. What did I say?

Patch, everything's going to be OK now.

Yes. I love you, Hannah.

I love you too, Patch, so much.

Then that's the only thing . . . he says, wanting to say something more. But there are no words left. To have loved her has made everything in his life shine, that's what he wanted to say. He hopes she heard him anyway.

Patrick can feel his breath leaving him now, the warmth of him ebbing away, everything beginning its return to the earth. Yes, it all makes sense. He is nothing but borrowed parts, pieces large and small that must be returned, some of them given and some of them taken—from the dust, from the oceans, from the fields, from the sky—but now it is the world's turn to take of him, soon he will come to be sustenance, this is how everything works.

Hannah blinks, the light of her eye falling on him like a raindrop as he thinks about the smallest pieces of him rolling away, stones spilling from the mountaintop, pebbles dropping into a lake, everything falling into the blue.

And the lake is the blue. And her eye is the lake. Because that's where he sees it, his life with her beginning, its light in the blaze of her eye as he falls deeper and deeper into the blue.

Where they kiss. For the first time, the last time, they kiss. And it surprises him how gently unfolding it is.

INTO THE BLUE

I bought it at a drugstore Saturday morning and wore it all day, noticing how it made the world swim as I bumped into things, stepping unsteadily from curbs and climbing steps clumsily, my feet looking sometimes too close to me and sometimes too far away. It was the same with my hands, which didn't seem to belong to me in this strange half-world.

At eight o'clock, I changed clothes and headed out into the dimming light, the sidewalks swelling with life as I walked the awkward mile or so to the Flatiron District, getting more and more used to it but still not at ease on my feet.

I was deliberately five minutes late. That night I would let you arrive first, Hannah, wanting you to see me make my entrance.

So before I went inside, I peered in through the restaurant window. And there you were, sitting at the table, so pretty it made me giddy with joy to think of spending even one minute in your company. What would it be like to spend half a lifetime with someone like you? It felt as if I had chanced upon something new in the world—love, happiness—and this discovery both thrilled me and terrified me. Because what if I couldn't find my way into your life? Now that I'd seen this prize shimmering in the distance, understanding at last that there truly is love in the world, what would happen if I lost my way and couldn't reach you? I felt sick and afraid and euphoric.

As the waiter led me toward the table, you glanced up, clapping your hands to your mouth in shock when you saw me.

I was about to wave hello when I misjudged how close the tables were on my left-hand side, my thigh knocking into a corner, cutlery rattling angrily, a wineglass falling over and its contents quickly staining the tablecloth. The man at the table yelled an oath at me as his wife let out a yelp. When I turned to apologize and the man saw my face, his expression changed quickly from enraged to sympathetic.

Dammit, I said, *I'm so sorry. Please, let me . . .* I reached for a napkin to mop up the spill.

Hey, that's OK, said the man. *Accidents happen, right?*

A small platoon of waiters were hurrying over to clear up the mess I'd made.

No, my fault, I said, *will you let me buy you a bottle of wine or . . . ? It didn't spill on you at all, did it?* I said to the woman.

No, it's no problem, she said, dabbing at a line of red spots on her cream-colored skirt. *Everything's fine.*

Are you sure?

Go ahead and sit down, said the man, waving me away. *Enjoy yourself. Hey, and here's a tip—the blue crab salad. Delicious!*

Thank you, I said. *And again, I'm so sorry.*

Don't mention it, said the woman. *Have fun.*

I turned, seeing that you still had your hands clamped over your mouth, and walked very carefully to our table. When I leaned in to kiss you on the cheek, you whispered, *It suits you, Patrick.*

I sat down and adjusted the eyepatch, which I was wearing over my left eye. *Don't you think it's time you started calling me Patch?* I said.

You laughed and tilted your head to one side as you looked me over. *It really is a good look,* you said. *It makes you appear dashing, slightly mysterious. And blue was a great choice of color. With that suit? Perfect.*

Are you sure? I said. *It's just that yours is black. I didn't want to go too matchy-matchy.*

Right, you said, *I hate those couples who color-coordinate their medical accessories.*

I just wanted to try and understand what it's like for you, I said. Then I started to tell you all about my day wearing the eyepatch, the simple tasks I'd found so much harder, the problems with depth perception, the soreness of my neck after turning my head to my blind side so often, the small children in the checkout line who'd asked me whether I was a pirate and how I'd told them that I was indeed, the delight on their faces when I added that my name was Captain Patch and asked if they'd like to hear a pirate joke.

You know pirate jokes? you said.

Only one, I said. *Why are pirates called pirates?*

I have no idea, Captain Patch.

Because they arrrrr.

You laughed again, an unsuppressed laugh that made me think life with you would be endlessly wild and spontaneous.

You know what else happened? I said. *People spoke to me. I mean complete strangers spoke to me. It was like I wasn't living in New York anymore. And something else weird—they were all nice to me.*

That's happened to me as well, you said. *Often people open up more when I'm interviewing them. Sometimes it's awkward with the lack of movement in my prosthetic, as if people aren't sure which eye to look at. That's not a problem when I'm wearing the patch.*

I reached into my jacket and took out an index card, notes I'd written earlier. *Right, Hannah,* I said, *I have one last thing to say about eyepatches and pirates and then I promise never to bring any of this up again.*

OK, what's going on? you said, a note of playful suspicion entering your voice.

I did a little research, I said. *Here we go, my top five fun facts about pirates. I think you'll be pleasantly surprised.*

You leaned in, your eye so bright it was like a light swinging toward me. And then, clearing my throat, I started. *Fun fact number one. Modern-day pirates are considered criminals but many pi-*

rates several centuries ago were state-sponsored fortune hunters. A letter of marque granted the holder permission to capture enemy merchant ships and therefore was effectively a license for piracy—these pirates were known as privateers. Some pirates-slash-privateers, such as Sir Francis Drake of England, were considered national heroes.

Wow! you said. *You can't beat national hero status.*

No, you cannot, I said. *Now, fun fact number two. The first captain to successfully lead an expedition to circumnavigate the globe was a pirate. By the way, if they told you at school that Magellan was the first person to circumnavigate the world, that wasn't quite true, he died halfway around in the Philippines and his crew finished the journey without him. No, it was the state-sponsored pirate Sir Francis Drake who completed the entire voyage as a captain when he sailed around the world in the* Golden Hind.

I'm liking the sound of this Drake guy.

According to rumor, so did Queen Elizabeth. But moving swiftly on, fun fact three. During a time when much of the world was controlled by uncaring monarchies, professional sailors were both underpaid and ill-treated. However, pirate life was based on fairness and democracy. This is true, ships were run according to their own pirate code, captains were often elected, loot was divided up according to strict rules and there was even a system of workers' compensation for pirates who lost limbs. For example, four hundred pieces of eight for the loss of a joint, eight hundred for a limb.

How much for an eye?

Actually, one of the codes did specify that. One hundred pieces of eight.

Damn, I knew I should have held out for a limb.

Should I continue?

Please. But I'll want my hundred pieces of eight by the end of the meal.

Fact number four, pirate-stroke-privateer William Dampier was a keen collector of plants and his bestselling book of observations made on his travels was considered a mine of information by Charles Darwin, who took Dampier's work with him on The Beagle. *William Dampier also introduced more than a thousand words to the English language including* avocado, barbecue, caress, chopsticks, posse *and* snug.

You know, maybe I am a pirate. I invent new words all the time when I'm drinking.

And lastly, number five, drumroll . . . There is no historical record of a pirate ever owning a parrot.

What, that's your last fun *fact? Way to end on a high note, Captain Patch.*

Sorry, you're right, I could have planned that better. But anyway, all I'm trying to say, Hannah, is that pirates have had a bum rap.

And didn't sport parrots as fashion accessories.

Yes, and no parrots.

So wait, basically you're pitching me the idea that I should become *a pirate? Is that what this is all about?*

Of course not, I said. *But I do think you should be anything you want and do anything you want, Hannah.*

For a moment I felt awkward. Had that sounded cheesy? Like some kind of lame pickup line? But then your face lit up and it felt like the room was shrinking around us, a curtain being drawn, only the two of us sharing this world.

Thank you, Patch, you said. *And you can take the eyepatch off now. It is a little strange, both of us wearing them, like it's a fetish or something.*

But that couple . . . I said, half turning. *They'll realize I was just . . .*

It's OK, they left a minute ago.

They were very kind, I said, taking off the eyepatch. *Didn't you think they were kind?*

Patch? You've made your point. No need to stretch it.

Sorry, Hannah.

Don't be sorry. That was all very sweet. But first something to drink. And then food, most important food.

I called over the waiter. I was in such a good mood the only thing that seemed appropriate was champagne. I opened the wine list and pointed at the Pol Roger. And I remember what we ate that time, you running your finger down the menu, looking up and asking me whether I wanted to share the rib eye for two before warning me that you liked your steak like your novels, bloody as hell. We ordered a bottle of Bordeaux.

As we shared the huge plate of beef, we spoke so much and ate so slowly that we had to order a second bottle of wine, our bellies full to bursting as we kept on talking and mopping up the red meat juices with the last of our fries.

Once we were done with our meal, we were too full for dessert. You asked me if I wanted to find somewhere quiet for another drink. Or a coffee, perhaps.

When we left the restaurant, I remember seeing the Empire State Building all lit up in blue, the sky indigo with a thin veil of cloud hanging over the tips of the tallest buildings. We didn't even think about where we were headed, just walked off together into the night, still talking and talking, until we found ourselves in Union Square, the lights of the park burning blue, and you reached out and took my hand. How warm you felt. How wonderful it was to be alive in that moment, walking through the park hand in hand.

But how strange the light. Sky, trees, streetlamps. Everything blue. Everything.

I remember what came next almost as if someone had choreographed our movements, both of us slowing down, stopping and turning, our lips coming closer as I fell deeper and deeper into the blue.

Your eye was as blue as a lake when you leaned in to kiss me. I closed my eyes and our lips met. And in that moment, embraced by the light of your kiss, I knew I would love you until the day that I died.

ACKNOWLEDGMENTS

I owe a considerable debt of gratitude to the following: my remarkable wife, Margi Conklin, who reads everything at the truly ugly stage and manages somehow to steer me lovingly into clearer waters; my indomitable editor, Stephen Morrison, who identified and polished my ugliness with the tact and skill of an empathic superhero; my beloved agent, Jessica Papin, who has never once been wrong; the baddest journalist in town, Michelle Gotthelf, who *is* the news in New York City; Debra Rosenzweig, for all your help and a particularly vital spark; my phenomenal team of readers, Sharon Pelletier, Jonathan Brown, Katherine Gleason, Jeffrey Williams, Shaun Pye, Sarah Crawford, Jemima Rhys-Evans and Paul Manes, whose kind and thoughtful insights helped me get past the mostly ugly stage; Bill J. Smith, John D. Trawick and Keith Lenart, without whose generosity in sharing their experiences of monocular life, this novel would be a less-than-half-baked thing; Naoisa Hoskins and Beth Peck, who saved me from being wrong about American schools a thousand times; the extraordinary team at Picador, Pronoy Sarkar, James Meader, Declan Taintor, Henry Yee (your cover took my breath away), Shelly Perron and Kolt Beringer (thank you for putting up with my irksome idiosyncrasies), and Jeremy Pink; for the loan of Too Happy Cabin, Sara Bernstein and Morgan Spurlock, a perfect place to write;

Gail Blauer for another happy cabin loan; Eric Bailey, Jason Kohn and Tom Keane, who helped me get my facts straight over and over again; and for their help in a number of other multifarious but vital ways, Laura Harris, Susan Conklin, Ted Conklin, Charlotte Fall, Katie Deabler, Alex Masucci, Kirsten Fleming, Charlie Rowlands, Emily Dziedzic, Mackenzie Dawson and Lauren Abramo.

ABOUT THE AUTHOR

CHRISTOPHER J. YATES was born and raised in Kent and studied law at Oxford University before working as a puzzle editor in London. His first novel, *Black Chalk*, was named a Must-Read by *The Boston Globe* and the *New York Post* and named a Best Book of the Year by National Public Radio. *Grist Mill Road* is his second novel. He lives in New York with his wife and dog.